FOR HIS
BROTHER'S WIFE

Published in Great Britain 2015
by Mills & Boon, an imprint of Harlequin (UK) Limited,
Eton House, 18-24 Paradise Road, Richmond, Surrey, TW9 1SR

© 2015 Harlequin Books S.A.

Special thanks and acknowledgement are given to Kathie DeNosky for her contribution to the TEXAS CATTLEMAN'S CLUB: AFTER THE STORM series.

ISBN: 978-0-263-25256-9

51-0415

Printed and bound in Spain
by CPI, Barcelona

Kathie DeNosky lives in her native southern Illinois on the land her family settled in 1839. She writes highly sensual stories with a generous amount of humor. Her books have appeared on the *USA TODAY* bestseller list and received numerous awards, including two National Readers' Choice Awards. Kathie enjoys going to rodeos, traveling to research settings for her books and listening to country music. Readers may contact her by e-mailing kathie@kathiedenosky.com. They can also visit her website, www.kathiedenosky.com, or find her on Facebook.

This book is dedicated to the talented authors of the
Texas Cattleman's Club: After the Storm series.
Ladies, it was a real pleasure working with you
and I hope we get to do it again very soon.

One

Colby Richardson—Cole to his friends and family—pushed his wide-brimmed Resistol back on his head and muttered a word he normally reserved for dire circumstances and locker room banter as he stood in the feedlot of the Double R Ranch and surveyed the damage to the outbuildings. His gaze strayed to the empty space where, up until six months ago, the main barn had stood. The debris had been cleared away, but it did little to erase the memory of seeing the barn he and his brother used to play in reduced to a pile of broken boards and splintered beams. The deadly twister that had leveled parts of downtown Royal, Texas, and several other small communities close by had skipped its way across the west Texas landscape, laying waste to everything in its path—including part of his family's ranch.

Glancing over his shoulder at the ranch house, he shook his head as he amended that thought. It didn't belong to his family anymore. When their father passed away a few years back, the ranch had gone to Cole's twin brother, Craig. Now it belonged to Craig's widow, Paige.

He sighed heavily as guilt and regret settled over him. He had always hoped that one day he and his estranged twin would be able to put the anger and resentment aside and, at the very least, establish a semblance of a relationship. After all, they were only thirty-two. There should have been plenty of time for that. But when the tornado tore its way through the area, his brother's time had run out, and with his passing any possibility of reconciliation between them had been brought to an end.

The devastation and loss of property were one thing, but the death of Craig—along with six other souls at the Royal town hall that day—was another. Cole and his business partner, Aaron Nichols, had used their Dallas-based construction company to help rebuild the town and make repairs to damaged property. But there wasn't a damned thing anyone could do to bring back the lives that had been lost. He wished with everything that was in him that there was.

Taking a deep breath, Cole unclipped the cell phone on his belt. He had put off making the repairs to the Double R long enough. The construction crew he had assigned to rebuild the Lone Star Bar and Grill would complete that job by the end of the day and could start on the repairs to the Double R first thing in the morning.

As he relayed the work order to the crew foreman and clipped the phone back onto his belt, he watched his sister-in-law leave the house and start across the yard toward him. A knot the size of his fist twisted his gut. The moment he'd learned about the tornado and Craig's death, he had rushed back to his hometown to do whatever he could to help Royal recover and to help Paige get through making the funeral arrangements for his brother. Right away it had become apparent that he'd have to keep his interaction with her brief and he knew she had to be confused by the strained encounters. But he hadn't anticipated the effect she still had on him.

The first time he'd laid eyes on her in his senior year of high school, Cole had been fascinated with her. Tall and willowy, she moved like a graceful dancer, and as he watched her walk toward him now, he found himself just as captivated as the day they'd first met. The slight breeze played with her long auburn hair and he couldn't help but wonder how the soft wavy strands would feel as he ran his fingers through them.

"I didn't realize you were coming by today, Cole," Paige said, smiling as she walked up to him. She used the name his family called him and it suddenly occurred to him, she was the only family he had left.

Shaking his head to dispel the last traces of his ridiculous introspection, Cole forced himself to concentrate on the reason for his visit to the Double R.

"I've scheduled one of the R&N work crews to start rebuilding your barn and making repairs to the other outbuildings first thing in the morning."

"Have the construction crews you brought with you from Dallas finished all of the work on the other projects first?" she asked. She had been adamant that the repairs the Double R needed could wait until permanent housing for the displaced families who had lost everything during the storm had been taken care of. Her selflessness hadn't surprised him in the least.

He nodded. "Aaron is in charge of overseeing those crews, but he assured me the last of the houses R&N Builders are contracted to rebuild will be finished by the end of the month."

"Good." She shaded her pretty gray eyes from the midafternoon sun with one delicate hand. "Stella and I were talking the other day about how important it is to get the families back into homes of their own and reestablish a sense of permanence and normalcy," she said, referring to Stella Daniels, the town's acting mayor and his business partner's new wife. "Children need that sense of belonging after what they've been through and all they've lost."

Cole detected the compassion in her tone. One of her most compelling and attractive traits had always been her thoughtfulness for others and he realized she hadn't changed much over the years. Paige was still the considerate, caring woman with a mile-wide soft spot for kids she had been in high school. It was a real shame that she hadn't had any children of her own. When she'd married his brother, she'd been pregnant.

Unfortunately, she had miscarried only a few weeks later and, to Cole's knowledge, she'd never become pregnant again. He fleetingly wondered why, but he wasn't about to ask. Cole had never been one to pry and he wasn't about to start now. What had happened between Paige and Craig during their ten-year marriage was their business, not his.

Not knowing much about what little kids needed, Cole nodded. "I guess it's important for them to feel that security."

"I think we all need that," she agreed, smiling sadly. "But especially after the tornado tore up everything familiar to us."

"How are you doing?" he asked, barely resisting the urge to put his arms around her for a comforting hug. It had to be extremely hard for her to lose her husband at such a young age and in such an unexpected way.

"I'm okay," she said, her gaze straying to the distant horizon. "In the past several years, Craig had had to go out of town on business a lot, so I'm used to spending time alone. But I always knew he would eventually be coming back home." Turning to meet his gaze head-on, she added, "It's knowing that won't ever happen and that I'm truly alone in the world that's the most difficult to deal with."

"I know it's been a big adjustment." Cole stated the obvious.

He wasn't sure what kind of business Craig had been involved in that would require a cattle rancher to make frequent trips out of town. But then he didn't know much about his brother's life beyond the fact that he belonged to the Texas Cattleman's Club—the same as Cole and most of their friends. Cole had even convinced Aaron to join the Dallas chapter after they had become friends and gone into business together. The connections they had made through their involvement with the TCC, as well as their reputation for excellence in quality and value, had helped propel R&N Builders to become one of the premier construction companies in the state.

They remained silent for several long moments before Paige glanced toward his truck. "Did you bring your things with you?"

"No, I'll just stay at the Cozy Inn," Cole answered, shrugging. "I have to get up pretty early and I wouldn't want to disturb you."

When he'd returned to Royal six months ago, Paige had offered for him to stay at the ranch while he was in town, but he had declined. He'd told her that it would be easier for him to stay close to the job sites where his construction crews worked. But the real reason he had stayed in Royal instead of at the ranch was due to the attraction he still felt whenever he was around her.

Paige gave him one of those looks that a woman gives a man when she thinks he's being overly obtuse. "Think about it, Cole. I live on a working cattle ranch. I get up before dawn every morning to give the hired hands a list of things I want done for the day."

"Don't you have a foreman to do that?" he asked, frowning.

"I do, but he's still dealing with his injuries from the tornado." She shook her head. "He was in the barn when the storm moved through and it's a miracle he survived. I assured him that he would have a job once he recovered, so I'm taking over for him until he's able to return to work."

"Couldn't you have one of the other men act as foreman until he recovers?" Cole asked.

"I could have, but with Craig gone I need to stay busy," she answered. "Besides, I want to learn more about managing the ranch since I'm going to be running it alone."

"You could always sell out and move into town," he suggested.

She looked directly at him. "I did think about it. But this is my home now and I prefer the country quiet over the sounds of a busy town."

Cole couldn't fault her for that. He had grown up on the ranch and when he'd gone away to college, it had taken him most of his first semester to get used to the noise of a bustling campus. Now, living in Dallas, he spent most of his weekends in a fishing cabin on a nearby lake just to get a little peace and quiet.

"Living in town would be closer to the charities you're involved in," he said, shrugging.

He hadn't discussed anything about her future plans with her since Craig's death. For one thing, he had made sure not to spend too much time with her once it became clear he was still attracted to her. And for another, it really wasn't any of his business what decisions she made or where she lived.

"And staying here at the ranch instead of driving back and forth to the Cozy Inn would be closer for you while your work crew rebuilds my barn and makes the repairs to the outbuildings," she shot back. "You said yourself that you liked to be close to the job sites you're in charge of overseeing. You couldn't get any closer to the job than staying here."

He hadn't expected her to turn the tables on him and use his excuse not to stay at the ranch against him. "I wouldn't want to impose," he hedged.

She shook her head. "That's ridiculous, Cole. This was your home long before it was mine."

Cole didn't want to go into the fact that he really hadn't missed the home he grew up in. He had too many memories of the altercations he had been in with Craig to be overly sentimental about it.

"But it's your home now," he countered.

"And I'm inviting you to stay here," she said, giving him a smile that caused every one of his male senses to go on high alert. "It will give us the chance to catch up."

As he stared at her, Cole realized that he'd run out of plausible excuses. He couldn't tell her the real reason behind his reluctance to stay at the ranch with her. She would probably think he was crazy, and to tell the truth, he really couldn't say she would be all that far off the mark. It was absolutely insane to be so damned attracted to his late brother's wife.

Resigned, he finally nodded. "All right." He turned toward his truck. "I'll bring my things with me tomorrow morning when we start the job."

"Would you like to stay for dinner?" she asked, walking beside him.

"Thanks for the offer, but Stella has a town council meeting and I promised I'd meet Aaron for dinner at the TCC clubhouse to discuss business." He felt guilty when he noticed the disappointment she couldn't quite cover with her smile.

"Okay, then I'll see you tomorrow morning," she said, turning toward the house.

"I'll be here for the next couple of weeks or so," he felt compelled to tell her. Maybe knowing it wouldn't be just a night or two would change her mind about having a houseguest for such an extended period. "Before I leave to go back to Dallas, you'll probably get tired of looking at me over the dinner table."

His words didn't seem to discourage her. If anything, her smile brightened. "I'll plan on making something special for dinner tomorrow evening to welcome you back home."

Cole's guilt at avoiding her the past six months increased tenfold as he watched her walk up the back porch steps to enter the house. He knew Paige had to be lonely. Her parents had both passed several years ago, and with Craig gone, charity work could only go so far to fill in the empty hours of a day. She was obviously anticipating having someone to talk to for a change.

Climbing into his truck, Cole started the engine and drove down the lane to the main road. The next few weeks were going to be a true test of his fortitude. From the time he'd seen her walking down the hall at Royal High School all those years ago, he had wanted nothing more than to make her his girl. But it was too late for that. She had married his brother and, even though he and his twin had never gotten along and hadn't spoken in more than ten years, Cole wasn't about to disrespect Craig's memory or his marriage to Paige.

The following morning when Paige got out of bed, she found that she looked forward to starting her day for the first time in longer than she cared to remember. What she had told Cole yesterday afternoon had been all too true. Craig had been away on business several nights out of each month for their entire marriage, but she had always known he would be returning home. And even though they had stopped sharing the same bed a few years ago due to Craig's restlessness while he slept, she had taken comfort in the fact that she wasn't alone—that he was just down the hall in the master suite. But the finality of his death not only forced her to face the fact that she had been lonely for a very long time, but also made her realize that their marriage had never been what she had wanted it to be.

She sighed as she walked into the bathroom for a quick shower. Maybe their relationship would have been different if circumstances had been less stressful when they'd gotten married and she hadn't lost the baby. But she'd had very little control of the situation. The minute Craig's father had learned she was pregnant, he had insisted that Craig do the right thing and marry her immediately. Her parents had been older and very conservative and the news of their only child being pregnant out of wedlock had broken their hearts. That was why when they urged her to accept Craig's awkwardly worded offer of marriage—she hadn't wanted to disappoint them further and agreed.

Unfortunately, only a few short weeks after she became Craig's wife, she'd lost the baby and had been unable to become pregnant since. She supposed she could have requested they end the marriage and go their separate ways. But she had made a lifetime commitment when she'd recited her wedding vows and she had been determined to be a good wife to Craig, even though they hadn't been in love.

As she finished drying her hair, Paige decided not to dwell on the past. Craig was gone and, although they might not have had the closeness she had always wanted for their marriage, they'd had a comfortable life together and gotten along well. That was more than some couples could say.

She went downstairs to the kitchen and started the coffeemaker. As she looked out the window above the sink, she noticed that Cole's truck was parked close to where the barn used to be. "When he says he gets up early, he means it," she murmured aloud. The pearl-gray light of dawn hadn't fully given way to the rising sun and Cole had already arrived and was ready to start work.

When the coffeemaker finished, she poured two cups of the steaming brew and left the house. She walked down to where Cole stood looking at a set of blueprints. "I thought you might need some of this," she said, handing him one of the cups.

"Thanks." He smiled as he took it from her. "Since most of the jobs I've been in charge of are on the opposite side of Royal, I couldn't see any sense in driving all the way across town and back every morning for coffee at the diner." Taking a sip, he nodded his approval. "This is the best coffee I've had in the past six months."

"Doesn't the Cozy Inn have coffeemakers in their rooms?" she asked.

He grimaced. "They do, but either I've been doing something wrong or they need to find a different brand of coffee packets."

"Well, you'll at least have decent coffee while you're here at the ranch," she said, taking a sip from her own mug.

"About that…" He hesitated. "I'm not sure it would be appropriate for me to stay here."

She frowned. "Why on earth would you say that? There's nothing improper about you staying here. This ranch has been in your family for five generations."

He stared at her for several long moments before he finally nodded. "I guess you have a point."

"I know I do," she stated firmly. "Did you check out of the Cozy Inn?"

"I have to go back into Royal to meet with the crew working on rebuilding the hospital wing that collapsed during the storm." He shrugged. "I'll check out then and bring my things with me."

The sound of a big truck had both of them turning to see a semi pulling a trailer full of lumber coming up the lane, followed closely by three R&N Builders pickup trucks. "It looks like it's time for me to go back to the house and let you all get started on my barn."

Cole handed her his empty cup. "Thanks for the coffee."

His hand brushed hers, and a pleasant tingling sensation zinged up her arm. "I—I'll have your room ready when you get back from town."

As she walked back to the house, she felt Cole's gaze following her as surely as if he'd touched her. Climbing the back porch steps, she entered the kitchen and took a deep breath. Maybe she shouldn't have been so insistent that Cole stay with her on the Double R, she thought as she set his cup on the counter. When she had been in high school, she'd had a huge crush on him. Perhaps it hadn't completely disappeared.

Thinking back, she could have sworn he had been just as smitten with her. But the one time he had asked her out, she'd had to explain that she wasn't allowed to date until she was finished with school. He had assured her that he would ask her out when he came home from college for the summer after she'd graduated. But he had apparently forgotten his promise and stayed at the university to take a couple of summer classes. By the end of summer, Craig had charmed her into going out with him instead and the following spring they had gotten married. The only time she had seen Cole after that had been when his and Craig's father had passed away.

She poured herself another cup of coffee and sank into one of the chairs at the table. The tension between the brothers at the funeral had been palpable and she never had learned why they were at such odds. She'd thought twins, even fraternal ones like Craig and Cole, were supposed to be close and share a bond that defied logic. But the Richardson brothers were as different as night and day. Whereas Craig had been outgoing and filled with restless energy, Cole was quieter and had a calming air about him. And the contrast didn't end with their personalities.

They looked absolutely nothing alike. Cole had beautiful dark green eyes, was a couple of inches over six feet tall and had a muscular build and straight, light brown hair. Shorter by at least three inches, Craig had pale green eyes, wavy, dark blond hair, and had been on the thin side. Both men were extremely handsome but in different ways. Craig's features were classic and he always looked as if he'd stepped right out of the pages of *GQ* magazine. But Cole had that rugged appeal that sent shivers up a woman's spine and had her imagining how it would feel to be in the arms of all that raw masculinity.

Her heart skipped a beat, and she shook her head as she rose to put their coffee cups in the dishwasher. She had no idea where that had come from, but it definitely wasn't something she intended to give further thought. She wasn't looking to find herself in the arms of any man, let alone Cole Richardson. Even though he was nothing like Craig, she had spent ten years with one Richardson brother and that had been enough to last her for quite some time.

Cole waited until the work crew left at the end of the day to move his things from his truck into the Double R ranch house. He wasn't looking forward to the next couple of weeks—especially after his reaction when his hand had brushed Paige's that morning as he'd passed her his empty coffee cup. If just that slight contact could cause his heart to stall and a fine sheen of sweat to bead on his forehead, what kind of hell would he go through being in such close proximity with her day in and day out?

Pulling his luggage from the back section of the club cab, he slowly walked toward the house. He hadn't been in the Double R ranch house in well over ten years and he wasn't entirely sure he wanted to go inside now. The memory of the night he'd left the ranch for good was an ugly one and had resulted in him severing all ties with his twin. They had managed to be civil with each other for their father's funeral a few years ago, but just barely. As soon as the service had ended, he had gone back to Dallas and, although Craig had started emailing him in the year or two before his death, Cole had deleted the messages unread. He hadn't been interested in anything his brother had had to say.

"I've got your room ready for you," Paige said, opening the door as he climbed the porch steps.

"Lead the way." He took a deep, fortifying breath as he stepped across the threshold and hung his black hat on a peg beside the door.

Cole did his best not to notice the slight sway of her hips as she preceded him down the hall to the circular stairs in the foyer, and he concentrated on looking around the house he grew up in. With the exception of some colorful Southwestern art on the walls, the house looked much the same as it always had. One of the terra cotta tiles at the foot of the steps had a hairline crack from the wear and tear of five generations of Richardson boys' roughhousing, and the honey oak banister still had nicks from where he and his brother had tried sliding down the thin rail.

"What's so amusing?" Paige asked as they started up the stairs.

Lost in the memories, he hadn't even realized he was smiling. "I was just thinking about the time I tried sliding down this rail and ended up wearing a cast on my arm for six weeks."

She grinned. "Not such a good idea?"

"Well, it had seemed like it at the time," he said, chuckling. "But I was only ten and quickly found out that it wasn't."

When they reached the second floor she showed him to the room closest to the stairs—his room when he'd lived here. "I hope you don't mind, but I boxed up the things you left behind several years ago and put them in a closet in Craig's...in the office just off the family room."

"You should have just thrown them away," he said, setting his suitcase on the bench at the end of the bed. He was surprised Craig hadn't insisted on her disposing of everything he had left behind. "I really wouldn't have cared."

"I couldn't do that. They weren't mine to get rid of." Shaking her head, she opened the curtains to let the late-afternoon sun brighten the room. "There were several sports trophies and medals. You earned those in high school, and I thought you might eventually want them."

"I'll go through the box while I'm here to see if there's anything I want to keep," he finally said, swallowing hard. Backlit by the sunshine coming through the window, she looked absolutely gorgeous, and if he hadn't already realized the extent of the attraction he still felt for her before, he sure as hell did now. Her dark auburn hair seemed to glow with shades of red and gold and emphasized her flawless peaches-and-cream complexion.

They stared at each other for several seconds before she started toward the door. "I'd better check on dinner. It should be ready in about twenty minutes if you'd like to wash up."

"Yeah, I'll be down as soon as I shower and change clothes."

When she pulled the door shut behind her, Cole took a deep breath, turned to get a clean set of clothes from his luggage and then headed toward the adjoining bathroom. It was going to cost him a fortune in overtime and his work crew was probably going to end up despising him for it, but he was going to push them to get the Double R job finished in record time. His peace of mind depended on it and for a couple of different reasons.

At one time the Double R ranch house had been his home, but there were too many unpleasant memories of the clashes he'd had with his twin for Cole to be comfortable staying there. When they were growing up, he had dismissed Craig's narcissism and need to win as just being overly competitive. But when his brother had involved others—unconcerned if they got hurt in his game of one-upmanship—Cole had quickly realized Craig was driven by a dark side that seemed to be directed exclusively toward him.

As he finished his shower and pulled on a clean shirt and jeans, Cole gritted his teeth when he thought of their last confrontation. Before he'd had a chance to ask Paige out, Craig had somehow figured out the extent of the attraction Cole had for her and it was as if he had thrown down a gauntlet that Craig quickly picked up. When Craig had taunted him with his intentions of bedding her before Cole had the opportunity to ask her out, they had come to blows. Cole had even tried to divert his twin from his mission by telling him that he was no longer interested in Paige. But it hadn't worked and the next thing he knew, Paige was pregnant and she and his brother were getting married.

Taking a deep breath, Cole tried to release the rage that still gripped him whenever he thought of the callous way Craig had used Paige. It was one thing for his twin to come after him, but when his brother had involved her in his vindictive game, Craig had crossed a line. In Cole's opinion, it was unforgivable.

But that was ancient history now. His window of opportunity with her had closed long ago. No matter what lengths Craig had gone to in order to win Paige, Cole had to accept the fact that she had remained with his brother for more than a decade. That had to mean they had been committed to their marriage, and whether or not he and his twin had gotten along, Cole was bound to honor that.

Two

"I hope you like country fried steak," Paige said, looking up when Cole walked into the kitchen.

The faint scent of his woodsy aftershave put her senses on full alert, but it was the way he looked that caused her pulse to race. His short, light brown hair was still damp from his shower, and he'd shaved off his five o'clock shadow. She barely resisted the urge to sigh when her gaze drifted lower. He was wearing a gray T-shirt with the R&N Builders logo in red, white and blue on the front; the knit fabric had to stretch to accommodate his bulging biceps and emphasized his well-developed shoulders and chest muscles. Her gaze traveled farther, causing her pulse to speed up. His worn jeans rode low on his narrow hips and clung to his muscular thighs like a second skin. She had to force herself to concentrate on removing the apple pie from the oven without dropping it.

Why did Cole have to be so good-looking and so darned masculine? And why on earth did *she* have to notice?

"I like just about anything homemade, but country fried steak is a favorite," he answered, seemingly oblivious to her wayward thoughts. "Is there something I can do to help you finish up dinner?"

She shook her head as she placed their dessert on the kitchen island to cool, then reached for the platter of steaks and bowl of garlic and herb mashed potatoes. Carrying them over to the table, she motioned for him to sit down as she placed the dishes beside the garden salad she had prepared earlier. "I have everything ready if you'd like to take a seat."

He remained standing as she poured them both a glass of iced tea, prompting her to ask, "Is there something else you'd like? I think I have a beer or two in the back of the refrigerator if you'd like one of those instead."

He shook his head and stepped behind her chair as she set the pitcher on the table. "Tea is fine. I'm just waiting to pull out your chair for you."

Paige tried to hide her surprise as she sat down. When was the last time a man had been chivalrous toward her? She couldn't remember if Craig had ever shown her those kind of manners. Maybe when they'd first started dating or when they had attended one of the holiday balls at the Texas Cattleman's Club and he'd noticed all of the other men pulling out their wives' chairs for them. But she knew for certain that he had never done it for her when it was just the two of them sitting down for dinner at home.

"Thank you," she murmured as Cole sat across the table from her.

He shook his head. "I'm the one who should be thanking you for making all of this. Everything looks and smells delicious."

"I love to cook but rarely take the time anymore," she said as they filled their plates. "Cooking for just myself isn't as much fun as it is when I'm cooking for others."

"You don't have someone to do the cooking and cleaning?" he asked, taking a bite of his potatoes.

"After your father passed away, Maria stayed on as the cook and housekeeper for a couple of years before she retired," Paige answered, smiling fondly as she remembered the sweet older woman who had helped her early in her marriage and had taken care of the house and helped raise the twins after the boys' mother had died when they were five. "Craig wanted me to hire someone to replace her, but I talked him out of it."

Cole frowned as he took a drink of his iced tea. "Why?"

"I'm not the type to spend a lot of time on the tennis court or golf course," she said, trying not to notice the play of muscles in his forearms as he used his knife and fork to cut into the steak. "And until the tornado came through, my charity work only kept me busy a couple of days a week." She shrugged one shoulder. "I had to have something to do to keep me busy."

She wasn't going to mention that she had hoped to fill her hours taking care of her children. But it didn't appear that she was going to have any. And it was too emotionally painful to think that she might never have a child of her own.

They fell silent for a time before Cole asked, "Do you still paint? If I remember correctly, you used to be a fairly good artist when you were in school."

"I hadn't put a brush to canvas in years," she said, surprised he remembered her love of art. "But I recently started painting again and thought I might turn Craig's den into a studio."

"Isn't that room a little too dark?" Cole asked, frowning. "I thought natural light was better for painting."

"It is," she agreed, smiling. "Craig converted the sitting room off the family room into his office."

"That would be a good place for a studio," Cole said, taking a bite of his steak. "With that wall of windows on the east side, the lighting should be perfect in the mornings."

"I thought so, too." His genuine interest made her smile. It was nice for a change to have a conversation while she ate, instead of dining alone in silence. "Craig gave me your father's den for my office when he converted that room and since I don't need two, I think it's the obvious choice for a studio."

Cole looked thoughtful. "You know, the lighting would be even better if the south wall was all windows, as well."

"I thought about that, but I wasn't sure it was structurally possible," she admitted. "What do you think?"

"It would need to be braced up in the attic since that's a load-bearing wall and a couple of beams added for support where the two walls meet in the corner, but I don't see why it wouldn't work." His smile caused her pulse to flutter. "I'll check it out for you before I head back to Dallas and let you know for sure just what would need to be done."

"I'd really appreciate that," she said, excited at the possibility of having an artist's studio with the perfect amount of natural lighting.

When she rose to cut them each a slice of apple pie, Cole carried their empty plates to the sink, rinsed them and placed them in the dishwasher. "No more work than I think it would take to make those changes, if you'd like, I could have my work crew get that done for you before we go back to Dallas."

"Really?" she asked, her excitement for the project rapidly building. Craig hadn't discouraged her love of art, but he had never encouraged it, either. "It could be done that soon?"

"Sure."

Cole's smile made her feel several degrees warmer. How could a man look sexy as sin with nothing more than a smile?

"There's no reason not to go ahead if that's what you want," he continued, seemingly unaware of the effect he was having on her. "The work crew will be here, and even if it takes a couple of extra days, I doubt they'll mind. It will just add to the small fortune Aaron and I have paid them in overtime and travel expenses over the past six months."

"Thank you so much, Cole." Thrilled that she was actually going to have her own art studio, she turned and, without thinking, wrapped her arms around him for a hug.

"No problem," he said as his arms lightly closed around her.

They both froze in place, and to say the moment was awkward would have been an understatement. Aside from the fact that she had embarrassed herself with her impulsiveness, the feel of Cole's solid strength surrounding her caused her knees to wobble. Staring up at him, she could tell that he was just as surprised by the embrace as she was. But it was an awareness in his dark green eyes that shocked her all the way to her core.

"I…um, thank you," she said apologetically, feeling heat color her cheeks. Taking a step back, she hoped he didn't notice her hands trembling as she dished up their dessert. "Would you like a scoop of vanilla ice cream on top of your pie?"

He shook his head. "Not this time. It looks and smells delicious just the way it is." She started to reach for the dessert plates, but he picked them up and carried them to the table for her. "As long as we'll be working on it, are there any other changes you'd like to make to your studio?"

His voice sounded just a bit deeper. Was he feeling the tension between them the same way she was?

"How much trouble would it be to put down a laminate or tile floor?" she asked, feeling a little more comfortable now that they were back on the subject of renovating the ranch house.

"No trouble at all," he said, taking a bite of his pie. He seemed more relaxed, as well. "While we get started on the barn, why don't you think about all the changes you want made and then let me know what you decide later on in the week?"

She smiled. "I'll do that."

As they continued to talk about the renovations to Craig and Cole's childhood home, Paige couldn't help but wonder again what had happened all those years ago. What had caused the twin brothers to have a falling out? And why had Cole left Royal without at least telling her goodbye?

Being an only child, she had no idea about the dynamics of sibling relationships. But she couldn't imagine anything so upsetting that it would make them stop talking to each other for more than a decade.

When they'd first married, she had asked Craig about Cole's departure, but he'd told her it didn't matter and they had never talked about it again. Of course, Craig had rarely discussed anything of importance with her. She had always felt a bit like an outsider within her own marriage.

"Thank you for going to the trouble of making dinner," Cole said, drawing her back to the present. He stood up and carried their empty plates to the sink, rinsed them and put them in the dishwasher along with the dishes from dinner. "It was the best home-cooked meal I've had in a long time." He chuckled. "Actually, it's the only home-cooked meal I've had in years."

"I'm glad you liked it, Cole." She rose to clear the rest of the table, but he was already reaching for their iced tea glasses. "I'm sure you're tired from working on the barn all day. I can take care of cleaning up."

He shook his head as he put their glasses into the dishwasher. "You cooked a great dinner. The least I can do is help with the dishes."

As she watched Cole finish collecting the dishes to load into the dishwasher, she couldn't help but note one more contrast between him and Craig. Her late husband had never voluntarily helped her with anything around the house and she'd gotten the distinct impression that he considered anything domestic to be "woman's work" and beneath him.

"If you don't mind, I think I'm going to call it a night," Cole said as she finished wiping off the kitchen island. "The crew will be here around dawn."

"How many men will there be?" she asked, turning out the light as they left the kitchen.

"Seven, counting me. Why?"

"Tell them not to worry about bringing their lunch after tomorrow," she said as they walked down the hall toward the stairs. "I'll have something ready for them every day they work until the job is finished."

"That's very generous of you." Cole placed his hand on the small of her back to guide her as they started up the steps. "But you don't have to do that."

"I know I don't." She barely managed a smile. "I want to do it." His hand at her back was only meant to steady her. But the heat from his wide palm seemed to sear her skin through her clothing and made it difficult to draw her next breath.

"We'll appreciate it," he said when they reached the top of the stairs. "But don't go to any extra trouble."

Stepping away from him at the door to his room, she nodded. "I'll be sure to keep it simple."

They stared at each other a few moments longer before Cole opened his bedroom door. "I'll try to be quiet in case you want to sleep in tomorrow morning."

"Sleep well," she said as she turned to enter her room across the hall.

Closing the door, Paige leaned back against it and took a deep breath. Why did she feel as if she was still that starry-eyed sophomore girl talking to the cutest senior boy in Royal High School whenever she was around Cole? And why had he broken his promise to ask her out when she graduated?

She shook her head at her own foolishness as she pushed away from the door and got ready for bed. She might have had a huge crush on him when she was younger, but that was ancient history. He had made his choice not to ask her out. Besides, some questions in life were just better left unanswered.

The following afternoon, Cole kept a close eye on the clouds in the Southwestern sky. They had been gathering since right after lunch, and unless he missed his guess, they were in for one of the legendary Texas gully washers. Hopefully the rain would hold off until they finished framing the barn, but he wasn't going to bet money on it. There was more than a fair chance he'd lose.

Twenty minutes later, the first crack of thunder rumbled overhead and he knew their workday had come to an end. He motioned for his men working on the rafters to climb down the ladders.

"Go ahead and start putting away the tools," he said when they were all safely on the ground. "We're going to call it a day. There's no sense in risking one of you being struck by lightning."

"See you in the mornin', boss," they all called as they hurriedly loaded their tools into the company trucks.

When fat raindrops began to fall, raising tiny puffs of west Texas dust as they hit the bare ground, Cole grabbed the blueprints for the barn from the tailgate of his truck, threw them into the front seat to keep them from getting ruined and slammed the door. Waving to his men as they drove away, he jogged across the ranch yard to the back porch. He'd no sooner sprinted up the steps than the sky seemed to open up and pour.

Staring at the curtain of rain just beyond the shelter of the porch roof, he clenched his jaw so tight he could've cracked a couple of teeth as he struggled to keep from cussing a blue streak. It was only midafternoon, and just the thought of being confined to the house for the rest of the day and night with Paige had him tied up into a tight knot. How the hell was he supposed to do what was honorable and right when it seemed the universe was throwing every obstacle it could in his way?

Considering the attraction he still had for her, he knew beyond a shadow of doubt the hell he was going to go through being alone with her. The urge to take her into his arms had been almost overwhelming, and if he hadn't realized that before, he did after she threw her arms around him for that tight hug last night in the kitchen. He had known it was her excitement over turning his brother's office into an art studio that had caused her impulsiveness, but that did little to prevent his body from feeling as if he'd been treated to the business end of a cattle prod. Then, when they'd walked upstairs together and he had discovered she was sleeping just across the hall from him, he'd lain awake half the night wondering what she wore to bed or if she wore anything at all. The other half had been spent speculating about why she wasn't sleeping in the master suite. Was the thought of lying in bed without Craig beside her more than she could bear?

"Cole, is everything all right?" Paige asked from behind him. "Why don't you come in?"

Turning, he found her standing just inside the open back door. "Everything's fine. I was just watching it rain," he said, knowing that his excuse for not going inside the house sounded pretty lame.

"You might be out here awhile," she advised with a slight smile. "It doesn't look like it's going to let up anytime soon."

Resigned, he took a deep breath and followed her into the house. "That's why I told the work crew to knock off for the rest of the day."

"That was probably a good idea." She walked over

to open the oven door and check on something inside. "I heard on the news this morning that the weather is supposed to be this way for the next week or so."

Why did she have to look so damned good to him? And why was he having such a hard time keeping things in perspective?

His heart thudded against his ribs when her words suddenly sank in. "The rainy season doesn't normally set in for another couple of weeks."

"I guess it's coming early this year." She closed the oven door and shrugged one slender shoulder. "But you know how it is around here in the spring. We'll probably have nice, sunny mornings and a pop-up thunderstorm just about every afternoon or evening."

It was all Cole could do to keep from groaning aloud. Due to the unpredictable Texas weather, this two-week job had every chance of becoming a month-long ordeal. At least for him. His work crew would reap the benefits in travel pay and overtime when the weather did let up. But he was going to face a lot of long hours confined to the house with the most alluring woman he'd ever known. His only consolation was once his men got the roof put on the barn, there was a little work they could do on the inside—rain or shine.

He supposed he could make a trip into town to see how Aaron and his crew were progressing on the hospital wing. Or he might stop by the TCC clubhouse to have a beer with one of his friends. But checking on the hospital rebuild would only take up an afternoon, and he'd never been one to start drinking in the middle of the day. What he needed was another project to keep him and the crew busy for several days—maybe even a week or two.

"We might be able to work around the rain," he said as a plan came to mind.

She looked skeptical. "How?"

"We could work on the barn and outbuildings when the weather permits and on your studio when it's raining," he said, hoping it would reduce the amount of time they'd spend alone.

"That sounds very efficient," she agreed. "Are you sure you don't mind the extra work? You were only supposed to take care of rebuilding the barn and repairing the outbuildings before you go back to Dallas."

He shook his head. "It will probably take a little longer to get the office converted to your studio because we'd only be working inside when we couldn't work outside," he warned. "But it would keep the work crew from being idle when it rains." He wasn't going to mention that part about cutting down on the amount of time he spent alone with her.

"I don't mind it taking longer at all," she said, smiling. "That room already has an outside entrance to the patio so it will be easy access for them, and since it's on the far end of the family room, it won't disrupt the rest of the house."

"Have you given any more thought to what you want done to the room?" he asked, warming to the idea more with each passing second.

"I really haven't had the time," she admitted. "Maybe we could go over some possibilities after dinner."

"Sure," he said, nodding. When she reached for a couple of pot holders on the counter, he stepped forward to take them from her. "Let me lift that out for you."

"Put it on the island," she said, pointing toward the marble top.

He set the cake pans where she indicated. When he turned back around, he found her staring at him. "What?"

"Nothing." She shook her head. "I was just thinking about possibilities for the studio."

Something told him that wasn't the reason, but he wasn't going to press the issue. Some things were just better left as mysteries of the universe.

"If you don't mind, I think I'll go upstairs for a quick shower and some dry clothes," he said, deciding to make a hasty exit before he did something stupid like wrap his arms around her and kiss her senseless.

She smiled as if she might be happy to have him out from underfoot. "Take your time. Dinner won't be ready for another hour."

"When I come back downstairs I'll help you finish up," he offered.

"That would be nice, but don't feel that you have to," she said, sounding a little breathless.

He nodded and, without another word, walked down the hall, climbed the stairs and entered his bedroom. With his pulse hammering in his ears, Cole made a beeline for the shower, stripped off his clothes and stepped beneath the refreshing spray.

As the warm water washed over him, he scrunched

his eyes shut, let his head fall back and tried to come to terms with what he'd just discovered. Staring into Paige's crystalline gray eyes, he had detected the same awareness he was certain was reflected in his own. And if he'd had any doubt about what he'd seen, the breathlessness he had heard in her voice convinced him that she was feeling the same magnetic pull he was.

So what was he supposed to do? How was he supposed to resist that? After all, he was a man with a man's needs, not a hapless eunuch. But giving in to his feelings wasn't an option, either. He and Craig might not have gotten along in life, but Cole was determined not to denigrate his brother's memory by putting the moves on Craig's wife such a short time after his death.

Cole's first and probably best option would be to leave the Double R as fast as he could. But where would he go?

He was certain his room at the Cozy Inn had already been taken. They only had so many, and with the influx of workers there to rebuild the town needing a place to stay, the owners had a waiting list for their rooms, along with every other hotel or motel in the area. And crashing at Aaron Nichols's place was out of the question. Even though he and his wife had just moved into a beautiful new home in one of Royal's exclusive subdivisions, Aaron and Stella were newlyweds. There was no way Cole was going to intrude on their time together.

The only other option he had was to stay on the ranch, hope the weather cooperated enough for him to work his ass off and get the job done as quickly as possible. Then he intended to get back to Dallas as fast as his truck could take him.

Gritting his teeth against the heat building in his lower belly, Cole reached out and turned the warm water into an icy spray. The next couple of weeks stretched out before him like a life sentence, and he was going to have to fight with everything in him to keep from acting on the attraction. But he was determined to do the right thing or die trying.

After a rather silent dinner, Paige poured herself and Cole a cup of coffee. "Would you like to go out on the porch to have our coffee while we talk about my studio?"

"Isn't it a little chilly for that?" he asked as he accepted the mug she handed him.

"I have a jacket," she said, laughing. "Besides, I love listening to the falling rain. It's very calming."

She omitted the fact that she needed the wide-open feel of being outside in the hope of easing some of the tension between them. With Cole in residence, the normally spacious two-story house felt a whole lot smaller and made her more aware than ever of the attraction still simmering between them. She might have been able to ignore it if she hadn't seen the heightened awareness in his eyes that afternoon when he'd helped her remove the cake from the oven. But all it had taken was one look and she knew they were both dancing around on thin ice.

"Here, let me help you with that," he said, setting

his coffee on the counter when she reached for her denim jacket on one of the pegs beside the back door.

When he took her jacket from her, Cole's hand brushed hers, sending a delightful tingle up her arm. "I—I was just going to throw it around me," she stammered.

Nodding, he stepped behind her to gently drape the garment over her shoulders. His hand seemed to linger a little longer than was necessary, and it was all she could do to keep from leaning her head to the side to lay her cheek against the back of it.

"Ready?" he asked, picking up his coffee mug. When she nodded, he reached around her to open the door. "Ladies first."

As they walked out onto the porch and sat down in the swing, Paige realized she'd made a serious error in judgment. She hadn't even considered how intimate it would feel as the sun went down and the dark night enveloped them.

"Besides the floor and another wall of windows, what do you want done to your studio?" he asked, setting the swing into motion.

"Would it be a lot of trouble to add a couple of cabinets for storing paints and canvas?" she asked, happy to focus on something besides the man seated on the other end of the swing.

"It wouldn't be any trouble at all." He took a sip of his coffee. "In fact, we could even add a sink for cleanup if you want."

She liked the idea, but she wasn't sure how difficult

that would be. "Wouldn't that be a lot more work adding the extra plumbing?"

Cole shook his head. "Not really. The north wall already has water and drain pipes running inside of it for the half bath on the other side. It's just a matter of tapping into those."

Enthused by the way the plans were shaping up, Paige set her coffee cup on the small wicker table beside the swing and turned to face him. "That would be fantastic. Since I mostly work with acrylics and watercolors, I'll be able to rinse and clean brushes without having to leave the room and run the risk of dripping paint on something."

"It's nice to see you're excited about it." His smile caused a tiny flutter in the pit of her stomach. "And I'm glad I'm able to help make it happen."

Suddenly self-conscious, Paige laughed nervously as she sat back in the swing to stare down at her hands. "I'm sorry. You probably think it's silly for a grown woman to be this enthusiastic about something as commonplace as redecorating a room."

He placed one index finger under her chin to lift her head until her gaze met his. "Not at all. Why would you think that?"

"I suppose it's because I've never done something like this before," she admitted. "Craig liked the way the house was and discouraged me whenever I mentioned wanting to change anything about it."

Cole's only reaction was a slight narrowing of his dark green eyes. "It's your house now, Paige. You can do whatever you want with it." His touch and the gentle tone of his deep voice sent a shiver up her spine and made her more aware than ever that there was still a spark between them.

Before she realized what was happening, Cole leaned forward to brush her lips with his. When he lifted his head, he seemed to search her face for a moment before he set his coffee cup beside hers on the wicker table, then took her into his arms.

Unable to find her voice, she simply watched as he lowered his head again to fuse their mouths. The feel of his lips as he slowly, methodically acquainted himself with hers was as erotic as anything she had ever experienced. Of course, she had only kissed one other man in her entire life, and although her late husband's kisses had been pleasant, they hadn't been anything like Cole's. Warm and pleasantly firm, Cole's lips caressed hers in a way that made her feel as if he was worshipping her.

When he softly traced her mouth with his tongue, then coaxed her to open for him, Paige couldn't have denied him access if her life depended on it. As she parted her lips, her heart beat double time and at his first gentle stroking of her inner recesses, she felt as if she would melt into a puddle. When his arms tightened around her, Paige automatically wrapped hers around him and held on as the feel of his strong body pressed to hers sent shivers of longing straight up her spine.

The unexpected sensation jolted her back to reality and quickly had her pulling away from him. Had she lost her mind? Cole was her late husband's brother and the last man she should be shivering over.

Cole immediately released her and, muttering a curse, got up from the swing. Walking over to the porch rail, he kept his back to her and remained silent.

Unsure of what else to do, she rose to her feet and picked up their coffee cups from the wicker table. "I... um, I'm pretty tired. I think I'll go ahead and turn in for the night."

As she started to open the back door, he finally spoke. "I'm sorry, Paige. I was way out of line. It won't happen again."

"It...wasn't entirely...your fault," she said honestly as she continued into the house.

After placing their cups in the dishwasher, she went straight upstairs to her room. Why did she feel so confused about Cole kissing her?

She had known what he intended to do when he set his coffee cup down and took her into his arms. He'd given her ample time to resist, but she hadn't made a single move to stop him. Why not?

Lowering herself to the side of the bed, she shook her head. She knew exactly why she hadn't protested. The truth of the matter was, she had wanted him to kiss her. And a part of her wished that he hadn't stopped.

Paige took a deep breath. Had she been so lonely that she fell into the arms of the first man who showed her the slightest bit of attention? Or was it the identity of the man that was responsible for her atypical behavior?

She suspected it might just be a combination of both.

Three

After spending a second sleepless night thinking about the woman across the hall, Cole was bone tired and more than a little irritable. Half of the crew was down with food poisoning from grabbing dinner out of a vending machine at a gas station the night before, everything on the build was taking twice as long because of their absence and the weather was threatening to end the workday early again. The only thing that seemed to have gone right the entire morning was his managing to get up and leave the house without running into Paige.

"Larry, watch what the hell you're doing!" Cole shouted as the man barely missed hitting another one of the workers in the head with a board.

When Larry Martin turned to give him a questioning look, Cole immediately noticed his pallor. A ghost couldn't have had less color. "Did you get a sandwich out of that vending machine last night like the others?" Cole asked.

Larry nodded. "We all had the egg salad sandwiches."

"What about you two?" Cole asked, turning to the other men.

"No way, boss." Harold Jenkins grinned. "Me and Terry had better sense."

"Yeah, we went through the drive-through at the Moo & Cackle and got a healthy meal," Terry Goodman chimed in. "We both had the macho man burger, a basket of chili cheese fries and a large chocolate milkshake."

"I'm glad you didn't decide on something unhealthy," Cole said drily.

"I think I'm dying," Larry complained, holding his stomach.

"Go ahead and pack it in for today," Cole said, resigned to the fact that with the majority of his crew out sick there was no way they could get anything else done on the build. "One of you call me in the morning to let me know how many of you are able to work."

While Harold and Terry loaded tools into the truck, Cole rolled up the blueprints. "Larry, I want you and the other three who ate from that vending machine to go to the urgent care clinic at Royal Memorial Hospital," he said, placing the barn plans in the seat of his truck. "R&N Builders will pay for the visit and whatever medication the doctor prescribes."

"Thanks…boss," Larry said, sounding worse by the minute.

"But do me a favor. Don't eat egg salad out of a vending machine again," Cole advised.

"I don't think…I'll ever eat…again," Larry moaned.

If he felt as bad as he looked, Cole couldn't say he blamed the man. "Just get to feeling better. You can worry about what you eat after that."

As he walked toward the house, he watched the R&N truck drive down the lane and felt first one, then another drop of rain land on his forearm. In no time, it was a steady shower and by the time he climbed the back porch steps, the sky opened up with another downpour. It wasn't even lunchtime and the rain had already set in for the day.

Staring at the back door, he wondered what he was going to say to Paige. Would she want to talk about last night? Or would she prefer to act as if the kiss never happened?

He guessed he could come up with some excuse to make the five-mile drive into Royal in order to avoid the situation entirely, but that would only delay the inevitable. Besides, he had never been the kind of man who avoided confrontations. He preferred to hit a problem head-on, deal with it and put the issue behind him.

He opened the door, entered the kitchen and looked around. He had expected to find Paige getting ready to make lunch, but she was nowhere in sight.

"Paige," he called, walking down the hall.

"I'm in Craig's off…in the room I'm turning into

my studio," she called back, correcting herself mid-sentence.

Cole walked across the family room to the door-way of what had been the sitting room when he'd lived there. When he realized Paige was cleaning out his brother's desk, he picked up a filled box. "Where do you want this?" he asked.

"In the den," she said, brushing a wayward strand of her long auburn hair from her cheek. "I wanted to get the room cleared out so your men can get started on the studio whenever they're ready. I can go through Craig's things later."

"I assume Craig had the accounting records and breeding registers on a computer?" he asked, picking up one of the filled boxes. "Do you need that moved, too?"

"Craig used a laptop for everything," she said, opening one of the desk drawers to poke around inside. "I moved it into my office the week after his funeral."

Carrying the box to the den, he realized that Paige hadn't yet looked him directly in the eye. He hated that she felt embarrassed or awkward about something that hadn't been her doing. He was the one who'd initiated the kiss, and he was going to take full responsibility for it.

"Paige, we need to talk about last night," he stated when he returned to find her sifting through the contents of a small tin box.

"I'd rather not," she said, continuing to give her full attention to the container.

He walked over to where she sat in the chair behind the desk and, moving the tin out of the way, took her hands in his to pull her to her feet. "Look at me," Cole commanded when she kept her gaze trained on his chest.

When she raised her gaze, he hated the embarrassment he detected in her dark gray eyes. "What happened last night was not your fault," he assured her. "I take full responsibility for it. I was the one who took advantage of the situation."

She surprised him when she shook her head. "I can't let you do that, Cole. I was just as guilty as you were."

"How do you figure that?" he demanded, frowning.

"Would you have stopped if I'd asked you to or given you the slightest indication that I was uneasy about it?" she asked.

"Absolutely," he said without hesitation. "I've never forced my attention on any woman and never will."

"Exactly my point," she said, nodding. "Don't you get it, Cole? I might have been a bit surprised at first, but I wanted you to kiss me. The only reason I put a halt to things was because I was frightened by that realization." She took a deep breath. "I'm still not sure that I'm comfortable with that little bit of self-discovery, but it's the truth."

He had known they were attracted to each other, but hearing her tell him that she had wanted his kiss sent a wave of heat through him at the speed of light. Cole felt his body begin to tighten and barely managed to keep himself from groaning aloud.

"I don't think my staying here is a good idea," he said, releasing her hands to take a step back.

She stared at him a moment before she shook her head. "That's nonsense. All the hotels and inns in Royal are still full of workers here to rebuild the town. It would be next to impossible to find a place to stay. Besides, we're adults. There might be a lingering attraction between us from when we were younger, but surely we have enough control to be objective about it."

As he stared at her, he had to agree that what she said made sense. They weren't and never had been hormone-crazed teenagers who couldn't keep their hands off each other. Hell, last night was the first time he had even kissed her.

"You're right," he finally said, nodding. "We can handle this."

And maybe if he repeated it to himself enough, he might even start to believe it.

After lunch, Cole checked to see what kind of bracing would be needed in order for his men to turn the south side of the room into a wall of windows for Paige's studio while she continued packing boxes. When he came back downstairs, he carried them into the den for her, and in no time they had Craig's desk and file cabinets completely emptied.

As they worked together to clear the room, Paige began to relax. They both seemed to have put last night behind them and were moving toward building a companionable friendship.

"The only things left to move to the den are a few boxes in the storage closet," Paige finally said, unlocking the door to gaze inside.

"Besides my sports trophies, what else is in there?" Cole asked, looking over her shoulder.

He wasn't touching her. He didn't have to. Just sensing his nearness sent a shiver of excitement sliding up her spine and caused a hitch in her breathing.

Paige gave herself a mental shake. The chemistry between them was nothing more than the remnants of a high school crush. All she had to do was keep that in mind and everything should be fine.

Besides, she wasn't interested in becoming involved with any man right now, let alone her late husband's twin brother. Since Craig's death, she had discovered a strength and independence that she hadn't realized she possessed. She wasn't willing to give that up, even for the man she'd had a crush on since she was sixteen years old.

"Other than your sports memorabilia and some of your father's personal effects, I have no idea what's in here," she answered, doing her best to focus on what Cole had asked her instead of the man himself. "Craig wasn't sentimental and never kept anything that he didn't think he could use or that served a purpose."

"If you don't mind, I would be willing to go through Dad's stuff for you," Cole said. "I don't have anything that belonged to him and, unlike my twin, there are a few things that I'd like to have that belonged to Dad."

"Of course. You can have all of your father's belongings," she said, her heart going out to him. Apparently, whatever had happened all those years ago to cause the two brothers' estrangement had prevented Cole from speaking to Craig about anything he wanted of their father's that hadn't been spelled out in Mr. Richardson's will. "I have several things that belonged to my parents and each time I look at them I'm reminded of a fond memory."

"Thanks, Paige. I really appreciate it." He gave her a resigned smile. "I'll probably get to go through everything as early as tomorrow since I expect the crew to still be out sick." Over lunch, Cole had told her about his workers suffering from food poisoning and that they might not be able to work for the next couple of days.

"Well, when they recover we'll be ready for them to get started on my studio." When she looked inside the boxes on the closet shelves, she frowned. "That's odd."

"What?" he asked.

"Why on earth did Craig keep this closet locked?" she asked, not really expecting Cole to know any more about his brother's reasoning than she did. "Yours and your father's things are all that's in here. I expected important documents or something else that would require a little more security."

"To tell you the truth, I never did understand why Craig did a lot of things," Cole muttered, reaching to lift one of the boxes.

As she watched him carry the carton out of the room, she had to admit that most of the time she hadn't understood her husband, either. She was sure it made sense to Craig, but he never went out of his way to explain what he was thinking, and if she asked, nine times out of ten he would tell her not to worry about it.

Deciding there was no way of knowing how Craig's

mind had worked, she picked up the phone to make arrangements for the thrift shop run by one of the TCC charities to pick up the office furniture. By the time she ended the call, Cole had finished taking the rest of the boxes from the closet to the den.

"Thank you for helping me," she said, smiling as she surveyed the almost empty room.

"You did all the work." He grinned. "All I did was supply the muscle."

Forcing a smile, she nodded. She'd done her best not to notice how the sleeves of his T-shirt stretched over his bulging biceps each time he picked up a box. Most of the time she had failed miserably.

"I hope you don't mind something quick for dinner," she said as they started toward the door. "I didn't realize it was getting so late."

"I'm fine with whatever," he said, following her into the kitchen. "Why don't we have a frozen pizza or sandwiches?"

"Pizza and salad sounds good," she agreed.

Going into the pantry, she removed a thick-crust self-rising pizza from the freezer. When she returned, Cole had already gathered the makings for a salad from the refrigerator and started tearing up lettuce into a couple of bowls.

Paige put the pizza in the oven, then helped Cole finish making the salad. She enjoyed the relaxed camaraderie as they worked side by side to prepare the meal and felt more confident than ever that they would be able to dismiss their attraction and might even become good friends.

Forty-five minutes later, as they cleaned up from dinner, Cole asked, "Are you ready for coffee out on the porch swing?"

Paige closed the dishwasher and turned it on before she looked directly at him. Considering that she still found him extremely tempting, she wasn't entirely certain it would be a good idea to put themselves in the same situation.

"Do you think that's wise?" she asked.

"To tell you the truth, I'm not sure. But I don't want you to stop doing the things you enjoy because of me." His slow smile caused her heart to flutter. "Besides, I gave you my word that nothing else would happen. That hasn't changed, Paige. The only way I'll break that promise is if you ask me to."

She could tell he was completely sincere. But he wasn't the one she was worried about.

"I'll make coffee," she said, determined to prove to herself once and for all that she could control the temptation he represented.

But the more she thought about it, the more Paige realized her apprehension was silly. They had worked together most of the day clearing out Craig's office and nothing had happened. But the real test would be whether they could be together in a more intimate setting without anything happening. Once she was convinced they could do that, then she was certain they would be able to move forward with renewed confidence and build a solid friendship.

When she poured them each a cup of coffee, Cole draped her jacket over her shoulders. His hand didn't linger as it had the night before, and Paige silently chastised herself for feeling a little disappointed. This was the way she wanted it to be between them—companionable without complications.

Once they were seated on the swing, she listened to the rain falling softly on the new spring leaves of the live oak trees surrounding the house and tried to remind herself to relax and enjoy the moment. "I think this is one of the things I love the most about the Double R," she said softly. "It's so peaceful out here."

"It's one of the things about living on a ranch that I miss," Cole agreed, his voice just as hushed. It was as if neither of them wanted to disturb the tranquility of the night. A cow bawled somewhere in one of the pastures, causing him to chuckle. "Even when the silence is broken by a cow calling to her calf or a coyote howling off in the distance, it beats the hell out of listening to the sounds of a city."

Taking a sip of her coffee, she nodded. "When Craig and I first got married and moved to the ranch, I didn't want to live outside of town and really wasn't all that happy about being here. Now I wouldn't want to live anywhere else."

"I wasn't aware that you two didn't have a place of your own before Dad died," Cole commented.

"Craig thought it would be best for me to be here with your dad when he had to go out of town on business." She took another sip from her cup. "Your father's health had already started to decline and I didn't mind staying with him. He treated me like a daughter and I don't know what I would have done without his comforting words when my parents were killed in the car accident."

"I'm sorry you lost your folks in such a tragic way," Cole said softly. "They were good people."

"Thank you," she murmured. "It was a difficult time for me."

Neither spoke for several minutes, and Paige wondered if Cole was upset that she had been there to take care of his father when he hadn't.

"I'm glad you and my dad had a great relationship," he finally said as if he'd read her mind. "He deserved to have someone he loved with him who wasn't a big disappointment to him."

Paige frowned as she turned to face him. "Cole, you were never a disappointment to your father. He used to talk all the time about the things you had accomplished and how proud he was of you."

She wasn't about to mention that his father's praise of him had caused a lot of tension between Mr. Richardson and Craig or that their father hadn't approved of Craig's business trips. There was no sense in focusing on Craig's faults when he wasn't there to defend himself.

"I know that things between you and Craig weren't good and whatever was going on kept you away from Royal," she said tentatively. "But your father seemed to understand and was happy that you had built a good life for yourself up in Dallas."

He gazed at her for several long seconds before he turned to stare off into the darkness. "I did manage to see my dad a few times over the years at the Texas

Cattleman's Club when I had to come down here for a meeting or when he came up to Dallas with a delegation from the Royal chapter. But he never talked to me about R&N Builders. All he wanted to know was if I was ready to come back to Royal where I belonged."

Paige could tell that it bothered Cole, but she wasn't going to ask what had happened between him and Craig to keep him away for so long. If he wanted her to know, he would tell her. Otherwise, it was none of her business.

"I think it's about time to call it a night," Cole said a few minutes later. "If the crew is back on their feet tomorrow, I'll need to be ready to work." He stood up and stretched his arms. "That's if the weather cooperates."

"That's a lot of 'ifs,'" Paige pointed out as she got up from the swing.

When he reached around her to open the back door, his arm brushed her breast, sending a tingling excitement throughout her body. His sharp intake of breath indicated that he'd felt it, too.

The air was suddenly charged with tension, and as they stared at each other, she watched his eyes darken with the same desire that she was certain shone in hers. Thankfully, neither of them commented on the moment as they entered the kitchen and she held out her hand for his cup. She noticed when he gave her the mug, he held it so that she could grip the handle without touching his hand. All things considered, it was a very wise choice.

She set the cups in the sink and walked with him down the hall to the stairs. As they climbed the steps, she could feel the heat from his hand close to her back, but this time he didn't touch her.

Reaching the top step, Paige released the breath she'd been holding as she turned toward her bedroom. "Good night, Cole."

"Sleep well," he said. "I'll see you in the morning."

Paige nodded and, without looking back, went into her room. They had passed the test, and he'd stayed true to his word. He had promised he wouldn't kiss her again unless she asked him to. She hadn't asked him to, even though she had been sorely tempted to do just that.

Sighing, she thought about how she felt now as opposed to the way she had felt as a wide-eyed teenager. At sixteen, her feelings had been those of an innocent, inexperienced girl with a crush on the best-looking boy in school. But now she was looking at Cole through the eyes of a woman, and her feelings were far from chaste.

A shiver slid up her spine as she undressed and pulled on her nightshirt. She and Cole were adults now, with adult desires and needs. And although she knew it was for the best that he hadn't kissed her, she couldn't help but wonder if he felt as let down and disappointed as she did.

Cole stopped gazing up at the ceiling long enough to glance over at the clock on the bedside table. He had gotten into bed more than two hours ago and he was still as wide-awake as when he'd first stretched out.

Punching his pillow, he turned to his side to stare at the closed bedroom door. Why did he have to be so damned honorable? He had given Paige his word that nothing was going to happen between them. And it hadn't. But he was paying a hell of a price for his nobility.

It had been nothing short of torture helping her empty Craig's office and not being able to take her in his arms. The sound of her soft voice, the herbal scent of her long, auburn hair and just the sight of her moving gracefully around the room had tied him into a knot the size of a basketball. But as torturous as the day had been, sitting on the porch swing beside her this evening and keeping his hands to himself had been pure hell.

Feeling as if he were ready to crawl the walls, he ground his teeth against the tightening in his lower body. Maybe he needed to make a trip up to Dallas this coming weekend and give Sally Ann Denton a call. Neither he nor Sally Ann were interested in a serious relationship, but they came together from time to time for a "no-strings-attached" night of relief from the stress and tension of their day-to-day lives.

But even as the idea came to mind, Cole rejected it outright. Sally Ann wasn't the woman he wanted. The woman who created the need burning through him at the speed of light was sleeping right across the hall.

How had his brother been able to spend one single night away from Paige? And what in the Sam Hill had Craig been into that kept him away from the ranch so often?

Cole clenched his jaw so tight it ached. He wasn't buying for a minute that his twin had been away on ranch business. There were the occasional weeklong stock shows a rancher needed to attend, but those only took place a couple of times a year. And he seriously doubted Craig was going to the smaller, local auctions. For one thing, those wouldn't require an overnight stay. And for another, a ranch the size of the Double R didn't normally buy or sell cattle at those because the smaller sales barns couldn't deal with the volume of livestock from a ranch that big. Besides, the Double R raised nothing but top-quality, purebred Black Angus cattle. They had contracts with processing plants to supply the beef for high-end restaurants and gourmet meat shops across the country. A marketing firm handled that end of the ranching business, so there was absolutely no reason Cole could see for his twin to be away from the ranch so often. At least, not on business.

Surely Craig hadn't been so stupid that he...

A sudden flash of light, followed immediately by what could only be described as the sound of a bomb exploding, shook the house. But it was the sound of shattering glass and Paige's terrified scream that rocked Cole all the way to his core and had him throwing back the covers to jump out of bed. He grabbed his jeans and pulled them on as he raced to jerk open the door.

He had just taken a step out into the hall when Paige ran headlong into his bare chest. His arms automatically closed around her to keep her from falling backward.

"I think lightning hit the house," she cried, wrapping her arms around him as if he were a lifeline.

"Did it break the windows in your room?" he asked, his heart pounding hard against his ribs.

It wasn't something that happened often, but he had heard of lightning coming through windows and striking people inside a house. She was clearly all right, but it was the thought of what might have happened that caused a cold feeling to fill his chest.

"N-no," she said, trembling against him. "It wasn't in my room."

"Stay here while I go check the rest of the bedrooms." He started to take a step back, but she continued to cling to him.

"N-no," she said shakily. "I'm going with you."

"It's going to be all right, sweetheart," he said, tucking her to his side as they started down the dark hall.

Paige was extremely frightened and he could understand why. He'd already been awake when the lightning struck. But to be awakened out of a sound sleep by something that loud had to have been a shock to her system.

As they made their way from one room to another, he opened the doors to a couple of bedrooms before he discovered where the damage had occurred. Apparently lightning had struck one of the trees surrounding the house, sending the top of it crashing through the bedroom's windows.

"There's nothing I can do about it tonight," he said, closing the door. "I'll take care of it tomorrow when I can clear the tree away from the house and see the extent of the damage."

"I think I'll just stay up," she said, walking beside him toward their bedrooms.

"It's barely past midnight," he pointed out. "You

worked hard clearing out the room for your studio, and I'm sure you're worn out. You need to rest."

She shook her head and the feel of her long, silky hair rubbing against his shoulder sent a shaft of longing from the top of his head to the soles of his bare feet. "I won't be able to sleep as long as it continues to storm."

He tried to concentrate on what she had said. "Why not?"

"I was never afraid of storms before," she said, sounding a little embarrassed. "But I was home alone the day the tornado came through and even though it missed the house, the sound of the wind and the way the house shook was terrifying. I've never been through anything like that before and I never want to go through it again."

Her fear was understandable, and he hated that she had been by herself the day the deadly twister caused so much destruction. It was nothing short of a miracle that it hadn't hit the house, and the thought of what might have happened if it had was more than he could bear.

"Where did you take shelter?" he asked, tightening his arm around her shoulders.

"I really wasn't sure where to go until I remembered the tornado drills they made us practice when we were in school. They always had us go into an interior hallway, sit on the floor and cover our heads." She shuddered against him. "I took a throw pillow from the family room couch to cover my head and crouched in the storage closet under the staircase in the foyer."

He nodded. "Other than a basement or storm cellar that was the safest place."

The storm outside thundered loudly, causing her to jump. "I hate being afraid," she said on a soft sob.

Taking his cell phone from the pocket of his jeans, Cole checked the weather app he had installed six months ago after the tornado had torn up the area. Other than thunder and lightning, there wasn't anything severe coming their way. Without a second thought, he steered her toward his bedroom.

"What are you doing?" she asked as they entered the room.

He stopped halfway to the bed to gaze down into her amazing gray eyes and gave her what he hoped was a reassuring smile. "Do you trust me, Paige?"

"Of course," she said without hesitation.

"I'm going to hold you while you sleep," he said, leading her over to the bed.

"I…um, do you think that's a good idea?" she asked, looking doubtful.

"It will be fine," he said. Cole briefly wondered if he had lost the last ounce of sense he possessed. But he would gladly suffer through whatever he had to in order to ease her fears. "I gave you my word this afternoon that nothing is going to happen between us and I meant it. All I'm going to do is hold you and make you feel safe so that you can get some rest."

"What about you?" she asked, looking uncertain. "Will you be able to sleep?"

"Sweetheart, I can sleep through just about anything," he answered.

It wasn't exactly a lie. Normally, after working with one of his construction crews all day, he was out like a light the minute his head hit the pillow. But with Paige in his arms, it was highly unlikely that he would be able to so much as blink an eye.

Thunder rumbled overhead and that seemed to seal the deal for her. "My nerves aren't going to allow me to argue the wisdom of this," she admitted, shaking her head as she got into bed.

Although it was dark in the room, Cole could make out her slender silhouette lying on the king-size mattress and her dark auburn hair spread out across the pristine white pillowcase. He swallowed hard and, taking a deep breath, stretched out beside her to hold her in his arms.

At first she remained stiff, and he knew she was as nervous about the sleeping arrangement as she was about the storm outside. But as she began to relax, he noticed a couple of important details that he had missed before. The fabric of her nightshirt was a lot thinner and the hemline a hell of a lot shorter than he had realized. Of course, his attention had been claimed by easing her fears and assessing the damage from the lightning strike when they were out in the hall. But now?

The last thing on his mind at the moment was a tree breaking a window or her fear of the storm. His focus had narrowed to the enticing woman with very little on lying next to him.

"Thank you, Cole," she said softly. "You probably

think I'm just being a big baby about this, but I really appreciate your consideration."

"We all have things that bother us." He chuckled. "You don't like storms. I'm not a big fan of snakes."

"I don't like those, either," she agreed.

When another clap of thunder interrupted the quiet, she snuggled closer and placed her delicate hand on his bare chest. It was all he could do to keep from groaning aloud.

Yeah, he was just a regular saint, he thought sarcastically. If she only knew how the feel of her soft hand on his skin made the blood in his veins turn to liquid fire or how her lush breasts pressed to his side had him throbbing with need, she would probably kick him out of bed, out of the house and off the Double R Ranch faster than he could slap his own ass with both hands.

Her delightfully warm body was quickly making him harder and hotter than he could ever remember, and he suddenly found it difficult to breathe. He did his best to hold himself away from her, but it was all but impossible when every time it thundered she moved a little closer to him. When she suddenly went perfectly still, he knew beyond a shadow of doubt that she had felt the bulge straining at his fly.

"I don't think this is going to work, Cole," she said, breaking the silence as she started to roll away from him.

"It's all right, Paige." He tightened his arm around her and briefly wondered if he had become a glutton for self-punishment. "I'm a man of my word. I promised that nothing is going to happen unless that's what you want."

"That's the problem," she murmured.

His heart stalled. "What do you mean?"

She was silent for a moment before she finally whispered, "I know it's insane, but I do want something to happen. I want you to kiss me again."

Cole didn't even bother to ask if that was what she really wanted. He didn't have the strength to hold out any longer.

Covering her lips with his, he slowly explored her perfection, then traced the seam of her mouth with his tongue to coax her to open for him. When she did, he once again savored her with all of the reverence she deserved.

He'd kissed a lot of women in his time, but none of them tasted as sweet as the woman in his arms. Cole wasn't going to dwell on what there was about Paige that was different from other women. He wasn't sure he wanted to know.

Unable to stop himself, he moved his hand from her back around to the underside of her breast. Cupping the soft mound, he gently caressed her as he chafed the hardened peak with the pad of his thumb. The thin cotton fabric of her nightshirt became an intolerable barrier, and without thinking he reached for the hem of the garment.

He brought his hand to an abrupt halt when he realized what he was about to do. Paige had asked him for his kiss, not his lust. But when he felt her hand move down his abdomen to the unbuttoned waistband of his jeans, his heart felt like it might jump right out of his chest and it sent a surge of heat straight to his groin. But when she reached for the tab at the top of his fly, he quickly took her hand in his to stop her.

"Paige, sweetheart, it's not that I don't want you touching me. Believe me, I do." He stopped to draw in some much needed air. "But besides the fact that I didn't bother pulling on underwear when that bolt of lightning took down the tree, I don't want us starting something we can't finish."

She kissed his collarbone. "All of my life, I've played it safe, lived by the rules and done what everyone expected of me. If I learned nothing else when that tornado came through it's that life can be over very quickly and unexpectedly. Just once I don't want to hold back and do what others think is appropriate or right. Tonight I want to break the rules and do what I really want to do."

Cole closed his eyes and waged an inner battle with himself. He knew it wasn't wise. Besides the fact that she was his late brother's wife, they were barely reacquainted. But he had wanted her for more years than he cared to count and his nobility only went so far. He had reached its limit and there was no way he could turn back now.

"I can't believe I'm going to say this, Paige," he finally said, forcing himself to ignore the complications making love to her would bring with the morning light. "Let's break a few rules."

Four

As she watched Cole get out of bed to remove his jeans, Paige knew what they were about to do was absolute insanity. But she didn't care. For once in her life she was going to throw caution to the wind and live for the moment. She briefly wondered if she was finally experiencing the rebellious stage that she'd skipped in her teens.

But as Cole tossed his jeans to the side, got back into bed and took her in his arms, she ceased thinking. There would be plenty of time to analyze her decision tomorrow. Tonight she just wanted to get lost in the comfort of his lovemaking and once again feel as if someone cared for her, as if someone needed her.

He immediately placed his mouth over hers and gave her a kiss so filled with passion and need that it took her breath away. As he tenderly explored her with the same thoroughness he had done the first time he'd kissed her, Paige gave herself up to the desire threatening to consume her.

The delicious sensations Cole was creating were electrifying, and she was only vaguely aware when he lifted her nightshirt over her head and tossed it aside. The feel of his calloused palm on her bare breast and the pad of his thumb gently chafing her tight nipple caused her head to spin. She had never experienced anything as amazing as his tender lovemaking.

When he skimmed his hand down her side to her hip, then slipped his fingers inside the elastic waistband of her panties, heat flowed throughout her body and sparks flashed behind her closed eyes. But when he parted her to softly stroke the tiny nub of intense sensations within, she felt as if she would burn to a cinder.

Wanting to explore him as he explored her, she caressed his firm flesh as she moved her hand from his chest down his abdomen and beyond. When she found him, she gently measured his length and girth, and then explored the fullness below. Her reward was a heartfelt groan rumbling up from deep inside him.

The strength of his need for her was overwhelming and the knowledge that she had created that kind of passion in him filled her with a feminine power she'd never experienced before. But when he moved to test her readiness for him, her hands stilled and she gave in to the delightful ache of her own building desire.

"Cole, I…need you," she pleaded.

"And I need you." He paused a moment before he

shook his head. "I don't think we'll be able to do this, Paige. I don't have anything to protect you."

"It doesn't matter," she said, feeling a little sad. "I miscarried over ten years ago, and I haven't been able to become pregnant since. I doubt that I ever will."

"Maybe one day you will," he said hoarsely as he parted her knees with one of his. "But right now, I want you so much, I'm willing to risk it. I'm going to love you now, Paige. Is that what you want?"

"Y-yes. Please…I think I'll go out of…my mind… if you don't," she said, her body burning with the need for him to make them one.

As she stared up at him, Cole took her hand in his and together they guided him to her. Without a word, he slowly moved forward and as he sank himself deep inside her, she realized that she had never felt as complete as she did at that moment.

Lowering his head, he gave her a kiss so tender it brought tears to her eyes as he began a slow rocking against her. His gentle movements and the passion in his kiss were an intoxicating combination and she knew for certain that lovemaking had never been as beautiful or as meaningful as it was at that moment with Cole.

All too soon the building tension inside her took on an urgency that only total fulfillment could relieve. Apparently Cole sensed she was close to finding the release they both sought because he quickened his pace, and in no time, Paige was set free by the waves of pleasure flowing through her. She wrapped her arms around him and held him tightly to her when she felt the surge of his body deep inside hers. A moment later he groaned and gave up his essence with one final thrust.

When he collapsed on top of her, she held him to her and scrunched her eyes shut as reality intruded. Cole was her late husband's brother and she had practically insisted that he make love to her.

Did he think she had used him as a substitute for Craig? That was the furthest thing from the truth, but how could she tell him something like that? She didn't even know how to go about starting that conversation.

She could count on one hand the number of times in the past several years that Craig had made love to her. And even though he had encouraged her to move into another bedroom because of his restlessness during sleep, she suspected the real reason behind his suggestion had been because he'd no longer desired her.

"Are you all right?" Cole asked, levering himself to her side.

"Yes, I'm...fine," she said, feeling unsure of what he might think of her. "Cole...I—"

"If you don't mind, I'm pretty tired," he said slowly, as if he felt as uneasy as she did. "Why don't we talk in the morning?"

Nodding, she started to get out of bed, but he tightened his arms around her and shook his head. "It's still raining and I promised I would hold you so you can get some rest."

"But it isn't storming."

"It might start again," he answered, sounding sleepy.

If the gravity of the situation hadn't already settled in, she might have laughed. But there was nothing funny about what she had done. She had practically insisted that Cole make love to her.

What on earth must he think of her?

Embarrassed by her uncharacteristic behavior, she feared she had destroyed the tentative friendship they had developed over the past week. She just hoped there wouldn't be an awkwardness between them that was so uncomfortable it proved insurmountable.

Around dawn, Cole pretended to be asleep while Paige gathered her clothes and returned to her room. He wasn't exactly being a coward about facing her in the morning light. He just didn't know what he was going to say to her. What could he say?

What he'd done was unforgivable. He had known she was vulnerable and shaken by the lightning strike, and she probably hadn't been thinking clearly. But he had wanted her so badly, he'd lost his perspective and taken advantage of her weakness. Hell, he'd even used her fear of the storm as an excuse to get her to stay in his bed after they'd made love because he hadn't wanted to let her go.

He had known as surely as the sun rose in the east each morning that in the light of day everything would change between them. And it wasn't going to be for the better.

Swinging his legs over the side of the bed, he sat up and buried his face in his hands. After she had drifted off to sleep, he'd lain awake the rest of the night, alternating between feeling guilty and hating himself for his own weakness. He wasn't feeling a lot different this morning.

He had done everything he'd told himself he wouldn't do. In less than a week he had abandoned his vow to respect his brother's memory and marriage, and he'd made love to Craig's wife. He might have even destroyed the tentative friendship he and Paige had started to build.

When his cell phone rang, Cole abandoned his self-loathing to glance at the caller ID. It was one of the members of his work crew.

"What's up, Harold?" he asked, taking the call.

"The rest of the guys are still sick as can be," the man reported. "Do you want me and Terry to come on out there to the ranch and see if there's something the two of us can work on?"

"Yeah, a tree came down and broke a couple of windows during the storm last night," Cole answered. He told Harold what replacement windows and other materials to pick up at the lumberyard to make the necessary repairs. "It shouldn't take more than a few hours to get the job done, then you and Terry can have the remainder of the day off. Maybe the other guys will be back on their feet tomorrow and we can resume work on the barn."

"Sounds good, boss. We'll see you in about an hour," Harold said, ending the call.

Tossing his cell phone back onto the bedside table, Cole got up, grabbed a change of clothes from the dresser and headed for the shower. He wasn't surprised that his men were still out sick, but he certainly wasn't happy about it. Besides the fact that building the barn would take that much longer, he wouldn't have the excuse of working to get him out of the house for a while to figure out how he was going to make all of this right with Paige.

He supposed he could drop by the TCC clubhouse for a few hours and see who was hanging out in the club's sports bar, but that wasn't going to give him the solitude he needed to think. Deciding he couldn't do anything until after his men repaired Paige's windows, Cole finished his shower, got dressed and headed downstairs to see if Paige was even talking to him.

As he entered the kitchen, he couldn't help but breathe a sigh of relief when he found a note by the coffeemaker, telling him that she had gone to the Texas Cattleman's Club for a breakfast meeting of one of her charities. She was going to be away most of the morning, but she had taken the time to see that he had a decent cup of hot coffee. Maybe by the time she returned, he would know what to say to her and how he was going to make it up to her for his weakness.

Three hours later, after clearing away the tree limbs and replacing the broken windows, Cole watched his men drive away and wondered how much longer it would be before Paige returned. He still hadn't figured out how he was going to make things right with her.

He stared at the herd of work horses grazing in the east pasture, and then glanced up at the sky. It wasn't due to start raining until later in the afternoon and there was just something about being on the back of a horse that had always helped him think things through.

Without hesitation, he walked down the porch steps and headed toward the shed, where he'd seen a few saddles that had been salvaged when the barn rubble had been cleared away. Checking to make sure the saddles were intact and any needed repairs had been made, he took one of them, along with a bridle, and headed toward the pasture.

After catching a bay gelding, Cole saddled the horse, mounted up and headed across the north pasture. He didn't have a destination in mind. He just wanted to roam. The Double R had more than a thousand acres, and he knew every inch of it like the back of his hand.

By the time he reached the creek, he had a good idea what he was going to do. He had ridden within a mile of Royal. He was going to continue into town and check to see if there was any chance of getting a room at the Cozy Inn. The way he saw it, removing himself from the ranch was the only solution. He was a guest in Paige's house and he had crossed a line. She might put up a token protest, but she'd probably be happy to see him leave. And if he couldn't find a room, he fully intended to talk to Aaron about overseeing the rest of the Double R build so Cole could head back to Dallas.

He checked his watch. Aaron would be at the TCC, meeting with Gil Addison, the president of the club, to discuss the last of the repairs to some of the clubhouse outbuildings. Maybe he would just skip looking for a room and make the arrangements with Aaron to take over.

Distracted by his dilemma and what he planned to do, Cole failed to notice how close the horse was to the edge of the creek until it was too late. All the rain over the past few days had caused the bank to be unstable and when it gave way under the gelding's weight, Cole was thrown to the ground as the animal struggled to regain its footing.

Landing at an odd angle, Cole felt a sickening crunch in his knee followed immediately by a searing pain. But like any good rancher, it wasn't until he saw the horse was upright and walking normally that he assessed the damage to himself. He hoped that his knee was only sprained, but as soon as he tried to get to his feet, he knew it was something a lot more serious.

Unable to stand, he used his cell phone to call Aaron.

"Hey there, Cole. How's the Double R build going?" Aaron asked cheerfully. Ever since the man had gotten married he seemed to be in a perpetual good mood.

"It's not," Cole answered, trying to move his leg to a more comfortable position. He gritted his teeth against the sharp pain the movement produced. "I need you to take me to the hospital."

"What happened?" Aaron asked, his voice turning serious.

Explaining the situation, Cole gave Aaron directions to a road the ranch hands used to haul hay from one pasture to another. It would bring his friend within fifty feet of Cole's location.

"You'll see a gate to your left," Cole instructed. "I'm sitting about fifty feet from that on the creek bank."

"I'll be right there," Aaron promised.

While he waited on his partner, Cole called the bunkhouse to tell the cook to send one of the ranch hands to the north pasture to get the gelding. When he hung up, he briefly thought about calling Paige to let her know about the situation but decided against it. Aside from the fact that he hadn't had the opportunity to talk to Aaron about overseeing the crew making the repairs to the ranch, he hated the idea of her seeing him like this. Nothing made a man feel lower than having a woman witness him at his weakest.

"Did Aaron say what happened to Cole?" Paige asked as she and Stella hurried through the emergency room entrance at Royal Memorial Hospital.

Stella shook her head. "When Aaron called all he told me was to find you, let you know that he was taking Cole to the hospital because he had gotten hurt and to make sure you met them here."

Paige briefly wondered why Cole hadn't called her, but then she realized that after the events of the night before, she would most likely be the last person he'd call. She was not only guilty of initiating their lovemaking, but she also had been so embarrassed by her actions that she hadn't been able to face him this morning.

It was true that she'd had a breakfast meeting of the planning committee for the Family Crisis Center's annual spring fund-raiser, but wanting to put off having to see the condemnation in Cole's dark green eyes, she'd left the house an hour and a half before it started. She knew she'd taken the coward's way out, and it wasn't something she was the least bit proud of. But she had no idea what she would say to him in the way of an explanation for her actions when she didn't fully understand them herself.

Her inner turmoil had seemed to set the tone for the rest of her morning. During the meeting she had learned she would need to present a program outlining the charity's objectives and accomplishments for the newer volunteers. Public speaking was something she hated doing and was much more comfortable working in the background while others took charge. But with so many in need of assistance after the tornado, all the volunteers were having to take charge of this or that in order to meet the needs of the people they were trying to help.

Now Cole had been injured and it wasn't quite noon. She was almost afraid of what the afternoon would bring.

"Could you please tell me if Cole Richardson has arrived yet?" Paige asked when she and Stella approached the reception desk.

"Are you family?" the receptionist asked politely.

Technically she supposed they were family, but Paige wasn't sure they would allow a sister-in-law in the treatment room or tell her anything about his condition. "I'm Mrs. Richardson."

The woman smiled. "Your husband was brought in about fifteen minutes ago by his business partner. Mr. Nichols is with him now, but you can go on back. He's in examination room twenty-four." She shook her head apologetically at Stella. "I'm afraid only two can be in the room with him at a time."

"No problem," Stella assured the woman. When

Paige started toward the entrance leading to the treatment rooms, Stella stopped her. "Please tell Aaron that I'll be in the waiting room."

"I will." Paige hugged her friend as she whispered, "And thank you for not correcting the receptionist's assumption."

"You and Cole are all the family either of you have left," Stella stated quietly. "Under similar circumstances, I would have done the same thing." She smiled. "Now, go back there to see what's going on and send my handsome husband out here to keep me company."

Smiling, Paige nodded and walked back to the room where Cole was being treated. "What happened?" she asked when she reached the cubicle where Cole lay on a hospital bed. His eyes were closed and she couldn't tell where he was injured.

Standing beside the bed, Aaron turned to smile at her. "He decided to try being a cowboy again and ride a horse. But he found out he's just a little rusty."

She frowned. "He went horseback riding?"

Aaron shrugged. "When he called he said he'd been riding along the creek and the bank collapsed. The horse went one way and Cole went the other."

"Does he have a concussion?" she asked, concerned that Cole hadn't opened his eyes.

"As hard-headed and stubborn as he can be sometimes, he might have been better off if he had landed on his head," Aaron answered, chuckling. "But he apparently tried a standing dismount and couldn't quite stick the landing. He screwed up his knee and we're waiting for Lucas Wakefield to examine him and let us know how bad it is."

"But this wouldn't be serious enough for Luc to be called in, would it?" she asked. Dr. Wakefield was head of the trauma department and the region's top trauma surgeon.

Aaron shook his head. "Aaron was with me when I got Cole's call, and you know how we all are. TCC members take care of our own. Once Luc found out Cole was injured, he wanted to see him first."

"Hey, sweetheart," Cole said, opening his eyes to give her a big grin. "Did you come to give me a good-night kiss?"

Shocked, Paige's cheeks burned with embarrassment. "It's not quite noon yet, Cole." When she looked at Aaron, she asked, "Are you sure he didn't land on his head?"

Winking at her, Aaron laughed out loud. "They gave him something for pain and I think he's starting to feel the effects," he explained. When Cole reached for her hand, Aaron nodded toward the door. "You can take over from here with Don Juan. I'll be out in the waiting room if you need me."

"Stella's out there waiting for you," Paige said as Cole took her hand in his to pull her closer. She waited until Aaron had left the room before she tried to extricate her hand from Cole's. She would have tried sooner, but she was afraid of what Cole would say. "Why don't you try to get some rest, Cole?"

"Why don't you climb into bed with me and we'll

rest together?" he asked, giving her another goofy grin as he tried to pull her closer.

"The nurses and doctor won't let me," she said, thankful that the bed rail was between them. Even with him under the influence of a painkiller, she was no match for his strength. "Besides, you don't mean that."

"Yes, I do." He looked for all the world as if he did indeed mean it.

"We'll discuss this later," she said when Lucas Wakefield walked into the room.

Confident that Cole was in good hands, Paige started to leave the room so Luc could examine Cole's leg. "I'll be in the waiting room with Stella and Aaron."

"Stay here," Cole insisted.

She shook her head. "I can't. Luc needs to examine your leg."

"You don't have to leave," Luc said, smiling as he lifted the sheet to look at Cole's swollen right knee. With practiced yet gentle hands, he tried to bend Cole's leg as Paige looked on. When it appeared that it was locked in place, Luc shook his head. "I'm almost positive you've torn the meniscus. I'm going to order a MRI and call in an orthopedic colleague of mine for a consultation. Depending on what the MRI shows and what the orthopedist says, we may be doing surgery."

"Okaaay," Cole said, sounding drowsy. Apparently the full effect of the drug was going to put him to sleep.

"Surely you won't do the surgery today, will you?" Paige asked, alarmed.

"Normally, we wait until we see if the problem resolves itself on its own. That usually takes two or three weeks," Luc explained to her after it was apparent Cole had fallen asleep. "But the way his knee is locked, I'm afraid a piece of the meniscus may have been torn off and possibly lodged in the joint. That won't get better without surgery." He walked to the door. "I'll go put the order in with Imaging and talk to you again after we get the results of the MRI."

Within fifteen minutes a technician from the imaging department arrived to wheel Cole down the hall for the MRI, leaving Paige to sit down in a chair in the corner and wait for his return. It was the first chance she had to think about his reaction when he'd opened his eyes to find her standing next to the bed.

He'd seemed genuinely glad to see her, and that surprised her. Of course, he was under the influence of strong pain medication, but she always thought that drugs tended to remove filters and revealed what a person really felt. Could it be that he wasn't as upset about last night as she thought he would be? If that was the case, why had he been so pensive after they made love? Was he as confused about what happened as she was? And why hadn't he called her instead of Aaron?

"Paige, I've admitted Cole and he's being taken up to the surgical floor," Luc said, walking back into the small examination room almost an hour later.

Lost in thought, she hadn't realized so much time had passed. "I take it that your diagnosis was confirmed?" she asked, standing up.

"It's not quite as bad as it could have been," Luc said as they walked out into the hall. "I used a little of my pull and had the radiologist give it a preliminary look.

He said the meniscus is torn and ragged and looks like it needs to be trimmed so that it doesn't get caught in the joint."

"When will you be doing surgery?" she asked.

"Tomorrow." Luc smiled. "I'll be observing, and Dr. Campbell will be the attending surgeon. He's the orthopedic specialist I called in. I'll only be observing because of my friendship with Cole."

"I suppose it's because Cole is a TCC member and so are you that you're going to be in the operating room with him?" she guessed.

Luc nodded. "Members of the TCC tend to look out for each other."

"Is that also why the surgery was scheduled so quickly?" There was a bond between TCC members unlike anything she had ever seen.

"Partly," Luc said. "If it was anyone else, we'd probably send him home and schedule the surgery within a week or two. But I know Cole. Given the opportunity, he'll put it off because he's too busy with work to be bothered. Unfortunately, that could cause more damage."

"In other words, you aren't going to give him a choice," she said, knowing that what Luc said was right on the mark. Cole was so dedicated to R&N Builders he bordered on being a workaholic.

"Well, let's just say instead of not giving him a choice, we're sending him a strong message that it's something he doesn't want to delay," Luc answered, laughing. "Besides, it will be arthroscopic surgery and relatively simple. You'll be able to take him home tomorrow afternoon. But he'll have to stay off that leg and keep it elevated for a few days to keep the swelling down."

Paige wondered how Cole would take the news that she was going to take care of his recovery. Because she was the closest thing to family that he had, she was the obvious choice. "Does Cole know about all of this?"

"I told him right after we took a look at the MRI." Luc laughed. "I thought I'd better tell him and get him to sign the consent forms while he was between doses of pain medication and relatively lucid."

Paige smiled. "That was probably a good idea. He's not quite himself once he takes that."

"Most people aren't," Luc said. "Looks like duty calls," he said as a nurse approached with a metal chart in her hand. "I'll see you first thing in the morning, Paige."

As she walked down the hall toward the waiting room to tell Aaron and Stella about the surgery, she couldn't help but think about the upcoming week or so. The first few days might not be too bad. Cole would be on painkillers to keep him comfortable. And if his behavior today was any indication, they wouldn't be discussing their indiscretion; she would be trying to avoid another one.

But there wasn't a doubt in her mind that there would be a day of reckoning when he had recovered enough to stop taking the medication. She just hoped things weren't extremely uncomfortable for either of them when that day came.

* * *

The following morning, Paige sat in a corner by herself in the surgical waiting area while Cole was in surgery. She had spent a restless night thinking about what would happen when she took him back to the ranch. There was no way she was going to try to get him upstairs to his bedroom. There were too many steps and she could only imagine how hazardous it might prove to be with him using a set of crutches.

"Have they taken Cole back to the OR?" Lark Taylor asked when she walked into the waiting room.

Looking up at the pretty registered nurse, Paige nodded. "They took him into surgery about ten minutes ago." She smiled. "I didn't expect to see you today, Lark."

"I'm on break and thought I would come out and check on you," Lark answered. "It won't take too long, and Cole's in the very best hands possible," Lark assured her as she lowered herself onto the chair next to Paige. "Dr. Campbell is the best orthopedic surgeon on this side of the state, and you know Luc Wakefield's reputation. Both of them are top-notch."

"I have no doubt everything will go well." Paige gave Lark a meaningful smile. "I'm just wondering how much of a bear Cole is going to be during his recovery."

The nurse laughed. "Men will be men. I haven't seen one yet who isn't a total grouch when he's sick or injured."

"How are the wedding plans coming?" Paige asked as their laughter faded. Lark was engaged to Keaton

Holt, another member of the TCC, and Paige had never seen the woman happier.

Lark's green eyes sparkled with excitement. "Our families are working together for a change and I think it's actually going to come together by June. Of course, it didn't hurt that Keaton told everyone they better not disappoint me or they'd have him to deal with."

Paige was a bit surprised that things between the two families were so harmonious. The Taylors and Holts had been feuding for some time and it had surprised everyone when Lark and Keaton had fallen in love.

As she stared at Lark, Paige couldn't help but feel envious. The woman was about to marry the man she loved with all her heart, and her excitement was palpable. Looking back on her own wedding day, Paige wished she could say that she had been happy about starting a new life with Craig. But all she could remember feeling was a deep sense of desolation. She had disappointed her parents and had been entering into a marriage with a man she didn't love and who didn't love her. It was supposed to have been the happiest day of her life, but for her it had been one of the saddest.

"You and Cole will be there, won't you?" Lark asked, looking hopeful.

"I can't speak for Cole, but I wouldn't miss your wedding for anything, Lark," Paige said, forcing a smile. "Do you have a gift registry at any of the shops in town?"

"Keaton and I really don't need anything, so I didn't bother," Lark said, shaking her head. "We've decided to request that in lieu of a wedding gift, we'd like for everyone to make a donation to the Royal Tornado Relief Fund or the Family Crisis Center."

"That's such a wonderful idea," Paige said sincerely. "There are still so many in need. I'm sure that both charities will be very appreciative. And I know firsthand they can put the extra money to good use."

"That's what we thought." Lark checked her watch. "My break is almost over. I need to get back to the ICU," she said, rising to her feet. "Good luck taking care of Cole while he recovers from his surgery. And if you need any help or have questions about it, please let me know."

"I will," Paige said, standing to give her friend a hug.

As she watched Lark, who was so thrilled about her upcoming wedding and future, walk out of the waiting room, she felt guilty. Even though she and Craig hadn't been in love, he had been a good husband and the only thing he had ever asked of her was to watch over his father while he was out of town on business. He couldn't help that her heart had been elsewhere on their wedding day or that she had felt as if she were marrying the wrong brother.

Her heart stalled and she gave herself a mental shake. It was water under the bridge now, and there was no sense in dwelling on the mistakes of the past.

As she sat back down to wait for Luc to come out and tell her how Cole's surgery had gone, she thought about the mistake she had made the other night with Cole. It wasn't so much that she felt their lovemaking was wrong. Nothing in her life had felt more right than what she had shared with Cole. It was the circumstances leading up to it that bothered her the most— the fact that she had practically thrown herself at him. What was there about the man that made her act so out of character?

"Cole came through the surgery just fine," Luc said, interrupting her thoughts. Still dressed in his blue surgical scrubs, he walked over to her and sat down. "He's just coming out of recovery and as soon as he gets dressed, you can take him home."

"Is there anything special that I need to do?" She shook her head. "Let me rephrase that. Is there anything I need to try to prevent Cole from doing?"

Nodding, Luc chuckled. "It probably won't be easy, but if you can, keep him off his feet for the next few days. Cole will be on crutches and that should help, but he needs to keep his leg elevated to prevent swelling. Dr. Campbell has a list of instructions that he sends home with his patients, along with a prescription for pain medication. He's also made arrangements for in-home physical therapy to start on Monday. You can call when you get home and set up a time." Luc stood up to leave. "Cole will have a follow-up appointment at the end of next week, but if you need anything or have a concern before then, don't hesitate to get in touch with me."

"Does that include calling you to come by and give him a lecture when he fails to listen to me?" she joked.

"If he gets too ornery, I'll come out to the ranch and help you hog-tie him," Luc said, laughing.

Listening to Luc, Paige decided there would be plenty of time later to analyze what there was about Cole that caused her to react the way she did. Right now, she needed to take him back to the ranch and see just how difficult it was going to be getting him to follow doctor's orders.

Five

"Dammit," Cole muttered as he tried to get up the back porch steps. He couldn't use his right leg and he was convinced his crutches were a bigger hindrance than they were help.

"Do you need to lean on me?" Paige asked from behind him.

"No, I can make it," he answered through gritted teeth. He was determined to get up the damned steps on his own or die trying. He wasn't about to accept her help.

By the time he made it onto the porch, sweat beaded his forehead, and he'd silently run through every cuss word he had ever heard. He couldn't think of anything more humiliating than for Paige to see his helplessness. No man wanted a woman to see how inadequate and weak he was—struggling to do even the basics. It didn't just bruise his ego; it took a seriously large chunk out of it.

While he stood there catching his breath and feeling lower than the stuff he scraped off his boots after a trip through the barnyard, she opened the back door for him to enter the kitchen. Following her through the house on the crutches was torturous, and by the time he got to the family room, Cole knew that physically he'd gone about as far as he could go without sitting down to rest.

"I anticipated climbing stairs being a problem for you," she said as he made his way across the room. "That's why we're not going to attempt getting you up to your room."

He shook his head. "I'll make it. I just need to rest a little."

"No, you won't." She pointed to the couch. "I've already pulled this out into a bed and I've added a four-inch-thick memory foam mattress topper to make it more comfortable for you."

"You didn't need to go to all this trouble," he said, secretly relieved that she wouldn't be watching him struggle to get up the stairs. He might have protested, but as he eyed the bed, he had to admit he was more than ready to lie down after the ordeal of getting from the car into the house.

"Don't be silly," she said, taking his crutches and setting them aside when he lowered himself to the edge of the sofa sleeper. "It's no trouble at all."

Even though he was having a hard time accepting

his limitations, he was thankful for Paige's foresight. She had not only made him a bed downstairs, she'd sent Aaron to the sporting goods store to pick up the pair of gym shorts he was now wearing. There was no way he could have gotten up all those stairs on crutches without falling and breaking his neck, nor could he have put on a pair of jeans. The bandage on his knee alone would have prevented that. But there was an added bonus in wearing the shorts. Because he was going to be in the family room and couldn't go to bed in the buff as he normally did, he could wear them to sleep in, as well.

"Thanks for everything," he said, being careful when he stretched out not to cause himself any more pain than he was already in. His knee was killing him, and he was more than ready for some of the pain pills Dr. Campbell had prescribed for him.

"You need some of your medication, don't you?" she asked as she arranged pillows under his leg to elevate it.

Nodding, he closed his eyes against the throbbing in his knee. "If you don't mind, I really would appreciate it."

As she left the room, Cole wondered how things could get more complicated. He was not only laid up for the next week or so, he was being cared for by his brother's wife—the woman he had taken advantage of when she had turned to him for comfort. And even though she had asked him to make love to her, he'd been well aware of the fact that she had been frightened and vulnerable. He should have been stronger—should have been able to keep his head and resist. He fully intended to talk to her and offer a heartfelt apology for his lapse in judgment when the pain in his knee calmed down to a manageable level. He just hoped like hell she accepted it.

When she returned from the kitchen with a glass of water and a couple of the pills, Cole didn't waste any time downing them as quickly as he could. But he hated having to rely on medication to escape the pain. It made him sleepy and he couldn't remember a damned thing from the time they kicked in until they wore off and he had to take more. But there was an added benefit. At least he didn't have to see the pity in Paige's pretty gray eyes—or if he did, he didn't remember it.

"Try to get some sleep," she advised as she carefully pulled the sheet up to his waist. She placed a small handbell on the end table beside the sofa. "If you need anything, all you have to do is ring this bell."

As he watched her leave the room, he breathed a sigh of relief. At least she hadn't asked why he'd gone out riding yesterday or mentioned anything about wanting to discuss the other night. It was something they needed and would do, but not until he felt as though he could talk without clenching his teeth against the throbbing in his knee.

Closing his eyes again, Cole felt as if he were floating and knew the medication was starting to kick in. As he drifted off to sleep, he smiled. Even though he was sure he came up lacking in her eyes, there wasn't a thing about Paige that he didn't find absolutely amazing. With her long, dark auburn hair framing her angel face and her gray eyes filled with concern for him, he didn't think he'd ever seen a woman as beautiful or enticing as his Paige.

Thirty minutes after she'd given Cole the medication, Paige went back into the family room to check on him. She knew that he was embarrassed and not at all happy that she was having to take care of him. But she enjoyed feeling needed again. Her own mother had always told her she was a natural-born nurturer and would be a wonderful mother someday. Because it appeared that was never going to happen, she had to be content nurturing others she cared for.

Craig had never made her feel that he really needed her, and if she hadn't had Mr. Richardson to focus her attention on while Craig was away, she couldn't imagine how boring her life would have been. But Cole and Craig's father had always made her feel as if she made a difference in the quality of his life, and toward the end, she was the one he'd asked to oversee his diet, medications and doctor's appointments. He'd even told her it was nice to have a woman fuss over him again—something he hadn't had since his wife had died when the twins were little.

As Paige walked over to the bed to stare down at Cole, she smiled. The boy she thought to be so good-looking when they were in high school was nothing compared to the devastatingly handsome man he had become.

Why couldn't he have been the Richardson twin to ask her out all those years ago? He had promised her that he would wait the two years for her to graduate from school. Why hadn't he come back home that summer and kept his promise? And why hadn't she waited for him?

Paige sighed over what might have been. If there had been even the slightest possibility of a second chance for them, she had ruined it. From the moment he came back to Royal over six months ago, Cole had avoided being with her, and it had been clear that he hadn't wanted to stay at the Double R. But she had pressured him into agreeing simply because she had been so lonely. Then when he'd tried to be a gentleman and help her through the fear she'd had since the tornado, she had pressed for more by asking him to make love to her.

Lost in thought, she was startled when Cole reached up to grab hold of her hand. "Hi, sweetheart. Where have you been?"

"In the kitchen," she answered, knowing that he had no idea where he was, let alone where she had been.

"Why don't you lie down with me and I'll hold you while it storms," he said, giving her the same grin he had when she'd first seen him in the hospital.

Her breath caught at the reference to their night together. But she immediately dismissed it. It was the medication talking, not Cole.

"It isn't even raining," she said, forcing a smile.

"We can pretend it is," he coaxed, pulling her down to sit on the edge of the bed beside him. He reached up to trace her lips with his forefinger. "That way we can make love again."

"Why don't you try to get some more sleep," she

countered, her pulse racing like a runaway train. To get her mind off his ramblings, she checked to make sure his leg was still elevated.

When he closed his eyes and she thought he had drifted back to sleep, she started to get up. But his eyes flew open, and he tightened his grip on her hand. "I sleep better and I'm a lot happier when you're with me." His grin widened. "We could make love again."

"That wouldn't be a good idea." Thinking fast, she added, "I don't want to run the risk of hurting your knee."

She knew his euphoria was drug-induced and that he didn't have a clue what he was saying. But that didn't keep her from wishing that he did.

"I, um, have a few things I need to do," she said, trying hard to come up with a convincing excuse. "Would it help if I sit here until you go back to sleep?"

He looked disappointed but finally nodded. "I just don't want to lose you again," he said sleepily.

He didn't want to lose her again? What did he mean by that?

She tried not to put too much stock in what Cole said. He wasn't himself on the medication and nothing he said was based in reality. Unfortunately, her heart wanted to argue the point.

Paige waited until she was absolutely certain Cole was asleep before she extricated her hand from his, stood up and left the family room. She had to call Royal Memorial Hospital to set up an appointment for the following week with an in-home therapist to start Cole's physical therapy. Then she needed to start the chicken soup she'd planned for their dinner. And if she could think of something else to do, she'd do that, too. The busier she kept herself, the less time she would have to think about the man softly snoring on her pullout couch.

Two hours later, she checked on the soup simmering on top of the stove and finished filling parfait cups with chocolate pudding when she heard the ringing of the bell she'd left beside the bed. Putting the cups into the refrigerator, she wiped her hands and hurried into the family room.

"You rang, sir?" she asked, smiling.

"Could you hand me the remote control?" he asked, his eyes not quite meeting hers. "I tried, but I can't reach it without putting pressure on my knee."

"Of course," she said, handing it to him. "Is there anything else I can get for you?"

He shook his head. "I won't bother you again."

"You're not bothering me," she said, smiling. "Just relax and watch the news. I'll bring dinner in to you in a few minutes."

Walking back into the kitchen, she shook her head as she placed bowls of soup, toasted cheese sandwiches and glasses of iced tea on a bed tray to carry into the family room. She had been right. Cole hated that he had to rely on her for the simplest of things. And she could understand that his pride was suffering because of it. But it wouldn't be forever, and if their positions were reversed, she was sure he wouldn't mind helping her.

"Let's get you propped up so you can have dinner," she said when she returned to the family room.

"Thanks, but I'm not really hungry," he said, continuing to stare at the television.

"You have to eat something," she said, setting the tray on the coffee table she'd moved out of the way when she'd pulled out the sofa bed before going to the hospital that morning. Reaching for some throw pillows, she smiled. "Do you need me to help you sit up?"

He finally looked up at her. "Really, Paige, I don't want to be a problem."

Frowning, she put her fists on her hips. "Let's get something straight, Cole Richardson. You are not a bother, a burden or a problem. You need someone to take care of you while you recuperate and, whether you like it or not, you're stuck with me. Now, sit up and let me put these pillows behind you so you can eat dinner. And don't tell me you aren't hungry. I happen to know you haven't had anything to eat all day."

He looked surprised by her outburst, but instead of arguing the matter further, he managed to sit up on his own without putting pressure on his knee and leaned forward for her to put the pillows behind his back. "I hope you didn't go to a lot of trouble."

She smiled. "None at all. The instructions Dr. Campbell sent home with you suggested a soft diet this evening because of the anesthesia, so I kept it very simple and easy." She picked up the bed tray and, being careful not to bump his knee, placed it over his thighs. "You have homemade chicken soup, a toasted cheese sandwich and iced tea." She picked up her dinner from the tray, carried it over to the armchair and sat down.

"Be sure to save room for dessert. I made chocolate pudding."

"Thank you," he said, picking up his spoon to taste the soup. After he swallowed, he said, "Normally I don't care much for soup, but this is really good."

She hid a smile as she watched him eat. For someone who claimed he wasn't very hungry, Cole had downed the bowl of soup and devoured the sandwich in record time.

"Would you like some more soup or another sandwich?" she asked, placing her empty bowl with his on the tray to take back to the kitchen.

"I think I'd rather have the pudding," he said, giving her the first smile she'd seen from him today that wasn't under the influence of pain pills.

"I'll be right back with it," she said, returning his smile.

While they ate their pudding, they watched one of the military investigation dramas on TV, and by the time the show was over, she could tell he needed more pain medication. After giving him one of the pills, she sat back down in the armchair to wait until Cole dozed off before she went back into the kitchen to clean up.

"If you have something else you need to do, go ahead," he said, yawning. "I'll be fine."

Rising to her feet, she motioned toward the kitchen. "I'll go ahead and clean up from dinner. If you need me—"

"I'll ring…the bell," he said, closing his eyes. He sounded extremely sleepy, and she knew he was moments away from going to sleep.

Fifteen minutes later, after wiping down the counter and starting the dishwasher, Paige returned to the family room. She gasped when she found Cole trying to get out of the bed. "Where do you think you're going?" she asked, alarmed that he might hurt himself further.

"I was coming to find you," he said, grinning from ear to ear. "I can't sleep without you."

"Why don't you try?" If he was going to attempt to find her whenever she wasn't in the room with him, it was going to be a big problem. She might just have to curl up in the armchair for the night.

He stubbornly shook his head and started to get up again.

"What if I sit beside you and we watch a little more TV together?" she suggested. Maybe if she humored him, he'd relax and drift off for the night. Then once she was sure he was sound asleep, she would get up and move back to the armchair.

That seemed to placate him, so she took off her shoes, went over to the other side of the bed and, propping some throw pillows behind her, stretched out her legs on the mattress. As they watched another crime drama, Paige couldn't help but think about the difference in Cole when he was on the pain medication. Once he took one of the capsules it wasn't long before he was as happy as a lark and willing to go along with just about everything she suggested.

But he wouldn't be zonked out on painkillers forever. Yawning, she briefly wondered how much longer he would need them. Probably not more than another day or so at best. She just hoped his disposition improved when his discomfort eased. The smiling, affable Cole was much easier to deal with than the grouch he could be when the medication wore off.

Maybe then they could discuss what had happened the other night, she could apologize for her role in the matter and they could move on.

When Cole woke up it didn't take long for him to realize he wasn't in bed alone. Paige's head was resting on his shoulder and his arm was around her. He briefly wondered how the hell they had gotten that way. The last thing he remembered was taking another dose of pain medication and lying back to watch an episode of his favorite television show. Paige had been sitting in the armchair just a few feet away.

How did she end up in bed with him and why? He'd bet every dime he had it hadn't been her idea. Did that mean the pain pills had him doing something besides just sleeping? If that was the case, he'd taken the last of the pain pills, no matter how much his knee hurt.

"Paige," he said softly, not wanting to startle her. "It's time to wake up."

He watched her blink a moment before she tilted her head to look up at him. Her eyes widened as she realized where she was.

"Oh, Cole, I'm so sorry," she apologized as she tried to pull away from him. "I must have fallen asleep while we watched TV. Is your knee all right? Is it still elevated? I'll get up and get you some more of your medication."

"Slow down, Paige," he said, tightening his arm

around her to hold her in place. "Yes, my knee is sore but it's not intolerable right now. Yes, it's still elevated. And no, I don't need any more of that damned medication. I have a feeling it's responsible for you being in bed with me." He took a deep breath. "Exactly what did I do or say while I was under its influence?"

"Let me get out of bed and we'll talk," she said, pushing on his chest again.

This time he released her and struggled to sit up without moving his knee. Glancing at the clock on the mantel, he realized it was just before dawn. Had they spent the entire night in bed together?

"What time did you get in bed with me?" he asked.

"I'm going to start a pot of coffee," she said, brushing her long hair back away from her eyes with both hands. "Then we can talk." If she was evading his questions like this, it wasn't a good sign.

"That might not be a bad idea," he said, hoping the caffeine would clear his head and help him remember the events of the night before.

He didn't like being unable to remember what he'd said or done. It made him feel out of control—something he tried never to allow himself to be.

A sudden thought had his heart pounding hard against his ribs. Surely they hadn't made love again. He glanced down at his T-shirt and gym shorts. He was pretty sure they hadn't. For one thing, they were both fully dressed. And for another, she seemed just as surprised to be waking up in his arms as he was to be holding her.

"Would you like for me to make your breakfast?"

Paige asked, walking back into the room with two mugs of coffee. "I know you must be hungry."

He figured her offering to fix breakfast was her way of putting off talking to him. "Not right now. I want answers more than I want something to eat."

She stared at him a moment before she gave a short nod and walked over to sit in the armchair. "What do you want to know?"

"Just exactly how bizarre do I get when I'm on the pain medication?" he asked, taking a sip of his coffee.

"I wouldn't really call it bizarre," she said, shaking her head. "The only thing I can think of that was a little scary was when you tried to get out of bed."

He frowned. "Do you know why I was trying to get up?"

She nodded. "You were trying to find me."

"Was there something I needed?" he prompted. Her abbreviated answers indicated there was something she didn't want to tell him. He was determined to find out what that something was.

She shook her head but didn't quite look him in the eyes. "You just wanted me to be in here with you."

"What else?" He set his cup on the end table and carefully lowered his legs over the side of the bed to sit on the edge. "And don't tell me there isn't something. You're too reluctant to talk to me about it for there not to be."

She took a sudden interest in the contents of the cup in her hand. "Really, that was the only thing you did."

"What did I say?" he asked, knowing when she

jerked her head up to look at him that he'd hit pay dirt. "And why were you in bed with me?"

"You kept asking me to get into bed with you because you said you slept better when I was there." She shrugged one slender shoulder. "You were so insistent that I told you I would sit beside you while we watched television. I must have fallen asleep because the next thing I remember was waking up with my head on your shoulder."

"I've been on that medication for two days," he said slowly. "There has to be more."

She sighed audibly. "You really want to know?"

"I wouldn't have asked if I didn't," he said firmly.

"You might not like some of it," she warned.

"Just tell me, Paige."

"In the ER you asked if I had come to kiss you good-night," she said, smiling as if she found the incident humorous. "That was the first indication Aaron and I had that this medication might be causing a personality change in you."

"Aaron heard that?"

His friend was never going to let Cole hear the end of that one. Fortunately, he had gathered a few things on Aaron over the years that were just as embarrassing and when mentioned would shut him up in a hurry.

She nodded. "But he walked out of the room just before you tried to get me to climb into the hospital bed with you."

Cole groaned. "Was that it?"

"That was all that happened at the hospital," she

said, nodding. "The majority of what you said was here after I brought you home from the hospital."

So far it wasn't as bad as it could have been. "You might as well tell me everything."

"Every time you take the medication you want me to get into bed with you," she said, her cheeks coloring a pretty pink.

"I'm nothing if not persistent," he muttered, disgusted with himself. "Is that it?"

She hesitated before she continued. "A couple of times when you tried to talk me into getting into bed with you, you wanted us to make love again."

Outstanding, he thought sarcastically. Apparently, under the influence of the drug he was quite chatty.

"I know you didn't mean it," she said hurriedly. She paused for a moment, and then took a deep breath. "And as long as we're talking about making love, I'm really sorry about the other night." She stared down at her hands. "I more or less threw myself at you and I take full responsibility."

He shook his head. "Paige, there's absolutely no reason for you to apologize. I took advantage of the situation."

"No, you didn't." She got up from the chair and reached for his empty coffee cup. "I practically begged you to make love to me, and the next morning I was so embarrassed by my actions, I left the house early to go to my meeting just so I wouldn't have to face you."

Cole knew she was going to try to escape to the kitchen, but he was determined to get everything out in the open. Taking the cups from her hand, he set them on the end table, then pulled her down to sit beside him on the side of the bed. To keep from taking her in his arms, he gripped the edge of the mattress with both hands.

"Paige, don't you get it? If I hadn't wanted to make love to you the other night, there's nothing you could have said or done to change my mind," he stated flatly. "Give me credit for having more control."

"You did try to talk me out of it," she insisted. "You were obviously reluctant and I ignored that."

"Did you hear what I just said?" he asked. "I just told you I wanted to make love to you, Paige. Hell, if the truth is known, I've wanted you since I first laid eyes on you walking down the hall at Royal High School."

"You wanted me?" she asked, looking as if she couldn't quite believe it.

Nodding, he gave up and put his arm around her shoulders. "You're my late brother's wife and the two of you would still be married if that tornado hadn't come through six months ago and taken Craig's life. I've disrespected Craig's memory and your marriage and I'm truly sorry for that. But as contradictory as it sounds, I'll be damned if I regret that it happened."

"I don't, either," she said, surprising him. "I still feel like we wouldn't have made love if I hadn't pressed the matter, but what we shared was absolutely beautiful."

They sat in silence for a few minutes as reality set in. "So where do we go from here?" he finally asked.

"I suppose we could go back to building a nice friendship," Paige answered, sounding a little unsure.

He shook his head. "Sweetheart, I don't think that's possible."

She looked disappointed. "Why not?"

"I know I shouldn't and I've fought it with everything that's in me because you're my late brother's wife, but I want to be a whole lot more to you than just your friend, Paige," he said, lowering his head to capture her soft coral lips with his. "That's why I don't think a friendship between us would even be possible."

Not wanting to start something he couldn't finish, Cole made sure to keep the kiss simple and sweet. It was still unclear how things were going to progress between them or if they even wanted to try for something more. And there was no way he needed to add a boatload of frustration to the discomfort from his throbbing knee.

When he raised his head, he smiled. "You mentioned something about making breakfast?"

She looked as unsure about his declaration as he felt when she nodded. "What would you like to have?"

"It doesn't matter to me." He grinned. "I'm about as hungry as a bear waking up from hibernation. Even though it was really good, soup doesn't stick with you for very long."

Her smile was one of the prettiest sights he'd ever seen. "I'll go see what I can whip up."

As he watched her leave the room, Cole had no idea where things were going with them or how it would all turn out. Even though Craig would have had no problem making a move on Paige if the situation had been reversed and she had been his widow, Cole still couldn't help but have some lingering guilt about his feelings for her. But he also knew that if he didn't stick around and find out where their attraction led them, he would end up regretting it for the rest of his life.

Six

"Cole, I don't think this is what the doctors had in mind when he said to take it easy and keep your leg elevated," Paige observed as they walked toward the men working on her barn. His progress was slow, but Cole did seem to be getting the hang of using the crutches.

"I promise if my knee starts to hurt more than it does right now, I'll have the guys help me back inside," he said, giving her a smile that caused her pulse to race.

As soon as his men had called to tell him they were all fully recovered from the food poisoning and ready to go back to work, he decided one of them could set up a couple of lawn chairs under the live oak tree closest to the barn so that Cole could oversee their work. After trying to talk him out of it with no success, she finally gave in and carried the pillow for him to put under his leg when he propped it up on the other chair.

"What if it starts raining?" she asked as he lowered himself into the lawn chair and laid his crutches on the ground beside him. "You're not supposed to get the bandage wet."

"Do you worry this much over everything?" he asked, laughing.

"Your father used to call it fussing." She smiled at the fond memory as she placed the pillow she had under her arm on the chair facing Cole. "He used to tell me I fussed over everything."

"Well, I'm sure he loved having you around 'fussing' over him," Cole commented. "Dad didn't get much of that after Mom died."

"That's what he'd told me." Helping Cole get his leg positioned comfortably in the chair, she added, "But I didn't mind at all. We became quite close over the years, and I really miss him."

When she turned to go back to the house, Cole caught her hand in his to stop her. "Thank you for taking care of my dad when his health started to fail," he said, his expression turning serious. "I'm glad he had you here with him."

"No need to thank me. I enjoyed spending the time with him," she said, smiling. As an afterthought, she warned, "Oh, I almost forgot to remind you. Don't be so stubborn about working that you overdo things. If you do, you might need to start taking the medication again."

"There you go fussing again," Cole teased. His

grin caused a tiny shiver to slide up her spine. "Don't worry. I'm done with those pills. I don't care how much it hurts—I want to remember everything I say or do from now on."

Impulsively, she touched his cheek. "Just please take it easy. I'd hate to have to get stern with you again like I did yesterday afternoon when you kept apologizing for being a problem."

He laughed. "Do you have any idea how cute you are when you're laying down the law?"

"I prefer to think of it as being assertive," she said, enjoying their easy banter.

"Boss, here's the blueprints for the barn," one of Cole's men said, walking over with several rolls of paper. He nodded at Paige. "Mornin', ma'am."

After returning the man's greeting, Paige smiled at Cole. "I'll let you get to work and I'll start thinking about what I'm going to make for you and your crew for lunch."

As she walked back to the house, she thought about her talk with Cole earlier that morning and how different he was than before he'd had his accident. He seemed more relaxed around her now, as if confessing that he felt guilty—but that he had no regrets about their making love—had been liberating for him. He had even started showing her small gestures of affection—touching her hand when he talked to her and freely calling her sweetheart. She found she enjoyed the attention and she couldn't help but compare how differently the twin brothers treated her.

Craig had never gone out of his way to be overly affectionate. She frowned at the memory. In fact, it had seemed as if he didn't see the need in showing her any kind of affection unless they were getting ready to have sex. And she couldn't remember Craig ever using an endearment instead of her name.

Her breath caught when she realized how different making love with Cole had been, as well. He'd been gentle and caring, and she'd actually felt as if he cherished her, whereas Craig had been only mildly interested in whether or not she found their times together satisfying.

Of course, she couldn't blame him entirely for the state of their marriage. She had stayed in the loveless union for two very good reasons. First of all, she hadn't wanted to add to her parents' disappointment in her by divorcing Craig. And second, she had made a lifetime commitment to stay with Craig when she'd recited their wedding vows. She had been taught all of her life that it was a promise that wasn't made lightly, nor should it be broken easily.

But Craig was gone and with his death, so was her commitment to honoring their wedding vows. Cole had mentioned wanting to be more to her than just a friend. Was he talking about a future that included her in his life? Or did he mean only while he was staying on the ranch with her?

If that was the case—if he only wanted a casual relationship that would end when he went back to Dallas—she was certain that wouldn't be enough for her. Maybe it was her conservative upbringing or the fact that she had only been with one other man in her life.

But it didn't matter. She never had been, nor would she ever be, the "no-strings-attached" type.

Deciding that only time would tell, she went about her morning as usual. After giving her hired hands a list of chores that needed to be done, she returned to the house to start making lunch for Cole and his men. As she put the finishing touches on a tray of ham-and-cheese sandwiches, she was startled to see one of Cole's men helping him through the back door. Glancing at the clock, she frowned. He had only been outside for a few hours.

"Is your knee hurting?" she asked as she accepted the pillow his worker handed her.

Cole shrugged. "Nothing I can't handle."

The sudden sound of thunder rumbling overhead provided a clue as to why he was returning to the house so soon. "It sounds like the rain is coming early today," she commented.

Cole nodded. "I figured as slow as I am on these damned crutches I'd better get inside before the downpour started." After he thanked his worker for carrying the chairs to the porch and opening the door for him, Cole grinned. "I didn't want to run the risk of getting another lecture."

Before the man helping Cole went back outside, Paige stopped him. "I already have sandwiches made. Why don't you take them with you for the crew's lunch." She quickly wrapped the sandwiches, put them into a bag and handed it to him. "I hope you like ham and cheese."

"Thank you, ma'am," the man said politely. He

grinned. "We'll eat just about anything but egg salad out of a vending machine."

"Very wise choice," she said, grinning back at the man.

After the worker left the house, she caught Cole staring at her. "Did I do something wrong?" she asked, confused.

He shook his head. "You like taking care of people, don't you?"

"Everyone needs to feel a sense of purpose," she said, smiling. "Mine is caring for those around me. Besides, I like doing it."

"You mean you like 'fussing' over them," he corrected, grinning.

"Whatever." She stopped laughing when she noticed him wincing. "Are you sure your knee is all right?"

"It's sore, but it's a lot better than it was yesterday," he said, slowly lowering himself to one of the chairs at the table.

She moved another chair in front of him, placed the pillow just so and pointed to his leg. "Elevate."

"Now you're being bossy," he said, laughing.

"No, that was me being assertive." She grinned. "There's a difference."

"What do you have planned for this afternoon?" he asked, lifting his leg onto the pillow as she'd instructed.

"I have to work on this month's program for one of my charity meetings." She smiled as she went to the cabinet for plates to set the table. "I'll bet you're going to take a nap."

When he shook his head, his warm smile made her

feel as if he'd caressed her. "I might do that a little later, but I thought I'd start going through some of those boxes we took out of the closet in your studio."

"It's not a studio yet," she said, laughing.

"It will be as soon as we can get into Royal to pick out new floor tile, paint for the walls and cabinets for storage." He looked thoughtful. "If we can get that done one day next week, then the guys can work outside when it isn't raining and inside when it is."

"How does next Thursday afternoon sound?" she asked, setting the table for lunch. "We can go to the lumberyard after your doctor's appointment."

"That will work." He picked up the glass of iced tea she set in front of him. "When is your next meeting at the TCC clubhouse?"

Paige paused for a moment. "Week after next. That's where the meeting of the Family Crisis Center volunteers is always held. Why?"

"I thought I'd set up a meeting with Aaron to discuss some plans we're considering for R&N Builders." Cole smiled. "We've been talking about opening a branch office here in Royal."

"That would be great." Grinning, Paige carried a platter of sandwiches to the table and sat down. "Now that Aaron is married to the mayor and they're expecting a baby, it would probably be a good idea for them to live in the same town."

Cole laughed. "Yeah, he mentioned that when he took me to the hospital the other day."

As they ate, it suddenly occurred to Paige that she still had no idea why Cole had been out riding the day of the accident. "Cole, you never did tell me why you took one of the horses out for a ride the day you got hurt."

"When I was a kid, I used to go riding whenever I needed to think things through," he answered as he covered her hand with his where it rested on top of the table. "I was trying to decide what I needed to do to make things right between us after making love to you."

She glanced at his knee. "Well, it probably wasn't exactly the way you thought it would work out, but the horse did play a role in our dealing with what happened."

He laughed. "Yeah, I guess you're right. If he hadn't stumbled, I wouldn't have a bum knee and we wouldn't have had our talk this morning about the things I said while I was on painkillers."

Loving the easier atmosphere between them, she grinned. "Do me a favor. The next time you need to think, why don't you try doing it from the porch swing? I don't think it would be nearly as hard on you."

He surprised her when he shook his head. "That wouldn't work."

"Why not?" she asked, her pulse racing when he began to trace slow circles on the back of her hand with the pad of his thumb.

"Because if I played it safe and never got hurt, you wouldn't have anything to fuss over." His deep voice sent heat coursing through her veins.

"I do love to fuss," she admitted, feeling a little breathless. *Especially whenever the one I'm fussing over is you.*

After lunch, Cole sat in the den with his leg resting on an ottoman in the wide space under his father's big walnut desk. Going through a few of the boxes, he found several things of his father's that he wanted to keep and more that could be donated to one of the thrift shops in town.

Staring at the pocket knife his father had always carried, Cole couldn't help but smile as he turned it over in his hand. He couldn't remember a time that his dad hadn't had it with him. The handle had been made from a deer antler, and then carved with a scene of a stag regally standing in the middle of a forest. Cole remembered his dad telling him that his and Craig's grandfather had carried that knife from the time he was twelve years old, and Cole had no trouble believing it. The intricate carving had been worn down over the years but it was still a work of art and something that Cole was more than happy to keep. He placed it alongside his dad's pocket watch and chain and the silver dollar with a bullet hole in the middle that had belonged to his great-great grandfather.

With all of the boxes containing his father's things emptied, Cole reached for the carton of his sports trophies. Along with the high school memorabilia, he found a couple of belt buckles he'd earned from junior rodeo and a baseball signed by a couple of Rangers ball players. But he was mystified at finding a com-

puter flash drive at the bottom of the box. He knew for
certain that it wasn't his. He hadn't left anything like
that behind when he went off to college. That could
only mean that at some point in the past several years
Craig had thrown it into the box. He didn't even consider the notion that it had belonged to his father. His
dad had hated technology and swore that computers
would lead to the ruination of the world.

The drive probably had pictures on it or maybe
music. Craig used to like collecting both.

Picking up the device, Cole put it into the USB port
of the laptop Paige had said belonged to Craig and
opened the directory. Most of the files were labeled
by month and it appeared that Craig had been keeping
a digital journal. But as Cole scanned the list, one file
stood out and caused a sickening dread deep in the pit
of his stomach.

Double-clicking on his own name, Cole opened the
file to find several documents. When he clicked on
the top one in the list, he realized it was one of many
emails Craig had sent to him in the past year or so.

A deep sense of guilt settled over Cole as he stared
at the heading. When his brother had sent the messages, Cole had deleted every one of them unread. At
the time, he hadn't been interested in a thing Craig had
to say to him. But now?

Cole stared at the computer screen for several long
minutes as he tried to decide what he wanted to do.
If he opened the email and discovered that Craig had
been trying to reach out and make things right between
them, he would never forgive himself for not meeting

his brother halfway. But the only way he would know for sure would be to read them.

Before he had a chance to talk himself out of it, Cole quickly read the first message, then sat back in the desk chair to stare off into space. What had he ever done to Craig to inspire such hatred? Why had his twin been determined to taunt and harass him with events of the past, even as adults?

In the email, Craig had been reminding him about the fight they'd had over Paige just before she'd graduated from high school. Cole had been home from college on spring break and somehow Craig had discovered that Cole intended to ask her out after graduation. His twin had apparently decided that he was going to spoil that for Cole and vowed that by midsummer Paige would be dating him and by Christmas he would be sleeping with her.

Cole had done everything he could think of to protect Paige from Craig's sick sibling rivalry, but nothing he had tried had made a difference—not even the broken nose Cole had given Craig with a solid right hook. When it became clear that his brother was still intent on executing his plan to use Paige, Cole had tried feigning indifference in the hope that Craig would think he had lost interest in her and give up. Cole had even gone as far as taking a couple of classes during the summer semester to stay away from Royal and prove he was no longer interested in Paige. But Craig had seen through the ploy and finally convinced her to go out with him for the first time that fall.

Cole had thought about telling Paige what Craig

was up to and the sick game he was playing, but Cole hadn't been certain she would believe him. It was so damned bizarre, even he had a hard time believing the extent of the jealousy that had driven Craig.

Looking back, his brother had always been that way toward him—even when they were small children. If Cole had something, it didn't matter what it was, Craig wanted it. If Cole did or said anything that garnered any kind of praise—either from their father or in school—Craig did his best to take credit for it or diminish Cole's accomplishment in some way.

Over the years, Cole had gotten used to Craig's need to be the center of attention and always be the one who came out on top of every situation. For the most part, he had ignored the rivalry and one-upmanship his twin seemed to thrive on. But when Craig went after Paige as a way to taunt and torment Cole, his brother had crossed the line. That's why Cole had cut Craig out of his life. And with the exception of having to see him at their father's funeral, Cole hadn't spoken to his twin in almost twelve years.

But why would Craig have started emailing him a couple of years ago just to dredge up events that had taken place all those years ago? Surely Craig had realized that Cole had moved on with his life.

The dread he had felt when he first saw his name on the file intensified. Craig never did anything without a reason and if it involved Cole, it was most likely a disturbing one.

As he stared at the list of documents, the last thing he wanted to do was read more of Craig's boasting about how he had won Paige and what a loser Cole was. But if there was the slightest possibility that his brother had shown even a tiny bit of remorse for using her the way he had, Cole wanted to know about it. He wanted to find some indication that somewhere beneath all of the spite and cruelty there was a kernel of good in his brother.

Praying there was something in one of the documents that redeemed Craig, even in the smallest of ways, Cole forced himself to read the rest of the messages. When he finished the last one—dated the day before Craig had been killed—Cole's gut burned with white-hot fury. The extent of Craig's depravity was sickening.

The only reason Craig had emailed Cole the past couple of years was to gloat and tell him that he had never loved Paige and had been unfaithful practically from the day they had gotten married. He had explained that when their father had forced him to marry her, Craig had insisted they move to the Double R Ranch on the pretense of watching over their father. Then, while Craig went out of town to find his pleasure with more exciting women, Paige had been left at home with their dad. He had even mentioned purposely avoiding sex during her most fertile times of the month because a baby would have only tied him to her even tighter than their farce of a marriage already had. Craig had closed the last email by telling Cole that he was planning on leaving her for another woman and that Cole could have her now that Craig was done with her.

Sitting back in the chair, Cole shook his head. How could his brother have been so callous? How could he have treated a wonderful, caring woman like Paige with such disregard?

If he hadn't known how Craig operated, he might have questioned why his brother had continued to send the messages when it was clear he wasn't going to get a reaction from Cole or why he had kept a record of them.

But Craig had always been that way. It was as if he liked keeping something—a trophy of sorts—to remind him of his sick escapades. And he had probably figured that when he and Paige were divorced he would send the box to Cole—increasing the chance that Cole would find the memory device and eventually read the messages. Craig had also known Cole well enough to be reasonably sure that he wouldn't tell Paige because he wouldn't want to hurt her.

Cole wasn't certain how long he sat there trying to come to terms with what he had learned. It didn't matter. Nothing would ever change the facts of what Craig had done, nor the impact it would have on Paige if she ever discovered it.

That's why Cole was going to do his best to see that she never found out what a snake she had been married to. He never wanted Paige to know that all of those out-of-town business trips Craig had taken over the years were nothing more than clandestine meetings with other women. Cole couldn't stand the thought of her going through the kind of emotional pain that revelation would bring about and once again becoming the victim of his brother's arrogance.

"Cole, are you all right?" Paige asked from the doorway.

"Uh, sure." He quickly closed out the file on the laptop, pulled the memory device from the USB port and shoved it into the pocket of his gym shorts. "Why?"

"You looked like you're a million miles away," she said, smiling as she started across the room toward him.

"I was just taking a trip down memory lane," he said, motioning toward the boxes of his father's things.

When she stopped beside him, he didn't hesitate to put his arms around her waist to pull her close. His brother might have been a damned fool, but Cole wasn't. He knew exactly what a wonderful treasure she was.

"Did you get the program for your charity group finished?" he asked.

"Y-yes," she said, sounding a little breathless. "And I had enough time to make dinner afterward."

"I didn't realize it was that late," he said, checking his watch.

Her pretty smile sent his blood pressure up a good twenty points. "How is your knee? Do you think you can sit at the table, or would you rather me serve you dinner in bed again?"

Releasing her, he grinned as he reached for his crutches. "I'm not going to lie to you. My knee hurts, but I think I can make it through dinner before I have to lie down."

"You should have taken a nap this afternoon," she said, preceding him across the foyer and down the hall.

"Actually, I'm glad I didn't," he said, realizing it was true.

As hard as it had been to read those emails, Cole couldn't say he was surprised at finding the evidence of his brother's duplicity. It just proved what Cole had thought for a long time. Craig was a narcissist with little or no conscience—maybe even a sociopath. He had uncaringly used Paige for the sole purpose of making himself feel superior, and Cole couldn't believe he had been beating himself up for the past several days because he felt he had disrespected his brother's memory and marriage.

Cole shook his head. He had no idea where things were going with Paige, but there was one thing he was positive of. From here on out, he was done feeling the slightest bit of guilt or remorse for anything that happened between Paige and him.

After dinner, Cole slowly retreated to the family room, while Paige cleaned up the dishes. He hadn't said as much, but she knew his knee was probably throbbing unmercifully. She had caught him wincing a few times during dinner when he didn't think she was looking, and he didn't try to argue when she suggested he lie down to watch the news.

But when she'd offered to get him some of the pain medication, he had refused. She could understand his reluctance, given the way he reacted to it, but she didn't like to see anyone in pain, especially not Cole.

She nibbled on her lower lip. They joked about her worrying over him, but the truth of the matter was, she wouldn't want it any other way. She loved that Cole allowed her to care for him, loved that he seemed to appreciate her efforts and was more comfortable with her doing things for him.

It was such a contrast to the way Craig had always been when she'd tried to do things for him. The few times he had been ill, Craig had been irritable and hadn't seemed to want her anywhere near him. She had been disappointed at first. But as the years passed by, it had ceased to matter.

Frowning, she chided herself for once again comparing Cole to Craig. They might have been twins, but their personalities were as different as their looks, and it was past time to stop noticing the contrast between the two brothers.

It bothered her a bit that Craig always seemed to come up lacking when she thought about them. He was dead and there was no sense in focusing on his shortcomings in life. Craig couldn't help it that she had fallen for Cole all those years ago before she had even met him.

Deciding to make a conscious effort not to compare the men from now on, Paige turned out the kitchen light and went down the hall to the family room to check on Cole. She found that he had fallen asleep, and she wasn't going to wake him.

But the moment she turned to go over to sit in the armchair, his eyes opened and he reached up to catch her hand in his. "Where are you going, sweetheart?" he asked, grinning.

"Did you take some of the medication?" she asked.

The sound of his rich laughter caused a warm feeling deep inside her. "No, and I don't intend to." He hooked his thumb toward the empty mattress beside him. "Why don't you kick off your shoes and stretch out beside me? We can watch the Rangers game together."

"Who are they playing?" she asked as she slipped off her shoes and sat down on the sofa sleeper's mattress.

He shook his head. "It doesn't matter who they're playing. It's the Rangers. I always watch their games."

"I would have thought you were more of a football fan," she said, arranging pillows behind her. "You were Royal High School's star running back and played varsity all four years." She paused as she thought back on their high school days. "And didn't you play in college?"

"Yup, I went to Texas State on a football scholarship. It's my favorite, but I played just about every sport Royal High had to offer," he said, nodding. "I was on the baseball team all four years, as well."

"I probably didn't notice because I was in dance class and always had practice for our spring dance recitals," she said, leaning back against the pillows.

"That's not surprising," he said, folding his arms behind his head. "You move like a dancer."

"You watch me move?" she asked, suddenly feeling a little self-conscious.

He turned his head to look over at her. "Sweetheart, I've always watched the way you move."

"Even when we were in school?" If the look in his

eyes was any indication, he must have liked what he'd observed.

"Actually, it was one of the first things I noticed about you the day I saw you coming down the hall toward me," he said, smiling. "You were wearing blue jeans and a green sweater that made your hair look a little more red than auburn."

She couldn't believe he had remembered so many details, but that wasn't what she'd been wearing the first day they'd met. "I probably wore that sweater another time. But the first day we met, I had on a peach-colored shirt and khaki slacks."

His slow smile sent a shiver of anticipation up her spine. "I didn't say it was the first day we met. I said it was the first time I saw you walking down the hall. It took me a couple of weeks after that to work up the nerve to introduce myself."

She couldn't believe Cole Richardson—the school jock and heartthrob of the Royal High School senior class—had been nervous about talking to a lowly sophomore girl, who was almost as flat-chested and taller than most of the boys her age. "I had no idea," she said, completely stunned by the revelation. "Why on earth were you nervous about talking to me?"

"Probably because I thought you were the prettiest girl I'd ever seen," he admitted. "And I wanted to ask you out. But I was afraid a girl as pretty as you would turn me down flat."

"But I wasn't allowed to date, as you found out," she said, wishing her parents hadn't been so strict. Maybe if they had allowed her to date at a younger age, she and Cole would have been high school sweethearts and her life would have turned out differently.

Cole shook his head. "Your parents were probably right about that. Although I had the best of intentions, I was still a teenage boy with more hormones than good sense. And no matter what guys say, at eighteen that's about all a boy has on his mind."

Deciding there was no better time, she asked him the question she had wondered about for more than ten years. "Why didn't you ask me out after I graduated like you said you would, Cole?"

He stared at her for several long seconds before he sighed heavily. "I had to take some classes that summer, Paige." He unfolded his arms and reached over to touch her cheek with his index finger. "Believe me, it was the last thing I wanted to do. But it was the only chance I had."

"I thought you had forgotten," she said, her skin tingling from the contact.

"No, I couldn't forget you," he said, pulling her over to rest her head on his shoulder. "After my classes were over, I had football practice and the season started."

"And I had started dating Craig," she said, unable to keep the resignation from her voice.

"Things don't always work out the way we plan," Cole said, wrapping his arms around her.

"No, they don't." She was supposed to have been happily married with two or three children by now. Instead, she was the childless widow of a man she hadn't loved.

"But sometimes, when you least expect it, we get a

do-over," Cole said, his tone philosophical. "We just have to be brave enough to take those second chances when they come along."

Was Cole telling her he wanted that for them? Or was he asking her if she had the courage to try?

Unsure, she remained silent as they settled back to watch the baseball game. She didn't want to assume too much or read something into his statement simply because she wanted it to be there. She also needed to decide if she wanted to enter into a relationship so soon after Craig's death. It had only been a little more than six months since that fateful day. Also, for the first time in her life, she was on her own. She was just beginning to realize her potential and who she was as a woman. And it felt good.

She yawned and closed her eyes as she snuggled closer to the man holding her to him. Was she willing to give up her newfound independence? Would Cole even want her to? Did he feel threatened by a woman's independence the way Craig seemed to have been?

Paige wasn't sure. Hopefully she would be able to think things through and find answers to her concerns before Cole left to go back to Dallas. She had a feeling that if they missed their opportunity to explore their feelings this time, there might not be another one.

Seven

When Cole woke up sometime after midnight, several things immediately became apparent. The baseball game had been over hours ago, Paige was sound asleep in his arms and he wanted her. Hell, if the truth were known, he'd wanted her since he'd returned to Royal over six months ago.

Unable to stop himself, he turned his head to place his mouth over hers. He told himself he was just going to give her a little good-night kiss and that would be it. But when her lips clung to his, he didn't even try to stop himself from continuing, nor did he consider that he was playing with a fire he might not be able to put out.

Soft and sweet, he traced her with his tongue as he savored the taste of her. Parting her lips on a contented sigh, Paige murmured his name and a surge of heat made a beeline straight to his lower body.

Deciding that he'd better call a halt to the caress before things went further than he intended, Cole moved to break the kiss. But it appeared that Paige had awakened with other ideas.

When she brought her delicate hand up to cup his cheek, her eyes locked with his. Cole could see the desire in the dark gray depths, and he felt as though he might go up in a puff of smoke right then and there. If he was reading her right, Paige wanted his kiss and a whole lot more. He couldn't have denied her if his life depended on it.

Bringing his mouth back down on hers, Cole deepened the caress to explore her thoroughly and completely. To his amazement, she kissed him back with the same degree of passion and need. His heart pounded hard in his chest when she engaged him in a game of advance and retreat, nipping at his lower lip with her teeth.

Some men might have found her taking control to be a threat to their masculinity. Cole found it sexy as hell. He was secure enough not to be intimidated and loved the fact that she wasn't afraid to show him what she wanted. He had a feeling that Paige was just beginning to discover her strength as a woman, and he wanted to be the man who helped her find it.

When he eased away from the kiss, he ran his fingers through her silky auburn hair as he rained tiny kisses along her delicate jaw and down her throat to her collarbone. "Paige, I want you." He raised his head

to gaze down at her. "I want you to take me deep inside you and make me feel like you're never going to
let me go. But if that isn't what you're feeling, too, tell
me now."

"I want you, too," she said, nodding.

"Are you sure?" He kissed her cheeks, her eyes and
the tip of her nose. "Because I don't want any awkwardness between us in the morning and no feelings
of guilt. My making love with you this time won't be a
way to escape the fear of a storm, it won't be a mistake,
nor will it be disrespectful to Craig or your marriage
to him. It will be just you and me sharing a special
moment together."

"I've never wanted anything more in my life than
to share that with you, Cole," she said without hesitation. "But what about your knee?"

He smiled as he lowered his head to brush his lips
over the satiny skin along the column of her neck.
"We'll have to be a little more creative. You can take
the lead this time and be on top," he whispered.

"I've never been…on top," she said, running her
hand down his side to the tail of his T-shirt.

Cole really wasn't surprised by her admission. His
brother had been a very selfish individual and hadn't
cared enough to encourage Paige's adventurous nature.
But Cole wasn't going to think about it now. There
would be plenty of time for that later. Right now, he
had the most exciting woman in the entire world in
his arms and he was determined to bring her as much
pleasure as possible.

"You'll do just fine, Paige."

When she lifted his shirt to run her hands over his abdomen, he quickly pulled it over his head and tossed it to the floor. As she continued to explore his pectoral muscles and abs, a wave of heat flowed through his veins, making him a little light-headed.

"That feels…good," he said, groaning.

"I love your body," she said reverently. "I love touching you and learning what you like."

"Part of the excitement of making love is trying new things and finding new ways to give each other pleasure," he said as he unbuttoned the top of her polo shirt.

Lifting the garment over her head, he tossed it to the side as he reached for the front clasp of her lace bra. He made quick work of helping her out of it, then tossed it to the floor with their shirts. He held her gaze with his as he slowly covered one beautiful breast with his hand.

"You're perfect," he said as he gently touched her tight nipple with his thumb.

Cole reveled in the growing spark of desire in her pretty gray eyes. Lowering his head, he kissed the tip of her other breast, and then took the peak into his mouth. As he explored and teased her with his mouth and hand, he loved hearing a tiny moan escape her parted lips, loved the glow of excitement coloring her porcelain cheeks.

Slowly sliding his hand down her smooth flat stomach to the waistband of her jeans, he worked the button through the opening and eased the zipper down. As he captured her mouth with his, Cole slipped his fingers beneath the elastic band of her silk panties and parted her, stroking her with infinite care.

"Y-you're driving…me…crazy," she gasped.

"The good kind of crazy?" he asked as he smiled down at her.

"That…depends," she said breathlessly as she caressed his chest.

"What does it depend on, Paige?" he asked, continuing his tender assault.

"On what you intend to do about it," she said, closing her eyes for a moment as if savoring the sensations he was creating inside her. When she opened them, the passion he detected in her gray gaze robbed him of breath. "If you don't do something soon, I think I'll go completely insane."

"Then let's get the rest of these clothes off," he suggested.

Between kisses, they helped each other finish undressing, and by the time he took her back in his arms, Cole felt as if he would go up in a blaze of glory. Her soft form pressed to his harder flesh caused him to feel as if he had been branded. Burning to make her his again, he had to take several deep breaths to slow down the fever building inside him.

"I need to love you now, Paige," he said, feeling as if he was close to losing the slender hold he had on his control. "Straddle my hips, sweetheart."

When she did, her smile was replaced by a look of pure ecstasy as she took him in. "I feel so…complete," she murmured, closing her eyes.

He tried to slow himself down, but his body was urging him to complete the act of making love to her. "You feel so damned good." Gritting his teeth, he struggled to hold himself in check. "I don't want to rush you, but I want you more than my next breath."

Placing his hands on her hips, he guided her into a slow rocking motion. No other woman had ever held him as tightly or as perfectly as Paige. Somehow he knew as surely as he knew his own name that no other woman ever would.

As the heat running through his veins began to gather in his loins, Cole felt Paige's tiny feminine muscles tighten around him and knew she was close to finding her satisfaction. Touching her where their bodies joined, he gently stroked her and watched as she slipped over the edge. Her release triggered his own, and he held her to him as waves of pleasure coursed through both of them.

When she collapsed on top of him, Cole stroked her long auburn hair and held her close. Now that he knew the truth about Craig and how uncaring he had been with Paige, Cole didn't feel a bit of remorse for making love with her. He cherished her as his brother never had and he saw no reason to suppress his attraction to her any longer.

He was pretty sure she felt the same way. Otherwise she wouldn't have made love with him. But he wasn't going to rush things between them, even though Paige was everything he'd ever wanted. He needed to make sure she was as comfortable with her feelings as he was with his.

Besides, he had a few things to get lined up with R&N Builders before they went any further. He and Aaron had talked about opening a satellite office in

Royal after Aaron and Stella got married. But they needed to have a serious talk about the future of their business if both he and Aaron remained in the area.

"That was beautiful," Paige said, raising her head to look down at him.

Deciding to push thoughts of R&N Builders future to the back burner, Cole kissed her chin. "You're beautiful."

When she moved to his side, Cole gathered her to him and covered them with the sheet. For a man who had never cared to share his bed for an entire night with a woman, he found that doing so with Paige felt like the most natural thing in the world.

As she snuggled against him, he closed his eyes and enjoyed the feeling of her lying against him. But a sudden thought had him opening his eyes to stare at the ceiling and kept him awake long after Paige drifted off to sleep.

What if he had gotten her pregnant?

Both times they'd made love, he had failed to use protection. The first time, they had both been distracted by the storm. It was a weak excuse, but he had taken Paige at her word that she didn't think she could become pregnant.

Tonight was an entirely different story. He could understand Paige dismissing the issue. But after reading Craig's emails, he knew the real reason she was childless and it had nothing whatsoever to do with infertility. Craig had purposely avoided having children with her by avoiding the fertile days of her cycle because when the time came, he had wanted to be able to make a clean break from her.

But Cole had known the truth and had ignored his responsibility of using protection. Was he looking to become a daddy? Just because Paige's first pregnancy had ended with a miscarriage didn't mean that another pregnancy wouldn't be successful.

Glancing down at the sleeping woman in his arms, he tried to imagine what it would be like to see Paige pregnant with their baby. With her inherent need to take care of her family, she would be a wonderful mother, and he would like nothing more than to give her the babies she had always wanted.

But she should be aware that it was a possibility and have a choice in the matter. He couldn't in good conscience continue to make love to her without using some kind of protection. It was one thing for him to know the reason behind her failure to conceive. But she had no idea about Craig's deception, and telling her would require Cole to explain how he knew why she had remained childless for the past ten years. As far as he was concerned that wasn't even on the table for consideration. He couldn't bear to see the devastation on her pretty face when she learned how little she'd meant to his brother or the cruelty of Craig letting her believe she was unable to have children.

As he felt sleep begin to overtake him, Cole knew his decision had been made. He was going to protect Paige from learning the truth for two simple reasons. For one thing, her knowing what his brother had done wouldn't change anything and would only add disillusionment to the emotional pain she had already suffered. And for another, dragging Craig's name through the mud and exposing him for the narcissistic sociopath that he was would make Cole no better than his twin had been.

After Cole's doctor's appointment on Thursday, Paige stood in the paint aisle of the Royal lumberyard and hardware store comparing colors. "Cole, what do you think of this color?" she asked. "I really like the warm cream, but white or off white might reflect the light a little better."

"Colors that reflect light are more your area of expertise than they are mine," Cole answered, looking over her shoulder at the samples she held. "Why don't you just go with the color you like best? I doubt there would be that much difference in the amount of light they reflect."

"You're probably right," she said, deciding on the warm cream color. "I'm probably overthinking things."

"Hey," he said, turning her to face him. "It's your studio and you should have whatever you want."

His smile warmed her all the way to her toes as he lowered his head for a kiss. His lips moved over hers with precision and care, and even though the caress was rather chaste, she felt a little breathless by the time he lifted his head.

"You're going to get us kicked out of the lumberyard," she said, laughing as she looked up and down the aisle to see if anyone had witnessed the kiss.

Cole laughed. "As long as R&N Builders keeps buy

ing our supplies from them, I'm pretty sure they'll turn a blind eye."

She could tell Cole was a lot happier than he had been for the past week. At his appointment this afternoon, the orthopedist had removed the large bandage covering his knee and he was now allowed to put partial weight on that leg. He still had to use the crutches, but it was much easier to steady himself as he walked. He also seemed to be happier now that they were browsing the aisles at the lumberyard than he'd seemed when they had stopped at the grocery store earlier. She supposed it was a guy thing, but he had definitely shown more interest in the cabinetry they'd looked at for her studio than he had in the broccoli and cauliflower she had selected in the grocery store's produce section.

"How does your leg feel?" she asked, realizing how long he'd been moving around on it.

"It's a little sore but nothing I can't handle," he said, repeating the same thing he told her every time she asked.

"I'm definitely going with the cream color," she said, handing him the sample. They had already picked out floor tile and her cabinets and with the selection of the paint she was almost certain they had everything for her studio.

"I'll put these on the list for R&N's next delivery for the Double R build," he said, putting the paint chip in his shirt pocket.

"Is there anything else I need to pick out before we

head back home?" she asked as they started toward the courtesy desk.

He looked thoughtful. "I can't think of anything here. But I do need to stop by the pharmacy."

She waited for Cole to give the store clerk a list of items to be added to the next delivery for the ranch. "Did the doctor give you another prescription to have filled?" she asked as they walked out of the store.

"No, I'm going to buy a box of condoms," he whispered close to her ear.

"But why?" she asked, frowning in puzzlement. "I told you that I don't think I'm able to get pregnant."

"And there's the key word," he said as they got into her Mercedes. "You don't *think* it's possible. But you don't know for sure."

"Well, no, I haven't had my suspicion confirmed by a doctor, but I haven't become pregnant in ten years," she said, a little less certain than she'd been a few minutes ago.

"Did you ever stop to think it might be Craig's fault?" Cole asked.

She shook her head. "If you'll remember he made me pregnant before we got married and I haven't been able to become pregnant since. That suggests that it might be my problem. I might not be able to sustain a pregnancy."

To her surprise, Cole shook his head. "It doesn't matter. Men can become sterile at any time and for a variety of reasons." He reached over to take her hand in his. "I just don't want to make you pregnant until that's what you want."

Her heart skipped a beat. It was something she hadn't considered, and she had to admit he had a valid point. But it was the way he explained his reasons for buying the protection that stopped her in her tracks. He didn't want to make her pregnant until she wanted him to? Did that mean he was all right with them having a baby?

Paige gave herself a mental shake. She always seemed to be reading things into what Cole said and it was past time she stopped. Men had a habit of phrasing things differently than women and their intentions weren't always what women perceived them to be.

"All right," she said, putting the sedan into Drive. "Next stop, the pharmacy and then home."

A few minutes later, while Cole went into the pharmacy, Paige waited outside in the car at his request. He didn't give her a reason, but she had a feeling he might think she would be embarrassed at the checkout when all they purchased was a box of condoms.

"That was quick," she said when he slid back into the passenger seat a few minutes later.

"A lot of men won't admit it, but they have a size and brand they prefer," Cole said, grinning.

"I thought those were a one-size-fits-all kind of item," she said, laughing.

Cole laughed with her. "Sweetheart, contrary to the observations of our country's founding fathers, all men *are not* created equal."

As their laughter faded, they each fell silent, and Paige couldn't help but marvel at how easy it was to be with Cole. They both liked many of the same things, they enjoyed rooting for the Rangers baseball team and their sense of humor was similar.

"Are we still on for our date tonight?" Cole asked as Paige steered the car up the lane leading to the ranch house.

"Date?" She shook her head. "I have no idea what you're talking about."

"You, me, propped up on the sofa bed with the Rangers playing the Yankees." His wide grin faded. "I figure it will be one of our last nights in the family room now that I'm able to move around a little easier and will be able to get upstairs to my room soon."

She nodded as she parked the car in the garage. "You're probably right. The physical therapist will be here again tomorrow afternoon."

"Yeah, and results are pretty quick. I'm amazed after each session at the progress I've made," he said as they got out of the car and went into the house. "And that's just fine with me. I'd like to get back to work."

"But you've been overseeing things from the lawn chair under the tree for the past several days," she reminded him.

"Yeah, but that isn't all that I normally do," he said. "I like to inspect things, and that requires climbing ladders and making sure the job is done right."

"You don't trust your men?" she asked as they walked through the mud room.

"I do trust them, but—"

"You like doing some of the work yourself," she guessed.

He grinned. "Well, there is that."

When they entered the kitchen, Paige looked at the clock. "I think I better start dinner." Turning, she caught Cole wincing. "And you had better stretch out for a while and elevate your knee."

He gave her a short nod. "I might have been on it a little too long today."

"Do you need my help getting your leg propped up?" she asked, taking a casserole dish from the cabinet.

"No, I think I can manage to stuff a couple of pillows under it," he said as he continued on down the hall.

Two hours later, after she watched Cole devour the steak-and-potato casserole she had made for dinner and a huge slice of chocolate cake for dessert, she cleaned the kitchen and started the dishwasher while he went to turn on the baseball game. But entering the family room for their date to watch the baseball game, she stopped short when she saw how busy he'd been. There were several candles lit on the mantel, and he had propped up pillows for her to lean back against when she stretched out beside him. And he was sound asleep.

Smiling, she went around the room blowing out the candles, then went upstairs to change into her nightshirt. Cole had to be exhausted from being on his feet for several hours and if he was able to escape some of the lingering discomfort in his knee by going to sleep, she wasn't going to wake him.

When she finished changing, she went back downstairs to the family room. Pulling the sheet back, she got into the bed beside him. She snuggled close and smiled when he pulled her into his arms and held her to him in his sleep.

At the age of nineteen, she'd envisioned her marriage might one day be this way. Unfortunately, after she'd gotten married and moved to the Double R she had never been able to see Craig as the loving husband in those daydreams.

Paige sighed as she felt herself start to drift off to sleep. She hadn't loved Craig, and he hadn't loved her. She had accepted that. But it hadn't kept her from hoping that one day he would give her a reason to care as deeply for him as she had always cared for Cole—the way she still did.

"What time will your meeting be over?" Cole asked as he and Paige walked through the doors of the Texas Cattleman's Club the following week.

The physical therapy had worked wonders, and he was down to using a cane. The therapist had assured him that by the middle of next week, he would probably be able to do without that as long as he took it easy and didn't try to rush his progress. And that suited him just fine. He was more than ready to get back to work full-time, even if it was with a few restrictions for a while.

"I'll give the program on the charity's mission to the new volunteers, then we'll break for brunch and have the business meeting after that," she said, sounding distracted as she checked her tote bag for at least the tenth time since they'd left the ranch. "It will probably be early afternoon by the time everything is over."

Cole put his hands on her shoulders and gazed

down into her amazing gray eyes. "Stop worrying. Your notes for the program are still in the tote bag, the same as they were the other nine times you checked." He kissed her forehead. "Relax. You're going to do just fine, sweetheart."

"What about you?" she asked. "How long do you think your meeting with Aaron will take? I hate to think you'll just be sitting around waiting on me."

"You're fussing again," he said, laughing.

She smiled. "I'll have to work on that."

He shook his head. "Don't work on it too hard. I kind of like having you fuss over me." He smiled. "Aaron and I are going to discuss plans for the new branch office and a couple of other ideas I've been mulling over. After that we're meeting Luc for lunch. I'm sure by the time your meeting is over, I'll be ready to go."

She took a deep breath. "I guess I'm as ready as I'll ever be, then."

"You look beautiful, you've got all your notes ready and you'll blow the socks off all those women," he assured her.

"Hey, you two," Aaron greeted them as he entered the clubhouse. "Cole, it's good to see you up and on your feet again instead of lying in a hospital bed with a goofy grin on your face."

"Now you know how you looked that time you fell off that ladder and had to take pain medication for your twisted ankle," he shot back good-naturedly. "Or how about the time I had to take you to the ER because you—"

"Never mind," Aaron said, laughing. "I get it. We've

both got enough on each other to ensure the other's silence from here on out."

Cole grinned. "Just so we're clear on that."

"I hope you get a lot accomplished," Paige said, smiling at Aaron. Then she turned to Cole, and the smile she gave him sent his temperature soaring. "I'll see you after my meeting."

He barely resisted the urge to take her in his arms. "We'll be in the club's sports bar."

As he watched her walk away, Aaron elbowed him in the ribs. "And you said I had it bad when I had my shorts in a bunch over Stella."

"Shut up, Nichols," Cole said, grinning.

Aaron laughed and started down the hall toward the meeting rooms. "I've reserved a private meeting room for us."

Cole nodded. "Good. I've got a new idea to run past you and I'd like to keep it on the down low for the time being."

As they entered and sat down at a small conference table, a door at the other end of the room opened and a waiter quietly carried over a tray with a carafe of coffee, cups and a platter of pastries. "If you need anything else, please let me know," the man said before turning to leave the room.

"Okay, what do you want to talk over first?" Aaron asked, pouring them both a cup of coffee.

"I know we agreed that we'd open an R&N satellite office here in Royal, but what do you think of moving the main part of the business down here and having the satellite office in Dallas?" Cole asked.

His coffee cup halfway to his mouth, Aaron stopped to stare at Cole. "Oh, man, you're in as deep as I am, aren't you?"

Cole didn't try to pretend he didn't know what his friend meant. "Paige is the girl I told you about having a crush on when we were in high school."

"But she married your brother," Aaron said, finally taking a sip of his coffee.

"It's a long story and maybe one day I'll tell you all about it," Cole said, unwilling to go into the details of his twin's character flaws.

He had never told anyone what had transpired between Craig and him ten years ago. Aaron knew there had been bad blood between them, but he didn't know why they'd had a falling out. For the time being, Cole wanted to keep it that way. He knew Aaron would understand. Aaron had had to conquer a few demons of his own before he'd been able to share the details of his first wife's and child's deaths in a car accident several years ago.

"You're thinking you might want to move back to Royal now that Paige is single again?" Aaron asked.

"Yeah, I do," Cole said, nodding. "Royal is my hometown and I've been away a long time. I've missed it."

"You mean you've missed a pretty auburn-haired rancher," Aaron said, grinning.

Instead of answering, Cole just smiled and sipped his coffee.

"So what does the lady have to say about it?" Aaron asked, sitting back in his chair.

"I haven't mentioned it to her yet," Cole admitted. "I wanted to talk to you first since it's a business decision we both need to agree on."

"I appreciate that," Aaron said, nodding. "But I'm good with moving the main office down here. This is where my life is now."

"That's probably because you're married to the mayor and expecting a baby in a couple of months," Cole said, laughing.

Aaron gave him a sheepish grin. "Well, yeah. That has a lot to do with it."

They fell silent for a moment before Cole finally admitted, "It would help if I knew how Paige felt about me being around all of the time." He set his empty coffee cup on the tray. "I'm pretty sure she wants that, but we haven't talked about it."

Grinning like a Cheshire cat, Aaron pointed to Cole's neck. "Yeah, if that little love bite you're sporting on the side of your neck is any indication, you haven't been doing a lot of talking at all."

Cole should have known Aaron would notice. It was just a tiny mark, but the man had the eyes of a hawk.

"Remind me again why we're friends and business partners," Cole said, scowling at his best friend.

Aaron laughed. "Damned if I know."

"If you're agreeable, we can keep the Dallas office open," Cole said, getting back to their discussion. "We could promote Jim Edwards to office manager. He's our best foreman and has been with us from the beginning. He knows the business inside and out and won't have any problem overseeing the projects and bringing in new business. You and I could take turns going up there once a month to check on things, and there's always internet meetings and telecommuting."

"That sounds good to me," Aaron agreed. "We've got enough builds lined up down here, we can put quite a few people to work right away, as well as keep everyone working up there."

"It sounds like we have a plan," Cole said, sticking his hand out to seal the deal.

Aaron shook his hand and stood up. "Now, let's go meet Luc for lunch and toast moving the business to Royal with a beer."

As he and his partner left the meeting room, Cole smiled. He had one more thing left to do and one more stamp of approval to make his plans complete. He needed to talk to Paige and find out if she was open to having him hang around indefinitely.

Eight

The following Monday morning as she made breakfast, Paige felt happier than she had in years. She and Cole had spent a wonderful weekend together. On Saturday afternoon, he had insisted they take a drive around the ranch for him to show her some of his favorite places to play when he'd been a young boy. She had enjoyed seeing his favorite fishing spot along the creek and hearing his story about falling in when he was ten years old and thinking he would drown until he figured out he could stand up and the water only came up to his waist. They had also seen some of the big live oaks and cottonwoods that the tornado had uprooted as it made its way across the land.

Then when they had returned to the house, he had grilled steaks and vegetables for dinner before they cuddled on the sofa in the family room to watch the baseball game. It was a glimpse of the way their life could have been and the way she hoped life would be for them in the future.

He had mentioned that he had something he needed to discuss with her, but they never seemed to get around to it. She smiled when she thought about the reasons why they hadn't talked. It seemed that they couldn't be in the same room for more than five minutes without having their arms around each other.

She briefly wondered if he wanted to talk about the future. They hadn't discussed what would happen when he and his construction crew finished the barn and the repairs to the outbuildings, but she was hoping they could work out something. His life was in Dallas and hers was on the Double R, but surely they could find a way to spend time together. Maybe he could come down to Royal one weekend and she could travel up to Dallas the next.

"Uh-oh," Cole said, entering the kitchen and walking over to where she stood at the counter cracking eggs to scramble for breakfast.

Looking over her shoulder at him, she smiled. "You didn't want eggs?"

"No, the eggs are fine," he said, grinning. Standing behind her, he wrapped his arms around her waist to pull her back against him. "I've seen that look before. What are you worrying about this time?"

"What I'm going to make for dinner tonight," she fibbed.

He had a work crew arriving soon and she didn't

want to get into a discussion about what the future might hold for them. That subject should be broached when they had plenty of time to talk about what they both wanted and where they felt their feelings for each other were leading them.

"As far as I'm concerned, I'd be happy having you," he whispered close to her ear.

A shiver of anticipation coursed through her. Since their talk the first morning they had awoken in each other's arms, they'd spent every night making love, holding each other while they slept and rising in the morning to greet the day together. And Paige had loved every minute of it.

"You're insatiable, Cole Richardson," she said, hoping he never changed.

"I can't help it," he said, turning her in his arms for a kiss that caused her knees to wobble. "You're amazing and I can't get enough of you."

She felt the same way about him, but his work crew chose that moment to drive up the lane to start work on the barn interior, so she decided to wait until later to tell him so. "It appears that we'll have to talk about your…appetite a bit later."

He groaned. "Duty calls." He kissed her soundly, walked to the back door and smiled as he took his wide-brimmed hat from the peg. "With any luck, we'll get the barn finished and start repairing the equipment shed before we break for lunch."

"Don't try to do too much," she reminded him. "Remember what the doctor said about—"

"There you go fussing again," he said, laughing as he opened the door. "But I promise I won't overdo it."

Turning the scrambled eggs she had planned for Cole's breakfast into an omelet, Paige only managed to eat a few bites before the queasiness that had plagued her for the past few mornings set in. Scraping the rest of the food into the garbage disposal, she frowned. What was wrong with her? Beyond an occasional head cold, she was normally very healthy and she never lost her appetite.

But as she stood there wondering if she was coming down with some type of stomach flu, a sudden thought had her rushing into the office to look at her personal calendar. After checking the dates three times, she sat back in the desk chair in disbelief. She was almost two weeks late. The only other time that had happened was when she had become pregnant before she got married.

Glancing down at her stomach, she shook her head. She was normally as regular as clockwork. Could she be pregnant again?

A mixture of emotion flowed through her at the thought. She had wanted a baby for so long, she was afraid to hope. What if she were pregnant? How would Cole take that kind of news?

"Stop it," she said out loud, forcing herself to be realistic.

She didn't know anything for certain and there was no sense in going over all the what-ifs until she did. Nibbling her lower lip, she decided there was only one way to find out.

Her hands trembled slightly as she dug through her

purse for her car keys, closed the door, got in her car and drove the five miles into Royal. Try as she might, she couldn't tamp down the nervous excitement as she drove straight to the pharmacy where Cole had purchased the condoms, bought the pregnancy test and drove right back home.

Ten minutes after she returned to the ranch, Paige stared at the two white sticks in her hand. Both digital windows showed a positive result. She had bought one of the latest and, according to the pharmacist, most accurate home pregnancy tests on the market. She had even made sure the package had two test sticks just in case she did something wrong and needed an extra. When the first stick showed a definite positive, she repeated the test just to be sure. There was no doubt about it. According to the tests that boasted 99 percent accuracy, she was pregnant.

Placing her hand protectively over her flat stomach, tears of joy ran down her cheeks. She was finally going to have a baby. A baby fathered by the man she had loved since he'd first introduced himself to her all those years ago in the halls of Royal High School.

Her heart skipped a beat as she thought about her feelings for Cole. She had loved him almost from the moment she met him. Since his return to Royal, those feelings had intensified to where there was no longer any doubt in her mind about how she felt. She loved him with all of her heart and soul. And he seemed to care a great deal for her.

But how on earth was she going to tell him she was pregnant? And how would he react?

He had said when he bought the condoms that he didn't want to make her pregnant until that was what she wanted. Did that mean he would be happy to have a baby with her? When should she tell him? And what was she going to say?

She couldn't very well throw that kind of news at him during an ordinary dinner conversation. Something like "the rain stopped early today and oh, by the way, I'm pregnant, and please pass the mashed potatoes" would never do. No, she needed to come up with the perfect way to tell Cole he was going to be a daddy.

Unable to figure out any answers, she decided to do the one thing that usually helped her think and work through whatever decisions she needed to make. Paige started cleaning.

Starting upstairs in her room, she cleaned the already tidy space, gathered the clothes that needed laundering and put them into a basket. Going across the hall into Cole's room, she cleaned there, as well. When she was done, she emptied his hamper into the basket and headed downstairs.

As she sorted the clothes to put into the washer, something fell to the floor. Picking it up, she wondered which one of them had left a computer flash drive in their pocket. It might be Cole's, but she doubted it. It looked just like the one Craig had given her a few years ago to use as a backup for her charity programs. Although she didn't remember putting it in her pocket, it must be hers. She'd had hers out the day she'd made notes for her presentation to the volunteers of the TCC

Tornado Relief Fund. She probably had just forgotten she'd put it there.

As soon as she started the washer, she walked into the den, booted up her computer and stuck the device into the USB port. She wasn't trying to be nosy, but she wanted to be certain it was hers instead of Cole's. All she needed to do was check the file directory and she would know for sure which one of them it belonged to.

As she scanned the files, her breath caught and her heart began to pound when she realized the memory device had belonged to Craig. She opened the first file, titled "My Marriage." It appeared to be a journal Craig had been keeping from shortly after they had gotten married until his death almost seven months ago. As she read the first entry tears pooled in her eyes. It made her realize how much he'd blamed her for his life turning out the way it had. He had resented his father making him marry her and had even written that he wished she'd had the miscarriage before the wedding instead of a few weeks later. If she had, he wouldn't have had to go through with their marriage at all.

As she read more and more of the files, it got worse. He talked about purposely avoiding making her pregnant by keeping track of her most fertile times of the month and avoiding lovemaking because the last thing he wanted was a brat to tie him to her even more so than he already was. In another one of the files he even seemed to find it humorous that he had been able to get her to move out of the master bedroom on the pretense of his being a restless sleeper.

All that time Craig had known how badly she had

wanted to have a baby and how sad she'd been when she hadn't become pregnant. He had even convinced her that she was infertile by pointing out that he had made her pregnant once and the miscarriage she suffered might be her body's inability to support a pregnancy. How could he have done that to her? And why had she listened to him?

As she continued going through the directory, Paige found file after file filled with intense blame and loathing for her and how she had ruined his life. Craig had also written extensively about his "business trips" and how convenient it had been that his father's health had started failing and how it had kept her busy taking care of the old man while Craig took his current mistress to a new spa or on a weeklong gambling junket to Las Vegas. After an hour of reading about his illicit escapades with other women, Paige lost count of how many affairs Craig had had over the years.

As she sat there staring at the computer screen, she had to admit that she'd wondered about his frequent out-of-town trips. Maybe if she had cared more for him she would have questioned him about them. But she hadn't, and if she were perfectly honest, she had been happy for some time to herself and hadn't minded his being gone all that much. Unable to read any more of the sickening passages, she started to exit out of the directory, but Cole's name at the bottom of the list caught her eye. Why did Craig have a file with Cole's name on it?

Clicking it open, she realized that Craig had been corresponding with Cole for the past couple of years.

She frowned. That couldn't be right. Cole had made it clear that he hadn't had anything to do with Craig since leaving for college.

Why hadn't Cole mentioned the email Craig had sent to him? And why had Craig saved the messages?

Unwilling to read more of Craig's disgusting thoughts than she had to, she only opened a couple of the documents. As she read the last one, her heart sank and by the time she finished, Paige felt as if the world had suddenly spun out of control as she read Craig's ramblings. He was telling Cole that he intended to leave her for another woman and that Cole could finally have his turn with her because Craig was done and moving on.

"Oh, my God!" she gasped.

How could she have been so gullible? Why hadn't she seen through Craig's deception and lies?

But of all the revelations, the one that shattered her heart into a million pieces was the realization that Cole had known what Craig had been doing and the hurtful things he had said about her. Tears poured down her cheeks as she thought about the last line of Craig's email. "Now that I'm done with her, you can finally have your turn with Paige."

Had she been a pawn in a sick game the twin brothers had been playing all these years? How could they do that to her? What had she ever done to them to make them want to ruin her life?

Her stomach lurched and she had to run for the downstairs powder room to be sick. She had married one brother because she was pregnant, and now she was pregnant with the other brother's baby. It appeared that history was repeating itself.

But she wasn't going to be trapped in another depraved game with another Richardson brother. Once was enough to last her an entire lifetime and then some.

As soon as she managed to compose herself, she had every intention of ordering Cole to pack his things and leave the ranch. After what he and Craig had done to her, the way they had manipulated her life, she didn't care that the Double R had been in his family for years. It was hers now and if he ever dared to step foot on the property again, she would have him arrested for trespassing.

When Cole entered the house, he expected to find Paige in the kitchen making sandwiches for him and the work crew to have for lunch. She was nowhere in sight. She wasn't in the family room or the room she wanted to turn into her studio, either.

"Paige," he called as he walked through the house.

When she wasn't in the den, he climbed the stairs and finally found her sitting on the side of the bed in his room. Her head was slightly tilted down as if she was studying her hands, which were twisted into a tight knot in her lap.

"Why didn't you answer me?" When she lifted her eyes to look at him, the abject pain in the crystalline gray depths made him feel as if he'd taken a head butt to the gut.

"Paige, sweetheart, what's wrong?" he demanded,

crossing the room to stand in front of her. When he reached for her hands, she jerked them away.

"Don't call me that," she said, her voice tense with emotion. "And I don't want you ever to touch me again."

Sensing that whatever had happened was going to take a lot longer to resolve than just his lunch hour, Cole turned to leave the room. "I'll be right back."

As he went downstairs, he took his billfold out of the hip pocket of his jeans and removed a couple of hundred dollar bills. Stepping outside, he called to Harold. When the man reached the porch, Cole handed him the money. "Take the crew to the Royal Diner for lunch on me, then everyone has the rest of the day off with pay."

Without waiting for the man to comment, Cole walked back into the house, closed the door and retraced his steps back upstairs to his room. "Now, why don't you tell me what's going on?" he asked, walking over to the bed.

When he sat down beside Paige, she rose to her feet and walked several paces away. "I want you off the ranch as soon as you can pack your things." She turned back to face him. "And I don't ever want you to come back. If you do, I swear I'll have Sheriff Battle arrest you."

"Do you mind telling me what I've done?" he asked calmly. If she knew him better, she would realize his demeanor was a facade he had perfected years ago to keep his brother from knowing just how much he was getting to him.

"I'm not going to go into everything," she said,

shaking her head. "It's too sordid to repeat. But I know what you and Craig were up to and the sick game you were playing at my expense. It was your turn to have me? Really, Cole? How could you?"

Cole's heart came to a complete halt. Without thinking, he asked, "How did you find out?"

He watched her close her eyes a moment as if she were struggling to maintain her composure. "Oh, dear Lord, Cole, does it matter?" Opening her eyes, she stared at him. "How I found out isn't important. I told you I know about your vile game and that's all that matters. Now please pack your clothes, take your men and leave."

"Who's going to finish the barn and repairs to your other buildings?" he asked, stalling for time. He needed to think of a way to get her to listen to him. But at the moment, it appeared hell would freeze over before that happened.

"I'll hire someone else to do the work." She shook her head so vehemently that her ponytail swayed back and forth. "I want nothing more to do with you or your company."

Deciding that she needed time to cool down and he needed time to think, Cole got up from the bed and opened the closet to get his suitcase. "I can arrange to have Aaron take over the job. There's no sense penalizing the workers because you have a problem with me. Besides, the barn is almost finished and all that's left are the repairs to the sheds and turning that room into your studio."

"I'll think about it and let him know," she said,

walking to the door. "I want no further contact with you." Then she left the room.

As he gathered his things, Cole searched for the gym shorts he'd worn the day he discovered the memory stick with Craig's journal and copies of the messages he'd sent to Cole. He had put it in his pocket when Paige walked into the room that day to keep her from seeing the damning evidence of Craig's depravity. When he failed to find the shorts along with several other items of his clothing, he bet every dime he had that she'd been doing laundry and had found it.

Stuffing clothes into the suitcase, he cursed himself for being a damned fool. He had been so sure he could protect Paige from learning about the ugly side of Craig's personality that he had been careless. Now she thought he had known and been in on his brother's twisted escapades all along.

Cole stopped packing for a moment as a thought suddenly occurred to him. How could he possibly prove that he wasn't involved and had no knowledge of Craig's scheme?

He had deleted all of the messages from his own email account without reading them and, with the exception of their father's funeral, hadn't had any contact with his brother since he'd left home after their fight more than a decade ago. Unfortunately, he could talk until he lost his voice and Paige wasn't going to believe him. At least, not now. His only chance was to put distance between them and hope that when he returned in a day or two she would hear him out and believe what he told her.

After he carried his suitcase downstairs, he found her in the kitchen staring out the window above the sink. When she turned to face him, he could tell she had been crying. The knowledge damned near tore him apart.

"Paige, I—"

"Please don't, Cole," she said, holding up one hand to stop him when he started toward her. "I think it would be best if you just leave."

He wanted to take her in his arms and make all the emotional pain go away, but it was clear she wouldn't welcome the gesture. And once he touched her, he knew he'd never be able to let her go.

"Let me know if you need me for anything," he said as he walked to the back door.

"Not that you or your brother ever have, but don't worry about me," Paige said. "I'm a survivor. It may take me a while, but I'll be just fine on my own."

With nothing left that he could say to change her mind—at least for the time being—Cole walked out of the house, got into his truck and drove toward the outskirts of Royal. Although it didn't sit well, he couldn't honestly say he blamed her for not wanting to listen to anything a Richardson had to say. She had just learned that everything she thought she knew about her marriage and the past ten years of her life had been a complete lie. And even in death Craig was manipulating both of them and ruining their chances of being happy together.

Cole suddenly brought the truck to a screeching halt in the middle of the deserted highway. Paige must have only read the last email Craig had sent to him. She had talked about him and Craig playing her for the fool and she mentioned knowing that it was his turn with her. But if she had read all of the emails, she would have realized from the very first one that he had fought to try and stop Craig.

Paige was emotionally devastated and he had a way to put a stop to some of the hell she was going through. And that's exactly what he intended to do.

Knowing he had found the evidence to prove that he was in no way involved in anything Craig did, Cole turned the truck around and headed back to the Double R Ranch. He had loved Paige from the moment he'd laid eyes on her in the halls of Royal High School, and he was almost positive she had loved him just as long.

He had intended to tell her how he felt and ask her to marry him this past weekend. But they hadn't been able to keep their hands off each other, and he'd put it off in favor of getting a ring and planning something to make his proposal special. Unfortunately, that was no longer an option.

Cole pushed the gas pedal all the way to the floor and raced back to the only woman he had ever loved. He'd lost her once, but he'd be damned if he lost her again.

Nine

As she watched Cole walk out the door without a backward glance, Paige felt her heart break all over again. When she'd confronted him with what she had discovered on the flash drive, he hadn't tried to deny it. He'd only wanted to know how she'd found out about it.

She picked up a box of tissues, climbed the stairs, went into her bedroom and curled up into a tight ball on her bed. Cole's betrayal was without a doubt the most devastating thing she had ever experienced. Nothing in her entire life even came close to causing her the emotional pain she was feeling at that moment.

How could the utter joy of finding out she was going to have his baby be replaced so quickly by absolute desolation?

What Craig had done, the vile game he had played

to ruin her life, had been despicable. But it was nothing compared to Cole's duplicity. If she were completely honest with herself, she had always known that Craig was shallow and self-centered, and on some level, she had even known there were other women. But she had completely believed in Cole's sincerity and that he truly cared for her.

How could she have been so wrong about him? Why had she allowed herself to believe he cared for her as deeply as she cared for him?

Clutching her pillow, she sobbed into it as she realized another one of her dreams had died at the hands of a Richardson brother. For ten years Craig had taken her hopes of having a family away from her. Then, just when she learned she was going to finally have a baby, Cole had shattered the dream that she would also have the love of a good man as they raised that child together.

"Paige?" She heard Cole call from downstairs.

Why hadn't he listened when she told him to go away and never come back? Was he so determined to destroy her life as it seemed his brother had done that he came back just to ensure he had accomplished his goal?

Before she could collect herself and get up from the bed to face off with him again, she heard his footsteps as he entered the room.

"Please don't cry, Paige," Cole said as his strong arms wrapped around her to lift her to him.

Lost in her misery, she hadn't had the strength to

move fast enough to evade him. "Turn me loose and leave or I'll—"

"Yeah, I know. You'll call Nathan Battle and have me arrested," he said, making no move to let her go. Nor did he sound all that concerned about his impending trip to jail.

"Why are you doing this, Cole?" she demanded, unable to stop the tears from rolling down her cheeks. "Haven't you humiliated me enough? What else do you want from me?"

"Paige, there's no reason to feel embarrassed or betrayed," he said, his tone as gentle as she'd ever heard. "All I want is for you to hear me out. I swear to you that what you think you know isn't what really happened."

"Please, just leave me alone, Cole." She hated that she couldn't stop crying. She didn't want him to see how badly he had hurt her.

"You need to listen to me," he insisted.

When she pushed against his wide chest, he finally released her. "Go away, Cole." She scrambled to the other side of the bed and out of his reach. "There's nothing you have to say that I want to hear."

"You have to know I would never hurt you, Paige," he said, his voice deceptively sincere.

"And just how would I know that?" she asked, her anger beginning to chase away a bit of her devastation. "Everything I thought I knew about you and your brother has turned out to be nothing but lies and deception."

"That might be true for Craig, but not for me," he said, shaking his head. "I've never lied to you, nor have I ever done anything that I thought would hurt you in any way."

"You've never lied to me?" she scoffed. "That's not the way I remember it."

He stubbornly shook his head. "If I've said something to you that wasn't true, it was completely unintentional."

With the evidence she had discovered, she had a hard time believing him. "Really, Cole? If I remember correctly, you've lied to me as long as I've known you."

"How do you figure that?" he asked, frowning.

"You promised that you were going to ask me out as soon as I graduated from high school." She shook her head. "We both know how that turned out."

"I'm sorry about that, Paige." Surprisingly, he still had the nerve to look her in the eyes. "I fully intended to do what I'd said. But I had good reason not to keep that promise."

Whatever it was, she didn't think she wanted to hear it. "I waited for you that entire summer and the only reason I finally went out with Craig was because I got tired of him asking all the time." From the expression on his handsome face, she could tell Cole was holding something back —something he wasn't telling her. "What was your reason, Cole?" she asked, deciding she did want to hear his lame excuse just before she kicked him out of her life for good. "And before you answer, keep in mind that I've had a lifetime of lies. I want the truth this time."

He took a deep breath and rubbed at the back of his neck. "I was trying to protect you from Craig."

"How on earth could you possibly think that by not asking me out you were protecting me from your brother?" she demanded.

Cole stared at her for endless seconds before he spoke again. "Let me tell you something about Craig you probably don't know. He had a mission in life and that was to try to make me miserable or to take anything away from me that I valued or cared for." He took a deep breath. "After we got out of high school, Craig found out that I had a crush on you and told me he intended to not only make you his girlfriend, he was going to take your virginity."

"Oh, my God!" Her breath caught on a sob as she thought of how cold and calculating Craig had been and how he had planned to ruin her life even before they married.

Cole stood up and began to pace the length of her bedroom as if it bothered him that he'd upset her. "That happened while I was home on spring break the year you graduated. The same week I broke Craig's nose."

Paige gasped. "The two of you fought over me?"

Cole shrugged. "It wasn't much of a fight. I told him to leave you alone. It pissed me off when he said no. So I stuck out my fist and he just happened to be closer than he should have been."

She shook her head. "I still don't see how you thought ignoring me was going to dissuade him."

"I had hoped that if he thought I'd lost interest in you, he would give up and leave you alone." Cole shook his head. "That's why I didn't ask you out and stayed away that entire summer."

She frowned. "You still haven't explained why you thought that tactic would work."

"Craig normally had the attention span of a flea," Cole answered. "As soon as he thought he had prevented me from having what I wanted, he moved on to trying to torture me with something else. Unfortunately, that was the one time it didn't work. Apparently, Craig saw through the ruse."

Cole looked as if he was being truthful with her. But she'd learned the hard way that appearances could be deceiving when it came to the Richardson brothers. And it was all so sordid, she had a hard time believing what he said.

"Why didn't you just tell me what he had planned?" she asked. "Wouldn't that have been simpler than playing head games with him?"

"You have to remember, a twenty-year-old isn't much more than a boy and doesn't normally have the reasoning skills of a thirty-year-old man. Besides, I didn't figure you would believe me," Cole admitted. "It's so damned twisted even I have a hard time believing how Craig's mind worked."

"You're probably right." She shook her head. "But I've seen the evidence. You knew what Craig was up to and were obviously in on Craig's scheme. In the email he said it was your turn to have me because he was done and intended to move on."

"Paige, you didn't read all of the messages, did you?" he asked.

"No. I only made it through a couple of them and they were more than enough to make me sick. Especially after reading Craig's journal." She shuddered just thinking about how vile his ramblings had been.

"That's what I thought." Cole walked over to stand in front of her. "If you had opened the first email in the file, you would have known about what I just told you. In it, Craig was gloating about the fight failing to dissuade him and how he had succeeded in ruining any chances I'd had with you. The rest of the emails outlined what his life had been like being married to you."

Tears filled her eyes as a thought suddenly occurred to her. "He started sending those emails almost two years ago. You've known all this time and you didn't tell me," she accused. "You must think I'm the biggest fool who ever lived."

"I've never thought that about you, Paige." Sitting down beside her, Cole shook his head. "And until I found that flash drive the day I went through those boxes from Craig's office, I didn't know anything that was in them. Apparently Craig hid it in the box with my trophies and probably intended to send it to me at some point in time."

"I can't believe that you didn't know anything about the messages," she stated flatly. "He sent those to you. You had to know what he was up to and the horrible things he said."

"I have no way to prove it, but I deleted every one of them unread," Cole answered.

"Not even one?" she asked, still skeptical.

He shook his head. "Not even one. I wasn't interested in anything Craig had to say." He gently took her hands in his. "Don't you see, Paige? We've both been victims in Craig's sick game for over ten years. And if we give up on what we've found together these past few weeks because of what he put in his journal and those messages, he's continuing to call the shots and make us victims—he wins again."

"What is it that you think we have together, Cole?" she asked, pulling her hands from his. Her faith had been shaken right down to the foundation and she wasn't certain of anything anymore.

"It's not what I think, sweetheart," he said, taking her into his arms. "It's what I know." When she started to push against his chest, the look in his incredible blue eyes stopped her. "I love you and I'm pretty damned sure you love me."

"You love me," she repeated. She had wanted to hear those words from Cole since she was sixteen years old, and now that he'd said them, she was having a hard time believing that she'd heard him correctly or that he meant them.

"Paige, I've loved you since I first I saw you walking toward me on your way to Mr. Matthews's geometry class," Cole said, holding her close. "You were the prettiest girl I'd ever seen. And that hasn't changed. If anything, you're more beautiful now than you were then."

He started to brush his lips over hers, but she turned her head slightly, causing him to kiss her cheek instead. "Cole, I don't want to be hurt again. I've recently discovered that in the past I've been too gullible and placed my trust too easily."

"I understand, sweetheart," he said, giving her a smile that curled her toes inside her cross-trainers. "But

I give you my word that everything I'm telling you is the truth. I love you more than life itself, and if you'll give me the chance, I swear I'll make sure no one ever hurts you again." He paused for a moment before he continued. "If you'll remember, I was able to tell you what you were wearing the first time I saw you, as well as the day I worked up the nerve to talk to you."

She nodded. "But what does that have to do with—?"

"To prove just how hard and fast I fell for you that day, I can tell you that your hair was pulled back from your face and clipped with two silver barrettes," he said, smiling. "And your backpack was purple with pink trim."

"How do you remember so many details about that day?" she asked, astounded that he recalled everything so accurately.

"Because I fell in love with you and didn't want to forget anything about you," he said as if it was as simple as that. "I never want to forget seeing the love of my life for the first time."

She bit her lower lip to keep it from trembling before she finally managed to get words passed the lump clogging her throat. "I think I've loved you just as long."

"Thank God!" He immediately brought his mouth down to cover hers with a kiss that left her breathless. When he raised his head, he brushed a tear from her cheek with his thumb as he stared into her eyes. "I never want you to doubt how much you mean to me. I'm going to spend every minute of every day for the rest of my life telling you how beautiful you are and how much I love you, Paige."

"And I love you, Cole," she said, knowing in her heart that everything he had told her was true.

He gave her a smile that took her breath away. "I wanted to wait until I had a ring and planned something special when I ask you, but I don't want to waste another minute. Will you marry me, Paige?"

"Yes," she said, throwing her arms around his wide shoulders. "I've never wanted anything more in my life than to be your wife."

"When? And please don't tell me you want a long engagement." He cupped her face with his palms. "We had more than ten years taken away from us, and I don't want to spend another minute without you."

"There's something I need to tell you," she said, knowing it was time to share her news with him. "I hope you're as happy about it as I am."

"What's that, sweetheart?" he asked, kissing her cheeks, her chin and the tip of her nose.

"You wasted your money the other day," she said, smiling.

He looked confused. "I'm not sure what you mean."

"At the pharmacy," she explained. "You bought a box of condoms because you'd read the journal entries and knew that Craig had purposely made me think I had a fertility problem."

Cole nodded. "I knew there was the chance that…" His voice trailed off, and she knew from the stunned look on his face that he had figured out what she was alluding to. "You're pregnant?"

"Yes."

"When did you find out?" he asked, glancing from her flat stomach to her face, then back to her stomach.

"I've been feeling kind of queasy the past few mornings and when I checked my calendar, I discovered that I was two weeks late," she said, loving the look of complete awe on his face. "I made a special trip to the pharmacy to get an in-home test this morning." She laughed. "I even took it twice with the same results."

"I know that having a baby on the way was the reason behind your marriage to Craig," Cole said, his expression turning serious. "And don't get me wrong, I'm happy about starting a family with you. But how do you feel about it?"

"Cole, I couldn't be happier about it," she said, touching his cheek. "I'm finally going to have a baby with the man I've loved for almost half of my life."

His wide grin thrilled her and she knew in her heart that her dreams were going to come true. She was going to marry the love of her life and finally have the family she'd always wanted. And he was as happy about all of it as she was.

A week later, standing in front of the fireplace in the family room, Cole handed Aaron the wedding band he would be slipping on Paige's finger. "Lose it and you're a dead man."

Aaron laughed as he slipped the ring into the pocket of his suit coat. "If I lose it, you'll have to be content with finishing off what's left of me after Stella gets done."

The pastor from one of the churches in Royal walked

over to stand on the other side of him, then Cole watched Stella enter the room and take her place on the other side of the minister. Looking toward the door leading out into the foyer, Paige stood there in a champagne-colored satin dress holding a bouquet of bright red roses and white daisies. Just the sight of her robbed him of breath and he knew it always would.

After they'd finally put the past to rest where it belonged, Cole had kept his word and spent every day since making sure that Paige knew just how much he cherished her. He had been given a second chance with the only woman he would ever love and he wasn't going to take that for granted.

As she walked across the room toward him, her loving smile sent a shaft of longing straight through him. "You're beautiful," he said when she stopped in front of him.

"And you, Mr. Richardson, are the most handsome man I've ever met," she said, her eyes reflecting a love that would last forever.

As they turned to face Reverend Holloway, Cole was glad that he and Paige had decided on a very small, intimate wedding with just Aaron and Stella for witnesses. A larger wedding would have taken a lot more planning and neither of them wanted to wait any longer than necessary to finally start their lives together.

In the week since he'd proposed, they had put a lot of plans into motion that both of them agreed would be the fresh start they wanted to get their marriage off on the right foot. The day he had taken Paige for a drive around the ranch, Cole had been scouting out the best place to build a new house—one that was free of ghosts from the past and unhappy memories. They'd met with an architect yesterday, and they already had the man drawing up plans for a new six-bedroom house that included an in-home office for Cole to take care of R&N business, as well as an art studio for Paige.

He and Aaron had also managed to hire several more men, adding a couple of new work crews to the new Royal office. With the additional help, they would be able to keep up with the demands of their existing contracts to rebuild the town, as well as build his and Paige's new house. But the real winner was the Royal economy. R&N Builders were helping to put people back to work who had lost their jobs when the tornado tore through the town.

The minister directed him to repeat his wedding vows, and Cole turned to face his bride. "Paige, from the moment I first saw you, I knew that we were meant to be together—to share our lives and always be there for each other. Your love makes me want to be a better man and I give you my word that whatever life brings our way, I will always love, honor and protect you." He took the ring he'd handed Aaron earlier and gazing into her eyes, slipped it on her finger. "With this ring, I pledge myself to you for the rest of my life."

Tears filled her pretty gray eyes as she smiled up at him. "Cole, you are my everything—my love, my best friend and my partner in life. You have given me more than I ever dreamed would be mine. In your eyes I've finally found my home." Taking his wedding band from Stella, Paige slid it onto his finger. "This ring is a symbol of my never-ending love for you and I promise to honor and take care of you for all the days of my life."

He'd waited for years to hear her say those words. He knew this day and the days their children were born would be the happiest of his entire life.

"By the power vested in me by the great state of Texas, I now pronounce you husband and wife," Reverend Holloway said. The man smiled at Cole expectantly. "You can kiss your bride now, son."

"I love you, Paige Richardson," he said, unable to tell her enough how much she meant to him.

"And I love you, Cole Richardson." Her smile lit the darkest corners of his soul. "You are my heart and my soul for all of eternity."

Epilogue

Six months later

On the first anniversary of the tornado that had destroyed so much of the town and taken the lives of so many, Paige and Cole slowly made their way down Main Street toward the crowd gathering on the lawn of the newly finished Royal Town Hall. As they walked along hand in hand, Paige was pretty sure she resembled a duck.

Early on in her pregnancy the doctor had suspected she might be having twins, and a sonogram had confirmed that she and Cole were indeed having a little boy and a little girl. They both were thrilled by the news, but only two and a half months away from her due date, her belly was already big enough that she had started waddling when she walked.

"Do you need to sit down for a minute or two?" Cole asked as they strolled past Drew and Beth Farrell, who were laughing as they arranged pumpkins around the fall decorations they had donated for the day's ceremonies. Last year Beth's patch had been destroyed by the tornado, but this season it appeared to have produced a bumper crop. Pumpkins in all shapes and sizes, along with bales of straw and corn shocks, made a stunning fall display and reminded Paige that she and Cole needed to get one of the bigger pumpkins to carve for Halloween.

"Paige, are you all right?" Cole sounded worried that she hadn't answered his question.

Shaking her head, she smiled. "I'm fine. I can make it to the chairs in front of the podium. But I'd like to make a trip over to Beth's pumpkin patch within the next few days to get one for a jack-o'-lantern."

"Are you sure you're all right, sweetheart?" Cole asked, looking worried.

"Now look who's doing the fussing." She laughed.

He brought her hand up to kiss it. "You and our kids are my world, and I'm going to protect and take care of all of you."

"How are you feeling, Paige?" Megan Daltry asked as she and her husband, Whit, stopped to talk to them. A friend of Cole's and fellow Texas Cattleman's Club member, Whit owned Daltry Management Company and had helped Megan find her daughter, Evie, after the storm laid waste to the Little Tots Daycare. They'd been together ever since.

"I probably don't look like it, but I feel great," Paige said, patting her bulging stomach.

"Who is your doctor?" Megan asked. When Paige told her, Megan nodded. "That's who I'm going to."

"You're pregnant, too?" Paige hugged her friend. "I'm so happy for you."

"Yeah, we decided to give our daughter a little brother," Whit said, looking hopeful as he grinned from ear to ear. "But I'll be happy with a baby girl as long as she and Megan are all right."

"Congratulations!" Cole slapped Whit's shoulder in a friendly gesture. "We can attend Daddy Day Camp at Royal Memorial Hospital together."

"At least I'll have someone I know in that how-to workshop for new fathers," Whit said, looking relieved. "We can learn how to diaper a baby together."

"We'd better get to our seats," Cole said as the couple walked on ahead of them. "I don't want you having to stand throughout the ceremony."

"The Holts have arrived," Paige commented when she saw Lark and Keaton arrive with Skye and Jacob. Skye and Jacob had been having a rough time in their marriage when the tornado came through, but when Skye was injured Jacob had been there for her and during the time they spent together, they had worked through their problems. And Lark and Keaton had had to overcome a feud between their families. But after a rocky start for both couples, they had finally worked things out and couldn't be happier.

Both of the women were pregnant, and Paige couldn't help but wonder if the town was having its own little baby boom since the tornado had come through. It seemed that everywhere she looked there was another pregnant woman.

Watching Skye waddle after her baby daughter, Grace, Paige smiled. In a little more than a year, she would be chasing after her and Cole's babies as they toddled around. She had wanted to be able to do that for so long, she could hardly wait.

When Cole found them seats close to the stage that had been built for the memorial service to remember the lives lost in the tornado and the dedication ceremony of the new Town Hall, he helped her lower her bulk into the chair before sitting down beside her. "Are you comfortable, Paige?"

"You're fussing again, Mr. Richardson," she said, kissing his cheek.

"You're looking well, Paige," Julie Wakefield said as she and her husband Luc sat down in the seats next to her and Cole.

"I'm glad we got to see you," Luc told Cole. "Your company did a great job on rebuilding the hospital wing the tornado flattened and I'd like to see you and Aaron put in a bid from R&N Builders for the new wing Julie and I are planning to propose to the hospital board in a few weeks."

"It sounds to me like we'll be attending another dedication ceremony next year," Paige said, laughing.

Smiling, Julie nodded. "We hope so."

"Stella has been so good for Royal," Paige commented as the town's mayor stepped up to the podium. "After Richard Vance stepped down and Stella became the official mayor, she's done a wonderful job of bringing everyone together to rebuild the town. I don't think she'll have any trouble being re-elected."

Cole nodded. "She's also been the best thing that

ever happened to Aaron. He's more settled now than I've ever seen him."

When Stella read aloud the names of those killed during the storm and asked for a moment of silence, Cole reached down and took Paige's hand in his. Looking at each other, they silently acknowledged the loss of Craig, and she knew that, although he had done some terrible things to her and Cole, they both wished for him to rest in peace.

As Stella gave her speech and cut the ribbon for the official opening of the new town hall, the crowd was subdued, reflecting on their losses. But the applause that followed the ribbon cutting seemed to express hope for the future. When Stella was done, she paused for a moment as one of the city board members handed her a piece of paper.

"Is Dr. Marin in attendance today?" she asked, stepping back to the podium.

"I'm here," the doctor said, standing up a few chairs down from where Paige and Cole sat.

"You're going to be needed at the hospital very shortly," Stella said, smiling. "I've just been informed that Lark Holt is experiencing contractions and will be in need of your services."

As the ceremony wound down and the crowd began to disperse, Aaron approached his wife and handed their baby daughter to her before walking toward his car to get the diaper bag.

Paige and Cole laughed as they thought of how panicked Aaron had been when Stella had gone into labor. The look on his face had been priceless.

"You know you shouldn't laugh," Paige told Cole as he helped her up from the chair. "You'll be wearing the same expression and taking me on a wild car ride in about three months."

Cole wrapped his arms around her and gave her a kiss that made her legs feel weak and shaky. Then tucking her to his side as they walked toward their car, he said, "Sweetheart, I'll be glad to give you as many wild rides as you want."

Paige looked at the man she loved with all of her heart and soul. Cole was a loving husband and he was going to be a wonderful father. Sometimes she had to pinch herself in order to believe it was all real.

"Are you happy, Cole?" she asked when he helped her into the passenger seat of the car.

"I can honestly say the past six months have been the happiest of my life, Paige," he said, leaning down to give her a tender kiss. After closing her door, he walked around the car to slide into the driver's seat and start the engine. "Now let's go home so I can fuss over you some more."

"Have I told you lately how much I love you?" she asked.

Laughing, he nodded. "Yeah, but I never get tired of hearing it."

"I love you, Cole."

"And I love you, Paige. Now and until the end of time."

* * * * *

"I've missed you," she whispered.

Arching her back, she pressed her body even closer to his. "I didn't want to, but I did."

Gavin nibbled a sensitive spot beneath her ear, making her squirm. "Why didn't you want to miss me?"

"I had plans to take over the world. To be somebody. You were a temptation I had to resist."

He knew the feeling.

Worse, now that he had tasted her again, he hadn't a snowball's chance in hell of pretending he didn't want her. One look at her sweet face and mischievous eyes and he was a goner.

He thought of the babies in her womb...and their mother.

Cassidy Corelli troubled him. He was vulnerable where she was concerned. And vulnerability was the enemy of control.

If he was going to navigate these next few weeks, then he had to stay away from her. No touching, no kissing and certainly no sex. He would make that very clear.

Convincing Cassidy was one thing. Convincing himself was going to be a whole lot more difficult.

* * *

Twins on the Way
is part of the Kavanaghs of Silver Glen series:
In the mountains of North Carolina, one family
discovers that wealth means nothing without love.

TWINS ON THE WAY

BY
JANICE MAYNARD

MILLS
BOON

Published in Great Britain 2015
by Mills & Boon, an imprint of Harlequin (UK) Limited,
Eton House, 18-24 Paradise Road, Richmond, Surrey, TW9 1SR

© 2015 Janice Maynard

ISBN: 978-0-263-25256-9

51-0415

Harlequin (UK) Limited's policy is to use papers that are natural, renewable and recyclable products and made from wood grown in sustainable forests. The logging and manufacturing processes conform to the legal environmental regulations of the country of origin.

Printed and bound in Spain
by CPI, Barcelona

Janice Maynard is a *USA TODAY* bestselling author who lives in beautiful east Tennessee with her husband. She holds a BA from Emory and Henry College and an MA from East Tennessee State University. In 2002 Janice left a fifteen-year career as an elementary school teacher to pursue writing full time. Now her first love is creating sexy, character-driven, contemporary romance stories.

Janice loves to travel and enjoys using those experiences as settings for books. Hearing from readers is one of the best perks of the job! Visit her website, www.janicemaynard.com, and follow her on Facebook and Twitter.

For Charles—
I enjoyed our Vegas/Zion trip. I'm not much of a gambler, but I won big when it came to you. :)

One

Gavin Kavanagh needed a woman. Badly. He wasn't very good at relationships. He was too damn selfish, and he had trust issues. Which meant his only choices for sexual satisfaction were typically one-night stands. Since he was too fastidious to find much pleasure in that, he usually endured months of self-imposed celibacy until the day or the week he finally decided he couldn't stand it anymore, and he cracked.

This time, what tipped him over the edge was being in Vegas. He'd pitched in at the last minute to help out a sick friend by giving an address to several thousand cyber-security experts. Though public speaking didn't bother him, he much preferred to be alone in his man cave back in North Carolina.

Winding his way past noisy slot machines and crowded gaming tables, he headed for the exit, desperate to inhale fresh air and see the sky. He'd been incarcerated in this over-the-top hotel since lunchtime, and it was now almost ten at night.

On the sidewalk, he paused, taking in the garish display of neon and traffic spread before him. Vegas. Land of opportunity and lost dreams. Home of wild bachelor parties, just-past-prime entertainers and the siren lure of the *big win*.

He could see the appeal. The outrageous city pulsed with an almost tangible energy. If New York was the city that never slept, then Las Vegas was its manic twin. With enough disposable income and plenty of unencumbered time, a man could entertain himself here indefinitely.

But not Gavin Kavanagh. He couldn't wait to go home. *Good lord, Kavanagh.* Bullshitting himself was a new low.

It wasn't entirely a lie. He *did* want to go home. But there was something else he wanted more. The need writhing inside him was a voracious beast, reminding him that he was smack-dab in the land of legal hookers. For a few hundred bucks, the primeval urge to mate with a woman could be appeased.

He wasn't going to do it. What kind of man had to pay for sex? Maybe one who was too much of a curmudgeon to play nice with a decent female? To compliment her dress and ask about her day?

If that was the cost of sex as normal people enjoyed, he was out of luck. Pressing his fingertips to his temples, he winced as a shard of pain lanced its way through his head. He'd been up since 3:00 a.m. to catch a flight out of Asheville. Hell, even with a hooker, he might fall asleep before he could take care of business.

Heaving a sigh, he strode off down the street, trying to avoid looking at scantily clad women and signs for "adult" clubs. It was like putting an alcoholic in the middle of a distillery tour.

Weaving his way among tourists and time-share hawkers, he marveled that no one batted an eye at the occasional eccentrically dressed pedestrian. Perhaps Gavin was the oddity tonight.

He walked swiftly, needing the exercise to clear his head and regain control of his libido. It was almost one in the morning back home in Silver Glen. Exhaustion made him weave on his feet, but he knew he wouldn't sleep unless he was tired to the bone, not as buzzed as he was by the craving to feel a woman's soft skin and curves.

If he had his way, he'd be able to sublimate his sexual desires. He was a loner. Which meant that women either thought they could change him or were a little scared of him.

As the middle child of seven brothers, he had learned to be self-sufficient at an early age. He'd viewed his younger brothers as babies and wanted to avoid their company. His older brothers had been far too cool to tolerate little Gavin hanging around.

Even the community had unwittingly isolated Gavin. The Kavanagh brood had been referred to as the Three Musketeers—Liam, Dylan and Aidan…and the Three Stooges—Conor, Patrick and James. Gavin was often overlooked, partly because he didn't make waves.

He liked school. He never got in trouble. And though he grew to six feet in height by the ninth grade and two years later had filled out his gangly frame with muscles, he was often found with his head in a book. He knew how to fight. He could hold his own in a brawl.

But why do that when there were so many more interesting ways to spend his time?

He cut down a side street and followed it several blocks. Then, reversing his original course, he headed toward the hotel. Back here, away from the strip, there were not as many streetlights…less activity…fewer temptations to do something he might regret later. Unfortunately, he was not the only one to choose this route.

As he drew even with an alley that accommodated delivery trucks, he overheard a heated exchange. Pausing just out of sight, he listened.

The female voice surprised him. This was no place for a woman. She made her displeasure clear. "Leave me alone," she cried. "You can't have everything your way."

Gavin peeked around the corner just as the man put his hands on the woman's shoulders and shook her. The guy was about twice her size. "Stay out of it, Cass," he said. "Or you'll be sorry."

That was enough for Gavin. Hurling himself into the alley, he shouted, "Let go of her."

The petite dark-haired woman struggled, but the man had her wrists now, holding her hands away from his body. Gavin's yell distracted the guy for a split second, enabling the woman to land a blow.

"*Ow*, damn it."

Gavin seized the opportunity. With one efficient uppercut to the chin, he caused the bully to stagger backward. The guy was huge and wouldn't have fallen, but his foot slid in loose gravel. He lost his balance and went down hard, his shoulder striking the ground first. He didn't move.

"Hurry," Gavin said, taking the woman's arm and dragging her behind him. "We don't want to be here when he wakes up."

"But what if he's hurt?"

Gavin paused beneath a security light to examine her face with incredulity. "Do you really care?"

Big dark eyes framed in impossibly long lashes stared at him. Small white teeth worried a lower lip that was plump and shiny. "I suppose not," she said quietly. But she glanced over her shoulder nevertheless.

She was not the kind of woman Gavin needed tonight. Innocence framed her in an almost visible aura. His gut responded to that innocence on a visceral level with caveman lust, but he wanted sex that was hard and fast and insane. This sweet young thing was not in his league. He would scare her to death.

Still…he couldn't resist the urge to touch her. Tucking her hair behind her ear, he brushed her cheek with his thumb. "You're okay," he said. "I won't let anything happen to you, I swear."

Her gaze clashed with his. He felt as if he knew her somehow, a strange sense of déjà vu as if he had dreamed this moment before.

"You're very kind," she said.

"No. I'm not. But I don't like men who use their size to threaten women." He could have stood there looking at her all night. She made him feel things that confused him. Aroused him.

Dragging his concentration back to the matter at hand, he touched her arm. "We should go now." He urged her along, glad to see that even wearing four-inch heels, she was able to keep up with him. She kept a death grip on the small purse slung over her shoulder. "My car is parked at the hotel," he said. "I can give you a ride home."

"No." The negative was forceful. "He knows where I live."

Hell's bells. "Okay, then. But we need to call the police. You should make a formal complaint."

It was difficult to carry on a conversation when both parties were almost running. And perhaps speed was no longer called for, because there was no sign they were being followed.

"My side hurts," she complained. "And I don't want to involve the police."

Slowing reluctantly, he exhaled as she leaned against a mailbox, her chest heaving.

He tried not to notice her breasts.

"How much farther?" she asked.

He named the hotel in the next block. "Did he hurt you?" Though the man's threat had sounded menacing, Gavin hadn't seen the guy do more than shake the woman, though that was bad enough. The argument had been escalating, however, so no telling what would have happened if Gavin hadn't been around to stop it.

The woman straightened. "I'm fine." Her steady gaze took him in with a head-to-toe inspection that made him mildly uncomfortable. "You could take me to your room," she said. "So I can calm down and catch my breath."

Gavin froze, his nostrils flaring as if he could actually inhale her scent like a wild animal recognizing its mate. "I don't know if that's wise." Was this some kind of sick cosmic test of his character?

"I won't bother you. Unless you want me to," she said with a quick mischievous grin. "But I don't want to be alone right now. Please."

God help him, there was sexual interest in those beautiful eyes. He cleared his throat. "If that's what you want. Let's go."

This time, as Gavin traversed the acres of gaming floor in his hotel, he barely noticed the crowd. All his focus was on the woman he had rescued. He held her narrow wrist in one hand, sure he could feel the blood pulsing in her veins as he threaded his way through the throng, pulling her behind him. In the elevator he finally had a chance to see her clearly.

While she stared at the carpeted floor, he studied her, his heart thudding, his muscles jerky with leftover adrenaline. Chin-length curly hair somewhere between dark brown and black framed a heart-shaped face. Though she couldn't be more than five foot four at most, she appeared taller thanks to the outrageous shoes.

God, he loved those shoes. He could see her wearing nothing *but* those shoes as he laid her out on his big soft bed.

Down, boy. He told himself he wouldn't take advantage of her vulnerable state. But he had lied to himself once tonight already.

She was rounded in all the right places, including generous breasts that threatened to spill out of the neckline of her low-cut silver dress. The material was some kind of metallic fabric that sparkled when the lights hit it. Every time she moved, the dress moved with her.

Gavin reeled from the punch of sexual hunger. Any woman would have affected him the same, he told himself. She was nothing special. "What's your name?" he asked.

When she lifted her head and smiled, the hunger intensified. "Cassidy. Cassidy Corelli. My friends call me Cass. And who are you?"

"Gavin Kavanagh."

The elevator dinged. Together, they stepped out. Gavin's room was down the hallway and around the corner. He inserted the key card, opened the door and stood back for his guest to enter.

Cassidy surveyed the plush suite with raised eyebrows. "You're either a high roller or somebody very important."

"Not exactly." He sprawled in an armchair, trying to appear relaxed. It was probably not a good idea to let her see the beast that rode him. "I don't gamble. My friend was supposed to do the keynote at a conference here, but he got sick. I'm subbing."

Casually, as if it were the most normal thing in the world, Cassidy slipped off her shoes and went to the minibar. Without waiting for permission, she extracted a soft drink and a jar of macadamia nuts. "Do you mind? I missed dinner, and I'm starving."

"Help yourself." When she took the chair opposite his,

he nearly swallowed his tongue. The skirt of her dress was unforgiving. As she curled her legs beneath her, he caught a glimpse of bare thighs all the way to the mother lode.

He swallowed hard. "Do you have a phone, or do you need to use mine?"

She took a swig of soda, managing to look entirely comfortable and yet ladylike. "Why do I need a phone?"

"To call the authorities?" Her artless stonewalling scraped his nerves. Was she deliberately tormenting him?

Cassidy wrinkled her small, perfect nose. "I'm not sure that would be a good idea. This is sort of a family squabble."

His gut tightened. "As in the mob?"

Her jaw dropped. "Good grief, no."

"Are you married to the guy?" She wasn't wearing a ring, but that didn't mean anything. The scene he had interrupted could have been a domestic dispute.

Cassidy stared at him. Her lips were painted the same deep red as her toenails. "I'm not married," she said, enunciating each word carefully. "I don't have a significant other. I'm entirely unencumbered. And I don't have to be anywhere until ten in the morning."

The look she gave him tightened the back of his neck… and other body parts. Still, caution won out. "Are you a working girl?" he asked. In Vegas it could be hard to tell. Cassidy Corelli more than lived up to male fantasy, but she seemed awfully young.

She pursed her lips, suddenly looking more like a schoolmarm than a woman for hire. "I *work*," she muttered, glaring at him. "But not like that. I don't know whether to be insulted or flattered."

"How old are you?" In other circumstances, he would never ask such personal questions, but he also didn't want to contribute to the delinquency of a minor.

"I'm twenty-three," she said flatly, erasing most of his misgivings.

"Good."

She cocked her head. "Why is that good?"

He gave her a gentle smile. "Because if I follow up on your invitation, I want to make sure I don't end up in jail."

"What invitation?" she asked, feigning innocence, though in those huge expressive eyes, feminine excitement lingered.

His customary distrust of unknown women cautioned him to slow down. But Cassidy was light and warmth and spontaneity, all the things that were missing from his life. He was irresistibly drawn to her vibrant personality like the proverbial moth to a flame. But he'd been burned once…badly. So the doubts remained.

"Don't be coy. A woman doesn't outline her relationship status quite so succinctly unless she wants a man to know the score."

"Ah." Cassidy popped a nut into her mouth and chewed it slowly before swallowing and taking another sip of her drink. "Why don't you gamble?" she asked.

The non sequitur caught him off guard. He shrugged. "I'm good at math. But the house always wins. I prefer to control the outcome."

She gave a mock shiver. "So intense. I like that in a man."

"Is that why you were hanging around with Bozo the Bruiser?"

"Trust me," she said. "There's nothing romantic there."

"What were you arguing about?"

"I'd rather not discuss it."

"You're willing to have sex with a stranger, but you won't answer a simple question?"

She tossed her head and stood up, cheeks flushing. "Who said I'm willing to have sex?"

He gazed at her intently, letting her see the arousal that had built since he looked her over in the elevator. "No games, Cass. You tossed out a pretty blatant lure. Stay or go. Your choice."

Cassidy shivered inwardly. Gavin Kavanagh was a man, not a boy. He'd rescued her from what he thought was a dangerous situation, not pausing to consider the consequences. Though she was more than capable of taking care of herself, Gavin's masculine assurance triggered all sorts of non-PC feminine emotions.

He was a beautiful man. Tall and broad...exuding confidence. The combination made her damp in places she'd rather not ponder. His streaky brownish-blond hair was short and spiky, not expertly styled, but like a man who didn't care to fool with anything he considered a waste of time.

His gray eyes with the hint of blue were cool and distant at the moment. "Which is it?" The question was rife with masculine demand.

"Grumpy, grumpy, grumpy." She wanted more time to think about this, but if she let the moment pass, she would never see him again. She was tired of being her father's good little girl. Everyone expected her to live like a nun. And she had. But why? Her whole life was about work, work, work, and earning the love that should be a gift.

She'd been edgy and stressed for weeks now, arguing with her brother and going head-to-head with her father. Perhaps if she'd had a mother, she could have talked frankly about the fact that she felt like the world's oldest virgin. About her choice to wait for the right man. And the fact that she'd never even met a guy who honestly tempted her.

Being raised in Vegas had exposed her to a whole lot of mature situations that gave her an insight into all kinds of adult behavior. But it also took some of the bloom off the rose when it came to romance. She was probably holding out for a fantasy that didn't even exist except in books and movies.

She took a deep breath, feeling a funny spin in the pit of her stomach. To hell with her status as the firstborn who never strayed from the straight and narrow. She could blame Gavin for her sexual epiphany, but truthfully, this moment had been coming for a long time. She'd been saving herself for some unknown white knight, but surprisingly, the tarnished armor of a gruff, no-nonsense, make-my-day kind of guy punched all her buttons.

Though it took a measure of courage and nonchalance she wasn't sure she could pull off, she went to him and perched on his lap, curling one arm around his neck. "You could kiss me. It might help me make up my mind."

A firm hand gripped her hip. He smelled amazing. Woodsy cologne and warm male skin. She wanted things from him. Wild things. Wicked things. And that was saying a lot for a girl who had grown up in sin city.

"I should toss you out on your butt," he muttered. "You're a menace to the male sex."

"Really?" Could he be telling the truth?

"You're playing a dangerous game."

The suspicion in his hard eyes was perhaps warranted, but it stung. "Don't be that way," she said. Putting a hand to his stubbly cheek, she smiled wistfully. "I'll go if you want me to. But I'd really like to stay."

He made her wait a miserably long time. Maybe thirty seconds. Or more. She actually *felt* the moment she won the standoff. Though she was technically on top, Gavin took control right out of the gate. One big hand settled in the curls at the back of her head, pulling her down until his lips could reach hers.

"Gavin…" She had no idea what she meant to say. When his mouth settled over hers, her brain short-circuited. He was a great kisser. World-class. On a scale of one to ten, a thirteen. The only unlucky thing about that number was that they were both fully dressed.

He took his time, drawing attention to the fact that her experience was limited at best. Unapologetic, he slid his tongue into her mouth, mimicking the act they both wanted.

When she was starved for oxygen, he pulled back, his heavy-lidded gaze searching hers. "I don't know why you're here," he said gruffly, with perhaps the slightest note of accusation in his voice.

"I can leave." It would probably be best if she did. What had started as a personal declaration of independence suddenly seemed far more serious.

"Do you do this often?"

The insinuation infuriated her. "No," she snapped. "How about you?"

He grinned. "Never. Maybe we're experiencing Vegas madness. I've heard about it."

"I wouldn't know," she sniffed. "I'm a native."

"And I'm a novice."

"You're not a *novice* anything," she said drily. "But I could show you the sights if you're interested."

"I fly home tomorrow."

"We have tonight." She was skating a fine line between taking what she wanted and being totally reckless. But after four years of college and two years of grad school without a break, she wanted to know how it felt to be a woman. In every way.

He toyed with the neckline of her dress. The feel of his slightly rough fingertips on her bare skin made her nipples pebble. "The only sights I'm interested in at the moment are in this room."

The words were flat. Unadorned with emotion. The blaze in his eyes more than made up for it. So much so that she almost chickened out. To him, she had been a damsel in distress. He had acted honorably, protecting her from a perceived enemy. Only a man with high moral standards did that…right?

She'd always been a good judge of character. It was a necessary skill growing up in Vegas, particularly when your family had a lot of money. Every gut instinct she possessed told her that Gavin Kavanagh was one of the good guys. He was leaving in the morning. Was there any point in starting something that would never amount to anything more?

Playing by the rules was a first-child burden. Good grades, never breaking curfew, always trying to satisfy the parental units. Tonight she was damned if she was going to miss out on something incredible because she was too afraid to take a walk on the wild side.

"I'd like to take a shower." The follow-up didn't need to be spelled out.

"May I join you?"

So polite. But it wasn't really a question. She swallowed hard. "I suppose."

He shifted her out of his lap onto her feet. Her legs felt like overcooked pasta and her heartbeat was none too steady.

"I like your hair." He ruffled his hand through it, mussing the style.

Every time she thought she had him pinned down, he surprised her. Men in general had little patience when it came to sexual gratification. At least the ones she knew. Gavin, on the other hand, possessed remarkable restraint.

"Thank you," she said.

"Don't get shy now." He chuckled, taking her hand and leading her across the thick carpet that made her toes curl.

The bathroom was palatial and decadent. She spared a glance for the hot tub, but Gavin shook his head. "Later."

He turned the faucet control in the glass enclosure. Triple showerheads sprouted streams of water. "Last chance."

They were both still fully clothed except for her shoes. Though he might not like it, she knew she could turn around and leave the suite. He wouldn't chase after her. Her confidence wavered. Was she really about to get stark naked with a handsome stranger in his opulent shower stall?

She spared a glance in the mirror, hardly recognizing the woman who stood there. "Do you have any wine?"

"Needing a bit of Dutch courage, are we?"

"Don't make fun of me," she said. "You're an intimidating man."

"Which is why you insisted on coming to my room and throwing yourself at me."

Hot color swept from her throat to her hairline. From where he was standing, it must have seemed that way. How could she explain that he had dazzled her without even trying? "You'll be disappointed if you think I'm a pro."

"I thought we already established that you're *not* a pro."

"That's not what I mean. I haven't *done* this kind of thing."

"Sex? Or seduction?"

"I have not seduced you," she said primly, secretly charmed that he thought she could.

He nodded briefly, his firm lips curved in a sensual smile. "I'll admit to being predisposed. You're a very appealing woman."

The die was cast. "How about fetching us some of that wine while I get undressed?"

Two

Gavin's hands shook as he opened a bottle of Zinfandel. He managed to pour two glasses without spilling anything, but it was a close call. In his bathroom was a naked young female...the most beautiful woman he had seen in a very long time. If he had to create a sexual partner from scratch, she would look a lot like Cassidy Corelli.

Her sun-kissed Mediterranean coloring and cheeky personality were irresistible. He'd never particularly believed in fate as the arbiter of his destiny. He was too much of a control freak for that. But some unseen force or quirk of timing had put him near that alley at exactly the right moment. It was his choice how to proceed.

He carried the wine into the bathroom and stopped dead in his tracks when he realized that Cassidy was already undressed. She had donned one of the hotel's signature bathrobes. It was much too large for her.

"Most people wait until *after* the shower to cover up," he said drily. The acres of terry cloth might as well have been armor. But what his guest didn't realize was that bare feet and flushed cheeks gave her an air of innocence. The juxtaposition of smart-mouthed banter with youthful naïveté brought tenderness into the mix.

"I was cold," she said.

Since the bathroom was steamy, he took that with a

grain of salt. Though he had turned off the water when he saw they weren't getting in immediately, the room was plenty warm.

"Drink some wine," he said, handing her a glass. "It will settle your nerves."

She scowled at him over the rim of her crystal flute. "Who says I'm nervous?"

Leaning a hip against the counter, he drained half his glass. "Aren't you? Shouldn't you be?"

"Not unless you're a twisted psychopath."

"It's a little late to worry about that now, don't you think?"

She set down the glass of wine she had barely touched and shoved her hands in her pockets. Her chin lifted. "I can read people."

"Do tell."

"You were a Boy Scout. Eagle, if I had to guess."

He lifted an eyebrow. "I'm impressed."

"So I'm right?" Her pleased smugness amused him.

"One lucky shot doesn't qualify you to read the Tarot cards."

"I don't need cards. You're an open book."

He emptied his glass and set it gently on the counter with a little *clink*. "Then what am I thinking now?" He unfastened his belt and drew it from around his waist. When he dropped it on the floor, he was pretty sure she gulped.

"Stop that," she said.

"I seldom shower with my clothes on." His solemn joke lightened the look of panic on her face, though she still eyed him warily.

"Maybe we should get to know each other first."

"Did I mention that I'm flying out in the morning? Leave if you want to, Cass, but soon. I don't want to go any further with this if you aren't sure."

She paled, her brown eyes round with a mix of emotions he couldn't decipher. "I *want* to be sure."

"But you're not," he said, reading her fairly well.

"I thought I could be spontaneous and adventuresome. But it turns out I'm not really that girl."

He swallowed his disappointment. "I understand. Get dressed and I'll take you wherever you want to go."

She took a step in his direction, placing her small hand on his forearm. "How about a compromise?"

It became painfully clear that Cassidy Corelli didn't know much about men at all. She was naked for all intents and purposes, in his bathroom, and yet somehow she expected him to play nice. Even her fingers on his skin made him shudder with hunger.

Moving out of reach, he ran two hands through his hair. "What kind of compromise?" He was asking for more physical torture, but he didn't have it in him to kick her out.

"This is your first trip to Vegas, right?"

"Yes."

"I could show you the sights for a couple of hours. Enjoy the ambiance."

"And then what?"

"Whatever we want to do next."

Her smile seemed genuine. Was she deliberately teasing him, or did she honestly want to go to bed with him but was uncertain about the wisdom of that plan?

He was hard and ready. It wasn't conceit to think he could coax her into having sex right now. But he'd been raised to be a gentleman. Despite the demands of his body, he was well aware that Cassidy was not 100 percent on board with the idea of intimacy. Even if she *had* been the one to come on to him in the first place.

The smart thing for both of them would be for him to boot her out before somebody got hurt. He couldn't give her anything beyond tonight. And it was pretty clear that she was not a woman who went in for casual sex.

But she fascinated him, intrigued him…and he couldn't remember ever wanting a woman more. He was not in the habit of picking up strange females, especially not ones like Cassidy. Too many unknowns. Too many warning bells.

He'd learned the hard way not to be taken in by a seemingly innocent come-on. Cassidy was more than that, though. He believed it, or told himself he did. Otherwise, he was about to break his personal code into tiny unmanageable pieces.

His desire for her and her undeniable appeal could be blamed on Vegas, but whatever compelled him was strong and urgent.

"Fine," he said tersely. "Put your clothes on, and we'll see the sights." He'd been awake for almost twenty-four hours, but what the hell. Carpe diem it was…God help him.

When they reached Gavin's rental car, Cassidy was delighted to see it was a convertible. "Why don't I drive so you can enjoy yourself?" she said.

Gavin yawned and nodded. "Probably a good idea. I'm sleep-deprived." He went around to the passenger side. "You're in charge."

She didn't think he meant that statement to be provocative, but the image it conjured made her shift restlessly as she settled behind the wheel. Gavin Kavanagh was an imposing man. Imagining him nude and at her mercy made her mouth dry and her cheeks hot.

Once they folded back the top and exited the parking garage, her passenger slumped in his seat with his head against the headrest. She drove down the strip, pointing out places of interest that were unique to Vegas. The fabulous architecture, the neon lights, the endless spectacle and the marquees touting famous entertainers.

When she paused at a traffic light, Gavin waved a hand. "You love it here, don't you?"

His perception surprised her. "I suppose I do. We take the good with the bad. There's nothing like it anywhere in the world."

"I wasn't too impressed with Vegas before tonight. You've convinced me it has a lot to offer."

When she glanced sideways at him, the look in his eyes made her shiver. He wanted her. And he planned to have her.

Sweet heaven. Without asking, she turned the car around and headed out of town. She barely remembered her name. Sexual arousal flooded her veins, hot and sweet. Exhilaration, laced with anticipation, made her feel as if she could fly.

Fortunately, gravity kept her grounded. Driving in the desert at night was a special pleasure. The road was straight, traffic sparse and the spring air invigorating.

She was a good driver, and she knew her limits. Pressing down on the gas, she watched the speedometer hit sixty, then seventy, then eighty. In her peripheral vision, she saw Gavin straighten. "I'm not paying for any tickets," he said.

The implied but laconic warning made her grin. She pushed it to ninety and laughed out loud as the wind tangled her hair. "Don't worry. I know every law enforcement official in a fifty-mile radius." She had to raise her voice for him to hear her.

A rush of adrenaline took over, encompassing an odd mix of sexual hunger and sheer fun. Her hands were steady on the wheel. Anticipation rose in her chest like a wave of bubbles. The night was hers...the open road, as well. Earlier, she had panicked, plain and simple. She had second-guessed her decision to change the status quo. But now she was ready. She wanted Gavin Kavanagh, and she wasn't going to let her inexperience stand in her way.

Only the late hour curtailed her road trip. At last, she eased off on the accelerator and dropped back to a more sedate speed. At a pullout on the right, she slid the car to a stop and turned off the engine. The sudden silence was deafening. Overhead, a million stars twinkled and sparked.

Gavin reached for her before she had a chance to take her hands off the wheel. His kiss was urgent. Thorough. Masterful. She had assumed he was half-asleep. Which proved how wrong a woman could be. This was a hunger that had been building since she went to his hotel room.

The kiss was firm and demanding. It sent little squiggles of lust into every cell of her body. His hands anchored her head, one on each side of her jaw. Tilting her face to his, he ravaged her mouth, barely giving her a moment to breathe.

For Cassidy, it was earth-shattering. She'd never been too impressed with foreplay. In the course of her limited experimentation, it had proven to be awkward and usually disappointing. Apparently her subconscious had recognized Gavin Kavanagh as the man to prove her wrong.

Desperately, she pondered the logistics of getting naked in the backseat. But while she didn't mind being pulled over for speeding, getting caught in sexual flagrante delicto was another matter entirely. This was Vegas, true. But her father would have a coronary, and this was not a time she wanted to court his displeasure.

Gavin had more control than she did, apparently. He eventually gentled the kiss and released her, though his chest heaved. "You dazzle me, Cassidy Corelli."

His rough praise stroked her ego. Coming from a man

like Gavin, that was a compliment worth savoring. "The feeling is mutual."

He snorted. "You sound like a little girl practicing her social etiquette. Tell me honestly. Why are you here in this car with me?"

"I really don't know," she said, recognizing the truth as she spoke it. "But I never had a choice. There's something about you I can't resist." She paused, grimacing. "We get lots of flimflam artists in Vegas. Con men, gaming sharks, wannabe Don Juans. So I've learned how to spot them. But you're different, Gavin Kavanagh. You're the real deal. Don't ask me how I know. I just do…"

He leaned back in his seat with a sigh, but he took her hand in his. "This is the first time all day I've felt comfortable. The stars are just as bright in North Carolina."

His thumb played lightly over the pulse point at the back of her wrist, making her dizzy. "Do you live at the beach?" she asked.

"No. In a place called Silver Glen. It's in the western part of the state…in the mountains. My ancestors discovered a silver mine back in the day and restored the family fortunes after the Depression." He pointed to a group of stars. "Do you know your astronomy? Those are the Pleiades…the seven sisters. And over there is Orion. The fuzzy spot in his dagger is a nebula."

"You're very smart, aren't you?"

He chuckled. "Any third grader worth his salt can spot those."

She half turned in her seat, forcing him to release her hand. She couldn't see his expression very well. "There's one more place I need to go, just a quick stop, and then I'd very much like to return to your hotel. For real this time. You know…to—"

He put a hand over her mouth. "Don't say it out loud. I'm on a hair trigger. But I'm trying to behave myself."

A sudden gust of wind made her shiver. At night the desert temperatures plummeted. She wanted to cuddle into the warmth of his embrace, but if she did, they might not make it back to the hotel. And while she was prepared to lose her innocence with him, she would prefer her first time to be in more traditional surroundings.

She settled for nipping his fingers with her teeth. The naughty bite drew a groan and a curse from him. He gripped her shoulders. "You're playing with fire, Cass. I'm not averse to taking you over the hood of the car. Is that what you want?"

The possibility that he might decide to do just that made her melt inside. She could see herself, spread-eagled, Gavin lifting her skirt from behind and moving against her. She felt lost in an emotional desert, desperate for water. The inside of her mouth was like sand. "No." *Yes. Yes. Yes.*

He released her and sat back in his seat. "Then let's get out of here."

Gavin wondered if she had spiked his wine somehow. He was more aroused than he could ever remember, his body trembling with the need to mate with hers. Perhaps it was the magic of this perfect night or her radiant beauty or the laughter they shared. But whatever the reason, he scarcely knew himself.

Going along with her lead was a signal of his trust, though he might be falling through a rabbit hole for the second time in his life. His hunger eradicated most of his reservations, though the wariness lurked at a subterranean level. Once they were back in sight of neon and fake water-falls and massive pleasure palaces, it occurred to him to ask where they were going.

Cassidy gave him an impish grin. "No visit to Vegas is complete without seeing an all-night wedding chapel. My cousin is an Elvis impersonator. I want you to meet him. Besides, I promised him I'd stop by and see him tonight, because he's bored."

"Now?" It was the wee hours of the morning.

"Yeah. Robbie is being punished with the overnight shift for a few weeks. He didn't renew his license when he was supposed to, and he *married* several couples whose weddings turned out to be illegal. He almost got fired over it, but the boss has a soft spot for him, because Robbie can actually sing. So while they're waiting for his new license, he's stuck vacuuming the chapel and doing paperwork."

"What happens if a couple actually comes in wanting to get married?"

"Robbie calls the boss and wakes him up so he can dash over here." She parked the car at the curb in front of an improbably pink edifice decorated with white doves. It looked as if a bottle of Pepto-Bismol had thrown up.

"Good lord. Do people actually do this?"

Cassidy shook her head as she got out of the car. "You'd be surprised."

Inside, Robbie was visibly grateful for the company. "How's it hangin', Cass? I haven't seen you since Uncle Bobo's birthday party."

"I'm good," Cass said. "This is my friend Gavin."

Robbie appeared to be about the same age as Cass, but it was hard to tell for sure. He wore a white Elvis suit with a matching cape lined in electric-blue satin. His hair, and it looked real, was coal black with huge sideburns. "Very nice to meet you, sir."

Gavin winced inwardly. *Sir?* Did he really look that old? "Cassidy has been giving me a tour of Vegas. She said we had to stop here to make the night complete."

Cass's eyes met his. She shot him a look to which Robbie was oblivious…a look that said something entirely different would make the night complete. Gavin's brow dampened. How long could a man wait for a woman like this?

Robbie lifted a hand. "Follow me. I'll show you the Chapel of Love."

When Gavin muttered under his breath, Cass smacked his hand. "Be nice," she whispered. "This is the first job Robbie has been able to keep. We try to encourage him."

Gavin curbed his impatience as Robbie gave them the grand tour. When they stood in front of the altar, Robbie donned a white robe and stepped behind the podium. "Take her hands," he said pompously.

"Is this a shotgun wedding?" Gavin was only half kidding. But he took Cassidy's hands in his and faced her.

His faux bride frowned. "Not to worry. We don't have the paperwork. But I'm pretty sure Robbie could use the practice, if you don't mind."

Robbie grimaced. "Forgot something already." He stepped to one side and picked up a bottle of champagne. Popping the cork with a surprisingly practiced motion, he filled two flutes and handed one to Cassidy and one to Gavin.

Cassidy took a sip. "Wait a minute. Are you going to charge me for this?"

"On the house," Robbie said, snickering.

Gavin drained his drink, eager to finish whatever it took to get Cassidy back to his hotel room. When the room spun just a tad, he second-guessed the champagne.

Cass set her mostly full glass aside and took his hand again. "Go ahead, Robbie. What comes next?"

"Um…" He fumbled for his notes. "Do you, Cassidy

Lavinia Corelli, take this man to be your lawfully wedded husband?"

Gavin grinned. "Lavinia?"

His bride scowled at him. "Oh, hush." She turned to
Robbie. "You're doing fine," she said. "And yes, I do."

Robbie gave Gavin a sober stare that lost something in
the translation thanks to his attire. "Do you, Gavin…?"
He stumbled to a halt.

"Gavin Michael Kavanagh…" Gavin felt sorry for the
kid if he was really this inept when it came to his job.

"Do you, *Gavin Michael Kavanagh*, take this woman
to be your lawfully wedded wife?"

For a split second, Gavin felt the earth shift beneath his
feet. His brain was mush, definitely impaired thanks to
lack of sleep and alcohol. But one thing was perfectly clear.
If he had ever daydreamed of his wedding day—and that
was something a guy definitely did not do—the woman he
might have envisioned would be a clone of Cassidy Corelli.

Clearing his throat, he forgot about the late hour and
the goofy Elvis and the fact that he hated Vegas. Instead,
he looked into long-lashed eyes that were clear and guile-
less. A tiny smile played around lips curved into a perfect
ruby bow. The only flaw he could see was her wind-tossed
hair, and even that wasn't so bad, because it made him
think of sex.

Robbie backed up and started again. "Do you, Gavin—"

Gavin held up his hand, stopping the vow prompt mid-
sentence. Gripping Cassidy's fingers, he imagined what it
was going to feel like when she was soft and naked in his
bed. "I do," he muttered. "I definitely do. And now I'm
going to kiss my bride."

Three

Cassidy had heard the term *swept off her feet*, but she had never actually experienced the phenomenon. The moment when Gavin scooped her up against his chest was both emotionally and physically exhilarating. Her heart pounded and her stomach fluttered.

It was ridiculously retro to be aroused by a man's physical strength, but damn...Gavin Kavanagh was a sexy beast. Ever since Rhett Butler carried Scarlett O'Hara up that grand staircase to have his wicked manly way with her, women had secretly judged a guy's swoon factor by how easily he could heft his lover.

Cassidy could stand to lose ten pounds. But Gavin lifted her as if she weighed no more than a child. Oh, my...

She tasted desperation in his kiss, laced with a nuance of the nice champagne. Her breasts were squished up against a hard rib cage. Kissing him back eagerly, she might have forgotten a thing or two. Like the fact that they had a witness.

Robbie moved restlessly. When she sneaked a sideways peek at him, he was slack-jawed, perhaps stunned. "I need to get back to the office," he muttered. "You two can show yourselves out."

Cassidy wiggled until Gavin released her. There was a look in his eyes that made her a little crazy. But she concentrated on her cousin. "Thanks for showing us around, Robbie."

"Thanks for stopping by to see me." He lifted a hand. "I now pronounce you husband and wife."

She hugged him and kissed his cheek. "You'll get the hang of this. Just stick with it."

Moments later, the little chapel was silent. Gavin crossed his arms over his chest and stared at her with an expression that could have meant anything.

Following an impulse, she held out her hand. "Let me have your phone. I want you to have a picture to remember me by."

She was somewhat bemused when he cooperated. Scooting up against him, she tapped a couple of icons and held the phone at arm's length. "We have to document this night."

Unfortunately, her arms were short and Gavin was tall. She couldn't actually hold the camera far enough away.

He took it out of her hand. "Give me that." With one hard arm curled around her waist and the other extended, he framed the two of them in the small screen. "Say cheese," he muttered.

Just as he hit the button, she reached up and kissed him on the chin. Afterward, she bounced on her toes. "Let me see, let me see."

The shot was surprisingly sweet. She studied Gavin's face in the image. Even if she hadn't met him in person, she would be impressed with the man in the picture. He looked like a throwback to the steely-eyed cowboys of the past. All brooding machismo and sizzling intensity. "I like it," she said. "You're very photogenic."

He lifted an eyebrow. "No. I'm not. Let's get out of here."

She followed him obediently, smothering a smile. Ap-

parently a man like Gavin took her compliment as an af-
front to his masculinity. Since she had wounded his pride,
she held out the car keys. "I don't have to drive."

He shook his head and slid into the passenger seat. "Yes,
you do," he said, his eyelids drifting shut. "I'm taking a
nap between here and the hotel so I'll have the energy to
rock your world."

Laughing out loud at his tongue-in-cheek boast, she
started the car. Maybe he was serious. He didn't even
flinch when she whipped out into traffic. But minutes
later when she eased into a spot in the parking garage, he
sat up and ran a hand through his hair. "What time is it?"
he asked, rubbing his eyes with the heels of his hands.

Cassidy glanced at the dashboard. "Almost four."

He grimaced. "There's something unnatural about a
city where no one sleeps."

"They sleep," she protested, vaguely defensive about her
hometown. "But not necessarily from midnight until morning." Though Gavin Kavanagh would never be anything
other than handsome, he definitely looked the worse for
wear. Dark circles beneath his eyes and a pale undertone
to his skin bespoke his exhaustion. "I should go," she said
impulsively, squashing her disappointment. "You need to
get some rest before you fly out."

The look he gave her sizzled nerve endings in some
very interesting places. "I can sleep when I'm dead," he
growled. "You're not going anywhere."

The arrogance was justified given her propensity for
throwing herself at him tonight. But it rankled nevertheless. "Is that a threat?"

He cupped her neck with one hand and pulled her into
his kiss. "Call it what you want, Cassidy Corelli. But if
I'm going to be a guinea pig in your goofy cousin's wedding charade, then I think I'm entitled to a fake honey-

moon, too." He claimed her mouth with knee-weakening mastery. "C'mon, Cass. I need a bed. ASAP."

"Because you're tired?"

He got out and came around to her door, helping her to her feet. "Because I need you. Now."

Gavin had never been more serious or more desperate to have a woman. Granted, it had been several months since the last time he'd been naked with a female. In addition to his youthful catastrophic history in misjudging the fairer sex, when he lost himself in his work, his hermit leanings tended to take over. He liked people. But solitude gave him energy. Sharpened his mind. Spurred his creativity.

When it came to Cassidy, however, he was neither clear-headed nor particularly intelligent. His brain was not in the driver's seat. He wanted her. Fiercely. Madly. In a way that wiped out all his normal reservations. With an insanity no doubt induced by sleep deprivation and champagne and recent celibacy. But insanity nevertheless.

Later, he would not be able to recall the exact sequence of steps that took them from the artificially illuminated parking garage to the thickly carpeted hallway where his room was located. But through it all, he kept Cassidy by his side, hip to hip, his arm around her shoulders.

She laughed at him when he fumbled the key card from his shirt pocket and took three tries to open the door. "Are you sure this is your room?" she whispered.

The door swung wide. "Don't you remember? You were here not that long ago."

She passed him, entering the suite with a swish of hips and a low chuckle that went straight to his gut and hardened his aching sex even more. "All these hallways look alike."

The door closed with a muffled sound. For the first

time, his charming, funny tour guide seemed momentarily abashed. Her eyes wouldn't meet his. Graceful hands fluttered as if not knowing where to land.

He restrained the urge to grab her, an odd feeling in the pit of his stomach. "Problem, Cass?"

She licked her lips. "No."

The simple negative didn't sound convincing. "What's wrong?"

"Nothing." She kicked off her shoes as she had earlier, still not looking at him. "Would you mind if I take a quick shower...alone?"

He frowned, immediately suspicious. "If you think waiting will make me want you more, you're crazy. I'm far past teasing, I promise you."

Her chin came up at last and she grimaced. "I've never showered with a man. It may not seem like it, but I'm shy in certain situations. I won't linger, I swear. I want this, too."

Something about the vulnerability and honesty in her bittersweet chocolate gaze convinced him she wasn't playing games.

Nodding tersely, he put some distance between them. "Go, then."

When she disappeared, he drew in oxygen with a sharp inhale. Was Cassidy Corelli some kind of scam artist? Would he awake to find his billfold missing? Or was she what she seemed...an artless, far-too-young-for-him ingenue with a propensity for flirtation?

He paced automatically, doing everything he could think of to get himself under control. The last woman he'd slept with had been an artist in Asheville. They'd met at the home of mutual friends and acted on a quiet attraction that proved to be physically satisfying. Despite having much in common, their relationship had ended after six months due to a lack of fire.

That wasn't going to be a problem with Cassidy. Though this current encounter had all the earmarks of a one-night stand, what he felt at this pivotal moment was far more volatile than simple attraction. It wasn't that he wanted Cass. He *craved* her…with an intensity that alarmed his well-ordered existence.

Thankfully, she was true to her word. She reappeared in a very short amount of time wearing the same robe she had modeled earlier. He cleared his throat. "All done?"

She nodded, staring at him.

"Give me three minutes," he said. In the shower, he washed rapidly. The taut skin covering his erect sex was almost too sensitive to touch. Imagining Cassidy's fingers on his body made him groan.

When he stepped out of the shower, he caught his reflection in the mirror. It gave him pause. His eyes glittered with feral hunger, and his cheekbones were slashed with hot color. Every vestige of civilized male had been stripped away. He shuddered, closing his eyes as he imagined the moment when his body would penetrate hers.

She was so alive. He wanted some of that warmth for himself. Whether he had isolated himself deliberately or whether it had been a quirk of his birth order, he found it difficult to let people get close. With Cassidy, it was the opposite. He wouldn't be satisfied until they shared the same space, the same air, the same hushed anticipation.

His hair was still wet when he tucked a towel around his hips and returned to the living room. He found Cassidy sitting on the edge of a chair, feet planted flat on the floor, knees pressed together. She looked like a schoolgirl waiting for punishment to be doled out.

"Are you ready?"

She jerked when he spoke, as if she had been lost in thought. He saw her throat move as she swallowed. "Of course." She stood up so fast she stumbled and had to catch herself on the arm of the chair.

If he could have reached out a hand, he would have, but he was afraid that if he touched her, he would take her right there on the carpet. Extending an arm in the direction of the bedroom, he gave her what he hoped was a reassuring smile. "After you, Cass."

When she slid by him, careful not to touch, he caught a whiff of the shower gel he had rubbed over his own skin. The scent got in his head, imprinting her in his psyche.

Beside the king-size bed, she paused, her back to him. "Do you have condoms?"

"Of course." Though he had forgotten to fetch them from his shaving kit in the bathroom. In moments he rectified that glaring omission. Tossing a handful of packets onto the small bedside table, he glanced at the clock. It would be dawn soon.

Placing a hand on her narrow shoulder, he turned her around. Without her outrageous heels, the top of her head barely reached his collarbone. Using one finger, he tipped up her chin so he could see her eyes. Though she was by no means a helpless woman, her small frame seemed delicate next to his.

The expression in her gaze was difficult to read. Despite the fact that her hands rested trustingly at his waist, he sensed defensiveness in her posture. Perhaps she, too, saw the disparity in their physical sizes and felt threatened.

"I would cut off my arm before I would hurt you," he said. "I may be under the spell of a wicked arousal, but I'm not an animal. All you have to do is say *stop*…anytime. Do you believe me?"

She searched his face. "Yes," she said. Only that one word, but it was enough.

She had tied the sash of the robe tightly at her waist. If

the knot was supposed to slow him down, she didn't know much about men. He dispatched it in seconds and slid the entire garment off her shoulders and down her arms. When it fell to her feet, he thought he heard her gasp. Or maybe it was him.

All night he'd been desperate to hold her…to take her… to make her his. Now that the time had come, he had to pause a moment to take it all in. "You're beautiful," he said. The compliment was trite and commonplace and totally inadequate to convey the truth.

A more feminine woman, he had yet to find. Her skin was golden, a light, warm color that conjured up Italian olive groves and barefoot maidens running laughingly from ardor-filled suitors. Her glossy hair, black as a raven's wing, curled around his finger when he tested a strand.

He tried to fix his attention above her neck, but it was impossible not to notice the bounty below. Full, rounded breasts…curved hips…pert bottom. He scooped her into his arms, though the bed was no distance at all. It was a ploy to test the softness of her skin, to relish the naked magnificence that was Cassidy Corelli.

Her arms linked around his neck. "When do I get to undress *you*?"

"It's only a towel. I'm pretty sure we can manage."

"I notice it's kind of *poochy* in front."

Her mischievous teasing made him want to smile in the midst of his sexual frustration. "Are you calling me fat?" he asked, eyebrow raised.

"You don't seem to be in other places," she said. "But there's definitely a bulge beneath that terry cloth."

He flipped back the covers and dropped her on the bed. Her breasts jiggled nicely when she bounced. "Feel free to investigate."

Sprawling beside her, he settled on his back. What he

wanted was to pounce and take. But then again, anticipation was half of the pleasure. It took everything he had, even so, to feign relaxation.

Cassidy reared up on one elbow, fascination in her gaze as she looked him over. "I guess you work out." When she placed a hand, palm flat, on his abs, he flinched. It was too much and not enough.

"I'm not much for gyms," he said. "But where I live we spend a lot of time outdoors." His skin was several shades darker than hers for that reason. Except for a pale strip around his hips, he was tanned all over. He and his brothers had ranged free as kids, playing wild in the woods until they'd heard the bell summoning them to dinner.

She traced a scar below his rib cage. "What's this?"

"My brother Dylan shot me with a bow and arrow when we were in grade school."

"That's terrible," she exclaimed.

When she ran a fingertip over the puckered, long-ago-healed wound, he squirmed. "He didn't mean to. He was aiming for a squirrel. I ran into the line of fire at the wrong moment." The words were guttural, barely audible. He had broken out in a cold sweat, every cell in his body leaning toward the moment when she would remove the towel that tented lewdly upward.

Finally, when he thought he couldn't bear it a second longer, Cassidy curled her fingers beneath the edge of the damp towel and tugged. He lifted his hips. She finished the job.

"Holy crap." Her eyes widened. "Do you have a license to carry that thing?"

His penis was neither abnormally large nor embarrassingly small. But Cass stared at it as if she had unearthed a rare and exotic treasure. Her rapt regard increased its length and girth another increment.

"Trust me, Cassidy. We'll be a perfect fit."

Without replying, she wrapped one small hand around his shaft and squeezed lightly. He closed his eyes, holding his breath, as yellow spots danced against a black canvas. *God in heaven.* He was a goner.

Fluid leaked from the head. His would-be lover touched the slick wetness. Then she placed her fingertip in her mouth, tasting the evidence of his arousal. She seemed enthralled. Or perhaps postponing the inevitable out of some misguided notion that she was in control.

His patience eroded like sand in the midst of a storm. "Enough," he groaned. Forcing her onto her back, he used one hand to spread her thighs. Her sex was perfection, pink and wet and inviting. She smelled like lemons and need.

It never occurred to him to warn her before he tasted her essence. Her shriek might have awakened half the hotel had not the walls been so very well insulated. She shoved at his head. "Stop that. It tickles."

He had told her she could call a halt at any point. He just hadn't expected it to be now. Resting his forehead on her firm, soft thigh, he breathed harshly. "What's wrong? Surely you've had oral sex before."

"Of course I have. You startled me, that's all."

"Then may I continue?"

Her silence lasted about as long as it took earth to turn on its axis. Eons. Decades. "Cass?" He shivered like a man with ague.

"Yes…"

Her response was a tiny breathless syllable.

Returning to his task, he set about making her absolutely as insane as she had made him. Even as he pleasured her slowly, images filled his head. Driving hell-bent on a dark Nevada highway. Kissing wildly in the middle of the desert. Watching her body move like poetry in motion beneath that silver dress. Standing in front of an Elvis impersonator and promising forever.

At this precise moment all of it seemed perfectly reasonable.

He felt the instant when she neared the edge. Her hips lifted off the mattress. He held her down. Her breathing accelerated. He bit gently at the spot where she was most sensitive.

Holding Cassidy Corelli as she climaxed made every criticism he'd ever expressed about Vegas fade away into nothingness.

This was her town. And he'd staked a claim.

Four

Gavin shifted up in the bed so he could kiss her. On the mouth. The room was dim. When he moved his lips over hers, he was alarmed to taste salty tears. "Are you crying?" he asked, aghast.

She cupped his cheek. "Only a little," she whispered. "I didn't know it could feel that good."

"I haven't even gotten started yet." He said it to make her smile, but damned if it wasn't the truth.

"You're a dangerous man, Gavin Kavanagh."

"Dangerous how?"

"Addictive. Like gambling or alcohol."

"Are you saying I'm bad for you?"

"Maybe. Probably."

"Isn't that why people come to Vegas? To sow their wild oats? To cast off convention and morality? To take a walk on the wild side?"

As he argued his case, he stroked her breasts. They filled his hands as if she'd been created just for him. Not too large, not too small. He was beginning to think everything about her was eerily perfect. As if he were dreaming and any moment he would wake up and find the TV running some lower-than-B-movie porn flick.

He shook his head, trying to clear the fog and the feeling that he was letting down his guard at the worst possible moment. Cassidy's pert nipples fascinated him. Her little pants and groans urged him on as he played with the sensitive nubs.

She tossed her head, her hands gripping the sheets as he tormented them both. He usually preferred long hair on women, but Cass's chin-length curls framed her face and suited her personality so well, he couldn't imagine her any other way.

At last, he knew he couldn't hold out any longer. Testing her readiness with two fingers, he found her damp and welcoming. He grabbed a condom and rolled it on. As he moved between her legs and positioned himself at her entrance, he felt a flicker of unease. "Do you want this, Cass? No regrets in the cold light of day?"

At twenty-three, he'd been an immature ass. But Cassidy seemed far older than her years. Surely she knew her own mind.

Her smile was small but genuine. "I've never wanted anything more."

Surging forward, he cursed softly as the welcoming caress of her body squeezed him like a velvet fist. But icy shock slithered down his spine when he met with resistance. "Cassidy? Hell, Cass... Are you a...? Is this your...?"

Disbelief rendered him speechless. Along with another shot of suspicion and cynical doubt.

Slender legs wrapped around his waist. "Don't be mad. I know what I'm doing, Gavin. I realized not long after I set foot in your hotel room earlier tonight that I wanted you to be my first. It took me a little while to make up my mind, but I'm so glad I met you."

Something about that statement struck him at a raw spot, but he didn't have the mental acuity to process why. Instead, he focused on her deliberate omission. "Why didn't you tell me?"

"You would have left. Accused me of being too young for you. Done the noble thing and denied yourself."

To hear her assess him so accurately stung. "Or I would have taken what you offered regardless."

Her smile was wry. "I don't think so."

It wasn't as if he had a choice now. It would cripple him to leave this bed. Dazed and exhausted, he didn't have the strength of will to call a halt to things. She said she wanted this. And lord knows, he did.

Gently, he pressed forward. Her helpless wince stopped him cold. "I've never done this with a virgin," he croaked. "It's going to hurt you, Cass."

"Only for a minute. We'll muddle through, sweet man."

He was selfish and emotionally withdrawn and often cranky. Clearly, she didn't know him at all. He was torn in a dozen different directions. His body clawed for release like a junkie craving a hit. His brain shouted a warning. But Cass had done something to him. He couldn't bear the thought that this moment might be as bad for her as it was good for him.

Her fingernails dug into his butt cheeks. "It's okay, Gavin. I like it, really."

It was a brave lie, but nothing could disguise her cry when he pushed the final distance and found himself seated fully within her inner embrace. "I'm sorry, Cass," he muttered. It killed him to know he had caused her pain.

She wrinkled her nose. "It's not so bad now. I like how you feel inside me. Big and thick. Filling me up." Little flutters caressed his length as she exercised muscles that would give them both pleasure. "This is good. Truly. You've already given me an orgasm. It's your turn. Take what you need. I won't break."

Her altruism was charming but misguided. He would only go the distance if he could take her with him. He began to move slowly, shallow thrusts that applied pressure where her recent climax had left her ultrasensitive.

"Gavin!"

He knew the moment she crested again. Determined to make her forget the initial unpleasantness, he moved in her with care, staving off his own release until he felt her shudder and cry out.

Then it was all or nothing. He took her wildly, almost insensate, his world flaring into a hot white light before going black as incredible pleasure washed over him and carried him to a place of peace and unconsciousness.

Cassidy had done her share of impulsive things during her short life, but this was the most cataclysmic. Her body still hummed with aftershocks of sensation that made her toes curl against the soft cotton sheets.

Gavin Kavanagh was magnificent. Too bad she hadn't met him at a different time and place. If her father discovered that she had initiated sex with a virtual stranger, he would freak out, and he would certainly never take her seriously. He would question her judgment, and rightly so.

Now that school was done, it was the pivotal moment for her to take her long-coveted position at her father's side, despite her brother's wishes. It wasn't exactly a job that could be transferred cross-country, even if Gavin had been interested in more than a fling.

Still, she didn't have any regrets. Most of the guys she knew were shallow and egocentric. Boys, really. Not men. Not like Gavin. She ran a hand over his hard male chest, feeling the faint dusting of hair, the delineation of muscles, the flat belly. He was beautifully built.

When she moved lower to touch him more intimately, a large male hand clamped down on her wrist. "Give me five minutes, Cass. I haven't slept in over twenty-four hours and you just turned me inside out." But even as his rough-toned voice asked for mercy, his sex flexed and lifted.

"I wasn't rushing you," she said politely. "Just browsing the neighborhood." His bark of laughter made her smile. Somehow, she got the impression that Gavin Kavanagh was a pretty serious guy.

He started to lift up onto his elbows, but she pushed him back. "This one's on me," she said. The last thing she wanted was for him to see her as awkward or gauche. She tucked away her feelings of insecurity. Any woman worth her salt could pretend to be good in bed. Even if the majority of her knowledge was gleaned from books and movies.

Gavin rolled on a condom, and when he was ready, she climbed on top. Sliding down on him from this angle was very different. The brief discomfort was a small price to pay for the pleasure that was to come. She bounced experimentally. Gavin made a sound that was halfway between a curse and a prayer.

His fingers gripped her butt. "Why, Cass? Why me? Why now?" His jaw was firm, his expression suspicious and stubborn...as if he were prepared to chuck her out of his bed if he didn't like the answers.

What kind of man asked questions like that with a naked woman sitting on his chest?

She put her hands on his shoulders, kneading his flesh with giddy excitement. Already she could feel the beginning ripples of another orgasm. Some kind of serious pheromones were at work, because she wanted this beautiful man as she had never wanted anything in her life.

"I'll tell you, I swear," she said, panting. "But can we do this first? I think I'm having beginner's luck."

After that, any urge to talk disappeared. Gavin took charge. His arms were strong and his hips powerful. He held her and moved her and filled her with thrusts that built her hunger to a fever pitch. When she couldn't bear to wait another minute, he reached between them, touched her firmly at a certain spot, and then cradled her against his chest as they both came until there was nothing left.

She must have slept. At least for a few minutes. When she roused, Gavin was leaning over her with a washcloth, gently cleansing the residue of their lovemaking. His eyes were dark with concern as he saw the evidence of her innocence. Their eyes met…his shadowed, hers uncertain. It was a more profoundly intimate moment than any that had gone before.

When Gavin was satisfied that he had taken care of her, he tucked her up against his side, one big masculine arm holding her close. In moments his breathing became regular, but she couldn't tell if he was awake or asleep.

For the first time, misgivings winnowed their way to the surface, making her wince inwardly. What if this experience ruined her for other men? She couldn't imagine any other male of her acquaintance making her feel like this. Gavin was an intensely exciting lover. Both masterful and tender. At moments, it had been difficult to remember that she was her own person. All she had wanted was to lose herself in him.

The thought was sobering. She'd spent the past six years trying to prove her worth to her father. To make him see that a woman could be just as intelligent and business savvy as a man. But this gallant rescuer, her passionate lover, had shown her that in certain situations a woman might be tempted to chuck everything for the chance to be intimate with a man like Gavin.

She had planned out her career. She had goals and dreams. One day when her father was gone, Cassidy would be in charge of the casino. It was all she had ever wanted to do with her life.

But Gavin, damn him, made her question the master plan. Still, she shoved the doubts aside. She had gone into this experience with her eyes wide-open. This might not be casual sex on her part, but it was definitely temporary. It had to be. Her future didn't include a man who might try to mold her and change her and sidetrack her with his crazy hot body and phenomenal sex.

Her lover stirred and yawned, glancing at the illuminated dial of the clock beside the bed.

"What time is your flight?" she asked, feeling all her fuzzy happiness slip away.

"Eleven. Means I have to be there at ten."

"Not very long from now."

He linked his fingers with hers and lifted her hand to his lips. "Plenty of time for the big three."

"The big three?"

"I want to take you in the fancy tub, and the shower, and probably the sofa in the living room."

She actually felt faint. "Oh, well…"

He tugged one of her curls, tickling her ear with his fingertip. "But first, we talk."

"Talking is overrated. Though I do have a confession to make," she admitted, shamefaced.

He nuzzled her hair. "Then we'll start there."

It was difficult to know exactly what to say. "You know the man in the alley, the one you punched when you came to my rescue?"

"He's kind of hard to forget."

"That was my brother, Carlo."

The dead silence was intimidating. "Your brother was attacking you?" Gavin asked, the words enunciated carefully.

"Not exactly. We were arguing…loudly. Our family does that. I'm sure to an outsider it must have seemed as if I were in danger. So when you swooped in and rescued me, it was so sweet and wonderful and chivalrous."

"I hit an innocent man and left him on the ground. Yet you didn't bother to tell me the truth?" Gavin's volume escalated, his words incredulous. He rolled out of bed and got to his feet, pacing like a caged tiger. "Damn it, Cassidy. What were you thinking?"

The open accusation on his face brought hot tears to her eyes, but she blinked them back. "It all happened so fast," she said. "And trust me, Carlo is built like an ox. You didn't hurt him. When you dragged me back to your hotel room, I was enchanted. No man has ever stood up for me like that. I wanted to get to know you."

"You made a fool out of me," he said, his scowl black with displeasure.

"No. No, I didn't," she said, climbing off the mattress and going to him, trying to ignore her nudity and the shivery way it made her feel. She put both hands on his upper arms, wishing she had the strength to shake him out of his mood. "You acted on instinct. If the situation had been different, you would have saved me from something terrible."

Gavin thought himself far past being taken in by a pretty face. Yet here he was, suffering from the effects of bad judgment and simple lust. He'd been down this road before. A pretty girl, sexual attraction, a series of bad choices. As a senior at an Ivy League school in the Northeast, he'd spent time in jail when a woman accused him of rape.

The incident had nearly killed Gavin's mother. Even his own brothers had looked at him askance as if not quite sure what to make of the situation. The woman had been extremely convincing. Right up until the moment her lawyer promised to drop the charges against Gavin if the Kavanaghs handed over a hefty settlement.

Gavin had been furious and embarrassed and disgusted by the whole thing. He'd refused to let his family bail him out or pay anything to silence the duplicitous woman. For his stubbornness, he'd spent an unforgettable five nights behind bars. In hindsight, he should have tried harder to proclaim his innocence. The irony was, he'd never even had sex with the woman. They had dated only once.

Looking back, he could see that she had crossed his path intentionally, flirted with him and led him on. Her partner in crime, the alleged lawyer, was a fellow psychiatric patient with whom she had slipped away and, in a lucid moment, hatched a plan to get some money and disappear.

Fortunately for Gavin, the girl's parents had come forward when the story hit the newspapers. They lived in a nearby town where their daughter was institutionalized at a long-term care facility.

Gavin's pseudo girlfriend, faced with her parents' presence, finally recanted her story and Gavin was released. But the gossip had lived on. He hadn't dated much after that. Because every time he met a girl at school, there was always a look in her eyes…a question about Gavin's nature.

He'd responded to the situation by withdrawing into himself. He'd finished school and returned home to set up his cybersecurity business. He was good, very good. And once he was officially an adult, no one really cared about the unsavory incident in his past.

Yet, despite all he had learned, here he was again, standing on shaky ground. What if all that business at the wedding chapel had been some kind of setup? Was there an angry father or brother waiting just around the corner to insist on a shotgun wedding?

If was difficult to ignore the fact that a curvy beautiful

woman stood toe to toe with him, her breasts almost brushing his chest. "Put some clothes on," he said brusquely.

When he tried to turn away, Cassidy launched herself into his embrace, her arms locking around his neck. Though he was angry, his body responded predictably. Hunger roiled in his gut like an unappeased demon.

"Don't be like this," she cried. "We don't have much longer. Come back to bed."

Though he was stingingly aware of every inch of her voluptuous body plastered against his, he rallied his defenses, staring down at her with glacial disdain. Removing himself from her stranglehold, he stepped away. Cassidy's expression was chastened. As he watched, she grabbed a silk throw from the end of the bed and tucked it around her body like a sarong.

The ruby color made her skin glow.

Needing some armor himself, he picked up the damp towel from the floor and wrapped it around his hips as he had earlier. Grimacing at the clammy fabric, he crossed his arms over his chest. "I want to know," he said, keeping his tone level and unemotional, "how a woman who looks like you can still be a virgin at the age of twenty-three."

Cassidy perched on the end of the bed, one leg tucked beneath her. She was beautiful in an extremely natural and vibrant way. "It's simple, really. My dad is an extremely strict Italian Catholic father. My mother died when I was six. So Daddy sent me off to boarding school, followed by an all-girls college. It was only when I enrolled for my MBA that I had much contact with the opposite sex. And I was working so hard the whole two years that I didn't have much time for romance."

"So you remained pure as the driven snow." His sarcasm was a defense mechanism.

"I'm not saying I wasn't curious," Cass said. "But I

never really met anyone who tempted me enough to incur my father's wrath."

"What did you think he would do to you?"

"I didn't know. And I was scared to find out. I had body-guards assigned to me around the clock from the time I was first shipped away from Vegas. Daddy was afraid his status would make me an easy target for kidnappers. I rebelled, of course. But the one and only time I ever successfully eluded my guards and had a night out with girlfriends, my father came to campus and yelled at me for an hour, non-stop. That kind of thing leaves an impression."

"And after you graduated?"

"I wanted so badly to go into business with my father. I thought the MBA would convince him, but he has yet to promise me for sure that I'll have a spot at the casino."

"What about your brother?"

"Well, that's the infuriating part. I was a mama's girl, so when she died, I was lost. I was always *her* favorite and Carlo was Daddy's. Even though Carlo partied through school and majored in fraternity parties and binge drinking and women, he could do no wrong. I, on the other hand, worked my butt off. Carried a 4.0 all the way through. I wanted to prove to my father how ready I was to become his second in command."

"And did it work?"

"No. That's what Carlo and I were arguing about. He told me Daddy thinks I should marry and raise a family and leave the business end of things to Carlo."

"Maybe that's wishful thinking on your brother's part."

"I doubt it." Her expression was glum. "Daddy's very traditional. One of the floor managers is taking a two-week vacation starting next Friday. I'm hoping to cover for him while he's gone and prove that I can be an asset."

"So we've covered the reasons for your surprisingly virginal state, but not the specifics of *why me*? *Why now*?"

Five

Cassidy found that it was not an easy thing to carry on an adult conversation with a large, angry, half-naked man. She could understand his suspicions, but they were using up precious time.

She decided that honesty was the only prudent way to go. "I'm wildly attracted to you. From the first moment you ran down the street with me. You're gallant and wonderful and unlike any man I've ever met."

"And I'm leaving in the morning."

Grimacing, she nodded. "That played into it. No strings attached. When we got to your hotel room I realized that for once in my life I was going to take what I wanted and to hell with the consequences. I feel a connection with you, though I can't explain why. You're not much of a talker. But I knew that sex with you would be memorable."

Still he stared at her like judge and jury. "That's a pretty big step for the good little Catholic girl."

"I do want to prove myself to my father, but I'm a grown woman. My choices are mine." She paused, wondering if she had the guts to push this next point. "Admit it, Gavin. Tonight never would have happened if you hadn't been feeling some of the same things I was. You wanted me, too. That's what made it all so exciting."

The flicker of emotion in his eyes told her she had hit on the truth. The spark had come from both directions.

He glanced down at the place where the towel lifted over his erection. "It's a hard thing for a man to hide."

"I'd like to think I was more to you than a convenient body."

The silence stretched for miles. Just when she thought she would have to crawl into a hole to escape the humiliation, he nodded grudgingly. "You're a fascinating woman, Cass. Intensely feminine, distractingly sexual. But from where I'm standing, this all seems a little too good to be true. I can't help wondering if there's a trap in here somewhere."

She stood up, hoping his compliments meant an end to hostilities. "I swear on my mother's grave that I am no threat to you at all. And I've told you the whole truth and nothing but the truth. Do you believe me?"

He ran his gaze from her head to her toes, making everything in between sizzle with excitement. Her skin hummed with the need to feel him inside her again.

"I want to believe you. Though I have damn little reason to do so. But even if you turn out to be my worst mistake, I can't walk away now. Your promises will have to do." When he ripped off the towel a second time, she should have been prepared. But his body was a sculptor's dream.

She swallowed hard. "I'm glad."

With his hands on his hips, he studied her. Then, before she had a chance to prepare, he closed the distance between them in two long strides and plucked away her only armor, leaving her defenseless and bare in more ways than one.

He scooped her into his arms. "The hot tub will help you feel better." He kissed her briefly, a butterfly brush of lips to lips.

His breath was warm on her cheek. She looked up into

his eyes searching for something…anything. Was he sorry to be leaving?

In the bathroom, he turned on the taps. The oversize faucet dispensed water generously. While they waited for the tub to fill, Gavin perched on the edge and stood her between his legs. With his hands on her waist, he proceeded to rekindle her need.

Rough tongue on sensitive nipples. Murmured words of praise and admiration. His thumbs rubbed her hip bones in a desultory fashion as if there was all the time in the world for foreplay.

She rested her forehead against his. For the first time, she realized with no small amount of dismay that grabbing for what she wanted had a downside. "The sand in the hourglass is almost gone," she whispered. "I'll never forget this night."

His body went rigid, his rapid shallow breaths audible. "Pretend we have forever, Cass." He buried his face between her breasts. "That's all you have to do."

Gavin put a hand to his head and groaned. The muted chirping of the alarm on his cell phone had awakened him. Studying the screen, bleary-eyed, he saw that he barely had enough time to shower and shave and head to the airport to turn in his rental car.

He rolled toward Cass, determined to take her one more time despite the time crunch. Last night had been amazing, perhaps the best of his life.

But when he reached across the bed, he found nothing but empty, chilled sheets. Abruptly, the sleep fog lifted. "Cass," he called out urgently, hoping she was in the bathroom.

Then he saw the note on her pillow. His stomach pitched

unpleasantly. The small rectangle of hotel notepaper had been folded once. He opened it and read:

Dear Gavin:
Last night was amazing. I've never met a man like you. I'm sorry for not being totally honest with you in the beginning…about everything…but I selfishly wanted a chance to spend time with you. I suppose you think badly of me, but I hope in time you'll be able to forgive me and to enjoy the memories of our one incredible night in Vegas.

I know you have a plane to catch, so I didn't linger. I never have liked goodbyes anyway. I hope the women in North Carolina appreciate you as much as I do. You are one in a million.
Fondly,
Cassidy Corelli

He dropped the Dear John letter on the bed and put his head in his hands. This was the kind of experience many men craved—the gorgeous woman, the no-strings sex, the night of unparalleled excess. He should be feeling on top of the world.

But the truth was, this trip to Vegas sucked, any way you looked at it. Stumbling into the bathroom, he splashed water on his face and then stared in the mirror as he grabbed a hand towel. He looked like hell. Bloodshot eyes underscored by dark circles. Stubbly chin. A headful of hair sticking up in all directions.

If he'd just scored #1 on the all-time list of guy fantasies, then why did he feel like crap? And why was his gut telling him he'd made a gargantuan mistake?

He slept his way across the country. Flying first class at least gave him room to stretch out his legs and get semi-comfortable. The young blonde flight attendant flirted with him. He passed up the offers for alcohol and peanuts and instead propped his head against the window.

Changing planes in Atlanta was a hassle, but at least no one paid any attention to him. He bought the latest hardcover crime thriller so he could use it as a shield if necessary.

Once he landed in Asheville, he sent a text to his brother Conor, who was picking him up. In Conor's hybrid SUV on the way to Silver Glen, all Gavin wanted to do was brood. But Conor was cheerful and chatty and interested in hearing about the trip.

Gavin answered in single syllables, hoping his sibling would take the hint, but it was not to be.

Finally, Conor shot him a frowning glance and called him on his crappy attitude. "What the hell's wrong with you, Gavin?"

"Sorry," he muttered, suddenly ashamed of his mood. "I guess I'm just tired."

"Don't try that on me. Something is chewing your ass and I want to know what it is. Did your speech crash and burn?"

"No. Everyone loved it."

"Don't tell me you gambled and lost a pile of money. That doesn't sound like you at all."

Gavin managed a grin. "I never even put a nickel in a slot machine. If I want to blow money, I'll toss it out the window on the interstate."

"Then what?" Conor demanded, changing lanes to avoid a semitruck going twenty miles under the speed limit.

"Did it ever occur to you that it might be personal?"

Conor whistled as his eyebrows shot up to his hairline. "Good lord. It's a woman, isn't it?"

Not just any woman, but a sparkling, funny, utterly de-

lightful female who made him second-guess everything he knew about himself.

"Of course not," Gavin lied. "It was being in Vegas. Everything artificial and garish and frantic. I didn't want to go in the first place, and I'm damn glad to be home. Give me a good night's sleep, and I'll be back to normal in the morning."

Conor frowned, but kept his eyes on the road. "Fine. Don't tell me. But you'd better be more convincing when you talk to Mom, because she can sniff out a lie better than a bloodhound."

Cassidy covered her mouth with one hand, swallowing hard to keep from throwing up. She sat on the end of a vinyl-covered exam table, her modesty protected only by a thin paper gown.

"Could you please say that again?" she whispered.

Dr. Landau, the man who had been her pediatrician since birth, gave her a look laced with considerable concern. "You're pregnant, Cassidy. Didn't you suspect?"

"No, sir. Daddy is finally letting me take on more responsibility at the casino, and I've been working crazy hours. I just assumed it was stress. I'm not all that regular anyway."

The gray-haired, kindly physician had been telling her since she turned eighteen that she needed to find a general practitioner and an ob-gyn, but Cassidy loved Dr. Landau. Where her father bellowed and blustered, Dr. Landau was invariably gentle and professional.

He shook his head, his expression wry. "I'm retiring at the end of the year, Cassidy. I appreciate the fact that you and I have known each other for two decades, but you're a grown woman and you must find appropriate medical care. You have another person to think about now."

"How far along am I?" She knew the answer down to a five-hour period, but she wanted to hear it from him.

"About ten weeks, I think. You'll want to get an ultrasound soon. I can prescribe prenatal vitamins, but I need you to promise me that you'll call and set up an appointment with an obstetrician. Soon."

"I will, I swear. I thought I had a stomach virus. I never dreamed…" She trailed off, feeling foolish and alone and frightened.

Dr. Landau frowned. "How long have you been sexually active, Cassidy?"

She shrugged, her face heating. "Just about ten weeks."

He shook his head. "Isn't that the way it works? Couples try for years to get pregnant and others who aren't even thinking in that vein wind up with a surprise on the way. You have options, of course. But you'll want to discuss those with the father."

"He's not really in the picture."

The doctor didn't seem particularly judgmental, but Cassidy felt guilty anyway. She'd spent her entire life playing by the rules, and one impulsive night had brought her to this.

Dr. Landau stood. "Go ahead and get dressed. I'll have my nurse bring in the vitamin prescription." He paused. "You know I can't discuss anything we've said here with your father. But he's my friend. And you're going to need support no matter which way you decide to go. To be honest, you shouldn't spend another hour working in the casino. Secondhand smoke can be harmful to your baby."

"I understand," Cassidy said as panic clawed at her throat. "Thank you for seeing me today." An era of her life was ending. Though she had considered herself focused and mature and ready to assume the full mantle of adulthood, clearly there were aspects she hadn't considered.

When the doctor exited the exam room, she put on her clothes and glanced in the mirror on the back of the door. She didn't *look* pregnant. She didn't *feel* pregnant. She was, however, miserably sick and confused and desperate. What was she going to do?

As she drove home to the elaborate house she shared with her father and brother, her brain ran in circles. She was supposed to stand by her father's side, preparing to run the business in his retirement. She had trained for that, worked hard for that.

A baby had never figured into the plan. In fact, she had assumed she wouldn't have children. She knew her father's traditional values wouldn't allow him to choose her as his successor if she had a family. He'd think she needed to be with her children. So she had focused on working toward her father's legacy.

Keeping one hand on the steering wheel, she placed the other flat on her stomach. A new life. A baby. No matter the upheaval in her world, she would never consider terminating the pregnancy. She couldn't. Clearly Gavin had no interest in a relationship with her since there had been no contact between him and Cassidy since he left.

So only two choices remained…becoming a single mother, or giving the infant up for adoption. Even as she pondered it, a wave of maternal instinct washed over her, bonding her for the first time with the tiny boy or girl growing in her womb.

This child was *hers*. Hers and Gavin's, to be correct. The only thing she knew for certain was that she would keep the child. She would have to tell him. Eventually. But not until she had time to get her act together.

After dinner prepared by the housekeeper and served in the formal dining room, Cassidy and her father and Carlo adjourned to the family room. It was an unabashedly masculine enclave, but in one corner sat the Disney toy box that had housed Cassidy's dolls and such as she grew up.

Carlo was busy on his cell phone. Gianni Corelli lit a cigar and sat back in his overstuffed leather recliner. The smell of the Havana tobacco sent Cassidy dashing for the nearest bathroom to lose the contents of her stomach. When she returned, she was shaking, but moderately in control.

Neither male paid her much attention. They saw each other at work on and off all day. The evenings were for winding down, though often one or all of them would return to the casino toward midnight to see how things were going.

She wanted to ask Carlo to leave. It was going to be hard enough to break the news to one person, much less two. Her father's reaction was going to be ugly. But she couldn't think of any plausible reason to ask for privacy.

Finally, when tension knotted her belly and anxiety dampened her forehead, she blurted it out. "Daddy... Carlo...I have something to tell you." It took a few seconds, but both men looked up and focused their attention on her face.

Her father smiled genially. "What is it, *mia bella figlia*? I have had many compliments on your job performance the last two months. I suppose all that fancy education I paid for was worth it."

Carlo scowled. "I work, too."

His father gave him a grin. "Of course you do. Mostly coaxing young pretty tourists to try their luck at the roulette wheel. We all have our strengths, son."

Cassidy could tell that her father's patronizing tone irked Carlo, but her brother held his tongue. Luckily for him, in a few moments he was going to be out of the line of fire.

"Thank you, Daddy. I'm glad you're pleased."

"So," he said, tapping his cigar in an ashtray. "You have my attention."

There was really no way to ease into this. She swallowed, feeling nausea swirl in her tummy again. "I'm pregnant."

In hindsight, perhaps a letter might have been the better choice. Her father's florid complexion turned an alarming shade of puce. "I will kill the boy," he said, his dark eyes flashing fire. "Who is he? Who dared defile my baby girl?"

Cassidy wanted to roll her eyes, but she restrained the impulse. Why was this household always filled with drama? "I'm not defiled, Daddy. I'm pregnant. There's a difference. And he's not a boy. He's a man. I made a mistake and now I have to accept the consequences. But I want this baby. I really do."

Carlo had been struck dumb, perhaps alarmed by his father's apoplectic rage. For once, Cassidy's competitive brother didn't speak up. Maybe because he could already see the benefits for himself in this situation.

Gianni Corelli got to his feet, his hands clenched in fists. "You will correct this situation," he hissed.

Cassidy backed up a step. "I don't know what you mean." It broke her heart to see the man who had raised her stare with such open antagonism.

"You will go to him," he said. "Find the bastard and tell him what he has done to you. And you will not set foot in this house again until you are either engaged or married."

"But, Daddy…"

He held up a hand, his body quaking with fury. "Your dear mother, God rest her soul, would turn over in her grave if she could see you now. You have shamed our home."

At last, Carlo spoke, surprisingly in defense of his sister. "Take it easy, Papa. This isn't the Middle Ages. You're going to have a stroke if you don't calm down."

Unfortunately for Cassidy, much as she appreciated her brother's support, it didn't help the situation.

Her father held out an arm, pointing at the door. "Go. Pack a bag. Be gone by morning. I will cancel your credit cards. You may use the money in your personal account."

Cassidy gaped. That would be less than two thousand dollars. Her father hadn't wanted her to work while she was in school. He'd insisted that she concentrate on her studies. "But I—"

"This isn't up for discussion, daughter. You will make this right or you will never again be welcome under this roof."

Cassidy began to cry. Never in a million years had she expected this reaction. She knew her father was old-school and traditional and strict. He had been twenty years older than her mother when they married, and he was very much set in his ways. But he loved his daughter…didn't he?

Carlo took her arm, steering her out of harm's way when she was too stunned to walk on her own. His bedroom was first down the hallway. He urged her inside and shut the door. "If you'll tell me where you need to go, I'll put a plane ticket on my credit card." He opened a bureau drawer and withdrew a wad of cash. "This should help. And you can call me if you need more."

Cassidy sniffed, her emotions all over the map. "Why are you being so nice to me?"

Carlo gave her a lopsided grin. "You're my sister. Father has pitted us against each other our whole lives, but those things he said to you in there are wrong. I love you, Cass. You'll get through this. Don't worry."

It was a strange and wonderful sensation to feel her brother's arms around her as she sobbed. She felt a little less alone. A little less desperate. At last, she pulled back and wiped her eyes. "Thank you."

"Where shall I book a ticket to?"

"Asheville, North Carolina." She had already studied a map when she had been moping over losing Gavin. Asheville was the largest town of any size near Silver Glen.

"One-way, or with an open-ended return?"

"One-way, I suppose. I have no idea how this is going to turn out. I can't just tell this guy he has to marry me."

Carlo tugged her hair as he had when they were kids. "You'll find a solution. You always do. And besides, your baby daddy may be glad to see you. Who knows?"

Six

Gavin swung the ax with all his might, feeling the reverberation in his shoulders as the sharp blade cleaved the oak log. Beside him lay a three-foot-high stack of firewood that would season over the spring and summer and be ready for his fireplace come fall.

Sweat poured down his back both from exertion and from the heat of the sun in a cloudless sky. No matter how hard he pushed himself, he couldn't escape the memories that tormented him. His luxurious house high on the mountainside was usually a refuge. Since returning from Nevada, though, it had become a prison.

Even his demanding work, normally a stimulating and distracting challenge, failed to keep him from thinking about *her*. Young, sassy, exuberant Cassidy Corelli. She had bewitched him. There was no other explanation. And though he knew for a fact that a man couldn't become a husband without a license and other legal considerations, he couldn't erase the memory of standing in front of an altar and promising to love, honor and cherish. It had been a silly, dangerous game.

The ax glanced off a knot in the wood, narrowly escaping the toe of his boot. This was not a good time to lose focus.

A half hour later, he called a halt. After a shower and

a sandwich, he was prepared to hole up in his office and work until he was tired enough to sleep without dreaming.

He was in the kitchen smearing peanut butter over a slice of wheat bread when the doorbell rang. Frowning, he wiped his hands on a dish towel and headed for the front of the house. His hair was still damp, and he wasn't wearing a shirt, but it was probably a delivery person of some sort.

When he swung wide the door, his hand clenched the edge of the frame until his knuckles turned white. "Cassidy. What are you doing here? How did you find me?"

She looked like hell, to be honest. Her skin had lost its glow and her beautiful eyes were dull with fatigue. Even the sheen of her wavy dark hair was dulled. At her feet sat a small rolling suitcase. The simple navy knit dress she wore was sleeveless in deference to the weather. Over one arm she carried a khaki raincoat.

"May I come in?" she asked.

The words were polite and proper. Not in the least intimating that the two of them had once upon a time been naked together. He wanted to grab her up and smother her adorable bow-shaped lips with wild kisses, but his innately suspicious nature kicked in.

"Of course," he said, stepping back.

Cassidy's gaze landed on his chest and danced away. She was careful not to touch him as she slipped past him into the formal living room. "Thank you."

He indicated a chair. "Have a seat."

It was disconcerting as hell to realize that he was hard already. Just from looking at her. Hopefully the heavy denim would disguise his ill-timed response. He didn't know why she had come, but judging by her expression, it wasn't to have another round of crazy, impetuous sex.

She put down her purse and bag and sat in silence, her gaze cataloging the contents of the room. He tried not to notice the way a single curl tickled her chin. "Is this a so-cial visit?"

At last, she looked at him. Her teeth sank into her lower lip. Small graceful hands twined in her lap. "Not exactly."

"How are things going at the casino? With your father… and your job?"

"Great. Or they were." Now she appeared stricken.

Rubbing a hand across the back of his neck, he sighed. "I don't mean to be rude, but you're confusing the hell out of me. I thought we were ships that passed in the night. You made it very clear that you were focused on your work and on getting ahead of your brother. You never gave me any indication that you wanted to see me again."

Tears welled in her beautiful eyes. "I'm pregnant, Gavin."

She saw him turn white. Any burgeoning hope that he might be glad to see her shriveled and died. "Say something," she said.

"Are you telling me you think I'm the father?"

Her stomach turned to stone. "Of *course* that's what I'm saying. You were there, Gavin. You know I was innocent."

The skepticism in his frigid stare cut deep. "That was weeks ago. Doesn't mean there hasn't been someone else in the meantime." He paused, his expression going from disapproval to grim suspicion. "Have you forgotten that we used protection every time?"

She sat there stunned, gaping at him. The man who had made love to her in a Las Vegas hotel room with such ten-der passion had nothing in common with this hard-eyed stranger. She'd naively thought he might be glad to see her. Her throat was so tight she couldn't speak for several long seconds. But she lifted her chin and met his gaze bravely. "Except for that time in the hot tub. Remember?"

From the flicker in his eyes, she could see that he did. But the memory did nothing to soften his stance. Despite the fact that he had been sexy and funny and wonderful and irresistible when he had claimed her beneath the swirling water that night, he was anything but at the moment.

When he said nothing, she held out her hands. "Why would I lie about this?"

"Maybe you found out that the Kavanaghs are wealthy. Maybe you wanted a free ride."

"My father has enough money to buy and sell Silver Glen several times over."

"Then why are you here?"

His stony gaze made her angry. "I thought you might want to know that you were going to be a father. It seemed like important information. But if you don't give a damn, I've wasted a trip."

She leaped to her feet, feeling like a naive idiot. The knight in shining armor who had rescued her in a Vegas alley had nothing in common with this antagonistic man.

Before she could reach the door, he blocked her exit, inserting his big, intimidating self between her and the escape route. "Wait."

One word. Flat. Unemotional.

She pulled up short. "I know this isn't something you wanted, Gavin. If I'm being brutally honest, I didn't want it, either. But I'm pregnant, and I'm not going to make an innocent child pay for my mistakes."

Something about the line of his jaw softened. "Is that what I was to you? A mistake?"

"What would you call it?"

He rubbed a hand across his chin, for the first time betraying a hint of rueful self-derision. "Momentary insanity?"

They stared at each other, the past vivid and alive. In

his eyes she saw the truth of what he wasn't saying. He remembered all too well. Just as she did. The laughter and intimate touches they had shared. Hushed groans. Wild cries of pleasure. Sated, drowsy satisfaction in the aftermath.

Now that he had momentarily dropped his guard, he looked far more approachable. He folded his arms across his chest. "I'm sorry if I've been less than welcoming. I want you to stay for a while. If you're telling the truth, we'll have things to discuss. Plans to make."

Despite the *if* in his response, his about-face in terms of hospitality sent relief washing over her. The nausea she'd been fighting for days resurfaced. "Bathroom," she said hoarsely, her hand clamped over her mouth.

He read the situation instantly. Pointing to a door across the foyer, he followed on her heels as she made a dash for the facilities. Emptying her stomach for the third time that day left her wrung out and exhausted.

Gavin helped her to her feet, handed her a damp washcloth and steered her to the kitchen, where he gently pushed her into a chair and poured her a glass of cold water. Through it all, he didn't say a word. But his quiet empathy took the edge off her embarrassment.

"Thank you," she muttered.

He propped a hip against the counter. "Has it been bad?"

"You could say that."

"You've lost weight."

The man had seen her naked. His dispassionate comment shouldn't have made her blush, but it did. "I could stand to lose a few pounds."

Gavin shook his head. "Not that I recall."

Suddenly, the world shifted and they were back in the desert on a dark night, racing along the highway. She experienced the same sense of anticipation, the same feeling of wonder.

When it seemed as if her stomach was going to coop-erate, she grimaced. "I want to be honest with you about everything. My father has kicked me out of the house. Carlo took my place at the casino. Apparently I've be-smirched the Corelli family name. I think I was supposed to walk out into the desert and die for my sins, but I've never been the self-sacrificing type."

Gavin still reeled from Cassidy's revelation, but grow-ing up with six brothers, he had learned to keep a poker face. Never had that ability stood him in better stead than now.

He'd spent only one night with her, but even he knew how important it was for her to win her father's approval. It was hard to imagine the hurt she had suffered and the feelings of being adrift with this latest development.

And then there was his own bizarrely blank reaction. He was going to be a father. No matter how many times he said the words in his head, they didn't seem real. His brother Liam had a kid. And Dylan had adopted his bride's little girl. Aidan and Emma were expecting. But that didn't make it Gavin's turn. Not at all.

He wasn't cut out for parenthood.

Looking at Cassidy made him ache. Even dimmed, her beauty and spirit tugged at his heartstrings. If anything, the touch of vulnerability in her weary posture added an-other layer to her appeal.

"You can stay as long as you need to," he said quietly, wondering if he was condemning himself to weeks of sexual frustration. He'd acted out of character once in his life, creating an enormous mess. No point in compound-ing the mistake.

"I'm sure my father will relent eventually. For once, Carlo is on my side. He'll plead my case."

"What exactly does Mr. Corelli want from you?"

Cass's cute turned-up nose wrinkled. "He told me not to come home until I was engaged or married."

Gavin froze, his heart pounding in his chest. "You're joking, right?"

"I wish I were. My father is very old-school traditional."

For a moment, Gavin wondered if Cassidy was going to bring up their visit to the wedding chapel. Again, he reminded himself he couldn't believe everything she said. What if this whole thing was a scam? A setup?

"I don't know you, Cassidy," he said flatly. "And you don't know me. I hope you'll understand when I say we need to get a paternity test.

Though she winced, she nodded. "It's not necessary, but if it will make you feel better..."

"Can we do it while you're pregnant?"

"It's possible, I think. One tests the placenta and the other the amniotic fluid. But both procedures carry a small risk of miscarriage."

"Then we'll wait."

"For months?"

"Do you have a better solution?"

She sagged into the chair. "I suppose not. But what am I supposed to do in the meantime?"

"I don't know. What do other pregnant women do? Read books? Design nursery plans?"

Her eyes flashed. "I worked my butt off for six straight years of college. Is that degree useless now? Just because you and I did something stupid?"

He sympathized with her plight. He really did. But no matter the equality of the sexes, a woman always had to bear a greater share of the burden when it came to children. Especially if she planned on nursing the baby.

Imagining Cassidy with an infant at her breast was not

a good idea. When he realized his hands were shaking, he shoved them in his pockets. "Your degree will keep. In the meantime, you can explore Silver Glen. We'll need to find you a doctor very soon. Have you had an ultrasound yet?"

"No. I'd like you to be with me for that." She looked at him with such naked hope, that he wanted to reassure her. This moment should be joyful. And it would be so easy to let her back into his life. Her presence in his house would ensure warmth and light.

Though he couldn't say it out loud, he reluctantly admitted to himself that he had missed her. He wanted badly to believe her…to accept that he was her baby's father. But he'd been naive about a woman's sincerity once before and had paid dearly for his mistake.

"I'll be happy to go with you," he said. There was tenderness in his voice despite his reservations. No matter how hard he had tried not to, he remembered every second of the time she had spent in his bed. And how she had made him feel. He hadn't allowed himself to acknowledge how special it was, because there had been no choice but to let her go. Now she was here, and he could no longer pretend that the night in Vegas was ordinary. If the baby *was* his, life was about to get very complicated.

"I'm tired." Cassidy's emotions were written on her face. Despair. Disappointment. Had she expected him to welcome her with open arms? Not even a sheltered twenty-three-year-old could be that optimistic.

"I'll show you to a guest suite. You'll have plenty of privacy. The room has its own bath." His house wasn't all that large. But he'd built it sparing no expense when it came to comfort and luxury. Top-of-the-line everything. At least he could offer Cassidy the safety and security of a pleasant place to lay her head.

He knew his reserve hurt her. Maybe she really was exactly what she seemed. Gavin had been her first lover. No doubt about that. But she might have moved on quickly. She was a sensual woman, and he had awakened her sexual nature. It wouldn't be unusual if she'd exercised her new-found knowledge with a longtime boyfriend.

He still couldn't explain why she'd chosen Gavin and that particular Vegas night to change her status, but he liked to think it was because she saw something in him that she wanted…that she needed.

The two of them together had been incendiary. Sexual chemistry off the charts. But that didn't mean she had been celibate in the meantime.

What did it say about him that he hoped desperately he was wrong? If he let her know how much he wanted to believe her story, he'd be handing over power he wasn't ready to cede. Better to advance cautiously and see what happened.

"If you're feeling steadier now," he said, "I'll help you get settled." He ushered her down the hall and opened a door. "Will this do?"

The room was neither masculine nor feminine. But its muted shades of lemon and eggshell blue exuded a sense of serenity. He'd had help with the decor, and he was pleased with how it had turned out.

Cassidy scanned the furnishings with a small smile. "It's lovely," she said.

"I'll fetch your bags."

When he returned to the guest room, he found Cassidy bent over, one hand on the bed, slipping out of her shoes. It was a maneuver he had come to expect from her. She didn't see him at first, so he studied her freely. Though she was competent and smart, he sensed that her impending motherhood was weighing on her.

What did a man know about such things? He would

never understand what it meant to carry a baby for nine months. To feed the little boy or girl. To form a bond long before the day of birth arrived.

As a quintessential middle child, he'd forged his own way in life. Though he loved his family, he'd never felt as connected as he ought to be. Would it be any different if he had a son or daughter? His own father had been selfishly obsessed with chasing dreams of long-lost silver mines. The pursuit had cost him his life.

Gavin lived alone and liked it. He worked all hours of the day and night, answering to no one, except maybe his mother, Maeve, who was constantly trying to keep him involved in family events and telling him he spent too much time as a hermit. Lord knows what she would think about Gavin's houseguest.

Having Cassidy beneath his roof would play havoc with his life. He'd be tormented by images of her just down the hall. Sleeping in a bed he'd provided, getting naked in a shower he'd designed.

Holy hell. He was doomed.

She must have heard him, because she straightened suddenly and faced him, barefoot and beautiful. "I thought I'd take a nap," she said. "If you don't mind."

"Of course not. My office is at the back of the house. Let me know if you need anything."

She didn't blink an eye at his unwittingly suggestive offer. "I will."

Seven

Cassidy didn't realize she was holding her breath until the door closed behind Gavin. She sank into a blue-and-white toile-covered armchair and put her hands over her face. *Well, that went well.*

Surely there was no greater humiliation than puking in the presence of the man to whom she'd just given not-so-welcome news. Gavin had been in turns stoic and quietly compassionate.

But what he *hadn't* been was happy to see her. Perhaps she hadn't admitted to herself how much she was hoping for a fairy-tale ending. Which made no sense at all, because she and Gavin had spent less than twenty-four hours together. He was right. They didn't know each other.

In his shoes, she would have demanded a paternity test, as well.

Even so, the day had lost its fizz. Despite the upheaval in her life, she had been excited about traveling to Silver Glen and giddy about the prospect of seeing Gavin again. But it was painfully clear that their brief encounter in Vegas had meant nothing to him other than physical release.

She certainly hadn't spent the intervening weeks doodling her initials and his on napkins. Responsibilities at the casino had kept her busy for a succession of fourteen-hour days. She'd thrown herself into the family business with gusto, convinced that her father recognized her worth as an employee and an equal. But amid all that, it had been impossible to forget meeting Gavin.

Images from the night they spent together popped into her head at random moments, making her cheeks heat and her core tighten. He was not an easy man to forget.

Now, stripping down to her underwear, she climbed under the covers and tried to rest. One of the biggest problems with her pregnancy so far—in addition to the nausea—was an all-encompassing fatigue. That was partly the reason she hadn't thought twice about the fact that she had missed a period. She'd been stressed and exhausted, but determined not to show it.

Today, however, she had slept on the plane. Because of that, she only dozed lightly now, her mind darting from one subject to the next. Where would she live? Would her father relent? How much, if any, of a role would Gavin want to play in his child's life?

She was normally an optimistic person, but it was hard to see a way out of this. She had never anticipated being a single mom. In fact, she had never planned on being a mom at all. Though several of her friends were eager to start families, Cassidy's main goal in life had been to become her father's right-hand man. Or in this case, woman.

But that was part of the problem. Though her father loved her, she knew he didn't really think a female should shoulder serious responsibilities in the workforce if she was of childbearing age. Italians loved children. And they revered Madonna figures. In Mr. Corelli's estimation, there was no higher calling than to be called *Mother*.

Well, Cassidy couldn't argue about the importance of that role. But she wanted more. Was that such a crime? Growing up without a mother had made her painfully aware of how important it was for a girl to have a female parent. Since Cassidy was a realist, she deduced that she couldn't pursue her goal of one day running the casino and being a mom at the same time, because of her father's old-fashioned values.

So she made a choice. She chose career over home and hearth.

But what happened now?

At last, when it became clear that she wasn't really sleepy, she climbed out of bed and rummaged in her suitcase for gray yoga pants and a hip-length solid T-shirt in bright teal. Though some of her clothes were only now beginning to feel a little tight, the ever-present nausea meant that a loose-fitting wardrobe offered a degree of comfort.

Barefoot, she tiptoed down the hall toward the rear of the house. It wasn't difficult to locate Gavin. The door to his office stood open. She paused in the doorway and gawked.

On the far wall, a bank of no less than a dozen television screens were mounted in three rows. One of them played a popular news program. A second was linked to the Weather Channel. The other ten or so displayed what looked to Cassidy like gibberish. Gavin was focused on his work.

Surrounded by laptops and desktops and stacks of paper, he appeared to be multitasking without breaking a sweat. Knocking lightly at the door so as not to startle him, she crossed the threshold.

He swirled to face her. "Cassidy. Sorry, I didn't hear you."

"You were deep in thought. Am I interrupting?"

He shrugged. "Not particularly." He waved a hand at the leather executive chair that matched his. "Sit down. Did you nap?"

"A little." The bland conversation was polite and frustrating. Gavin looked masculine and gorgeous in jeans and a cotton sweater in a pale shade of green.

He ran his hands through his hair, rumpling it and making him look even sexier…as if he had recently rolled out of bed. "I forgot to mention that the kitchen is pretty well-stocked," he said. "You should help yourself to anything that sounds good to you."

"Do you cook?"

"Only when necessary. I have a weekly housekeeper who leaves things in my freezer that I can heat up. Sometimes I go eat at the Silver Beeches Lodge. And if I'm in the mood for pub food, my brother Dylan owns the Silver Dollar Saloon. I don't starve."

"I could fix some meals while I'm here. It would make me feel like I'm earning my keep."

"It's not necessary. But please feel free to do anything that entertains you."

"I'm not a child," she snapped, his last comment catching her on the raw. "I don't have to be distracted with pony rides and ice cream."

Her temper elicited a grin from her oh-so-serious host. "I don't own any livestock, and I'm lactose intolerant."

"Don't patronize me."

The madder she got, the more genuine his smile. It infuriated her.

"You know why we're squabbling, don't you?" he asked, cocking his head and staring at her with a gaze hot enough to make her squirm in her chair.

"Because you're an ass?"

"Ouch." He shook his head. "I brought you in and offered you food and lodging. And this is the thanks I get?"

She took a deep breath. "I'm sorry," she said formally. "I've disturbed your work. I'll go back to my room."

Without warning, Gavin stood up. Suddenly the office shrank in size. His personality and masculine presence sucked up all the available oxygen. Pacing so near her chair that he almost brushed her knees, he muttered beneath his breath.

"What did you say?" Probably something uncomplimentary about his unexpected houseguest.

He shot her a look laden with frustration. "We need some ground rules, Cassidy. First of all, we're going to forget that we've ever seen each other naked."

She gulped, fixating on the dusting of hair where the shallow V neckline of his sweater revealed a peek of his chest. "I'm pretty sure that's going to be the elephant in the room. Our night in Vegas was amazing. Maybe not for you, but for me. Telling me to forget it is next to impossible."

"Good lord, woman. Don't you have any social armor at all?"

"I am not a liar. If you want me to pretend we haven't been intimate, I'll try, but I make no promises."

He leaned over her, resting his hands on the arms of the chair. His beautifully sculpted lips were in kissing distance. Smoke-colored irises filled with turbulent emotions locked on hers like lasers. "I may be attracted to you, Cass, but I don't completely trust you. It's too soon. So, despite evidence to the contrary, I do have some self-control."

Maybe *he* did, but hers was melting like snow in the hot sun. His coffee-scented breath brushed her cheek. This close, she could see tiny crinkles at the corners of his eyes. She might have called them laugh lines if she could imagine her onetime lover being lighthearted enough and smiling long enough to create them.

"You're crowding my personal space," she said primly.

For several seconds, she was sure he was going to steal a kiss. Her breathing went shallow, her nipples tightened and a tumultuous feeling rose in her chest. Not nausea.

Something far more volatile. For the first time, she understood that whatever madness had taken hold of them in Las Vegas was neither a fluke nor a onetime event.

Gavin still wanted her. As much as she wanted him. But he wasn't happy about it.

At long last, he moved away. "I'm sorry."

She was sorry, too. Sorry he hadn't dragged her to the carpet and had his wicked way with her. Pregnancy hormones could be a blessing and a curse. Right now she wanted Gavin with every fiber of her being. For two cents, she would throw herself at him and let nature take its course.

But her pride got in the way. She was damned if she would let him think she was using sex to win him over. Either he trusted her, or he didn't.

Her mood plummeted. She had gone from fear of rejection upon her arrival to joy at seeing him again to disappointment that he wasn't prepared to believe her story.

"I'll try to stay out of your way," she said. Gavin's antagonism laced with unwilling arousal was insulting.

He folded his arms across his chest. "I doubt that will solve anything." He paused, frowning. "What would you say if I told you I believe you about the baby?"

"The baby is real," she said, deliberately misunderstanding him. "You don't have to believe me."

"You know that's not what I meant. This isn't a joke, Cass."

She inhaled sharply. "Believe me, I know that. I'm scared spitless."

His expression tautened. "Is that how you really feel?"

She hadn't meant to reveal weakness to him. "This isn't what I wanted…what I planned for. My life has run off the rails in one big, dramatic train wreck. I don't know anything at all about kids."

"I think it will come naturally."

"That's a myth perpetuated by sappy commercials and greeting cards. Babies poop all the time and scream for no reason. They're impossible to understand, and from what I can tell, their entire raison d'être is to drive otherwise functional adults to the brink of insanity."

"Have you thought about giving the child up for adoption?"

His face was a mask. She had no clue where he stood on the matter. But hearing the option spoken aloud made her realize one thing beyond any doubt. "No. He or she, poor little kid, is my flesh and blood. For better or worse. I may suck at this, but I want to be the best mom I can be."

His expression softened, and for a moment she thought she saw admiration in his gaze. "I'll help you any way I can…even if I'm not the father."

"Quit saying that," she yelled. "You *are* the father." Suddenly, several weeks' worth of anxiety and fear caught up with her. Though she scorned women who manipulated men with emotion, she was completely unable to stem the flow of salty tears and the ugly, gasping sobs that shuddered through her chest and left her raw.

Her hands were over her face, so she didn't see him come close.

"Shh," he said, gathering her into his arms. "You'll upset the baby. Everything is going to be okay. I promise."

His quiet support only made her cry harder. She hated feeling so desperately inadequate. All her life she had been the A student, the perfect daughter, the kid other kids' parents wanted their offspring to emulate.

She'd had a plan, and she'd worked hard to attain it. But now she'd lost her dream job, her home and her father's blessing. And in the process gained a responsibility for which she was definitely unprepared.

This was what happened when you broke the rules. Some people were able to pull it off without consequences. But not Cass. She should never have believed she could walk on the wild side with impunity.

Resting her cheek against Gavin's hard shoulder, her arms around his waist, she inhaled a deep breath and let it out slowly. He smelled the same as he had the night they met. A mix of aftershave and warm masculine skin and wildly erotic pheromones.

If he would hold her like this forever, she might try to squeeze out a few more tears. But the cataclysm had run its course. When she was reduced to sniffing and wiping her nose on the back of her hand, Gavin fished in his pocket for a soft cotton handkerchief, handing it to her without comment. The cloth was still warm from being close to his body.

He brushed the hair from her face. "You okay now, Cass?"

She sighed. "As okay as I can be. Nine months is a long time to be in limbo."

"Don't exaggerate," he said, eyes dancing with humor. "Surely it's only seven now."

"Easy for you to say," she muttered. "You're not the one who's going to swell up like a cow and have heartburn and need to pee constantly and—"

He put his hand over her mouth, halting her litany of dismay. Kissing her forehead, he rested his chin on top of her head. "You're going to be the most beautiful pregnant woman the world has ever seen. Men are going to stop in the street to stare at your gorgeous breasts. And women everywhere will sigh in envy at your maternal glow."

At last she chuckled. A weak laugh, but a laugh nevertheless. "You are so full of it."

"I call 'em as I see 'em."

"I'll go now," she said, pulling free of his embrace though she would gladly have stayed there forever.

"You don't have to. You can stay and watch me work."

"As lovely as that sounds, I'll pass. What is it you do anyway?"

"My cyber defense company is called The Silver Eye. I access high-end clients' servers remotely and try to breach them. When I succeed, I share the results and together we work toward a way to shore up their privacy and security."

"You must be awfully smart."

"It's a longtime hobby of mine. The fact that I was able to make a business out of it was a bonus." He glanced at his high-tech equipment and then back at Cassidy again. "What if I take you up to the hotel for dinner? China and candlelight and real linen tablecloths. You'll love it."

"It does sound nice."

"Then it's settled."

She handed him his soggy handkerchief. "What time?"

He took it with a grimace. "My mother usually arrives around seven. We'll eat with her if you don't mind. She chews my tail if I don't show up at least once a week… and I'm overdue."

"Your mother?" The words came out on a squeak of incredulity.

He shrugged. "I'll introduce you as an out-of-town friend. Your pregnancy is no one's business but ours at the moment."

"I've wondered when I'll start to show."

"Is there a formula for that?"

"Not really. It depends mostly on body type. And I've been sick so much I've actually lost weight."

"I'll make you a milk shake tonight before bed. We'll fatten you up in no time."

"Every girl's dream," she said, shaking her head at his cluelessness.

Gavin's gaze warmed to intimacy. "Most men I know like curves on their women...something to hold on to. A soft place to rest."

"For a computer geek you surely have a poetic turn of phrase."

"Maybe you inspire me."

They stood there in silence, each weighing the other's motives. In his eyes she saw the need to protect himself with emotional distance. But his body language spoke a different dialect. Already, he had touched her, comforted her, imprinted himself on her skin.

The only thing he hadn't done was kiss her. The omission seemed glaring. And regrettable.

Going up on tiptoe before she could change her mind, she captured his mouth with hers, pressing a kiss gently against his firm masculine lips. With her tongue she teased the seam until he inhaled sharply and opened to her, letting her in.

She was under no illusions. Her awkward, inexperienced seduction was neither graceful nor polished. But it did the job. Gavin growled deep in his chest and captured her nape in one big hand, pulling her close against his chest, shoving one hard thigh between hers.

"You're a brat," he muttered. But since his erection throbbed against the cleft between her legs, she didn't put much stock in his criticism.

"I've missed you," she whispered, arching her back so she could press her body even closer to his. "I didn't want to, but I did."

He nibbled a sensitive spot beneath her ear, making her squirm. "Why didn't you want to miss me?"

"I had plans to take over the world. To *be* somebody. You were a temptation I had to resist."

"Is that why you walked out of my hotel room?"

The trace of masculine pique in the sharp words told her he had been wounded by her defection. In the next second, she actually felt the change in him. The walls going up. The defenses snapping into place. Kissing her made him vulnerable, and that was the last thing in the world a man like Gavin Kavanagh wanted to feel.

"It seemed like the thing to do at the time," she said, hoping he'd understand.

"And once I was gone, how long did it take you to find another man to take my place?"

After a split second of shocked silence, she backed away sharply, tears springing to her eyes. "You're cruel and hateful and I don't know why I came here."

He scowled. "Maybe you couldn't stay away from me. Maybe there's no baby at all. Maybe that was a ploy to get into my house."

Even knowing he was fighting an attraction he didn't want, the accusation hit its mark. "Go to hell," she said, her chest heaving in wretched hurt and anger. "I don't even like you."

"Yeah," he said, his jaw rigid and his eyes stormy. "I don't like you, either."

Eight

Gavin wasn't worth a damn after that. How in the devil was he supposed to carry on with business as usual when the siren who had lured him onto the rocks in Vegas presently occupied a bedroom right down the hall?

Even worse, now that he had tasted her again, he hadn't a snowball's chance in hell of pretending he didn't want her. The need was like a tropical disease, striking without warning long after he had left the neon jungle. One look at her sweet face and mischievous eyes, and he was a goner.

Once again he allowed himself to consider the possibility that he had planted a child in her womb. *Dear God.* He should be pissed and angry and worried, but all he could latch on to was an emotion that felt a lot like euphoria. A baby. Was it possible?

He sat down hard in his chair and stared at the laptop readout in front of him. It might as well have been written in Sanskrit. The words and symbols danced across the screen, mocking his lack of comprehension. He was a man who could work for hours and never lose focus or concentration. His brain thrived on difficult puzzles.

But never had he faced a situation like this. For a moment, he saw his younger self behind bars, his fate and his reputation hanging in the balance. He'd felt utterly lost and alone.

Was he walking into another trap? Cassidy Corelli was not mentally ill. She had no need of his family's money. Yet still his unease remained. He kept going back to that night in Vegas. Why had he responded to her so viscerally? Why did she set him on fire? Not being able to understand his reactions made him uneasy. Why did a young, attractive woman wait so long to experiment with sex? And why choose a stranger?

He wasn't a whimsical man. He dealt in hard numbers and immutable equations. Over the past year or so he'd watched his brothers fall in love. In every instance, he could say without a doubt that his siblings had found mates who were perfect for them. Dylan and Aidan had reconnected with women from their pasts. Liam had discovered a female who didn't let him take life too seriously.

None of them had initiated relationships based on a one-night stand and an accidental pregnancy.

Gavin had taken several psychology classes in school. Freud would say that there *were no* accidents. That perhaps unconsciously, Gavin knew when he made love to Cass in the tub that he'd forgotten birth control and didn't care.

Was it true? Had Gavin wittingly contributed to the current situation? Or was Cassidy using that omission to coax him into believing that she carried his child?

What would have happened if he hadn't had a plane to catch that morning? Would Cassidy have stayed in his bed? From all he could tell, she was ambitious and determined to pursue her goals. He couldn't fault her for that. It was one thing they had in common.

But when she walked out of his hotel room that day, had she felt even a fillip of remorse for not saying goodbye? Or regret that she wouldn't see Gavin again?

He didn't claim to understand the fairer sex. They were

complicated and mercurial and no two were alike. How was a man ever supposed to gain the upper hand?

In the current situation, however, Gavin was determined not to let himself be swayed by physical attraction. Keeping his distance from Cassidy was a matter of self-preservation. Even if the baby *was* his, there were numerous hurdles ahead.

Did he honestly want to consider a shotgun marriage to repair her relationship with her father and give the baby Gavin's name? What chance did they have under those circumstances? Even the best of marriages failed at an alarming rate. He and Cass would be handicapped from the start. She would no doubt end up resenting him and the baby for destroying her dreams of working side by side with her father. And Gavin would always wonder if he was a means to an end.

He was tempted to believe every word she spoke, wanted to quite desperately, in fact. But if he dismissed his doubts and took her to bed again, what then?

Cassidy Corelli troubled him. He was vulnerable where she was concerned. And vulnerability was the enemy of control. The incident when he was in college had taught him to build a wall around his emotions.

If he were going to be able to navigate these next few weeks, then he had to stay away from her. No touching, no kissing and certainly no sex. He would make that very clear.

Convincing Cassidy was one thing. Convincing himself was going to be a whole lot more difficult…

Cassidy unpacked her things and tucked them into the drawers of a beautiful armoire. Gavin's home was sophisticated and lovely, not at all what she had expected when she tracked him down at the end of a private mountain road.

Maybe she had been expecting a masculine cabin with hunting trophies on the wall or a cluttered residence with big-screen TVs and recliners and pizza boxes stacked high.

The truth pointed out how little she knew about him. He was a deep river with strong undercurrents. His home reflected his love for beauty and his predilection for solitude. High ceilings, arched doorways and large windows created pleasing spaces that radiated tranquility and offered peace and the chance for reflection.

Curled up on a cushioned bay window seat, she looked out into the forest. It was the kind of scene where unicorns and centaurs might wander by. Or even a knight on a fiery steed.

As a young girl Cassidy had lost herself in books. Because her father—in his grief—had removed all pictures of Cass's mother from the house, Cassidy had often daydreamed about her mom. She had imagined the two of them weaving daisy chains and playing with puppies and stretching out on a quilt to watch cloud pictures in the sky.

Already, she found herself making lists of things she wanted to do with her baby. Books they would read together. Songs they would sing. Games they would play. God willing, her child would never have to grow up without a mother's love.

It scared her, though, to think about giving up her dreams and her career. Did she really have to? Was there a way to have it all?

And what about Gavin? Would he ever be as determined as she was to give their little one a perfect childhood? Even as she spun dreams, she acknowledged wryly that parenting was not going to be all rainbows and lullabies. It would be hard work…and at times unrewarding.

Her body was changing. Soon the evidence would be impossible to hide. What was Gavin thinking? Could he trust her without the test? Did he have any feelings for her at all? Or was she no more than an unpleasant disruption of his ordered life?

She would stay only until she had a chance to figure things out. And she would do her best to keep her distance as long as she shared Gavin's home.

When it was time, she dressed carefully for dinner. If she was going to meet her child's paternal relatives, she wanted to make a good impression...even if they had no clue what was going on.

The dress she had worn for travel was wrinkled, so she picked a sleeveless boat-necked top in black lace and paired it with a multicolored above-the-knee skirt in flirty silk. Strappy gold sandals made the look a bit dressier. The elastic waist guaranteed comfort if dinner didn't settle well.

She was ready and waiting when Gavin knocked on her door at six-thirty.

His eyes widened when he saw her. She saw the muscles in his throat work. But he didn't comment on her appearance. "Ready to go?" he asked gruffly.

She nodded, following him out into the hallway. He had shaved recently. The scent of lime tickled her nose in a pleasing fashion. His broad shoulders stretched the seams of a navy sport coat. The jacket, teamed with dark khakis and an open-necked white shirt, made him look like an ad for the successful young entrepreneur.

It was hard not to drool. She found herself wanting to strip away the trappings of conventional society and have him naked and all to herself for at least a week. Maybe then she would know where she stood.

While she was in her room dressing, Gavin had brought his car around from the garage in back of the house. Parked beside her nondescript rental was a sleek, fire-engine-red Porsche convertible, the top already stowed away.

She pulled up short. "Wow. This is yours?"

"Well, I didn't steal it if that's what you mean."

Ignoring his sarcasm, she ran a hand over the sleek hood. "I am *so* jealous," she breathed, reverently completing a circuit around the stunning vehicle. "*This* is what we should have had for our desert drive. I'm getting excited just looking at it."

Gavin had a funny look on his face. "I'm glad you approve."

"May I drive?" She looked at him beseechingly, her fingers itching to touch the controls.

He shook his head. "No, Cass. These mountain roads aren't like your straight desert highways. And this is a lot of car to handle."

She faced him toe to toe. "Please? Pretty, please? I'll be as careful as an old lady on her way to church."

They were so close she could feel the heat of his body. That heat brought back a lot of memories. They weren't touching, not at all. But they might as well have been. Arousal bloomed hot and vicious, making her catch her breath. When she would have backed away, Gavin took her wrist, his thumb pressed firmly against her wildly racing pulse.

"If it means that much to you, then okay. You can drive." The words were husky, as though his throat was as constricted as hers. "But keep it under thirty-five."

"Yes, Gavin," she said meekly.

His snort of laughter told her he wasn't fooled by her docility.

As she slid behind the wheel, Gavin went to the passenger side and sat down, handing her the key fob. When she started the engine, she felt the power vibrate through her veins. She closed her eyes for a moment, enjoying the sensation.

Her companion tapped her on the cheek. "Hello in there. Do you think we could get this party started?"

She shot him a look. "You're so impatient." Stroking the dashboard, she sighed. "This is one sexy car. It deserves to be appreciated."

"Appreciate it on your own time. I'm starving."

Gavin liked his car. A lot. But it took on a whole new persona with Cassidy behind the wheel. Her face was a study in delight. She showed no hesitance at all in backing around and sending the car hurtling down the driveway. When Gavin grabbed the door handle instinctively, she laughed out loud.

If Cassidy thought his car was sexy, that was nothing compared to how he regarded the whole experience from the passenger seat. Watching her drive his Porsche was almost as good as taking her hard and fast and hearing her cry out when he made her come.

Perhaps dinner en famille was not the best idea he'd ever had. What would she say if he asked her to turn around and go back to his house?

He never had the chance to find out. They arrived at the Silver Beeches Lodge in no time at all. Cassidy eyed the elegant hotel with appreciation. "Fancy," she said, climbing out of the car.

"It's the family business. My oldest brother, Liam, and our mother, Maeve, keep it filled to capacity. Don't be surprised if you bump into a movie star or a politician."

"I get the impression that your family owns a big chunk of the town."

He took her arm as they climbed the wide, shallow front steps. "Kavanagh ancestors built the town of Silver Glen. So in a way, yes. But it has expanded over the years."

"But hasn't lost its alpine charm."

"That's the idea. The business owners want to attract a certain clientele, so the shops are high-end and the paparazzi aren't welcome."

In the grand lobby of the hotel they ran into Conor. Gavin introduced Cassidy to his younger brother and watched as Cass dazzled him, as well. Conor looked gobsmacked. Since Conor had a certain reputation with the ladies, that was saying a lot.

Cassidy bubbled over with enthusiasm, giving Conor a quick blow-by-blow of driving the Porsche.

Conor looked over at Gavin with a raised eyebrow. "You let her drive your precious car? Damn it, man. You won't even let me *think* about driving it."

Gavin cuffed Conor on the back of the head. "Cass is a lot cuter than you are. Buy your own damn car."

The brothers squabbled amicably as they flanked Cass arm in arm and headed for the hotel dining room. The obsequious maître d' unbent enough to offer a smile as he led them across the floor to where Maeve Kavanagh was already seated at a table for four.

Maeve stood and greeted both of her sons with a kiss. "You've made an old woman very happy. I've been looking forward to this all day."

Given that Maeve was a vibrant woman in her early sixties, neither Gavin nor Conor paid much attention to her theatrics. Cassidy, however, blanched. "Oh, I'm so sorry. I shouldn't be intruding on family time."

Maeve had the grace to look abashed and backpedaled quickly. "I was thrilled when Gavin told me he was bringing a guest, my dear." Once everyone was seated, Maeve continued. "I love to see my boys, but we get overloaded with testosterone around here. It's a treat to have another woman at the table. Where are you from, Cassidy?"

Cassidy glanced at Gavin quickly, but answered easily

enough. "I met your son when he was in Vegas for a conference. My father owns a large casino there."

"I see."

Gavin could practically feel the wheels turning in his mother's head. She lived for matchmaking. Gavin could have hidden Cassidy away indefinitely, but by trotting her out at the first opportunity, he was hoping to demonstrate that he had nothing to hide.

When Conor reached for a second roll, his mother tapped his hand sharply. "You'll ruin your dinner. Chef has prepared something special for us."

Gavin grinned widely, glad to have his sibling around to deflect some of the maternal radar. Though all of Maeve's seven sons were grown with lives and careers of their own, Gavin's mother saw no reason to let them off the hook if she thought they were making mistakes, large or small.

"Tell me, Cassidy," his mother said. "What do you do for a living?"

Cass sat primly, her spine rigid as she answered. "I recently finished a business degree. My plan all along has been to step up beside my father in the family business."

Gavin smiled at his mother. "You and Cass have a lot in common. Both of you are astute businesswomen."

Maeve leaned conspiratorially in Cassidy's direction. "Beware compliments from a Kavanagh male, my dear. There's usually a hidden agenda."

"I'm not a bit surprised." Cassidy gave Gavin a look that made him squirm.

Fortunately, the server arrived with Caesar salads, and the conversation drifted to less volatile subjects. Cassidy seemed hungry, which Gavin took as a good sign. She'd told him she usually felt better later in the day, so he hoped she would enjoy tonight's meal.

"What are we having, Mom? You mentioned a chef special?"

"You'll see," Maeve said with a smile. "But let's just say he had it flown in this morning from Prince Edward Island, so it's fresh and wonderful."

When the salad plates had been cleared away, the server returned, bearing a large silver tray. He deposited it carefully in the center of the table with a flourish. "Colville Bay oysters. Enjoy!"

Maeve thanked the man. Conor whistled in delight. Gavin felt a sharp pang of hunger and couldn't wait to dig in.

Cassidy, however, had a far different reaction. She jumped to her feet, nearly overturning her chair. Her face turned an alarming shade of green, and her eyes filled with panic. "Excuse me, please."

In the wake of her abrupt departure, Gavin felt two sets of eyes on him. "I'll go see if she's okay," he said, feeling his throat flush with embarrassment and anxiety.

Maeve laid a hand on his arm, her gaze thoughtful but kind. "She's probably in the ladies' room. I'll check on her. You two boys eat. But save some for me."

Conor rubbed his chin. "Anything you want to tell me, bro?"

Gavin stared at the mucous-like crustacean and felt his own stomach flip-flop. "Nothing," he said. "Nothing at all."

Nine

Cassidy hunched over the commode, dry-heaving. If she had ever been this miserable, she couldn't remember. But when she opened the door of the stall and found Maeve Kavanagh sitting in a small chair at the ornate vanity, her stomach plummeted even farther.

"Mrs. Kavanagh. I didn't hear you come in."

Gavin's elegant mother, her auburn chignon only slightly threaded with gray, smiled gently. "Are you pregnant, dear?"

Cassidy swallowed hard and tried not to think about oysters. "No, ma'am. Of course not."

Maeve shook her head. "I'm not completely oblivious to the fact that my sons have sex lives. I choose not to dwell on the subject, but I am not naive. Gavin has never brought a girl home before."

"He didn't bring me, either. I showed up at his house for a visit, that's all."

"And that explains why you rushed from the dinner table?"

"I'm sorry. I didn't mean to be rude." Cassidy was disheveled and ill and upset, but she couldn't fault Maeve's concern for her son. "I may be coming down with something. You probably shouldn't be near me."

Maeve grinned, taking fifteen years off her age. "Are you carrying Gavin's child?"

"No. Really."

"Your commitment to the lie is impressive, but I can do this all night. Tell me, honey. Tell me the truth."

Cassidy's legs lost their starch and she sank onto an ottoman that matched the decor. "Okay. Yes. I'm pregnant."

"And is Gavin the father?"

"Yes. But he doesn't think so…or to be exact, he's not sure. He wants a paternity test."

Maeve winced. "How old are you, Cassidy?"

"Twenty-three."

"And did you want to become pregnant?"

"No, ma'am. Not at all. But now that I am, I'm going to do everything in my power to take care of this baby."

"And what do your parents think about all this?"

"My mother died when I was very young. My father is furious."

"Poor dear." Gavin's mother shook her head. "I would like to help you, if I can."

Cassidy held out her hands. "I know you mean well, but this is something Gavin and I have to work out between us. Please don't be angry. You're very kind. But I feel disloyal enough already for telling you without Gavin's consent."

"I understand. And I won't let on that I know. But I think I can shed some light on my son's attitude. Why don't you come to tea with me tomorrow? Here at the hotel. We can get to know each other."

"I'm pretty sure Gavin wouldn't like that."

"He brought you here for dinner tonight, didn't he? He may not be willing to admit yet that he's going to be a father, but deep down I'd say he acknowledges the truth."

"There are things you don't know," Cassidy said. Like

the fact that she and Gavin had been impetuous and foolish in the midst of a night of wild, crazy sex.

"I could say the same. I'll expect you tomorrow, Cassidy. Don't disappointment me."

By mutual consent the two women returned to the dining room. Cassidy was relieved to see that the oysters had disappeared. In their place were four servings of innocuous chicken piccata with fresh asparagus and brown rice. The scent actually made her stomach growl in a good way, something she thought was a statistical impossibility on this particular occasion.

As the men stood and helped the ladies to be seated, Gavin gave her a searching look. She smiled weakly. "Sorry about that." What else could she say? To attempt any sort of explanation would only make matters worse.

Fortunately, Maeve took over the conversation, directing the attention away from Cassidy. "Tell us about your trip, Conor."

Gavin jumped in eagerly, clearly happy to add to the diversion. "I haven't seen you since you got back."

Conor, too, seemed content to oblige. "I had a great time."

"Where did you go?" Cassidy asked.

"Switzerland. Lucerne to be exact. I was one of five judges in a junior alpine skiing event."

Gavin passed Cassidy the basket of homemade rolls. "Conor used to ski competitively. Now he runs the ski resort here in Silver Glen."

"Did you ever ski for the US?" she asked, studying the physical similarities between Gavin and his brother. Both men were muscular and fit, but Conor was a bit taller and leaner.

Conor shook his head. "I thought about it, of course. But I ski for the love of it…and sometimes competition gets in the way. I did make the US team as a sixteen-year-old, but I blew out my knee before I had a chance to take it all the way."

"I'm impressed," Cassidy said. "I've been known to fall off a bicycle. Sports were never my thing. I'm more of a bookworm, I guess."

Conor leaned forward, enthusiasm on his face. "I bet I could teach you to ski. We have a great bunny slope, and once you build up your confidence, you'd be surprised how much you'll enjoy it."

"I don't think so." Gavin's abrupt comment drew three confused stares.

Cassidy kicked him under the table. "What Gavin means is that I'm probably a hopeless cause. And I won't be around long enough for lessons. But it's sweet of you to offer."

Apparently Gavin thought learning to ski was not on the list of approved activities for expectant mothers. But if he wasn't even willing to believe that he was the father of her baby, she sure as heck wasn't going to take his advice on what she could and could not do.

Over dessert, Cassidy's energy level plummeted. Suddenly it was all she could do to keep her eyes open.

Gavin noticed right away and made their excuses. As everyone stood, Conor and Maeve gave Cassidy a hug. Maeve patted Cassidy's arm. "Don't forget our teatime tomorrow."

"I won't," Cassidy said, wincing inwardly.

As they left the hotel, Gavin took her arm. "Do you want the top up?" he asked. "It will be cool now that the sun has set."

In the mountains, even a warm spring day turned chilly after dark. "No," she said. The valet had the car waiting.

As Cassidy slid into the passenger seat, she leaned back and sighed. "I have my scarf. And I want to see the stars."

Gavin drove home on a slightly different route than the one they had taken earlier. At a pull-off overlooking Silver Glen, he stopped the car. Below them, the little town looked like a postcard, serene and beautiful.

"You're lucky to live here," Cassidy said. "I love the desert and the excitement of Vegas, but this is charming."

"It's home," he said.

The laconic response was all she was going to get out of him. His silence seemed ominous. Her heart sank as she realized that Gavin was no closer than ever to embracing her news. Any enjoyment she had squeezed out of the evening winnowed away beneath a wave of depression.

If she could only believe he would come around to caring for her and believing her, she would take a chance and stay. But she was deeply afraid that his past had damaged his ability to love and trust anyone other than his immediate family.

Now that Maeve had guessed about the baby, things were going to be even more complicated. Gavin would no doubt believe that Cassidy had blabbed the truth against his wishes. He would see that move as an attempt to ingratiate herself with his mother.

Back at the house, she excused herself and said goodnight. She didn't realize Gavin had followed her until he appeared in the doorway to her bedroom, a scowl on his face.

"What are you doing?" he asked, the words harsh.

She shrugged, stepping out of her shoes and wiggling her toes in the carpet. "What does it look like? I'm packing. There's no reason for me to stay after I have tea with your mother tomorrow. I came here to give you the news face-to-face, and I've done that. When the baby comes, you can give me the name of a lab you trust, and I'll show up when and where I need to."

"I told you I'd let you stay for a while."

She faced him bravely, hurt by his deliberate aloofness, but unable to find a way forward. "It's better if I go home."

"You can't go home, remember? Your father kicked you out."

"I have friends. I'm sure one of them will take me in."

"Male or female?"

Her temper flared. "Does it matter?"

On Gavin's face she saw a mix of emotions that was impossible to decipher. The only one she recognized clearly was hunger. He didn't *want* to want her, but he did. His trousers tented unmistakably.

The clear evidence of his need should have reassured her. Instead, it made her sad. If all they had between them was lust, she might as well cut Gavin loose and make her own way.

A baby needed stability. And as for Cassidy, she needed a man who at least respected her. Not someone who thought she was laying a trap.

He took a step forward with a look in his eyes that sent a shiver of primal apprehension down her spine. "Yes," he said, the word hoarse. "It matters."

Dragging her up against his chest, he wrapped his arms around her and found her mouth with his. Yearning. Excitement. An intimate knowledge of what it felt like to be possessed by this man. All those things made her melt against him despite the antagonism between them.

They might be at odds over her pregnancy, but this one thing hadn't changed.

Gavin held her firmly, his kisses coaxing and insistent. His body was telling her something he wasn't ready to admit. She was made for him and vice versa. It was as if the universe had picked out two people with the best possible sexual compatibility and tossed them together to see what would happen.

He nuzzled the side of her neck, making her squirm, breathless and wanting. "Let me go," she said.

The fact that she wrapped her arms around his neck tightly probably negated the demand.

Gavin walked her toward the bed. "You're already pregnant," he said. "It's not like we're going to make it worse."

She laughed, though it wasn't really funny. "If that's your pickup line, it sucks."

He bit her earlobe. "You'll have to forgive me. I may not be in possession of my right mind. Something about you makes me insane."

When they fell together onto the bed, it was clumsy and painful and altogether wonderful. His elbow whacked her shoulder. Her fingers ripped at his buttons. He dragged her top off over her head. In some small corner of her brain she knew she should stop him. But she couldn't bear to do it. At least this was honest. A need for a need. Two people giving and receiving pleasure.

If her heart broke in the meantime, surely it was worth the price.

He paused to stare at her bare chest, his gaze hot. "Your body is changing already," he said. The words held a note of wonder. When he cupped the sides of her breasts with both hands and gently pushed them together, a shock of heat stroked through her center, leaving her breathless.

"They've been swollen. And tender."

He brushed a nipple reverently. "Will it hurt if I taste them?"

"No." She was stunned that she could speak that single syllable. His question sent her body into a shuddering spiral of blissful anticipation. When he suckled gently, her sensitive flesh beaded tightly in his mouth.

"Gavin..." It was a whisper, a prayer.

He looked up at her, his head propped on his hand. "Too much?"

"Not enough."

His feral smile should have warned her. Abandoning his project for a moment, he shoved her skirt to her waist and stripped away her satin underpants. The cool air on her overheated skin added a layer of pleasure.

He had already shrugged out of his mangled shirt and was bare from the waist up. The bronzed chest sculpted with sleek muscles revealed both his physical capabilities and his masculinity.

Beside him she felt small and pale and helpless. That last adjective spooked her. She'd never leaned on anyone in her life. But now she was making decisions for two. Knowing that Gavin was around to stumble through this experience with her would make things so much easier.

When he touched her between her thighs and teased her with a fingertip, she gave up rational thought. At the same moment, he returned to her breasts, his lips and teeth closing over first one tip and then the other. The dual stimulation shot her over the edge of a blinding orgasm.

Gavin didn't wait for an engraved invitation. He left her only long enough to shed his pants and boxers and shoes before wedging his hips between her open thighs and positioning his firm length at her center. "I've dreamed about this," he muttered. The words were barely audible...as if they had been dragged from him unawares.

She didn't know what to say in return, so she simply held him. Already her body recognized him as its mate. Her sex welcomed his eagerly, sealing the bond that was physical, but for her even more. A great deal more. She was only now beginning to understand how much.

Gavin braced his hands beside her shoulders, his strong hips thrusting powerfully, his hard shaft filling her until her womb ached. For Cassidy it was a revelation.

In Las Vegas, she had not analyzed too carefully why she had met Gavin and wanted him desperately. Now, hazily, she understood that her soul had recognized him instantly as *the one*. No other man had ever affected her that way. She was beginning to think no other man ever would.

As his skin heated, he smelled of sex and spicy after-shave. Even blindfolded, she would know him now. She lifted into his thrusts, making him groan, feeding her own pleasure.

Her second climax climbed lazily, hitting every spot along the way, rolling over her like a tide of molten honey. She bit her lip hard enough to draw blood when it caught her by surprise. As she arched beneath him, he came as well, filling her with his release.

When it was done, they each breathed heavily. Though it was dark outside, the room was almost too bright. The overhead fixture beamed down on them. Cassidy was bashful suddenly, having no idea what Gavin was thinking. Without speaking, she scooted to the bathroom, washed up and donned the robe on the back of the door. It was thick and comfy and emblazoned with the logo of the Silver Beeches Lodge.

When she returned to the bedroom, Gavin sat with his back against her headboard. He had turned off all the lights except for a small table lamp, thus making it hard to read his expression.

Courageously, she tossed back the covers and sat beside him, unsure of the postcoital etiquette. "Now what?" she asked, her throat tight.

"I guess that's up to you. I'm willing to let you stay until the baby is born. But I think it would be best if we not repeat—" He stopped suddenly.

"You're saying we shouldn't have sex." The words were like sharp stones in her chest.

"Correct."

"You came to my room. Not the other way around."

His jaw was granite. Since they were seated hip to hip, she couldn't look at his face full-on, but he radiated strong emotion. "That was a miscalculation on my part. It won't happen again."

"Why?" She put her pride on the line, aching to get at the truth.

"Isn't it obvious?"

"Not to me," she said quietly.

"We aren't a couple, Cassidy. We have a tenuous connection at best. Even if the baby turns out to be mine, it doesn't mean we have a future."

"You think that's what I'm here for?"

"You said your father told you to get married and have babies. And you've spent your whole life working to please him."

She was insulted and ashamed and pissed. "There are any number of men who would be happy to put a ring on my finger, baby or no baby. I don't need your charity, Gavin."

"How's your cousin doing?"

The odd question caught her off guard. And deflated her anger effectively. "He's fine. The state renewed his license and backdated it to the expiration date of the old one, so his boss is happy."

Gavin got to his feet and wrapped the sheet around

his waist. But not before she got an eyeful of his considerable assets. He knotted the swath of cotton and stared at her, eyes narrowed, hands on hips. "Are you telling me that when we stood in front of him and repeated marriage vows, he was a legal celebrant for the state of Nevada?"

Suddenly, she saw where his mind was going. "Yes. But don't jump to conclusions, Gavin. You didn't sign anything. There was no license. We were only goofing around. I didn't trick you into marrying me. Your conspiracy theories are ridiculous. And you have far too high an opinion of yourself. We had a fling. That's all."

"Why did you take me to the chapel that night?"

"For exactly the reasons I told you. Robbie's my favorite cousin. I promised I would stop by and see him that night. And I thought it would be fun for you to get a taste of the whole Vegas experience." She paused. "Listen, Gavin. I have a baby to think about now. So as much fun as it is to burn up the sheets with you, it's not my priority. I'm going to go home and get a job and an apartment. One of the other casinos will hire me to work in their offices. When the baby comes, I'll be in touch."

He glanced at her open suitcase on the floor. "I have a vested interest in your pregnancy. I want you close by to keep an eye on you."

"In view of your cynical suspicions, I don't give a damn what you want. Besides, are you really prepared to attend doctor's appointments and childbirth classes?"

He blanched. "Yes to the first…no to the second. I'm calling for a truce for the next six-plus months. It's in the baby's best interests."

Gavin was everything she wanted and everything she needed. But he wasn't hers to keep. "Maybe so," she said. "But what if we kill each other in the meantime?"

"We'll have to take our chances. Call it our first parental sacrifice."

He'd boxed her into a corner simply by making her an offer she couldn't refuse. "Don't make me regret this."

His masculine shrug was a study in nonchalance. "I could say the same to you. Good night, Cassidy."

Ten

The fabulous sex should have relaxed Gavin and sent him off to dreamland, but it had the opposite effect. He tossed and turned for hours, unable to get the images of Cass out of his head.

He was infatuated with her. And that was dangerous. In other circumstances, he would simply screw her until he got her out of his system. But this pregnancy thing brought other factors into play.

At three, he got up and turned on the television. As he stared at a rerun of a 1950s sitcom, he asked himself the question he'd been avoiding. *Was* he willing to be a father to Cass's baby?

Perhaps the more pressing question was, could he let her go if the baby *wasn't* his? Right now, he had a legitimate claim, based on her insistence that he was the only man with whom she'd been intimate.

He wanted to believe her. But everything about that night in Vegas seemed surreal. The fight in the alley. The drive out in the desert. Coaching Robbie at the wedding chapel. Even the incredible sex.

Couples were supposed to have to learn each other's likes and dislikes before reaching that kind of mountaintop. Hell, he would give each and every time he and Cass had done it a best-in-show ribbon.

He took his phone and clicked on the photo icon. Scrolling back only a few spots, he found the selfie Cassidy had insisted they take in the chapel. Gavin studied the image. Though he wasn't smiling in the picture, something about his posture was relaxed. Cassidy radiated fun and happiness as she kissed his chin.

The photograph was more fiction than documentary. The real Gavin was neither spontaneous nor reckless. Even his kindest critic wouldn't describe him as fun-loving. He worked hard. He cared about his family. He kept up with his responsibilities.

But he wasn't impulsive. He wasn't lighthearted. He wasn't a match for Cassidy Corelli.

At last accepting the fact that he wasn't going to sleep, he headed for his office. He'd pay for it tomorrow, but at least he could lose himself in work and try to forget the feel of Cass's soft skin beneath his fingertips.

Cassidy dreamed that night. Brilliant, vivid dreams in full color. When she got up to go to the bathroom, she replayed every part so she could remember it in the morning. The sequence that left her shaky and confused was the one where she and Gavin stood beneath a white trellis woven with pink roses. There was no baby in sight…only Gavin in a tux and Cassidy in a sexy, close-fitting white dress that clung to her every curve.

As she climbed back into bed, she fretted. What did it mean? Did she secretly not want this baby at all? Had she come to Silver Glen to find her lover, Gavin, instead of her baby's father?

The questions persisted throughout the night and were with her still the next morning when she stumbled to the kitchen in search of crackers or dry toast. In hindsight, she should have made sure she had something to nibble on in her bedroom.

Praying she wouldn't bump into Gavin, she moved stealthily through the house. The faint light of dawn filtered through windows here and there. She was sick and shaky, a cold sweat dampening her forehead, as she rummaged through cabinets. When a hand touched her shoulder, she jumped a foot and cried out.

Gavin took her by the elbows and steered her to a chair at the kitchen table. "Sit," he muttered.

She rested her forehead on her crossed arms. For a bleak moment she wished she could roll back the clock to a time where she had never met Gavin...a moment when her biggest worry was whether or not she was going to get an A on her graduate thesis.

He didn't turn on the lights, and for that she was grateful. The pale early-morning sun was bad enough. Though she kept her eyes closed tightly, she was aware of him moving around the kitchen. After a few minutes her nose twitched at the smell of toast.

Gavin set a plate at her elbow. "You'll feel better if you get something in your stomach," he said. His words were gruff but not unkind. She made herself sit up, inhaling sharply when the room spun. While she concentrated on steadying the gyroscope that made her insides tumble like clothes in a dryer, Gavin finished brewing a cup of hot tea.

He loaded it with sugar and brought it to her, snagging a chair for himself and turning it backward. "Come on, honey," he cajoled. "Try a sip of the tea first."

She knew he was right. But she hated the prospect of another run to the bathroom. The fragile china was painted with a delicate Greek key design in gold and navy. Lifting the cup to her lips, she managed a taste. The tea was hot and strong, just as she liked it. When the first sip stayed down, she tried a second. Five minutes later, she started on the toast.

Gavin was amazingly patient and surprisingly intuitive. He kept quiet, content to monitor her progress from across the table. Unshaven and heavy-eyed, he was as handsome as ever. The pale yellow cotton button-down he wore was soft from multiple washings. He had rolled the sleeves to his elbows, exposing tanned forearms dusted with golden hair.

The fact that even his big manly hands turned her on was distressing.

Finally, she sighed and wrinkled her nose. "Thanks. I'm better now."

Though he'd been careful to keep physical distance between them, his smile held sympathy and admiration. "I don't know how women do it. Whoever called you the weaker sex was an idiot."

The gentle praise shored her spirits. That and the fact that he didn't seem as angry this morning.

He reached in his shirt pocket and pulled out a scrap of paper. "Here are the names of three good ob-gyns in Silver Glen. You can research them online. Let me know when you schedule the ultrasound, and I'll clear my calendar."

"Why do you work so hard?"

"You mean because I don't have to?"

"Yes."

"Why do you want to be your father's second in command?"

She pondered his question. "Fair point. If I wanted to, he'd have been happy for me to sit at home doing needlepoint or whatever the twenty-first-century equivalent is..."

"I like what I do. And it helps people. Seems to me like those are reason enough." He paused. "I have a full schedule today. Will you be okay on your own?"

"Of course. Remember that your mother has invited me to afternoon tea, so that will be nice."

He frowned. "I'm glad you didn't tell her about us last night."

"Well, I…"

He carried on, oblivious to her distress. "I know we'll have to say something sooner or later, but why cause a commotion before we have to?"

"She knows," Cass blurted out. "She guessed."

"Well, hell."

"She promised to pretend she *doesn't* know. I suppose *you* can pretend you don't know that she knows. One big happy family."

His jaw worked. "Is that supposed to make me feel guilty?"

"Not at all. You're entitled to your feelings."

"And what about you?"

"I'll get used to the idea. I really don't have much choice, now, do I?" She said it defiantly, hoping to provoke a reaction, but as usual, Gavin was not easily ruffled.

"I'll get someone to return your rental car. While you're here in Silver Glen, you can use one of mine."

"The Porsche?" she asked hopefully.

At last, his serious facade cracked. "In your dreams. You'll have to settle for a safe and sturdy Subaru."

"In other words, a *mommy* car."

"Might as well embrace your new status. From what I hear, it's a lifetime role."

"If you're trying to cheer me up, you're really bad at it."

He patted her hand and stood up. "More toast? More tea?"

"No. I'm fine. Thank you."

After carrying the dishes to the sink, he returned to the table and stood beside her, running a hand through her rumpled hair. Although she hadn't bothered to peek in a mirror this morning, she knew she must look like a bag lady.

His touch made her shiver.

"Take it one day at a time, Cass. You'll get through this."

The pronoun didn't escape her attention. *You'll* get through this. Not *we'll* get through this. Even now, and despite his hospitality, Gavin was no more open than ever to the idea that he was about to become a father.

It hurt. A lot. But since there wasn't a darn thing she could do about it, she put on a brave face. "Shall I throw something together for dinner tonight?"

"I don't need anyone to look after me, Cass. Rest. Read a book. I rarely remember to eat dinner anyway…at least not until eight or nine. I think it would be better if you didn't wait on me."

She nodded stiffly. "I understand. I suppose I'll see you when I see you." Before he could say anything else to upset her or make her feel like an interloper, she walked out of the room.

Gavin pressed his fingertips to his temples, feeling the unmistakable beginnings of a tension headache. Despite his decision to maintain an emotional distance from Cassidy, seeing her so downcast and wretched made him feel like scum.

He wanted to cuddle her and comfort her, but that would take him down a road he wasn't prepared to travel. Sex made a man stupid. He wasn't going to let himself be emotionally manipulated.

Though he worked several hours in his office, he was keenly aware of Cass's presence in his home. He spent a lot of time alone and liked it that way. Having her so close kept him off balance.

He heard the front door slam when she left to meet his mother. That in itself was disturbing. Was Maeve simply being sociable as was her habit, or did the fact that she guessed Cassidy was pregnant put her on high alert?

Doggedly, he forced himself to concentrate. Like an alcoholic counting days sober, Gavin was determined not to touch Cassidy again. Cold showers, working out in his home gym, battling Liam on the hotel's racquetball court…whatever it took, he would deny himself pleasure in exchange for knowing he was not tempted to do something stupid. He couldn't be sure, even now, that Cassidy was telling the truth. He wouldn't be duped. Not again. No matter that her smile lit up the room and her laughter soothed his soul.

The situation would become untenable if Cassidy realized how much he wanted her physically. So the solution was simple. He had to keep his wits about him, and he had to be celibate as long as she was in Silver Glen.

The prospect was unappealing at best. But he would make it work. He had to. If he let her see his weakness, she would worm her way into his ordered, solitary life. And if her claims of paternity turned out to be a hoax, he'd be screwed. It was better this way.

Cassidy found the car keys on the kitchen table with a brief note from Gavin. Apparently he couldn't even be bothered to stop by her room and drop them off. Perhaps he was afraid she would lure him into her bed like some femme fatale. Since she could count the number of times she'd had sex on one hand, his caution was ludicrous.

She dressed for her invitation to the lodge as carefully as she had the night before. Temperatures were supposed to hit the lower eighties by mid-afternoon—a heat wave for spring—so she donned a cheery sundress in poppy red and topped it with a crocheted ecru shrug. Canvas espadrilles and a straw market tote completed her ensemble.

Maeve Kavanagh met her in the hotel lobby. Gavin's mother was an impressive woman. She didn't try to dress below her age, but neither was her sense of style dowdy. Cassidy knew her hostess had been widowed many years ago. It was a marvel that some other discerning man hadn't snapped her up.

"We'll eat in my office," Maeve said, taking Cassidy's arm and steering her down a hallway that led to the back corner of the building.

Office was somewhat of a misnomer. Maeve's quarters were lovely and bright. An antique rolltop desk occupied one wall, its paper-laden surface evidence of Maeve's active role in running the lodge. But by far the largest portion of the room was given over to a feminine sitting area.

The furniture was upholstered in flowery English chintz. On a low table sat a silver coffee service. Above a gas-log fireplace, what looked to be a genuine Mary Cassatt hung proudly, its colors accenting the room's decor.

Cassidy took a wingback chair at Maeve's urging. The older woman chose a spot on the sofa just opposite her guest.

Maeve poured a cup of coffee and handed it across the table. "I forgot to ask if you are limiting caffeine. I can ring for something else."

"It's fine. I drink just enough coffee to be sociable. Otherwise, water is what keeps me going."

Maeve filled her own cup and sat back. "You're probably very wise. I grew up in a generation that mainlined this stuff. I try to keep it in check, but I'll admit to being addicted. So tell me, Cassidy," she said. "What are your addictions?"

Sex with your son seemed like an inappropriate rejoinder, so Cass reached for something more socially acceptable. "Well, I spend a great deal of time at our family's casino. I've been learning the business in hopes of becoming my father's second in command. If I have any spare time, I like to bicycle...and I get a kick out of organizing my friends' closets. I guess that makes me sound hopelessly dull."

"Not at all. Perhaps I'll let you take a crack at mine."

Cassidy let that one pass. Getting overly chummy with Gavin's mother seemed like a surefire way to get under his skin. "I think Gavin was worried about me coming here today."

Maeve eyed her over the rim of the cup. "Oh, really? How so?"

"He thanked me for not letting the cat out of the bag last night. I had to confess that you guessed that I'm pregnant."

"That must have been awkward."

"Yes, ma'am."

"I wouldn't worry about it. What you and I talk about is really none of his business."

"Are you sure about that? I think Gavin would disagree."

"Men and women usually disagree. That's what makes the battle of the sexes so much fun."

"I don't think I'm prepared to wage a war. All I want Gavin to do is trust me."

Maeve sobered. "That's not going to be easy, Cassidy. He had a terrible incident with a female when he was in college. It left him not a misogynist, but a skeptic, I suppose."

"What happened?"

"A woman accused him of rape."

Cassidy's heart sped up. "That's preposterous. Gavin is an honorable, decent man. He would never force anyone."

Maeve stared at her. "I wish his brothers and I had been so fiercely loyal. We believed him, of course. But the woman was so very convincing. There were odd moments when I wondered if Gavin saw doubt in our eyes, and it wounded him."

"You were human."

"Yes. But he was my boy. And I let him down. We all did. Gavin refused to be bailed out. When the woman's lawyer demanded a huge settlement in exchange for dropping the whole thing, I finally realized Gavin was being set up."

"How dreadful."

"Turns out, she had never even slept with Gavin. She was a patient at a mental institution in the next town. One night she and a cohort, who posed as the lawyer, slipped away. Her partner convinced her that with the money they squeezed out of an outrageous claim against an innocent man, they could run away. Gavin spent five nights behind bars before her parents tracked her down and the truth came out."

"I don't know what to say. It's so sick and cruel."

"Well, that's the point, I guess. She *was* sick. In order to find a mark at random, she spent time at the university and as luck would have it, she latched on to Gavin. It was after their first date that she made the accusation. He was blindsided."

Cassidy reeled inwardly. No wonder he was so upset to find out that he hadn't really rescued her from an attacker. And that she was a virgin. And that she had cajoled him into playing bride and groom with Robbie, the Elvis impersonator.

In his shoes, she might have been just as suspicious. Everything that had transpired between her and Gavin was innocent. But Cassidy was a stranger to him. And the crazy wonderful night they had shared could be construed as some kind of setup, particularly since she wound up pregnant. What a mess.

"I think I should probably go back to Vegas," she said, heartsick and discouraged.

Maeve disagreed. "Give him time, my dear. You each need time…time to see if you could actually make a go of this."

"I didn't come here to get a husband. I only thought Gavin should know about the baby."

"Nevertheless, something drew the two of you together when you met in Vegas. Don't underestimate the value of powerful sexual attraction. Many good marriages have started with less."

"I'm so confused."

"That's natural. I had seven babies, and every time I was pregnant, I felt as if I were wandering in a fog. Growing a human life is difficult. The process makes demands on your body, and it plays with your mind."

"Were you sick?"

"For the first three months, yes. But after that things improved. To be honest, though, I had friends who struggled with nausea the whole time. So don't be shocked if that's the case."

"Oh, goody. Something else to look forward to…in addition to heartburn and stretch marks and sleepless nights."

Maeve chuckled, her expression wry. "No one ever said being a woman is easy. But I'm here for you, Cassidy. All you have to do is ask. I want my son to be happy, and I think you're the woman to make that happen."

"How can you be so confident?"

"I saw the way he looked at you. Possessive. Worried. Gavin is halfway in love with you already."

Eleven

Cassidy barely saw Gavin for two solid days. On the third day, she headed out the door right after lunch for her ultrasound. She had barely made it to the car, when Gavin came strolling out of the house dressed and ready to go.

She put a hand on the driver's door. "What are you doing?"

"Going with you." He took the keys from her hand and motioned her around the car. "Come on. We don't want to be late."

She stared at him, bemused. She'd put the information on a piece of paper and laid it on his dresser yesterday with no comment. She wasn't even sure if he had seen the note. Yet here he was.

They didn't talk on the way to the doctor's office. Gavin was withdrawn, and Cassidy couldn't think of any topic that wouldn't lead to trouble. The visit to the specialist was a lesson in patience. First there were papers to fill out. Then they took her back for blood work and urinalysis. Finally, they returned her to the waiting area where Gavin sat and said that someone would be with her shortly.

Shortly must have been a euphemism, because an hour elapsed from the time they arrived until the moment a harried nurse appeared to get Cassidy settled in an exam room. Gavin had insisted on going along for this leg of the journey, so Cassidy didn't quibble, especially since he stayed out in the hall while she put on a gown.

There was no seating except the doctor's rolling stool, so Gavin leaned against the wall, his hands shoved in his pockets. It was a good thing the nurse had already checked her blood pressure, because Cassidy's heart rate was through the roof.

Fortunately, the doctor appeared after only ten minutes or so. She grimaced. "I'm Doctor Mensch. Sorry for your wait. We had an unexpected delivery, and my colleague who was supposed to be on call came down with a stomach virus. We've been scrambling to cover everything." She glanced at the chart the nurse had started. "I see the date of your last period. Are you fairly regular?"

Cassidy shrugged, her cheeks turning red. "Actually, I know exactly when I got pregnant. It was just the one night." She named the month and day.

The doctor's eyebrows went up, but she didn't ask for elaboration. "In that case, it looks like you're not quite eleven weeks. Let's do an ultrasound and see how things look."

Cassidy had expected the blob of jelly on her abdomen, but the physician shook her head. "We'll get more information from a transvaginal ultrasound. It won't hurt at all." The doctor glanced at Gavin. "Are you the father?"

Gavin opened his mouth, but Cassidy rushed into the breach. "No. He's not. Just a friend." Over the doctor's bent head, Cassidy shot Gavin a stubborn look. He had refused to accept the truth. She didn't want to hear any polite lies from him now.

Though his face darkened and his eyes flashed, Gavin remained silent. His expression, however, said there would be hell to pay later.

Cassidy squeaked when the instrument was inserted. It was cold. Her hands gripped the sides of the exam table.

The older woman noticed and smiled encouragingly. "This is rarely uncomfortable. Try to relax."

Easy for her to say. It wasn't every day Cassidy saw a tiny being who might turn out to have her hair or Gavin's eyes. For some reason, the room fell silent. It wasn't as if the doc needed to concentrate. Moving a wand inside a confined space wasn't exactly rocket science.

Three sets of eyes locked on the computer screen. But Cassidy was torn. She kept an eye on Dr. Mensch, too, waiting to see a nod of approval.

When a tiny frown appeared between the doctor's eyebrows, Cassidy's heart clenched. "What is it? What's wrong?"

The ob-gyn studied the screen. "Nothing at all. Everything looks good. And based on what you told me about the date of conception, we're right on target."

"But?" Cassidy had always had a knack for reading people, and there was something the doc wasn't saying. "But what?"

Moving the wand and applying pressure here and there, the doctor finally zeroed in on one grainy image. "There. Look at that."

To Cassidy, the readout might as well have been an M.C. Escher drawing. "I see blobs and spots. Help me out here. Does the kid have two noses? An extra set of hands? You're scaring me."

The doctor smiled, her expression mischievous. "In a manner of speaking. It's twins, Cassidy. Two babies. Congratulations. You're going to be doubly blessed."

Gavin felt as if someone had punched him in the chest. It was hard enough trying to convince himself that he might have fathered one child. Now fate had anted up to two. He glanced at Cassidy. She was almost as pale as the white paper cover on the exam table.

He put a hand on her shoulder. "You okay?"

She looked up at him, panic in her eyes. "What am I going to do, Gavin?"

The doctor glanced from Cassidy to Gavin and back again. "Is there a problem?"

"No problem," Gavin said. "She's a little shell-shocked, obviously." He swallowed hard, wondering how in the heck he had arrived at this juncture in his life. "We both are. But it will all work out." He took Cass's hand in his and squeezed it, trying to convey solidarity.

The doctor gave Cassidy a tissue and helped her sit up. "We'll print out a set of photos for you to take home. I'll want to see you back here in a month. Sooner if you have any problems. You're young and very healthy. This should be a straightforward pregnancy."

When the doctor exited, Gavin exhaled. "Well, that was a surprise."

"Uh-huh." Cassidy sat on the end of the table, her hands twisting in her lap. She stared at a spot on the far wall, her gaze unfocused. His bet was that she was in shock.

He put an arm around her shoulders. "We need to go, Cass. They'll need the exam room."

When she looked up at him, her pupils were dilated. "I don't feel like I'm having twins. How can it be possible?"

"Put your clothes on. We'll discuss it in the car. I'll buy you a milk shake and we can drive over to Asheville and look at nursery furniture. They have one of those baby superstores. I went there once with Dylan when he wanted to surprise Mia with a toy box for Cora."

Cassidy was silent as she handed over her co-pay and then let him lead her out to the parking lot. She winced at the bright sunshine. When she donned sunglasses, he could no longer read her emotions.

They picked up shakes at a drive-through window, vanilla for Cass and black cherry for him. Out on the interstate, he chose an XM station that played classical music. Cassidy still hadn't uttered more than a dozen words since the doctor gave them the news.

He drove carefully, suddenly conscious as never before that he was carrying not one but three lives in his hands. As they reached the outskirts of the city, he finally asked the question that had bothered him since Cassidy arrived on his doorstep. "Cass?"

"Hmm?" She sounded sleepy.

"Is there someone you should call about today's news?"

"You mean my father?"

"No. I was thinking of any other guy who might be a daddy to your twins. Shouldn't you give someone a heads-up?"

Slowly, she removed her sunglasses and turned sideways to face him. "No," she said flatly. "You're it. Get used to the idea."

Her militant attitude didn't bother him. For the first time, he wanted to believe her without reservation. But his old biases held him back.

At the baby store, they wandered the furniture aisles. Cassidy's eyes brightened when she spotted a traditional Jenny Lind crib and changing table in solid cherry. Unlike most of the mass-produced items, this was handmade by a local North Carolina craftsman.

When she flipped the tag to look at the price, she blanched. "I can't afford this. Especially times two. We'll have to try a thrift store."

"You're kidding, right?" Her dad owned an enormous, popular casino.

Cassidy shrugged, her expression resigned. "I'm unemployed, remember? And my father canceled my credit cards. I'll need to watch my spending."

He pulled the paper tags for the various items. "I'll buy the baby furniture and put the delivery on hold until you know where you'll be living."

She grabbed his wrist. "Why would you do that? According to you, it's not your responsibility."

The words had teeth. Guilt pinched, but he wasn't quite ready to cave. He wanted to believe Cass, but this was too big a decision to make lightly. If he wrapped his head and his heart around those two little beings growing inside her and they turned out not to be his, he wouldn't be worth a damn. "Let's just say I can afford it. What good is having money if you can't make life easier for your friends?"

"Who said you and I are friends?"

He raised an eyebrow. "Don't press your luck, Cass."

"Well, in that case…" With a scowl, she started tossing stuff in the shopping cart. Crib sheets, wall hangings, burp cloths, pacifiers, a high-tech baby monitor.

The stubborn tilt to her chin said she was waiting for him to stop her. But he wanted to see how far she would go. In ten minutes, the cart was almost too heavy to push. When a precariously balanced box of diapers began to slide off, Gavin caught it and put it underneath.

"You done now?" he asked.

Cass pushed a stray curl from her forehead. She was flushed, her forehead damp with perspiration. "I'll pay you back," she said, her stormy gaze daring him to disagree.

He eyed the trove of baby paraphernalia. "You may have to work the streets of Vegas, after all, to cover this."

"That's not funny."

When he saw tears in her eyes, he suddenly remembered everything he had ever read about expectant moms and hormones. Poor Cassidy. Her whole life had been turned upside down. And this was only the beginning.

"I'm sorry. Bad joke," he said, heading for the checkout lanes. "Let's get you home so you can take a nap."

As it turned out, she slept in the car. Gavin heard her gentle snore before they had been on the road fifteen minutes. He drove slowly, in no hurry to get back to Silver Glen. As they headed up into the mountains, he pulled off at a scenic overlook and parked.

Cassidy never stirred. The tiny frown on her forehead disturbed him. Were her dreams unpleasant, or was she still mad at him?

For the first time, a novel thought occurred to him. What if he accepted the babies regardless of their parentage? Was it enough that Cassidy was their mom and Gavin wanted Cassidy?

He watched her sleep and felt a shift in his thinking. Cass wasn't the only one whose reality was changing. Like it or not…father or not…Gavin was reaping the results of his one wild night in Vegas.

It was an unexpected pleasure to be able to study her intently without her knowing. Asleep, she looked closer to eighteen or twenty than twenty-three. He was only six years older than she was, but it felt like a much wider gulf than that.

She'd been innocent when it came to physical intimacy. He still hadn't come to terms with that. If both of them had acted out of character that one crazy night, what did it say about the chances for any kind of long-lasting relationship?

No matter the difficulties and the questions, he couldn't turn his back on Cassidy. Her father had thrown her out. Gavin never would. Not unless some other man came to claim her.

Imagining that scenario hurt. A lot. The severity of

his mental reaction told him he was in far deeper than he wanted to admit.

He wanted to touch her…if only to ruffle her dark hair or straighten the shirt that had rucked up to reveal a slice of soft golden skin at her waist. The urge was almost uncontrollable.

Soon, very soon, she would start to show. When that happened, his whole family would speculate. They weren't shy about asking questions. While it was comforting to know that he and Cassidy had a circle of support when it came time for the babies to be born, one part of him wanted to hide her away and keep her for his own.

She stirred and sat up, a crease on her cheek where she had rested against the seat belt. "Sorry," she said, yawning. "I seem to keep doing that."

"It's good for you and the babies."

She paled, her eyes dark and wide. "I thought maybe I dreamed that."

"No such luck. Try to think of it as efficiency…two for the price of one."

"It's too early to joke about this," she muttered. "Somebody up there made a big goof. I'm not the maternal type. The prospect of one baby freaked me out, much less two."

"I have faith in you, Cassidy."

"Why are you being so nice to me?"

The grumpy note in her voice made him want to smile, but he held it in. "It seemed like you were having a rough day. I'm trying to be supportive."

"Unless you can push two watermelons out of your female parts, you're pretty much useless to me now."

This time he did chuckle. "Women do it every day. How bad could it be?"

"Maybe like giving a guy a mammogram on his family jewels."

He winced and held up a hand. "I stand corrected." He started the engine and backed out of the parking space. "When we get home I have a proposition for you."

Cassidy yawned and rummaged in her oversize tote for a bottle of water. "I think that was what got us into this mess. Don't you remember?"

He *did* remember. In stunning detail. And that recollection made it very difficult to be objective about Cassidy's pregnancy. Or his own role in the situation. In fact, his life would be a whole lot easier if he could erase every moment of the time he'd spent in bed with Cassidy Corelli.

Easier maybe. But not nearly as much fun.

Twelve

Back at the house, Cassidy planned to hide out in her room and try to come to terms with the soap opera that was her life. But she and Gavin were still in the driveway when her phone rang.

She muttered an unladylike word.

Gavin shot her a glance. "Who is it?"

"My father."

"Are you going to tell him about the babies? Plural?"

The phone continued to ring. "No. Not yet." She didn't want to answer, especially with Gavin listening in. Getting another lecture from her father about the need for a husband and a wedding ring was an embarrassment she'd just as soon not share. "I'll call him back in a minute."

Inside the house, she was ready to disappear when Gavin took her arm. "Not so fast. I want to show you something."

He led her down the hall where her bedroom was located. His was farther back. And across from it was a door she hadn't opened.

She came to a halt. "Are you about to show me your collection of baseball cards and workout equipment?"

His lips quirked in a half smile. "No. Those are in the garage. Take a look. I thought you could use this as a temporary nursery when the babies first arrive."

"Oh." She peeked inside and was pleasantly surprised. The room was easily fourteen by fourteen, plenty big enough for two infants. At the moment, the furnishings consisted of a set of twin beds and a bedroom suite that was probably used for guests.

Gavin leaned against the door frame. "Some of my clients like to have face-to-face consultations. I occasionally offer them a room here."

"How would that work if the house is full of babies?"

"They're tiny at first, right? We can manage. There's the Silver Beeches Lodge, of course, and also half a dozen B and Bs in town. It's not a problem."

"And I won't be here for all that long." She said it deliberately, to goad him, to get a reaction…any reaction.

For a moment, she thought she had failed. His expression was blank, closed off. But before she could blink, he reeled her into his arms and kissed her hard. The embrace left them both breathless.

Gavin brushed her cheek with the back of his hand. "One day at a time, Cass."

Her phone rang again, shattering the moment of intimacy. Same caller. "I'll take this in my room," she said, her stomach curling.

Gavin kissed her one more time, this one gentle and sweet. "Don't let him be a bully. You have options."

Cassidy had been on the line with her dad for fifteen minutes, and not once had he mentioned her pregnancy. She squelched the stab of hurt. Apparently the impetus for this call was a far more pressing concern.

"I need you to come back, right away," her father bellowed. "I've lost half a million dollars already."

Letting him ramble and bluster for several minutes, she finally got the picture. Someone had infiltrated the casino's computer systems and was siphoning money into an offshore account. Gianni Corelli had spotted the missing cash, but that was as far as he had gotten.

Cassidy was sympathetic, but she wouldn't be a doormat. "You threw me out, remember? Why can't Carlo handle this?"

Her father's volume rose two decibels. "That pup can barely even *turn on* a computer," he yelled "You're the one with the brains. Come home, Cassidy. I need you."

Interestingly, he hadn't realized he needed her until she wound up on the other side of the country. "I'll think about it, Daddy." She sensed his rage, but beneath it was fear. Her father had built a mighty empire. It must be maddening to see it threatened.

Part of her was angry that her only parent hadn't acknowledged her pregnancy at all. Or admitted that he was wrong to throw her out. Or at least shown some appreciation for her talent and her dreams for the casino. But she told herself it was just as well, because she was no closer to having any answers than when she left Vegas.

He spent another five minutes demanding her immediate presence, but Cassidy stood firm. "I'll call you tomorrow," she said. "But I make no promises." He knew what he had done. It wouldn't hurt him to spend a few hours learning to regret that he had booted his only daughter to the streets.

Over dinner prepared by Gavin's housekeeper, Cassidy told Gavin about the crisis in Las Vegas.

His forkful of lasagna stopped halfway to his mouth. "So he wasn't calling about your pregnancy...or to check on how you were feeling?"

"Never even mentioned it," she said wryly. She swallowed a bite of the garlic bread that was to die for. "But I let him know that he couldn't order me around like a child."

"Good for you."

"I need a favor," she said. The request was really rather ballsy considering all he had done so far, but he *was* her babies' father. And this request would indirectly benefit them.

Gavin took a sip of his Chianti and wiped his mouth on a napkin. "Okay." He seemed cautious but resigned.

"Do you think you could hack the casino's security protocols and help me figure out who's doing this?"

He caught on immediately. "That's brilliant. If we succeed, your father would take you back with open arms."

"That's what I was thinking." But was that truly what she wanted? She was confused and adrift. If her father changed and her goals were back on track, where did that leave her relationship with Gavin? And what about the twins? She knew she wanted to be at home with them, at least for a few years.

"Do you have the appropriate access codes?"

"If they haven't updated them. And I doubt they have. I haven't been gone that long."

"Then let's give it a try."

In Gavin's amazing office, he offered her a high-backed leather chair that matched his. She sat beside him at the console while he booted up one of his computers. One of the things she liked about him was that he wasn't scared off by her intelligence.

In college and grad school, she'd sometimes started dating a guy only to get dumped when he found out that her looks didn't equate with being a party girl. And the smart ones…the boys she would have enjoyed going out with, rarely asked her out *because* of her looks.

Gavin, on the other hand, seemed to enjoy the whole package. It made her feel good. Really good.

He pulled up a screen and glanced at her. "You ready?"

She nodded, her heart racing. What they were attempting was probably illegal…unethical at best. But the casino was part of her life, part of her birthright. She had a vested interest in seeing it succeed.

As she rattled off username and password, Gavin entered all sorts of characters and letters that looked like gibberish to her. "What are you doing?" she asked, frowning. This didn't seem like the usual log-in procedure.

"We don't want anyone to notice that we're poking around. I'm essentially camouflaging our access."

She leaned forward, fascinated by his matter-of-fact knowledge of things that were Greek to her. Soon, he pulled up a visual of the security suite. She and Gavin could see the multiple television screens that monitored everything happening in various parts of the casino. "Amazing," she whispered.

Gavin shot her a grin. "You don't have to be quiet. No one knows we're here."

She punched his arm. "Don't make fun of me."

In that moment, she realized this was the first time since she had arrived in North Carolina that she didn't feel at odds with Gavin. He was more like the man she had met in Vegas.

Who knew how long his good humor would last…

After forty-five minutes, she began to get bored. Gavin was deeply immersed in his task. But since she hadn't a clue how he was doing it, and because she had nothing to contribute at this point, she decided to bow out. "I think I'll go now."

Gavin barely acknowledged her departure.

With a sigh, she wandered down the hallway to the room he had offered as a nursery. Sitting on one of the twin beds, she tried to imagine what this space would look like with two babies in residence. Her pregnancy still didn't seem entirely real, even after seeing the evidence on an ultrasound.

What did seem *very* real were her feelings for Gavin. She cared about his opinion of her. And she wanted to be a part of his life. She might even be falling in love with him, though her mind shied away from that thought. Too much room for heartbreak.

What was she going to do? She had some big decisions to make and no road map. Even if she understood Gavin's reservations about accepting his paternity on faith, it didn't make things any easier for her. He'd told her she could stay until the babies were born, but that wasn't a viable solution, was it? If she hunkered down in his home, seeing him every day, the outcome would be inevitable. She would want to stay in his house and in his heart. It was easy to hope he might give up his doubts about her trustworthiness. Easy, but not realistic.

Given what Maeve had shared with her about Gavin's past, trust wasn't a commodity he shared easily. Perhaps even the attraction that burned so brightly between the two of them increased his misgivings.

Cassidy wanted a father for her babies, but even more than that, she wanted a man who loved her unequivocally. Once Gavin saw legal proof that the babies were his, he would do the right thing. She had no worries there. But that wasn't enough. It never would be.

She'd given her innocence to a wonderful man. But was the sexual chemistry between them a sign of something deeper? For her part, it was becoming more and more clear that the answer was yes. Gavin was smart and funny and sexy and masculine in a way that made a woman feel protected…even if she could take care of herself.

Staying in his home would almost certainly increase

the intimacy between them, with or without sex. Which would make Cassidy incredibly vulnerable to deep hurt.

She had to come up with another plan. One that didn't involve Gavin. She was a mature, well-educated woman. She could figure this out. But how could she leave Silver Glen when her heart was trapped here?

Gavin stretched and craned his neck, working out the knots from sitting too long. It hadn't been easy, but he'd done it. He knew who was stealing from Cassidy's father. Telling her was a task he'd rather not face.

Surely it could wait until morning.

He yawned as he shut everything down and prepared to head to bed. It was almost 2:00 a.m.

The house was quiet when he left his office. Some part of him wanted to make sure Cassidy was okay. When he saw that her door was open, he peeked in. His heart stopped. The room was empty, the bed neatly made. She wasn't in the bathroom. All her things were still in the closet and drawers.

Crazy thoughts rushed through his mind. Did she sleepwalk? Could she be outside? Had she taken his car and gone for a joyride? Was she so upset about her pregnancy that she might consider desperate measures?

It took him a full sixty seconds to get hold of himself. There had to be a plausible explanation.

He would search the house first. If that produced nothing in the way of answers, he might have to involve the police.

Fortunately for his galloping pulse, he found her almost immediately in the extra guest room. She was curled on her side in one of the narrow beds. Still on top of the covers, she was fully dressed except for her shoes that lay tumbled on the floor.

He leaned against the wall, breathing harshly. The kind of fear that had swept through him wasn't logical. But then again, none of his reactions to Cassidy Corelli fell into the realm of rationality.

The depth of his anxiety shocked him. In a very short time, she had done something to him…something unfathomable. She had made him want to love her.

But as much as he yearned to let go and wallow in the sunshine that was Cassidy Corelli, he was bound by his past. By the memory of getting burned. By the prospect of finding out that everything he thought he knew was a sham. What did it say about him that he couldn't take her bubbly charm and artless innocence at face value?

Was he too cynical for such a woman?

When he regained a modicum of control, he picked her up gently. His heart clenched when her head lolled against his shoulder. In her bedroom, he tossed back the covers and deposited her gently on the mattress.

She roused despite his care. "Gavin?"

"You conked out in the other room." He brushed the hair from her forehead. Her cheeks were flushed, her gaze heavy with sleep. "Close your eyes, Cass. It's late."

Her hand gripped his wrist. "Don't go."

The quiet entreaty undid him. Chances were she wouldn't have said it if she had been fully awake.

Chances were he could have refused it in broad daylight.

But the hour was late and his walls were down.

He leaned over her and found her lips. The taste still baffled him. Both exotic and sweet, the combination hit his weak spots. The need to pounce warred with the desire to cherish. She was so damned adorable.

The kiss lengthened, deepened. His mouth moved over hers lazily, as though they had all the time in the world. The room was quiet except for the sound of their breathing.

Her arms came up around his neck. "I want you, Gavin."

How could any man resist such a raw, honest statement? She asked for his unquestioning belief about her babies, and he couldn't give her that…not yet. But this he could offer. Pleasure. Connection. Two people meeting in the comforting dark and trying not to think about the struggles they faced outside these walls.

Deliberately, he reached out and turned off the bedside lamp.

Undressing was a dance, a slow, wistful ballet. First her clothes, then his. In the light from the hallway all he could make out was the shape of her. Any nuances of expression were lost in the shadows.

Probably just as well. He didn't want to see disappointment or regret in her beautiful eyes. She asked for faith and he had none. All he could give her was this.

Moving over and into her stopped time for a moment. He forced himself to release the breath he'd been holding. Strong, slender legs wrapped around his waist. "The babies?" he croaked.

He'd heard the doctor's assurances. Sex was fine. Sex was healthy for the mom and for the dad. But still he worried.

Cassidy cupped her hand behind his neck and pulled him down for a kiss. "They're good. I'm good. It's all good, Gavin."

Maybe it was and maybe it wasn't. Falling so deeply into the dream of having Cass forever wasn't good at all. He couldn't believe life happened in such a way. A chance meeting in an alley. A reckless night of sex and laughter. That was the stuff of movies.

Cassidy squeezed him with her inner muscles. "You're thinking," she complained. "Come back to me."

That she read him so well was also unsettling. Shutting

his brain to the endless sequences of events that could lead to disaster, he chose to live in the moment. She was warm and soft, so soft. Would he be able to take her like this in another four weeks? In eight?

Perhaps it would have to be from behind soon. That notion made him shudder. Tonight he had done his best to go slowly…to slide with purpose over the spot that ensured her pleasure.

But the madness beckoned now. His lungs strained for air. His loins ached. "Come with me, Cass," he pleaded. She didn't answer, not verbally. But he heard her breath catch and felt her tremble against him.

Wildly, he thrust, chasing something just out of reach. She was his. He wanted it to be so. It *had* to be so. The fleeting thought that some faceless man might have fathered her babies made him insane.

He cried out her name when he came. The physical release was something more than pleasure, something less than peace. He felt incomplete and incoherent. Wanting something so badly and knowing he was the only obstacle in the way.

Cass's hands petted him, smoothed his shoulders, glided over his back. "Sleep with me," she cajoled.

It was the easiest request she'd ever asked of him.

"Yes," he muttered. He was loath to separate his body from hers.

In the end, he simply rolled to one side and dragged her against him before covering them both with the quilt.

Cassidy yawned. "Did you have any luck with the computer stuff?"

She was relaxed and warm and on the verge of sleep. "We'll talk about it in the morning," he said.

"Okay…good night, Gavin."

I love you, Cass…

Thirteen

Gavin awoke sometime later to the realization that Cassidy was climbing out of bed. "Where are you going?" he mumbled, not happy about losing his bedmate.

"I have to pee," she whispered.

He grinned in the dark. Being a woman was no easy task. But then he sobered. Cass would need someone at her side to care for her in the months ahead. She was strong and self-sufficient, but pregnancy was hard, especially with twins. He would keep her here as long as she would stay.

His present circumstance pointed out the flaw in his plan. He'd said *no more sex*…and yet here he was. A little voice inside his head posited the notion that Cassidy might be trying to lull him into complacence. That perhaps she thought by appealing to his masculine hungers she could win him over and make him believe what she wanted him to believe.

When she returned to the bed, her feet were cold. He rubbed them with both of his, shoving aside the thoughts that troubled him. He couldn't hold her without wanting her. His sex rose strong and eager.

"Cass?"

"Hmm?"

"You feel up to round two?"

She reached between them and gave him a naughty squeeze. "I could be persuaded…"

As Gavin eased her thighs apart and caressed her before entering her, Cassidy blinked back tears, hating the ready emotions that ambushed her without warning. Growing up, she'd never been a girlie girl when it came to feelings. Her dad had been very fair in that way. He expected Cassidy *and* Carlo to *suck it up*.

Scraped knees, disappointments with school friends, anything that could upset a kid…Gianni Corelli insisted his children put on a brave face. Cassidy had received no exemption for being a girl.

These past few weeks, she barely knew herself. Laughter turned easily to tears and vice versa.

The hardest thing right now was not letting Gavin see how emotional she was about their lovemaking. Being intimate with him made her soar with happiness. But in the aftermath, her doubts and worries returned full force.

He brushed his thumb across her cheek, finding dampness. "What's wrong, Cass?"

Inside her, he flexed and thickened, their connected bodies a precious reminder of her pregnancy. "Not a thing. Don't mind me. I've never been pregnant before. These mood swings take some getting used to."

"You could have said no."

"I didn't want to say no. I wanted you."

"It's tough on a guy's ego when the woman cries."

"Haven't you heard of happy tears?"

"Is that what these are?" He caught one with his fingertip. "Are you happy right now?"

She swallowed hard. *Was* she happy? She was making love to the only man she'd ever been with, the man who had—with her—created two miracles. Two new lives. She should be over the moon. But life wasn't that simple. Not when she knew Gavin wasn't prepared to take her word about the paternity of her children. His children.

Even knowing the reasons behind his inability to trust, it hurt.

She swallowed her reservations and her disappointment. *Suck it up.* "I'm happy," she said, only half lying. "I already love these babies, and I'm happy to be here with you."

He didn't answer. At least not verbally. But he rolled to his back and took her with him, settling her astride his hips. "Cry if you have to, Cass, as long as they're happy tears."

She wasn't able to climax this time. And she was pretty sure he realized it. Exhaustion and worry and a brand-new her combined to rob her of the response she wanted to give.

As he went rigid and choked out her name, his hands bruising her hips, she leaned forward and kissed him, feeling the trembling he couldn't hide. Maybe Gavin didn't trust her. Maybe he didn't love her. And maybe he didn't want to be a dad.

But one thing was clear. He wanted her. Every bit as much as she wanted him.

Morning found her once again hunched over the kitchen sink. Only this time Gavin accompanied her from the bedroom. In fact, as soon as he realized she was in distress, he scooped her up and carried her down the hall, both of them naked as the day they were born.

When he fetched saltines and plain tea and put them at her elbow, he kissed her nape. "Will you be okay if I go get your robe?"

She nodded, her breathing shallow as she willed away the nausea. But this time she lost the battle. While he was gone, she emptied her stomach. When he returned, she had just finished cleaning up the sink. Weak and weary, she let him tuck her into the robe and tie the sash.

"I need to sit down," she muttered. At least she wouldn't have to worry about gaining too much weight if this trend kept up.

Gavin had donned a robe that matched hers. He brought her untouched tea and crackers to the table. "Try to eat something, Cass. You'll feel better."

"My head knows that, but my stomach keeps voting *hell, no*."

Gavin chuckled quietly. But he was smart enough to let her be miserable in peace as she nibbled and sipped. It was a full half hour before she could actually swallow without any fear of gagging.

By that time, the sun was all the way up and Gavin's cozy kitchen was filled with warm, beautiful light.

He leaned his chair back on two legs and studied her face. "Your color is better. More death-warmed-over than zombie corpse."

"You do know how to flatter a girl."

"Should I tell you how nicely that robe shows off your cleavage?"

She glanced down, mortified. The lapels gaped, exposing her chest almost to the navel. "Why didn't you say something?"

His quick grin was full of masculine appreciation. "I was enjoying the view."

Slowly, she stood up, gratified that the room spun for only a couple of seconds. "I think I'll go take a shower."

Gavin touched her hand. "I have something to tell you about the casino. It's not good. Do you want to hear it right off or when you've had a chance to get dressed and your stomach quits doing acrobatics?"

She stared at him. Now the queasy feeling in the pit of her belly had nothing to do with pregnancy. "How bad?"

"Bad enough." His expression was sober.

Sinking back into her chair, she braced herself mentally. "I've always believed in ripping off the Band-Aid as quickly as possible. Don't keep me in suspense. What did you find out?"

"It took longer than I expected. You'll be glad to know that the casino's online security is actually damned impressive. I had to dig pretty deep to find answers."

"You're stalling."

He shrugged. "It's your brother."

She gaped at him. "Carlo?"

"Do you have another brother?"

The news was too incredible for her to quibble over his sarcasm. "But why?"

"I haven't a clue. Your father was on target about the amount. From what I could tell, the money has been moved ten to twenty thousand dollars at a time to three separate offshore accounts."

"I can't believe it." She *knew* Carlo. He might not have her work ethic, but he wasn't a criminal.

"The only other explanation is that he might have inadvertently given someone access by sharing his passwords and usernames."

"He wouldn't have done that. My father taught us from the time we were in high school to keep that stuff absolutely private." Yet she had shared hers with Gavin. She had infinite trust in him.

"Well, then, I think we've found the source of the theft. How do you want to handle this?"

A shiver ran down her spine as she imagined her father's reaction to the news that his beloved son was stealing. "I'll have to tell Daddy in person. This is not the kind of thing you can do over the phone."

"We, the Kavanaghs I mean, have a small jet that we share with a couple of other businesses. It's parked on an airstrip outside of town. My brother Patrick is a licensed pilot if you're game. It would be quicker than flying commercial out of Asheville, and more comfortable than first class."

"You own a jet?" Even Gianni Corelli wasn't that much of a high roller.

"We *share* a jet," Gavin said.

"Same difference," she muttered. She had barely adjusted to the change in time zones and now already she was going to head back across the country. The idea made her tired just thinking about it. But there was no point in delaying. Especially if money was continuing to disappear.

"How soon can we leave?" she asked.

"I'll contact Patrick. Depending on his schedule and if the jet's not already spoken for, we could fly out this afternoon."

"Make the call," she said, her stomach in a knot.

Gavin leaned across the table and squeezed her hand. "I won't let your father badger you or upset you. It's not good for you *or* the babies."

His gentle kindness in the midst of everything that was going on made her want to throw herself into his arms. Instead, she summoned a smile. "Thank you, Gavin. I appreciate your help."

Gavin did his best to keep an eye on Cassidy without her catching on that he was hovering. She sat in her wide comfy seat with her legs curled beneath her. They had both dressed for the upcoming meeting with her dad. Cass wore a scoop-necked, short-sleeved ivory angora sweater with black dress pants and chunky coral jewelry. With her hair pulled back in a loose ponytail, she looked young and beautiful.

He'd seen the look in his brother's eyes when he introduced Cassidy to Patrick. It was a masculine reaction that couldn't be masked. Cass made an impression.

She'd been charming and friendly before Patrick took the pilot's seat. Now her gaze was glued to the small window as they soared across the miles. He had a feeling she wasn't really seeing anything in particular. She was pale and subdued.

Her profile made him ache. So feminine, so sweet. But not weak. Far from it. She was smart and focused, despite the recent upheaval in her life. Once this business with her father and brother was settled, Gavin had a decision to make.

He knew in his gut that Cassidy's babies were his. And he knew there was no conspiracy. Or at least he was almost sure. Making love to Cassidy last night had stripped everything down to life's most basic level. She wasn't a liar or a cheat. He'd known that all along, though he hadn't been willing to admit it. Now life had dropped something wonderful in his lap. Something he hadn't asked for... something he hadn't expected.

Maybe sometimes, *knowing* someone had nothing to do with the calendar and everything to do with recognizing a person's character. If he followed up on his one wild night in Vegas...if he gave himself over completely to the idea that he and Cass were soul mates, his whole life would change.

Was he willing to place his trust in such an ephemeral dream?

Quietly, he unfastened his seat belt and crouched in the

aisle beside her seat. "Hey," he said quietly. "You feeling okay?"

She had her arms clasped around her waist in a protective posture. She nodded slowly. "I'm fine."

"I'm not so sure you are."

"Since when is the oh-so-practical Gavin Kavanagh a mind reader?"

"I'm beginning to figure out how *yours* works."

Finally, he coaxed a smile from her. "It's dangerous for a man to think he understands women," she said.

"Is that so?"

She patted his arm. "We are mysterious creatures."

"Like unicorns?"

"Don't make fun of me. Besides, there's a difference between mythical and mysterious. I'm very real."

Their gazes clashed, hers mischievous, his rueful. "It's taken me a little while to accept that. Everything about that night in Vegas seemed like a dream."

"For me, too, Gavin. I am a pretty responsible person most of the time. So I can't really explain what happened except to say that you were so terribly earnest and sweet when you rescued me."

"I'm not sweet," he growled, insulted by her description. "I did what any man would do."

"My brother is big and brawny and three inches taller than you. But even though you thought he was some kind of thug, you rushed in and did battle for my honor."

"Somebody's been reading too many romance novels."

"Don't disparage an entire genre. Whether you like it or not, you acted like a hero."

He shook his head, wishing he hadn't gone down this particular path. Which meant that changing the subject was in order. "Have you planned out what you're going to say to your dad?"

She rubbed her temples, the line of her mouth grim. "I'd like to say yes, but the truth is, I'm dreading it. The last time I saw him, he was yelling and throwing me out of his house."

"Would you like me to be there with you when you talk to him?"

Shock colored her face. "In what capacity?"

He knew what she wanted him to say. But he couldn't do it. Not quite yet. Maybe he had it in him to face down a bully, but this thing with Cassidy was another story. "As a friend," he said. "For now."

Seeing her disappointment at his answer made his stomach hurt. She called him a hero, but the truth was, he was afraid. Afraid to find out that he was being used…that he was blind to her faults…that she'd lied about who she was.

Only moments before, she had laughed and teased him, despite her anxiety about this trip to Vegas. Now, thanks to him, she had closed herself behind a veil of indifference.

"Yes," she said. The single word flat. "That would be helpful." She deliberately turned her face away from him, shutting him out.

But he deserved it.

When they landed in Vegas, Patrick stayed behind to take care of the formalities. Gavin had ordered a car to pick them up. It whisked them in short order to Cassidy's father's casino.

Gavin paid the fare and took Cass's arm. "How do we do this?"

She stood on the street, staring up at the building as if she had never seen it before. "I sent a text to my father's secretary. He's in his office. We'll go up and get it over with."

With his hand at her back, he followed her through the crowds to a private elevator at the back of the building. As the small cube whisked them upward, he leaned against the wall and studied his companion. Was it his imagination, or could he see a small baby bump?

The thought made his heart race. Imagining Cassidy rounded and glowing in the advanced stages of pregnancy was a kick to the gut...in a good way.

"Cass," he said impulsively.

She lifted her chin. She had been studying her shoes intently. "Yes?"

"When we get back to Silver Glen, you and I need to settle some things." He was trying to tell her that he was on board...that he was ready to accept fatherhood. But she took it the wrong way.

What little color there was in her cheeks faded. He saw her throat work as she swallowed. "You're right," she said quietly. "But let me get through this first."

He tried to answer, to correct whatever misconceptions she had, but the doors to the elevator opened, and the moment was lost. As they made their way down a long hall, he was impressed by the elegant Oriental runner and the silken wallpaper. Even in areas of the casino closed to the public, no expense had been spared.

Gavin put a finger beneath his collar and tugged. He'd worn a suit and tie as befitted his role in this upcoming drama, but he was tense and uneasy. Not for himself, but for Cassidy.

Though she had glossed over it when she came to North Carolina, he knew she had been deeply hurt by her father's reaction to her pregnancy. Cassidy was determined to be the one to break the news about who was stealing the money. But if her dad was verbally abusive to her in any way, Gavin would intervene.

He was not about to let anyone make Cassidy feel bad about herself. Or to be insulted or belittled.

He stood by her side as she knocked. Turning the knob, she opened the door and they both stepped inside. "Hello, Daddy," she said. "I need to talk to you."

Fourteen

Cassidy could feel Gavin at her back, his warm, solid presence a silent comfort. Perhaps she should have done this on her own. Perhaps it was cowardice to need backup. But she couldn't be sorry he had come with her. It was the only thing propelling her forward at the moment.

Gianni Corelli rose to his feet slowly, his gaze darting from his daughter to Gavin and back again. His bushy eyebrows drew together. "Is this the scoundrel who—"

Cassidy cut him off with a chopping motion of her hand. She wouldn't lie outright to her father, but today was not the time to dissect her untimely pregnancy. There were more urgent matters at hand.

She touched Gavin's arm briefly, feeling the strength of muscles beneath his jacket sleeve. In dress clothes, it was readily apparent that he was a man from a privileged background. He was comfortable with wealth. But not owned by it.

"Daddy," she said, "this is Gavin Kavanagh, a friend of mine. His company deals with cyberattacks of all kinds. I asked him to dig into the money being stolen from you. He found the source of the theft."

Gianni Corelli sat down hard in his chair, his daughter's failings forgotten for the moment. He seemed older suddenly, almost frail, though he weighed almost two hundred and fifty pounds. "Tell me," he croaked.

Cassidy took a small chair and dragged it to the edge of the large desk. Sitting down quickly, she wondered if there was any easy way to do this. She took a deep breath, gazing at him with all the love she could muster. "It's Carlo, Daddy," she said, her heart aching for her parent.

Gianni frowned. "What do you mean, *it's Carlo*?"

"Carlo has been stealing money from the casino…from you. Don't ask me why, but it's true."

The old man stared at her aghast. His hands began to shake. She reached out and gripped both of them, trying to steady him. "Daddy…don't get upset. We'll get to the bottom of this."

He stared at her. "I love that boy. And he stabs me in the back?"

Cassidy had expected fury and outrage. But the reality was even worse. Her father was heartbroken. And perhaps for the first time in his life, at sea. His vigor and infuriatingly dictatorial personality changed in an instant. To Cassidy, it was astonishing. But the metamorphosis was clear proof of how much Gianni idolized Carlo.

Gavin appeared at her elbow. "Drink this, sir. It will help." He had poured a shot of whiskey from the decanter on the sideboard. Cassidy was so intent on her father she had almost forgotten Gavin's presence in the room. "Thank you," she whispered, brushing his hand with hers.

Gianni tilted his head and swallowed the amber liquid. When his chest rose and fell in a giant sigh, she knew they had turned a dangerous corner. He gathered himself visibly. After a moment of hushed silence on the part of everyone in the room, he leaned forward and pressed the button on his intercom. "Find my son. I need him in my office ASAP."

* * *

Cassidy looked to Gavin automatically for support. His encouraging smile helped calm her nerves. She knew he was worried about her. This stress couldn't be good for her or for the babies. Outwardly, she was calm and resolute, but inside, she was a mess.

The three of them were silent as the minutes ticked away on an antique mantel clock. Her father's fireplace was for show and far from necessary in Vegas, but he leaned toward the traditional when it came to decor, as in most other things in his life.

It was exactly twelve and a half minutes before Carlo knocked briefly at his father's door and entered. He stopped short when he saw his sister and Gavin.

"Cassidy," he said, his face lighting up. "I didn't know you were here. Is everything okay?"

Carlo's look of love and concern as he hugged her seemed genuine. She hugged him back. "I'm fine, Carlo. But Daddy needs to talk to you about something." She paused awkwardly, hoping the alley had been too dark the night Gavin punched Carlo for Carlo to recognize him. "And this is my friend Gavin." She waved a hand in Gavin's direction.

Gavin nodded, apparently content for the moment to stay out of the limelight. The two men were standing far enough apart to make shaking hands unnecessary. Carlo returned the nod and looked at his father. "What's up, Pop?"

Gianni rose to his feet, putting one hand on the back of his chair. "I know, Carlo." The three words were ice-cold. But Carlo didn't get it.

He frowned. "Know what?"

The genuine puzzlement on her brother's face made Cassidy wonder for one hopeful second if Gavin was mistaken. She stayed silent, waiting to see how her father would handle this dreadful moment.

Gianni scowled. "I know about the money."

Carlo tensed, his body language unmistakable. "I don't know what you mean." But there was no doubt in anyone's mind that he did. He paled beneath his golden tan, his expression hunted.

The older Corelli stepped out from behind his desk and walked toward his son, with Cassidy at his side. She wasn't sure what she could do, but she wanted to be close in case her father needed physical assistance.

To Carlo's credit, he didn't back up.

Gianni poked a finger in his son's chest. "You *stole* from me, boy. Don't you know that I would have given you anything you asked for?"

Carlo blanched, wild-eyed. "I can explain."

Cassidy inhaled sharply. "So you admit it?" Up until that moment, she had prayed there was some mistake, some confusion.

Her father shook his head, seeming to age before her eyes. "It makes no sense. You deliberately decimated your own inheritance? Or were you trying, perhaps, to make sure you received more than your share?"

Carlo was sweating now, though the room was cool. "I had a plan, Papa. Truly, I did. Let me tell you."

Cassidy's father folded his arms across his chest. "I fail to see how you deserve a hearing, given your appalling villainy, but let no one say that Gianni Corelli is not fair. Speak, boy."

"Can we sit down?" Carlo asked.

Cassidy breathed an inward sigh of relief when her father consented. The stress of this confrontation taxed her strength and threatened a return of the morning's queasiness.

The three of them settled into seats around the fireplace, Cassidy and her father on the sofa, Carlo in an adjacent armchair. Though she lifted an eyebrow and motioned for Gavin to join them, he gave a negative shake of his head.

Carlo leaned forward, elbows on his knees, head in his hands. "I wanted to make you proud of me," he muttered.

His father looked at him as if he were an alien species. "I do not think I have reached the age of senility," he said, shaking his head. "But you are speaking foolishness."

Cassidy felt a wave of sympathy for her younger brother. Growing up, he had been spoiled by their father. Though Carlo had always been a bit immature, this latest escapade took his peccadilloes to an alarming new level. "Carlo," she said softly. "Why don't you start from the beginning?"

At last he sat up straight, his broad shoulders filling out the dress shirt and expensive sport coat he wore. He was too handsome for his own good. Females everywhere swooned when faced with that sexy smile and dark-eyed gaze.

Cassidy understood that he had coasted through life up until this point on his looks and his charm. But if he were going to be her father's right-hand man, he sure as heck had better offer some kind of a decent explanation… and quickly.

"It was because of Cassidy," Carlo said quietly.

She blinked, shocked by the seeming attack.

Her father saved her from having to respond. He glared at his son. "I do not like the direction this is going."

"Hear me out, Papa." Carlo had regained his equilibrium, but was visibly troubled. "When you sent Cass away, I knew you were wrong to do so. But I didn't say anything, because I knew this was my chance to finally work by your side. All my life I've heard you say how smart Cass is and how ambitious…how much you admired her responsibility and her drive and her instincts for business."

Cassidy stared at her father. "You did?"

His sheepish nod astonished her. "Of course. You're my daughter. It made me proud that you were just like me."

Carlo shrugged, looking at his sister with resignation. "See? I could never live up to that. But suddenly, you blotted your copybook by getting pregnant…with no husband or father in sight. I had to do something quickly to solidify my spot as Corelli presumptive."

"But I was gone," Cass said. "The job was yours."

"Maybe, maybe not. But I knew if I could make Papa see me in a new light, I had an opportunity to impress him with my worth."

Gianni slammed a fist on his knee. "So you decided that defrauding your papa of half a million dollars was going to make me happy?" His voice rose to a shout at the end, renewing Cassidy's fears that her father's health might be at risk.

Carlo winced. "I knew you would be upset when you realized the money was missing. I was going to offer my help in finding the culprit. When I 'discovered' the stolen cash, my plan was to return it to you and reap the benefits of your gratitude. So help me God, that's the truth."

The room fell silent. Gavin wanted to believe the kid's story, though there was no real hard evidence to do so. But Carlo was seemingly transparent, his contrition real and touching. Though he wasn't all that much younger than Cassidy, he had a lot of growing up to do.

A man needed to pave his own way in the world, though certainly not at the expense of the innocent. Gavin found it in his heart to feel sorry for Carlo. But his most pressing concern was for Cassidy.

Her brother's actions had to be a slap in the face.

Gianni stared at his son, his expression inscrutable. "Who taught you how to do such a thing?"

"I fooled around with computer stuff in college. I'm good at it, Papa."

"Good enough to rob me blind." But the rejoinder held little heat. The old man looked at his daughter. "Do you believe him, Cassidy? You've always been good at reading people. Is Carlo telling me the truth?"

Gavin frowned, taking an instinctive step forward. Gianni was being cruelly unfair. Why should Cass be asked to implicate or exonerate her own brother?

Cassidy stood up, her expression hard to read. "Excuse me, please." She made a beeline for the private bathroom that occupied a large corner of Gianni's office.

Neither Gianni nor Carlo seemed perturbed by her abrupt departure. Gianni shook his head. "I want the money back in the casino accounts by tomorrow morning at eight. Are we clear?"

Carlo nodded. "Yes, sir. Does that mean you believe me?"

Gianni scowled. "I need time to think about it. I will consult with your sister and let you know."

It was the most painful thing he could have said. Carlo slumped in his chair, defeat in every line of his posture. It had become very clear to Gavin in the past half hour that Gianni's brand of parenting was manipulative at best. He had pitted his children against each other, and sadly, the consequences were emotional bloodshed.

Cassidy's tenure in the bathroom was longer than Gavin would have liked. His radar was already on high alert when she finally emerged. In an instant he knew there was trouble.

"Cass," he said urgently, going to her and putting an

arm around her waist despite the eyes watching. "What's wrong?"

She leaned into him, hands clinging to his forearms, her brown eyes wide with panic. "I'm bleeding," she said. "Oh, Gavin, I'm bleeding."

In an instant all thoughts of the stolen money or Carlo's perfidy were forgotten. Cassidy's brother had his cell phone in his hand. "I'll dial 911."

Gianni shook his head vehemently. "It will take too long with traffic." He pointed at Gavin. "You, boy. Take her yourself. The closest hospital is only three blocks away. I'll have a car meet you downstairs at the back door service entrance. Carlo and I will be right behind you."

Gavin scooped Cassidy into his arms. She didn't protest. That scared him most of all. "I'll take care of her," he said, giving the two Corelli males one last glance. The two men, so much alike in build and coloring, had identical expressions on their faces. Fear.

It was a good bet that Gavin's face looked exactly the same.

Reversing the route he and Cass had followed to access her father's office seemed to take forever. He held her tightly, as if he could literally keep her safe. But today's danger was not something as clear-cut as a bully in an alley. It was internal...potentially devastating.

In the elevator, he looked down at his precious cargo. She was crying. "Ah, God. Don't, Cass. I can't bear it. Everything is going to be okay."

"You keep saying that," she whispered, "but it seems to be getting worse. This is my fault," she said.

"No." He didn't know how to comfort her.

"Yes. It's true. In the very beginning I didn't want this pregnancy. Now I'm being punished."

"The world doesn't work that way. Neither does God

or fate or any other force of nature. Not every woman is ecstatic when she finds out she's pregnant. But would you give those babies up now if you could?"

"Of course not."

"Then hush, sweetheart. Don't upset yourself more. This has been a hell of a day."

With Cassidy's help, he located the door to the delivery bay. As promised, a car was waiting. Gavin tucked Cass into the backseat and ran around to the other side of the car to join her. Only then did he realize this was the spot where he had first met her.

At another day and time, he might have paused to smile at the irony. But now was not the moment for reflection. He leaned toward the driver. "To the hospital. And hurry."

The medical facility was modest in size, but completely modern and fully equipped. Everything worked like a well-oiled machine. The wait time in emergency was only fifteen minutes, which seemed like a miracle to Gavin. He was prepared to do battle, but when they took Cassidy back, he followed and no one protested.

The nurse, however, did oust him while she helped Cassidy into a gown and checked her stats. When he was allowed to return, the woman in scrubs gave him a smile. "The doctor will be in very shortly. Hopefully ten or fifteen minutes. You picked a good time to come. It's been pretty quiet here today." She exited the room moments later.

Cassidy looked pale and small in the hospital gown. "Hold my hand," she said, stretching out her arm.

He gripped her fingers with his, trying to telegraph courage. She didn't speak, and he didn't know what to say to her. Finally, when the burden of silence became too great to bear, he sighed. "Are you hurting?"

"No."

"Is there much…uh…"

"Not a lot…but not a little."

"Is it because we had sex last night?" The possibility tormented him.

"I don't know. Miscarriage is fairly common in the early weeks."

"You're not having a miscarriage," he said firmly. "Don't think that way."

Finally, the doctor came in. Although it had seemed like a long wait, when Gavin glanced at his watch, he saw that the nurse's estimate had been spot-on.

The emergency room physician looked barely old enough to be out of med school. But he seemed confident and knowledgeable. "Let's see what's going on," he said as he pulled out the stirrups.

Cassidy glanced up at Gavin. "Would you step outside, please?" She tried to pull her hand free.

He tightened his grasp instinctively. "But I…"

The doctor nodded, though his gaze was kind. "We won't be long."

Gavin had no choice but to cooperate. He went into the hall and shut the door. In the old days, emergency rooms had curtains. But now that privacy laws were so stringent, even these cubicles had standard doors.

What was happening inside? Why had Cassidy asked him to leave?

It seemed like eons before he was summoned. The doctor poked his head out the door. "You can come back in now."

When Gavin returned to the small room, he found Cassidy sitting up on the end of the exam table and the doctor washing his hands. The man spoke over his shoulder. "Everything looks perfectly fine. It's not uncommon for fluctuating hormone levels at this stage to prompt some bleeding. She'll be fine. It wouldn't hurt to rest tomorrow, but after that, resume activity as normal."

Gavin cleared his throat. "So it was nothing we did?"

The doctor's smile was professional but sympathetic. "Not at all. Ms. Corelli said she's been under a lot of stress...and I understand she flew cross-country today. But to be honest, I would seriously doubt that this was anything other than an isolated incident. We'll do some blood work to make sure. I don't think we have any reason to admit her, though."

When the man in the lab coat exited, Gavin wanted to talk to Cassidy. But before he could do so, Gianni and Carlo arrived. Cassidy's father leaned down to kiss her. "What's happening? Are you okay?"

Cassidy nodded. "The doctor says so. He thinks it's a hormonal thing and very normal."

"Thank God." Gianni touched her hand, his smile tentative. "I owe you an apology, my daughter. I reacted poorly when you told me you were pregnant. I want you to come home. You and Carlo will *both* work by my side. I take some of the responsibility for his foolishness. I thought it was a good thing for the two of you to compete, but I see now that I was wrong."

Cassidy stared at her father. "But you believe that women should stay home and raise children."

Gianni shrugged. "I am old-fashioned, what can I say? If you want to be a mother to your children and still work at the casino, I will try to adjust. I don't want to lose you, Cassidy. You are my dear daughter, and I see your mother in you every day. Besides, practically speaking I need your instincts and training to help me keep up with the times."

"This is a big turnaround for you."

"Yes. But today I saw what my stubborn ways drove

my son to attempt. I would hate for you to do anything so foolish. We are a family, we three Corellis. We belong together."

Carlo spoke not a word during all of this. Finally, Gavin saw Cassidy stare at her brother. "Say something, Carlo."

His smile was rueful. "I want you to come home, too. And I'm sorry for being such an idiot."

Cassidy shook her head. "The funny thing is, I was always jealous of *you*, Carlo. If we actually try to work together instead of against each other, imagine all we can accomplish."

Gianni nodded. "We will get out of here now. Give us a call when you're ready to come home."

Fifteen

Cassidy reeled. A huge portion of her life had done a one-eighty turn. Instead of being the disgraced child, Cassidy had heard a retraction with her own ears. Her father actually said he needed her. Perhaps if she looked out the window, she would see pigs fly.

Only Gavin remained a problem. And sadly, this relationship was not going to be tied up so neatly in a bow. The exam room was tiny. Four adults had occupied the space, and yet not once had her father acknowledged Gavin's presence.

Surely he wondered why the cyber expert who tracked down Carlo's culpability was hanging around in the midst of a pregnancy scare. Anyone with half a brain could figure out that Gavin and Cassidy had some kind of relationship.

But Gianni Corelli, for once, hadn't butted in. Perhaps it was his silent way of finally acknowledging that Cassidy was a grown woman and capable of making her own decisions.

She took a deep breath. "Would you mind stepping outside again so I can get dressed?"

Gavin straightened from where he had been leaning against the wall. "I've seen you naked."

The statement was flat…uninflected. But it made her flush nevertheless. "This is different."

She held his gaze with difficulty. Finally, he nodded. But on his terms. "I'll turn my back, Cass. That's all you're getting."

Dressing hurriedly was an act of cowardice. She couldn't bear the thought of being vulnerable in front of him. There were things to be done, and she needed whatever armor she could find.

When she was decent, she muttered, "Okay."

Gavin faced her, his hands in his pockets. "That's it? Carlo is forgiven? I thought you said your father would be upset."

"He was. He is. But everyone makes mistakes, Gavin. Carlo is family. He did a stupid thing, but Daddy won't kick him out."

"He kicked *you* out."

"Yes." She sighed. "But he apologized. I don't want to spend my life being mad at him. He's my children's grandfather."

"So what now?"

With a tiny prayer to the patron saint of acting, if there was such a thing, she smiled normally. "You and Patrick go home. I appreciate all you've done. When the babies are born, I'll contact you and we can arrange for a paternity test if you are still interested. After that you can make a decision about how much or how little involvement you would like to have."

His eyes narrowed. "So pragmatic. Problem solved. You're really going to ignore the fact that we have this insane chemistry between us?"

What did he want from her? Was she supposed to blurt out her love when he had been nothing but suspicious of her from the beginning? She might be brave, but she wasn't that brave.

"Of course I care about you, Gavin," she said calmly as

her heart was breaking. "But I have my life to lead and you have yours." She couldn't stay with him for the twins... not without something beyond sexual attraction. It would destroy her. She needed more than a father for her babies. She needed Gavin's love and trust.

"So that's it? You're staying here?"

"You heard Daddy. Everything is forgiven. I appreciate your taking me in when I came to North Carolina, but thankfully your house can get back to normal. If you would ship my things to me, I would appreciate it."

Now ice replaced the heat. "God, you're a piece of work. You never would have sought me out if it weren't for the pregnancy, would you?"

"I'm not the one who left Vegas and never looked back."

Where had it sprung from? Such bitter enmity? The memory of their first night together in this very town was so sweet and wonderful. Yet they had come to this.

She wanted him to say he loved her...to beg her to marry him...to demand that she return to North Carolina and claim her rightful place as the mother of his children.

But Gavin did none of those things. He simply stared at her with hot eyes, eyes that judged her and found her wanting.

At last when she couldn't bear the standoff one second longer, he put his hand on the door. "Have a nice life, Cassidy."

The angry sarcasm flicked her on the raw. "Don't forget to send me a bill for the jet trip. I'm a Corelli. We can afford it."

Whatever bleak expression she saw in his gaze must have been mirrored on her face. She couldn't believe she had been so nasty to him. Maybe they were not good for each other at all. Perhaps if they stayed together, his cynicism would drag her down.

He shook his head as if trying to free himself from a bad dream. "It's on the house," he said, the tone glacial. "Consider it payment for our one wild night in Vegas."

Gavin walked the streets of the neon city for an hour before he was calm enough to go in search of his brother. He found Patrick at Mandalay Bay feeding quarters into a slot machine.

Patrick looked up in surprise. "Where's Cassidy?"

Gavin couldn't quite meet his little brother's gaze. He was still raw inside. "She's with her family. Where she belongs. If you're up to it, I'm ready to fly home."

Patrick's face fell. "I thought we were staying a couple of days."

"Maybe another time." Maybe when hell froze over. He never wanted to set foot in Vegas again. Cassidy had given him the ephemeral promise of happiness and warmth, but it was all a sham. He'd made another mistake with a woman. And this time, he might never recover.

Cassidy found healing in work and in the steady, burgeoning presence of her twins. She talked to them constantly. Every night before bed she read them stories.

Her relationships with her father and her brother improved daily. Carlo's faux pas had given him a dose of humility. And Gianni Corelli was trying to change his attitude about women. Both men had Italian blood in their veins…and centuries of chauvinistic history. But even so, they were making an effort, and Cassidy appreciated it.

In the dark of the night when there was no work to do and no stories to be read, she thought about Gavin. She told herself the pain would get better…that she wouldn't crave his touch every second of the day. But in that arena, she hadn't made much progress. No crying, though. It wasn't good for the babies. Cassidy would be strong for them. She and her twins would build a family together.

Whenever she thought about the future, it was in terms of how she would manage to be mother and father at the same time. She'd waited her whole life for a man to come along who would be her perfect ideal of a mate. Someone strong and caring and decent and kind.

Maybe that was asking too much. Maybe that was her problem. It wasn't really fair to ask Gavin to be an instant father. Not when the only contact he'd had with her was that one night in Vegas.

Admittedly, since then he had shown a marked interest in taking her to bed, but sexual attraction wasn't strong enough glue to hold a relationship together when neither of the parties really knew each other. That wasn't quite true, though. She *did* know Gavin, maybe more than he realized. She had seen his relationship with his mother and his brothers. She'd witnessed his attempt to help her and shelter her even in the midst of his doubts.

There were so many reasons she had fallen in love with him. But she made the choice to cherish the memories and not be sad. Gavin needed someone in his life. She was convinced of that. But clearly, it wasn't her.

She thought about moving out of her father's house and getting her own place. She would need help after the birth, though, so that wasn't really practical. Her father wouldn't be much assistance, but Carlo was actually getting excited about the twins.

The day the beautiful baby furniture arrived unexpectedly from North Carolina, Cassidy broke her no-crying rule. After Carlo helped her assemble the crib, he took off to play basketball with some friends. Gianni was at the casino. Cassidy sat in the middle of the floor in the babies' room and sobbed.

The day she and Gavin had picked out those pieces, she really hoped everything was going to be okay. She'd even begun to imagine how she might use her training and talents to start some kind of business in Silver Glen.

But she'd been both misguided and naive.

Twice now she'd thought about flying to Silver Glen to see if there was any kind of chance with Gavin. But twice she talked herself out of it. If he wanted her, he would have come. His silence spoke volumes.

The day arrived when she had to put away her stylish clothes and don maternity tops and pants. She wore them proudly, not at all worried about gaining too much weight. Heartbreak had a way of keeping the pounds in check.

Still, it took her by surprise when she walked past a mirror and saw her rounded belly. Being pregnant was both magical and exhausting. The morning sickness had finally abated, but the fatigue remained.

She found herself counting the days until her due date, in part because she was excited, but also because once the twins were born, she would have an excuse to contact Gavin.

What would he say when that day came? Would he even consent to a paternity test? The man was an enigma…

Gavin acquired three new clients in the weeks following his return from Vegas…big clients. He stayed busier than ever, troubleshooting problems and making suggestions for improvement to the businesses in his care.

The thing with Cassidy felt uncomfortably like failure. And failure was rarely part of his vocabulary. He had been almost ready to confess to Cassidy that he believed her about the babies and that he wanted her to stay…maybe forever. But then her father had taken her back with open arms and Gavin had lost his bargaining chip.

If Gavin thought there was a chance she could fall in love with him, he would have said something. But he'd trapped her with an unintended pregnancy. She was young and bright and beautifully alive, and she deserved a man better than he was, a man who hadn't spent far too many years bound by his cynicism. He told himself things ended as they should have. But deep down, he didn't believe it, particularly in the middle of the night when he was aching and sleepless.

Cassidy had brightened up an existence he hadn't even recognized as gray. She'd made him want…had made him feel.

He was accustomed to keeping his own counsel, but the situation ate away at him. He should talk to somebody. Anybody. But his pride got in the way.

So he couldn't decide if it was a good thing or a bad thing when Conor showed up one afternoon. Gavin had just changed into running clothes and was sitting on the back porch tying his shoes. His brother was attired similarly. Gavin eyed him with suspicion. "This is a little coincidental, don't you think?"

Behind Gavin's house, a three-quarter-mile trail led up the side of the mountain. The route was steep and rocky and challenging. His custom was to run up and back three times.

Conor grinned and shrugged. "You're a creature of habit. And I could use the exercise. Race you to the top."

Before Gavin could stand up, Conor took off, his long legs eating up the distance. Gavin's competitive instinct kicked in. No way in heck was he going to let his baby brother beat him.

Conor, however, was a skier and a natural athlete. Gavin was determined, but Conor had a head start. They made it to the top and turned around, hurtling downward on the narrow trail at breakneck speeds. At the bottom, they started all over again.

At the start of the fifth trip to the top, Gavin began to question his sanity. Sweat poured down his back and dripped into his eyes. His thigh muscles screamed. His lungs burned.

Conor's pace had slowed noticeably, but so had Gavin's. They changed position frequently, either elbowing each other out of the way or sliding past if the other one paused to breathe.

At the completion of five circuits, Conor held up his hand. "Enough." He leaned forward, both hands on his knees, his labored gasps audible.

Gavin joined him, mimicking his stance. "What was that about?" he asked.

"You've been hiding out. It's not good for the soul."

"Since when did you become a philosopher?"

Conor didn't bother to answer the rhetorical question. He straightened and swiped his arm over his forehead. "Humidity's a bitch today."

Gavin agreed, but that was hardly the point. "Why are you here, Conor?"

Conor's eyes danced with mischief, despite his fatigue. "Patrick told me he met your sexy visitor. Said he took the two of you to Vegas."

"Patrick should mind his own damned business."

"He told me Cassidy is a sweetheart."

Gavin felt his neck tighten. "Patrick can stay the hell away from Cassidy."

"Why? You don't want her."

Gavin saw red. Literally. His response was gut-deep and fierce. He swung his fist at Conor's jaw and connected with a satisfying crack that sent pain shooting down his arm. Conor staggered backward, but remained standing.

His younger brother rubbed his chin, his expression no longer lighthearted. "You are one screwed-up sonofabitch."

Gavin agreed with him, but a man never showed weakness. "I'm doing just fine."

"Listen to me, Gavin. I know you. You're a perfectionist. You never allow yourself to make a mistake because of what happened when you were twenty-one."

"You mean when I was a credulous fool and ended up in jail?" Even now the memory was raw, though buried deep.

Conor leaned against a support beam for the porch. "Maybe I never told you, but Patrick and I admired the hell out of you back then. Still do for that matter."

"I don't want to talk about this."

"You went to *jail*, Gavin. For five long nights. Because you knew you were innocent and you wouldn't let your own family bail you out. It wasn't your fault the woman you met was psycho. It was your first date. You paid for it with a hell of a big tab. From where I'm standing, you're still paying."

It pissed Gavin to hear his little brother lay out the truth so neatly and with such painful accuracy. "I should have known," he muttered.

"*Any* guy would have done the same. She was cute and sexy and she came on to you. How were you supposed to anticipate that she would cry rape?"

"Did you know Mom wanted to pay the hush money?"

"Not because she thought you were guilty."

"Then why?"

"She couldn't bear the thought of your being in jail. None of us could."

"You had doubts." It was the first time Gavin had ever said it out loud. The *only* time he had ever given voice to the stunning, sick feeling in the pit of his stomach.

Conor stared at him intently, as though trying to do

some Vulcan mind meld thing. "No. We were in shock and upset and worried. But we knew you weren't a rapist. God, Gavin. Give us some credit."

Gavin stared into the distance, unable to meet his brother's earnest gaze. The worst of what happened was in the past. His slate was wiped clean. What remained was the fear of being duped again.

"I barely know Cassidy."

Conor understood what he wasn't saying. "It's like being hit by a drunk driver, Gavin. The victim goes through all the what-ifs. But in the end, the accident is a quirk of timing. Sheer bad luck." He paused. "You did nothing wrong. You met a pretty woman on campus and asked her out on a date. She targeted you, but it didn't work. The likelihood of another such *accident* is less than nil. You've *been* with Cassidy, even if not for months and years. You know her. Trust your instincts. They won't steer you wrong. You're a mature man, not a kid anymore."

"Thank God." Gavin's muttered response was more of an honest prayer than Conor realized. "Thanks for the pep talk, little brother."

Conor rubbed the heel of his sneaker in the grass. "So what are you going to do?"

"About what?"

"Don't be dense. About Cassidy."

"I appreciate your concern, Conor. I really do. But I don't need help with my love life."

"Do you? Love her, I mean?"

There was no humor on Conor's face, no teasing, no sibling jostling for position. Only a deep compassion that made Gavin ache. His brother's empathy made him feel naked, stripped of all defenses.

Gavin swallowed hard. "How can I? If you add up the

time she and I have spent together, it wouldn't even equal a week."

"That's your excuse?"

"It's not an excuse, damn it. It's the truth."

Conor shook his head. "This is a worst-case scenario for you, isn't it? Love at first sight. Throwing caution to the wind. Poor Gavin. Maybe you should leave her alone after all. I'm not sure you can handle the fallout if you really are in love. Good luck, bro. You're gonna need it."

Sixteen

Gavin stood beneath the stinging spray of the shower and wrestled with his desires and his fears. Cassidy was a fun one-night stand. He had acted completely out of character that night. He needed time to decide what to do. But the clock was ticking, because Cassidy carried two small lives in her womb. Those babies wouldn't wait for Gavin to make a decision.

Conor's words had impacted Gavin. In a good way. But they didn't change the facts of the case. Cassidy wanted nothing more than to work by her father's side in the family business. She didn't need Gavin's money, because she had plenty of her own. Las Vegas and Silver Glen were miles apart in every way that counted.

So, the questions were pretty simple: *Did* Gavin love Cassidy? Did he trust her completely? Did he want to step out of the dark into a world of light and happiness? And was he willing to do whatever it required to make her his?

As she drove the short distance from the casino to the Corelli mansion, Cassidy thought about something Carlo had said recently. She'd been trying to convince him that she and her father had forgiven him. But Carlo had pointed out that it was much harder to forgive himself.

He was so right. Cassidy could forgive Gavin *his* doubts,

but she had a hard time excusing her own actions. She should have been completely honest and told Gavin that she had fallen in love with him. Maybe her admission would have made it easier for him to embrace his impending fatherhood and to admit he had feelings for her, as well. But maybe not.

She pulled into the garage and shut the door behind her. In the kitchen, she kicked off her sandals and poured herself a large glass of water. Drinking it slowly, she stood at the island and gazed around the room she had come to take for granted. She'd spent much of her time here over the years. Doing homework, playing cards with her brother, begging the housekeeper to teach her how to cook.

Now she was going to be a mother. But she had no guide to follow. Her own mom had died a long, long time ago.

She wanted more than anything for her babies to grow up knowing they were loved. Sharing custody was not ideal, but she hoped Gavin would be a real father. Someone for the children to lean on. And selfishly, she clung to the hope that one day Gavin might find it in his heart to trust her and forgive her and give her another chance.

She finished her drink and put the glass in the dishwasher. The sofa in the living room was comfortable, so she headed that way with the thought of taking a nap. But when she rounded the corner in the hall, she stopped dead. Gavin Kavanagh sat in one of the velvet-covered wingbacks, his hands behind his head, his legs outstretched in front of him.

Everything about his posture shouted relaxation.

"Gavin. You scared me to death."

"Carlo let me in. Sorry," he drawled. But he didn't look sorry at all.

His gaze zeroed in on her protruding stomach. Slowly, he rose to his feet. "My God. You're really pregnant."

The awe and wonder in his voice touched her. "Pretty sure you already knew that."

He shook his head. "That's not what I meant. *Really* as in *very*. Very pregnant." His hand hovered over her belly. "May I?"

"Of course." Most people didn't even ask. For whatever reason, pregnant women seemed to be fair game. But Gavin had helped create the little duo she carried.

Gavin settled his palm against the curve of her considerable baby bump. "Do you know yet about the sexes?"

His hand hadn't moved, but being so close to him was arousing. "No. Next week, I think."

At that exact moment, one of the twins kicked…hard.

Gavin jerked his hand away. The momentum nearly made him trip over an ottoman. "Was that one of the babies?"

She took his hand and put it back. "Yes. Be patient and you'll feel it again. It's amazing."

As she had promised, another large ripple briefly distended the surface of her belly.

Gavin's eyes met hers. "Incredible," he said hoarsely.

They were standing so close she could inhale the scent of him. His streaky brownish-blond hair was longer than when she last saw him. She touched the silky strands just above his ear. "You need a haircut."

"No time," he muttered. He took her hands in his. "Cassidy?"

"Yes?"

"I know the babies are mine."

Shock left her speechless.

He grimaced. "I've known it all along in my heart, but my head was slow to catch up. I'm sorry."

"I understood. It hurt. It *really* hurt, because you were the only man I'd ever trusted enough to be intimate with.

I understood, though, after talking with your mother, that I was paying for another woman's sins." His admission healed a tear in her heart, but it wasn't what she really wanted.

He shook his head. "That whole business when I was about to graduate from college…well…let's just say it shook me…made me doubt myself when it came to women."

"I can't imagine what you went through."

"The thing is, Cass…" When he stumbled to a halt, she frowned. She had never seen Gavin unsure of himself.

"What are you trying to say?"

He shrugged, his expression bleak. "I fell in love with you. I *am* in love with you. I know I hurt you by not trusting you about the babies, but I want you to know the truth. Even if you don't feel the same way."

She wanted to throw herself at him, but he looked more miserable than lovesick. "We both had some hurdles to face, Gavin. This situation has been tough for both of us."

"Spending five nights in jail was tough. But spending even five more minutes without you in my life will kill me. I love you, Cass. So damned much." He ran his thumb over her cheek. "My body recognized the truth that very first night. You were this perfect woman I had dreamed up, but you were real."

She had to blink to clear tears from her eyes. "Trust me, I'm not perfect."

"Perfect for me," he said, the words deep and firm. His gray eyes were clearer and more open than she had ever seen them.

"Oh, Gavin." She wrapped her arms around his neck, feeling a deep tide of gratitude wash over her. "I can't hug you like I want to," she complained. "I feel like a cow and I'm only five months along."

He kissed her softly, his lips lingering over hers until they both sighed. "It might be easier lying down."

She grinned. "Spoken like a man."

"Am I wrong?" He lifted an innocent eyebrow.

"Not at all."

Hand in hand, they walked down the hall to her bedroom. She wanted to shove him up against the nearest wall and demand that he ravage her, but this sweet reunion disarmed her completely.

With the door safely locked behind them, his hands went matter-of-factly to his shirt buttons. They undressed in silence as a huge lump of emotion clogged her throat. "I love you, too," she whispered. "Why else would I still be a virgin all this time if I hadn't been waiting for Mr. Right?"

He was nude now, his erection lifting against his abdomen. Freezing for one long second, he took a deep breath, staring meaningfully at her stomach. "Not exactly a virgin, Cass."

"You know what I mean." She wanted to cover herself with her hands, but as a full-fledged adult with a family on the way and the most amazing man in the world about to make love to her, she stood proudly in front of him.

Sweetness winnowed away, replaced by raw passion. The look in his eyes made her tremble.

He raked both hands through his hair, his expression agitated. "Is it okay? I don't want to hurt you...or them."

She went to him, resting her cheek against his chest, hearing the steady thump of his heart. "You won't. You can't. Be with me, Gavin. In all the ways there are. I want you so much."

He lifted her into his arms, not visibly strained by the fact that he carried not one but three individuals. Folding back the covers on her bed with one hand, he put her down gently and joined her.

"I won't ever walk away from you again." Reclining on his hip, he bent and kissed her belly. "You're beautiful inside and out, Cass. Funny and smart and full of life. We have things to discuss, but first things first."

He wouldn't move on top of her even though she coaxed. Instead, he spooned her. Lifting her leg over his, he entered from behind.

The position was interesting. But she soon lost any interest in Sex 101 when Gavin began to move inside her. The weeks of grief and stress melted away. Against all odds, she and Gavin were together again.

He held her firmly but gently, his body worshipping hers. The desultory pace began to make her frantic. Moving restlessly against him, she tried to get him to take the hint. "Please, Gavin. I'm so close."

He nipped the back of her neck with sharp teeth. "Don't rush me, woman. I've missed you. I want to savor the moment."

With his body surrounding her, she had no recourse but to close her eyes and reach for the tantalizing ripples of completion. When the end came, there was no doubt. She cried out, the whip of pleasure sharp and wicked. Already Gavin groaned and shuddered as they rode the wave together.

Gavin's heart thundered in his chest. His mouth was dry as cotton. But he held Cass's breast in his hand, so he didn't move, not even to disconnect their bodies. His head rested on her pillow, his thighs cradling hers.

When he thought he could speak, he muttered in her ear. "How do you feel?"

She yawned and stretched, turning on her back to look up at him. Her molten chocolate eyes glowed with happiness. "Shattered. Complete. Sexually sated. Giddy. Shall I go on?"

"Brat." He plucked at her nipple. The temptation to initiate round two was strong. But he had things to tell her.

When it looked as if she might fall asleep, he said her name. "Cassidy."

"Hmm?" She didn't even open her eyes.

"I know how important it is to you to work alongside your father and your brother. I'm prepared to move my entire business to Vegas so you can fulfill your dream."

Her eyes flew open. "You can't do that."

"Why not?"

"Because I won't let you. I don't want to take you away from your family and Silver Glen. I won't."

He could see that her indignation was genuine. The generosity it encompassed humbled him. "In that case," he said, "I have one other proposition to offer. What if we split our time between both states? And what if you join me as an equal partner in The Silver Eye?"

Any trace of drowsiness fled from her gaze. "Why?"

"I like the thought of working with you."

"I'm sorry, but the answer is no."

His heart fell to his knees. "Oh."

Cass shook her head with a rueful smile. "My whole life has been focused on the Corelli casino, in part because of competition with my brother. But the truth is, I've found other goals, other dreams. Carlo and I are in a good place now, and he's going to make my father and me proud."

"So what will you do?"

"That depends on you, I think."

He stared at her blankly. "How?"

"Did you perhaps intend to propose to me? But you forgot that part?"

He put a hand to his forehead, feeling the gradual return

of hope. "It's entirely possible," he said, his smile rueful. "Seeing you again scrambled my brain. Will you marry me, Cassidy Corelli, and have my babies?"

"Only if you understand that my being pregnant and in love with you is not a sacrifice. That I'm a grown woman making a decision about my future without coercion or regret."

"Then you're saying yes?"

"With pleasure, my sweet Gavin."

"There's one more thing," he said, stroking her rounded belly.

She rolled her eyes. "Sheesh. And they say women talk too much."

"Don't be a smart-ass when I'm being romantic."

"Sorry," she said, trying to look penitent and failing miserably. The happiness she felt was written all over her face.

Some of the sparkle even rubbed off on him. He ran his fingers across her brow, through her short, dark curls, his chest tight with emotion. There were so many ways he could have missed out on meeting her. If his friend hadn't gotten sick. If Gavin hadn't agreed to do the speech. If Gavin hadn't decided to take a walk around Vegas that night.

And now here he was...with Cass...having babies together. Making plans to get married. In love. It wasn't anything he'd anticipated, or anything he'd thought he wanted. But it was the best thing that had ever happened to him.

He tried not to let the sight of her soft, warm, curvy body sidetrack him. "What would you think about going to the wedding chapel and letting your cousin marry us? For real this time."

Cassidy's chin wobbled. "Seriously? I'd love it. But what about your family?"

"We can have a big fancy reception later…in Silver Glen. But today, I only want you, my love."

"Oh, Gavin…"

"Oh, Cassidy…" He mocked her teasingly, but he knew how she felt.

"There's only one thing."

His shoulders tensed. What now?

"Tell me," he said, bracing for the worst.

Long lashes fluttered in sync with a cajoling smile. "Can I please take a nap *before* we get married?"

Five hours later, Cassidy walked by Gavin's side as they approached Robbie's Elvis-themed wedding chapel. Gavin squeezed her hand. "Are you sure about this, sweetheart?"

She nodded, leaning her head against his shoulder. "Not a doubt in my mind." While she napped, Gavin had checked out marriage procedural details. With no waiting period and no blood tests, all they had to do was show up in person and procure the license.

After that, Gavin had spirited her away to an extremely posh maternity boutique to shop for a wedding gown. Despite trying on at least a dozen possibilities, in the end she had chosen a 1920s style dress in ivory pleated silk that left her shoulders bare except for narrow straps. The empire bodice was covered with bugle beads and antique crystals that caught the light when she moved.

A small fascinator concocted of lace and a single faux magnolia blossom perched on the side of her head, completing the look.

She looked in the trifold mirror, glancing over her shoulder to get the back view. "What do you think, Gavin?" She had pooh-poohed the idea that it might be bad luck for him to see her gown. She had been separated from him for several long weeks. Now she didn't want to let him out of her sight.

His eyes glittered with desire. "It's perfect...almost."

She frowned. "Almost?"

She stood on a six-inch-high circular platform. Gavin went down on one knee and drew a red leather box from his pocket. "I forgot to give you this."

This was a flawless solitaire set in a plain platinum band. The clarity and purity of the stone shot a thousand tiny rainbows across the room when he slipped the ring onto her left hand. "Now it's official," he murmured, kissing her knuckles.

When the door of the wedding chapel swung open, Cassidy snapped back to the present. Robbie's expression was priceless. "More games, Cass?" he asked with a baffled look.

She shook her head. "Nope." Handing over an envelope of cash, she smiled. "This is the real deal. Gavin and I want you to marry us."

Robbie glanced down at her very pregnant belly, revealed tastefully in ivory silk. "Left it a bit late, didn't you?"

She laughed. "Better late than never."

This time, although the setting was familiar, everything else seemed brand-new. Gavin's deep voice repeating vows. Robbie's much higher tenor stumbling only slightly as he spoke his parts of the ceremony.

When it was her turn, she wasn't nervous at all. *"To have and to hold, from this day forward..."* She spoke the words reverently, steadily, so very grateful that her family was going to be complete.

Through it all, Gavin stared at her with a look she never thought to see from the quiet, brooding Kavanagh male. It was one part fierce possession and one part pride.

Afterward, when the paperwork was signed and the formalities completed, Robbie got a funny look on his face.

Cassidy stared at him. "What is it? What's wrong?"

Sheepishly, her cousin reached under the counter and produced a bottle of very familiar-looking champagne. "I forgot the bubbly," he said. "And you actually paid for it this time."

Gavin plucked the green glass container out of his hand and kissed his bride. "Mrs. Kavanagh can't have alcohol at the moment, but we'll save it for when the babies are christened. Besides," he said, taking Cass's arm and walking her down the aisle, "it's gonna be one wild night in Vegas, with or without champagne."

Epilogue

Cass lay with her eyes closed, feeling as if her body was floating over the bed. She ached in every cell...in every hair follicle. But beneath the physical discomfort was a deep vein of peace.

The door opened quietly and a man's voice called. "Wake up, Mama. Your son and daughter are here."

When she opened her eyes, Gavin had one baby and the nurse the other. Carefully, they each tucked a snugly wrapped infant into Cassidy's arms. The nurse excused herself.

Gavin pulled up a chair beside the bed and sat down. "Have you ever seen two more perfect infants?" He was rumpled and fatigued, but he beamed. They had made the joint decision *not* to find out the sex of the twins ahead of time.

"We still have to pick names," she said. "And our list is growing instead of shrinking."

"How about Elvis for the boy?"

"I am *not* naming my son Elvis," she said firmly, looking at Gavin's face to make sure he was kidding.

"Then what?"

"I was thinking Lola for my mother and Reggie for your dad."

"I thought you wanted unusual names, something that stands out."

"I changed my mind," she said, trying to imagine what it was going to be like when two babies toddled around the house.

"Well, I like it," Gavin said firmly. "I'm going to fill out the birth certificates before you change your mind again."

Cassidy's heart swelled as she looked from the pink-capped head to the blue-capped one. "I can't believe we did it," she said. "It's all over."

Gavin laughed out loud, wincing when the babies scrunched up their noses. "No," he whispered, stroking her elbow as he stood and carefully leaned over to kiss her. "It's only begun, Cass. It's only begun."

* * * * *

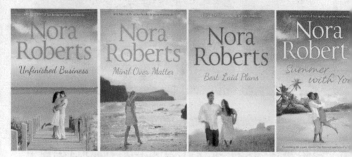

MILLS & BOON®

The Chatsfield Collection!

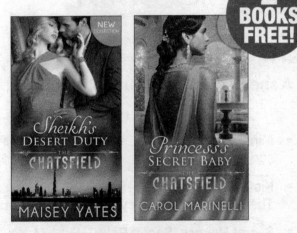

Style, spectacle, scandal…!

With the eight Chatsfield siblings happily married and settling down, it's time for a new generation of Chatsfields to shine, in this brand-new 8-book collection! The prospect of a merger with the Harrington family's boutique hotels will shape the future forever. But who will come out on top?

**Find out at
www.millsandboon.co.uk/TheChatsfield2**

MILLS & BOON®

Desire™

PASSIONATE AND DRAMATIC LOVE STORIES

A sneak peek at next month's titles...

In stores from 17th April 2015:

- **Minding Her Boss's Business** – Janice Maynard *and* **Triple the Fun** – Maureen Child

- **Kissed by a Rancher** – Sara Orwig *and* **The Sheikh's Pregnancy Proposal** – Fiona Brand

- **Secret Heiress, Secret Baby** – Emily McKay *and* **Sex, Lies and the CEO** – Barbara Dunlop

---

Available at WHSmith, Tesco, Asda, Eason, Amazon and Apple

Just can't wait?
Buy our books online a month before they hit the shops!
visit www.millsandboon.co.uk

These books are also available in eBook format!